HERE IN COLD HELL

TANITH LEE

HERE IN COLD HELL

Book Two of the 'Lionwolf' Trilogy

TOR

First published 2005 by Tor
an imprint of Pan Macmillan Ltd
Pan Macmillan, 20 New Wharf Road, London N1 9RR
Basingstoke and Oxford
Associated companies throughout the world
www.panmacmillan.com

ISBN 1 4050 0635 8

Maps by Raymond Turvey

1 3 5 7 9 8 6 4 2

A CIP catalogue record for this book is available from
the British Library.

Typeset by IntypeLibra, London
Printed and bound in Great Britain by
Mackays of Chatham plc, Chatham, Kent

For Asma Yasmin Sharfi,
who provided such a significant clue

Translator's Note

This text has been translated not only into English, but into the English of recent times. It therefore includes, where appropriate, 'contemporary' words – such as *downside*, or even 'foreign' words and phrases such as *faux pas* or *soupçon*. This method is employed in order to correspond with the syntax of the original scrolls, which themselves are written in a style of their own period, and include expressions and phrases from many areas and other tongues.

As with the main text, names, where they are exactly translatable, are rendered (often) in English, and sometimes both in English and the original vernacular – for example the name/title, *Lionwolf* (*Vashdran* in the Rukarian). Occasionally names are given in a combination of exactly equivalent English plus part of the existing name where it is basically *un*translatable, as with the Rukarian Phoenix, the *Firefex*.

The passage of Kraagparian philosophy that prefaces Volume 9 has already been expressed in our world, and for the right to quote it, in translated Kraag syntax, the author thanks the Michael Group of California.

Note on Intervolumens

The three books of the trilogy make up, in the original format, *one* long book, composed of scrolls – here represented as Volumes. The *Intervolumens* are interpolated adventures and developments from other richer sources – since, in the scrolls of Lionwolf, many of these events are detailed sketchily, and in a sort of shorthand.

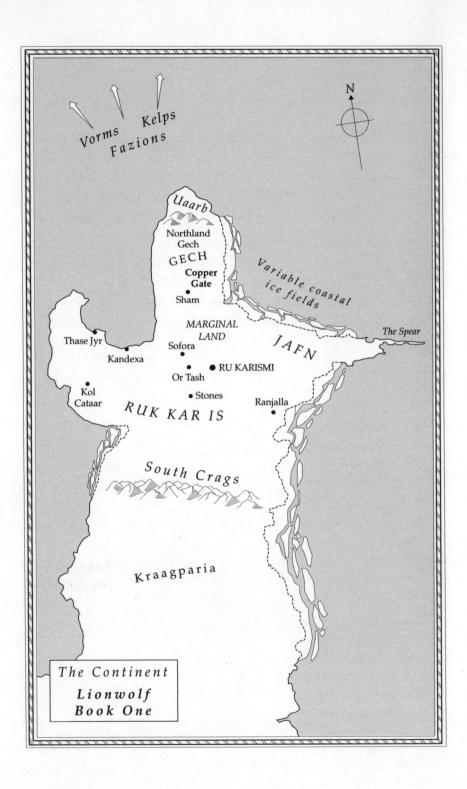

Vorms

Kelps

Fazions

N

Uaarb

Northland
Gech

GECH

Copper
Gate

• Sham

MARGINAL
LAND

Variable coastal
ice fields

The Spear

Thase Jyr •

Sofora •

JAFN

Kandexa •

• RU KARISMI

Or Tash •

Kol
Cataar •

• Stones

Ranjalla •

RUK KAR IS

South Crags

Kraagparia

The Continent

Lionwolf
Book One

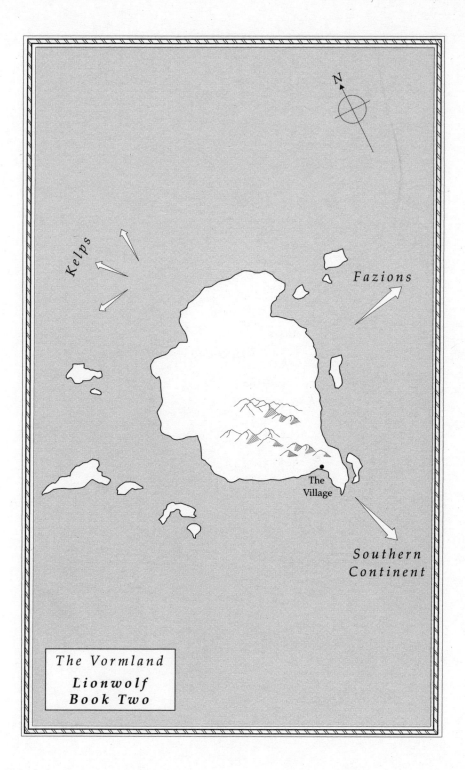

N

Kelps

Fazions

The
Village

Southern
Continent

The Vormland
Lionwolf
Book Two

I sent my Soul through the Invisible,
Some letter of that After-life to spell:
And after many days my Soul return'd
And said, 'Behold, Myself am Heav'n and Hell.'

Omar Khayyám
The Rubáiyát, quatrain LXXI
(translated by Edward Fitzgerald)

Sixth Volume

PLACE OF STONES AND DARK MOON

'So dark it is, how can I see my way?'

'You will find the path more easily if you are blind. If you are blind, you will *have* to.'

Song of Lalt: Simisey

ONE

The sun was blue.

He lay staring up at it, because it did not dazzle him; yet it gave light.

After a while he turned his head a little on the hard, smarting surface, to see what the sun gave light to.

Stones, shards and flints lay all around him, save in one direction where, about four shield-lengths off perhaps, they ended in dull and viscous water. That was the open sea. He thought so. But it did not really move, there were no waves, only an occasional sluggish rippling.

So cold. So cold . . .

He had been deep inside the sea, which was like a deadly beating womb. Then he must have been cast ashore. A ship – he must have been on a ship, which had foundered.

He could not remember any ship, except one with seventeen masts stuck in ice and grounded. And even the ice – not so cold – as this.

The man lying on the long broken beach closed his eyes, but his hand reached out emptily across the stones, and closed inadvertently on something that was of a different, smoother shape. At first he examined it only by touch. What was it? Was it his? He drew it in and held it to his face to look. But he was still unsure what it was. Nevertheless, for some reason his hand shut tighter on it and tears ran out of his eyes.

The next time he woke it was because a baleful sound, like that of a mooing beast or of a trumpet, was echoing out across the vast space inland, behind him.

Slowly now he sat up, and gazed inland, but it was a sort of nothingness, the beach of shards stretching for ever, and in the distance clouds, maybe, slowly moving, low against the earth.

He put the unknown wooden thing he had found inside his shirt, under his heavier outer clothing, which seemed made of leather and wool.

Just then terror came, glittering and wild, into his mind and he thrust it away.

Where was this country? He did not know.

Who am I? He did not know.

The trumpet or beast mournfully called again, inland.

His shadow fell from him, transparent in the sapphire sunlight.

When he stood up, it was because a disturbance started in the sea-pond. Unlike the pure fear which had to do with confusion, no alarm rose in him at the twisting waters. Actually he was quite glad to see it. It might give him something to do.

He put his right arm across his body and located a sheathed knife thrust in at his belt.

The water parted, thick as soup. A dark round object rose from it. A seal? But the roundness gave way to a head containing features, a mane of hair, a pillar of neck and wide shoulders – a muscular man of some height and girth was striking up now from the depths. Swiftly he stood clear of the sea and stepped out on the beach.

The newcomer was not wet. Neither his clothing nor his shaggy black hair had any liquid on or in them. His look was bleak, and blank. He took a single further step, then fell straight down on his face on the shore.

I too did that. So it must have been.

Even as he thought this, another figure started to come up out of the thick and turgid sea – and then another and another.

Watching them he thought instantly, *I'm no longer alone. I must have a name.* He put his hand to his face. It was a brown, young hand, with long strong fingers and a callused palm.

4

Looking at it a moment, he knew what each callus represented – use of a sword, a bow, the reins of a chariot . . .

The other new arrivals – there were ten by now and still others plunged up and in – took no notice either of the man already standing on the shore, or of any of those who had also just come there. But each man, reaching the stones, fell over, on to either his face or his side, and one, dropping initially to his knees, curled up in the position of the unborn foetus.

I must have a name . . .

Twenty men now were on the beach. Two more came wading in, and of these one glanced into the standing watcher's eyes. The watcher did not know this man – and yet there was something familiar about him. His hair was white although he too was quite young. The white-haired man raised one hand uncertainly, as if in greeting.

Unlike all the rest, additionally, he stayed upright after he had got out of the sea, despite heavily swaying this way and that.

'Where did it go?' he said, in a language the watcher knew very well, but could not name either.

'What?'

'The – city – the Gullah – the world – where?'

Something flashed in the watcher's mind. He remembered a chariot. He remembered speed and shouting and his own red hair blown like a flag, and now, putting back his hands, he pulled this long hair in over his shoulder, to stare at and be sure. Yes, it was red and savage as fire.

'If I answer where all that went, my friend, then you must name me before I tell it.'

'Oh. A riddle? Then you are – you are . . .' White-hair faltered. Great trouble smoked over his pale eyes. 'I can't,' he said, 'tell you your name. Though I saw you often, once . . . But then,' despairingly he added, 'who am *I*?'

The watcher felt a pulse of heat run through his blood, strengthening him. He said, 'For now, you'll call me Nameless.'

'Nameless . . .'

'And, for now also, until you recall your own name, you

shall be called Kuul. Which means One, or First, but in another tongue than that we speak now. As for the city and the . . . *Gullahammer*, the Brotherhood – that was lost. It's been left behind.' Nameless paused, considering what he had said, and that he seemed to know yet did not understand it. 'Here too there'll be things to accomplish.'

The man with white hair, Kuul, looked about the shore at the other men who had fallen over, swooning or sleeping. He yawned suddenly, then shook his head, as if both to clear it and to deny. 'I was a long while in that filth of a sea. I couldn't find my way. I won't waste time asleep like these fools. They must be western trash. Or Olchibe. We're Jafn, you and I. We only really sleep when we are dead.' And then his eyes widened. A deep agony filled his face and hung there. He repeated, quietly, 'We are dead.'

Nameless laughed. He had to force the laugh from him, but it sounded convincing enough. And Kuul smiled a little, wanting to be steadied.

'Do you *feel* dead, Kuul?'

'No – no.'

One further man had emerged from the sea and sunk down. No more appeared. The pond was flat, sullen and ungiving.

But the beast or trumpet brayed again abruptly, and much more raucously, over the shingle. It seemed closer than before.

'What's that?'

'God knows,' said Nameless, monotheistically in the Jafn manner. 'But I think someone else is on their way. So probably we'll learn.'

They checked their garments and weapons, of which last both men, and all the others from the look of it, had plenty, though some were of odd designs. Kuul clubbed back his hair and bound it with three strips of dried dog-gut.

Hair-tying for battle – that will make no difference to me, Nameless thought. Why was that? It must be he was benignly spelled, some witch or mage had made him invulnerable.

Of course, for surely he had been a king?

The idea of a fight was cheering, was it? He had fought a lot, previously, in the area beyond the dead sea, the world they had lost or left behind.

He noticed the men strewn on the beach were waking up again, some quite quickly, others slow and melancholy, as he had been.

Nameless was glad none of them had seen him lying weeping there on the cold shore, like a little boy wanting his mother.

'Yes, something's coming,' said Kuul. He turned to the waking men and shouted in a solid brazen tone, 'Hey, get up, you dreamers. Some urgent business is galloping towards us. Do you want to be caught on your backs like girls?'

And each of the men began scrambling upright, rubbing his face, searching out his personal armament of bows and daggers and spears.

Warriors, all of them. Perhaps they had been in a sea-battle with reivers . . . Vorms? Yes, that was the barbarian name, Vorms and Fazions – but no, these peoples had allied with the Brotherhood, the Gullahammer. Some other rubbish of the outer seas then.

Nameless looked upward at the sun again. It had moved a little, like a proper sun, and faint cloudlets were blowing across it.

He had seen a blue sun before. But not, he thought, in the sky—

The ground rumbled. The lesser stones began to jump, some of them, small pebbles and flinders flying up. As yet, however, nothing was visible of what approached.

All the men ranked themselves alongside Nameless and Kuul. Some of them even called out the name of *Nameless* – the Jafn version of it. Had they heard in sleep?

He turned to the big, black-maned man who had come out of the sea the first, after Nameless himself.

'I've forgotten how you're called, brother. Excuse me. It's been a long journey.'

'Years,' agreed the black-haired man. 'But call me, for now, Choy.'

Nameless nodded. *Choy* meant Two, or Second, but only in

the language of Gech, or sometimes Olchibe. And this man's skin was not yellow. He came from another nation.

It seemed also then Nameless had somehow *named* them all. He called along the line, 'Every man, say your name. We may need to shout to each other in the war that's coming.'

And they cried back their names – all numbers, though all in different tongues, and he believed all in tongues not their own – Olchibe again, or Jafn, or Urrowiy – like the unJafn name of *First* he had coined for Kuul, the first who spoke. Others had number-names which were from languages and dialects the Nameless one had never known.

Whatever else, they were a named band now, First and Second, and otherwise three to twenty-three.

By then a sort of haze was visible in the distance, murkier than the clouds which still drifted along there over the land. The rumble in the ground became a roar.

Then out from the fog burst a wall of rushing shapes, grey-black and golden, burning oddly in the cool sunlight, and the material of the beach flew off from either side of it like wings of water or ice.

Nameless flexed his body. He felt pleasantly hot now, and limber, ready to spring forward and leap among the enemy.

He raised the long knife, which was Jafn from its look. And next raised himself on to the balls of his feet to sprint.

In that second the amalgam which raced towards the twenty-four men on the shore exploded into visibility and nearness.

The waiting men howled. Yet none of them broke the line or fled. Instead, voicing berserk screams, they rushed forward, Nameless just ahead of them, his blue eyes wide as two furious suns.

The clash came awesomely, and reverberated along the shore for thousands of uncharted miles.

Nameless found himself lying now on his back, just as Kuul had warned the others not to be. Something stood on his chest and belly, panting hypnotically into his face.

It was heavy as lead, but in form lean, almost emaciated. Its muzzle and jaw dripped a scalding, stinging, stinking saliva.

There were thin white teeth. The rest was bluish, a bluish hound, but it had no eyes.

Even pinned as he was, this blind fanged thing's mouth an inch above his throat, Nameless thought, *I've seen such animals before – not dogs – but creatures without eyes and needing none.*

The bellow of the numbered fighters had dropped, through fast stages of other noise, to silence.

One of the riders loomed, nearly above Nameless. Like the hound he was dark bluish, clad in black and coiled in strands of golden metal. He had a human similarity, but his hair seemed to be made of gold snakes, tied back rather as Kuul had done it, but hissing and struggling. And his eyes, if he had eyes, were masked by a sombre vizor.

The other riders were the same, and Nameless saw them sitting astride their mounts all along the line of now fallen men. As for what they rode, Nameless thought of the fish-horses the sea-peoples favoured. But then Nameless forgot those. These horses had neither scales nor single horns; they did not reek of herring either. They were metal, black and gold, and each of them had eight legs. At first he told himself, a fallen hero, that the shell of these animals was only armour, and maybe the legs only artistic extras added on to frighten any foe. But he saw how they moved, how the legs moved, and that in the holes the gilt blinders left bare white sparks spattered, and nothing else.

The eyeless dog panted, not tearing out Nameless's throat. The snake-haired rider who towered over him on the eight-legged horse spoke in a soft, emotionless, peculiar voice.

'When the jatcha lets you go, get up. You will run before us, to the Place.'

'What pl—' Nameless began to say.

At once the hound – the jatcha – thrust its dripping muzzle against and almost into his mouth.

It smelled of butchery and old death. Nameless – and several men who had tried to speak and got the same treatment – retched and choked, unable to roll aside.

Then the jatchas padded off them. Men vomited into the stones. Nameless did not. He spat and stood up.

He looked into the face of the vizored thing on the unhorse with spider legs, and nodded.

Turning to the fallen men as they realigned themselves snorting, wiping mouths, raging and in an extreme of horror, Nameless then shook his head: *Do not resist what is irresistible.*

They obeyed him. What option?

On their feet they trotted through the crowd of mounted beings as it made way for them, and out along the sharded shingle.

'Where the clouds move,' said the soft omnipresent voice. Nameless saw that each of the several riders uttered at once and as one. 'There is the Place. Run now. Run along.'

Nameless and his men ran along. Towards the Place.

He had seen cities. He recalled that he had. He could not exactly picture them, but knew he had thought them small, quaint perhaps, and far less than what had been described by those who did so beforehand. After the hours-long jog over the broken shore, they ran among thick cloud, the sort encountered only on the tops of high mountains, and not always there. Then for another hour they ran inside the cloud, the obscene riders and dogs only glimpsed behind them, but sounding always with the jingle of their harness and battle-mail. The cloud dissolved without warning. And there was the Place.

Nameless stopped. All of them staggered to a halt.

Their guards did not prevent this, or try to force them on. They brought their spider-horses to a standstill, dismounted, and stood clasping their mailed fists to their hearts, shouting out a single word, which must be the true name of the Place. *'Shabatu! Shabatu!'*

'Face of God, what is it?' whispered Kuul.

Choy, on Nameless's other side, said, 'A great cliff, carved—'

'A city,' said Nameless. 'It's a city.'

Up it swarmed, far into the crystallized grey sky, vanishing there in a tapering perspective, while the blue sun perched on the highest limits, and lit it in streaming blue rays. It was pale,

walled – walls within walls – up and up, on and on. One vast
gateway broke the smooth frontage, and had doors of iron, fast
shut. Above the gate was carved an open bestial mouth, fringed
by black iron teeth. And from this mouth now erupted the
beast-trumpet note heard on the far shore. Here it rang the air
like a colossal bell.

Men covered their ears, moaned.

'Don't bother,' said Nameless. 'It can't hurt you now.'

Because, he thought, *we are, as Kuul noted, dead.*

The city had convinced him, it seemed.

But then anyway the guards were there, thrusting each man
down on his knees.

'Greet the Place. The city of Shabatu.'

'I salute Shabatu,' said Nameless, flat as a slate.

The other men of his band followed his example, and in the
same way.

Nameless thought, *I can't fathom the meaning of its name . . .*

But everything now was names, known and unknown, to be
invented or lost in amnesia. Also shapes, and new discouraging
events. This was what a child must deal with, every second,
once it had been born. But children lived and grew tough,
throwing off their shackles.

Nameless glanced around at his men. 'Cheer yourselves up,
my warriors,' he said, 'think how fortunate we are, to witness
such sights denied to other men. Think of the tales we can tell
when we go home.'

*I was a king. A king inspires and never shares his trouble, save
with some close relative or friend. Did I have those, ever? It's my duty
to hold these few together. They've been given into my hand.*

He took a step towards the city called Shabatu, and immediately one of the blind-yet-seeing jatcha hounds came around
him and was in his path, blocking it.

It was not, then, permissible to go on.

He looked at the dog, at the area where its eyes should be.

'Good hound. Thanks for your kind instruction.'

It was dog-size, but a very large dog, like the greatest and best bred of the Jafn hunting hounds, or the Urrowiy pack-dogs that carried whole travelling kitchens on their backs.

As the jatcha sidled by, returning to its station with the guards, Nameless put his hand towards its muzzle. It paused, sniffing at him.

'Know me,' said Nameless. 'I will be your friend.' The hound still paused, and no one had called it away. 'Your name,' said Nameless, 'shall be Star-Dog. A secret. Only I and you will know.' He leaned down then to the dog's ear and it growled, a strange gravelly menace. But Nameless only said, 'Live well, brother.'

The instant he straightened, one of the guards was there, clouting him across the back.

Nameless found again he fell. No, he was *not* spelled invulnerable. At least, not for the moment.

Yet he leapt upright again, facing the guard who had struck him.

'You should tell us, sir,' he said, 'what's disallowed. Then we won't disobey and annoy you so.'

'Everything is or may be disallowed,' said the guard, the guards, for just as before they all spoke at once.

Nameless looked round. His men watched him. He smiled at them. The blow had not hurt him.

Over the last of the shingle shore, another note sounded on the long beach. The tall black gates of the city were undoing themselves. A procession was emerging.

Some sort of priest was at the procession's head, like the priests of one of those lesser cities Nameless had visited elsewhere. The Jafn, of course, did not have priests, nor the other nations of the north and east, except the Olchibe, whose leaders were also the priests of their vandal bands. They relied instead on the powers of their magicians. Again, he had remembered something.

This priest figure wore deep blue, and lifted his arms to the sky. Behind him came others, all male, holding golden cups in which smouldered some type of incense. The aroma of it reached Nameless. It was like burning flowers.

12

The procession halted about a hundred paces away.

Only the foremost priest, thin as a stick, still advanced, walking over the stones and smiting them as he came with a long black staff.

Nameless watched him carefully. The man's face was pallid and had such small flattened nose, mouth, chin and brows it seemed unformed, or constructed by some careless god. The others were too distant to be certain if they were the same.

The priest's long hair resembled crawls of tallow. Like the snakes of the guards, this hair too appeared to be made of some other substance.

Now the priest was in front of them.

'Shabatu welcomes you.' A reedy voice, like a weak wind shivering through a hole in a narrow cave. 'Here is what you have earned and deserved. Shabatu is a Place of War. Behold the Battle Gates of Shabatu. Go now, join your Brotherhood, your Horde, your Gullahammer, your Army, your Legion, your Cesh, your Valmat, your Jihax, your Vandal-Sack . . .' The list went on. New names, new words, all of which meant war, meant the pride and prowess and honour and glory of war, and men banded together to make it.

I am at the Battle Gates. Where I belong.

Bitterness flooded Nameless. He embraced it. He was remembering, and *must* remember. But for now – for now they were driven aside, and along under the endless soaring walls of the city called Shabatu, Place of War, to join their regiment, the king and his twenty-three men.

A war camp. It lay in the lee of the walls, northwards, Nameless had concluded from the angle of the sun that now was setting.

Rank on rank of tents and bivouacs were spread out, some neatly positioned, and many haphazard and untidy. Fires burned between, flames anaemic in the light, but gaining in redness as the sun clotted in cloud and went down.

The sky to the west – it must be the west – was richly blue, a peacock colour. To the east, where night was starting to stir, a few campfire stars woke above, very big but not so brilliant. Maybe the unremitting cold had robbed them of their sparkle.

Moons would rise. Or would they? Nameless had known three moons, and nights of triple moonrise when dark was vivid as day. That was when he had been a king and ruled many thousands of men.

He stood up on the slope in the stone-littered landscape, looking mostly away to the north, or the west. In those two quarters, other lights than stars were becoming dimly visible. Presumably they blazed in the war camp of Shabatu's enemies.

All the men who had come with him from the sea, the men called by numbers, were accustomed to fighting. They had dropped easily into a pre-battle stance, part tension, part bravado, and part resignation. They had no tent, but made a fire down the slope, using flints from the beach, and sat there now, below.

There *was* food. Thin, small-featured persons, like the priests but dressed in secular style, brought round baskets of bread and citrus fruits, while others turned spits over several larger fires, roasting carcasses that seemed to be those of deer or some bovine animals. There was liquor too, wine and beer, even raw spirits. You could discover what you wanted, what you liked. One man – Seventeen – had already asked a passing snake-haired guard if tonight women would be available. The guard failed to answer. Nor did any women manifest. 'We haven't earned them yet,' said Eighteen. 'It'll be tomorrow, after we fight.' The guards must have said this at some point – or else other men already in the camp had said it. It seemed there had been for the camp a wait, an interval, until enough men were present to provide an equal force to that of the enemy. A couple of the men already in the camp had complained that Nameless's band had kept them hanging about for a year. 'A year? Can it be?' 'No. He's cracked.'

The camp was very great, as befitted an army under such gigantic walls as Shabatu's. And also, going on the fires, the enemy camp seemed enormous. Had all these warriors had to linger on the advent of twenty-four more men?

14

Kuul had come up the slope. He brought Nameless a chunk of roast meat that smelled enough like beef, and a jug of black Jafn-like wine.

They ate and drank for a time in silence. Then Kuul said, 'You are a Borjiy. I've recalled. You were my Chaiord. I think that was it.'

'What garth are you from?' asked Nameless, finding that the right words came now, or seemed to.

'Irhon.'

'Yes, Irhon. I know you – but still I can't remember—'

'My name. Nor I. Nor can I yours. Only my people. Oh, and I think I can recollect my wife, but *her* name's gone too. I can only see her hair and breasts and her sweet lower mouth.'

'Not too bad a bargain, then.'

They laughed.

All through the camp men were laughing, play-sparring, wrestling, shooting at marks, telling tales, burnishing and honing weapons.

Familiar, this, as his own skin.

And across the landscape, in the second camp, no doubt it was just the same.

'They don't know or won't say who we're to fight,' said Kuul, very low. 'Do you reckon it's human? I've seen no seefs or glers or such here, but God only knows. This is a weird and wondrous spot. It's like a dream – or a legend.' Nameless said nothing. Kuul swigged wine. He said, 'We *are* dead. I believe so.'

'Then,' said Nameless, 'if dead, death means life, for we live.'

'You think this is the Other Place? The land beyond the world? I thought that would be merry. And not so biting cold.'

'I think I live, and you live. I can smell you, Kuul. Even *in* the biting cold.'

Kuul grinned.

The sun was all down. The sky was growing luminously black, and more huge stars scattered out, thick as the shards on the beach, but even now not bright. As yet there was no sign of any moon.

'Look there,' said Kuul.

Nameless gazed behind him.

Shabatu, the War City, was slowly lighting up. It was not that torches, lamps or windows appeared. The walls themselves began to gleam and glow with a pale golden translucence. Around their fire, all twenty-two of Nameless's other men had got up and were staring, impressed, at this spectacle. But everyone else either took no notice, or mocked the newcomers' amazement.

'Tomorrow,' murmured Kuul, 'I mean to fight my best, and take the damned leer off their faces. We are Jafn.'

But the city shone like radiant golden ice. Who would need a moon, with such a city? Perhaps none, for no moon rose all through the long, cold night.

During the night, too, much of the camp slept. The slumber involved most of the men from Nameless's group. The Jafn Kuul naturally spurned sleep as most nights Jafn did, and Nameless felt no need of it. But eventually the one called Choy came up the slope with another man, Lifli – Five – who seemed to be a Kelp of the north seas. His nation was known for going seven days and nights awake at a stretch. The Kelp's face was sad and bewildered, but he had painted it with stripes for war. Nameless did not know him, nor did the Kelp know Nameless, but they sat down together on the slope and drank, looking at the city, or away to the east for sun-up. Choy too kept awake with the others. He said he had never slept very well.

If we live, how do we stand this extreme of cold? If we are dead, why do we need sleep or to stay insomniac?

'We are far from home,' lilted Kuul, who had a fine light singing voice. After the song he told them the Jafn story of the hero Star Black, made by God from snow to aid the garth of the Kree. 'When he came alive at God's breath, he also became blacker than night.' Later, Choy said that in his country there were black men, though not perhaps as black as that. They were all remembering – their women, their sons, their histories and fights, their myths and peoples. Only Nameless, despite his earlier optimism, felt the sightlessness still enfold acres of his memory in dense ice. *He* recalled no kindred, no lover, no friend. He recalled no Jafn stories, and certainly not his own. He waited for the dawn.

TWO

In the morning the sun that rose was transparent as a glass. Its edges only had any blue, and from it poured beams of frigid light.

Nameless saw how the sky was like a piece of palest grey marble, veined and polished, probably tactile, if you could reach.

After all, Choy had lapsed asleep.

Lifli was praying to a small image made of shell, with four arms and the head of a wicked-looking bird.

Kuul had gone but now came back with bread and beer. 'They're on the move.'

'The enemy.'

'Yes. See – you can make out the sun catching points on spears – or shields—'

'That's a big Cesh,' said Choy. He meant, Nameless knew, a war force. It was one of the words the priest had used. Choy scowled and for a split second reminded Nameless of . . . *someone*.

But already the hideous mouth-trumpet was yowling from the gates of Shabatu. All around men were prancing up. The cold, colourless air was also full of shouts and curses.

The snake-heads were coming too, riding through the disrupted tent lanes on their spider-horses with the jatchas running to heel, lean heads down, seeing their way by *scent*.

Nameless swung about among his men. He drank with them, passing round the cup, and reviewed the weapons they demonstrated. All were eager now, or to seem so. He congratu-

18

lated them. Nameless this far felt no excitement such as he had known on the beach. He guessed that would change, once he could properly make out their foe.

Despite the guards, no other here was mounted, and there were no chariots. What of the enemy?

'Come on,' said Nameless. 'Let's get down. We'll take the front. There's no organized plan – they don't know what they're at, but we do.' He put his hand on their shoulders, and they looked at him in the way he remembered, and did not know why. He had bound them to him. Therefore he must take care of them.

They advanced, loping, exchanging banter with those they passed, some of whom then trotted after, through the sprawled camp, out on to the plain of stones. No one now turned any of them back or tried to argue.

'You stay with me,' called Nameless. 'I go ahead, then you. Hold together. Look out for each other, as I will.'

'We'll be first – more glory.'

'Listen,' said Nameless, 'we're immortal now. Not one of us can die.' Their faces barely altered. Some smiled, nodding, others flinched, afraid of *that* where danger had not distressed them. But it was tepid and soon over. 'This,' said Nameless, 'is to prove us to be what we know we are. *Warriors*. Stay together. This enemy – we'll smash their fucking souls to pulp. Tonight, women and feasts. If not, we'll take what we need and go on to where they appreciate us. Either this is the Afterlife, or we're still in the world under some magic limitation. We have only to *fight* to be free.'

They sent up a cry for him, even those who had only followed his twenty-three did that. But all across the amassing armies other such affiliations rose. There was no coherence, and no commander over all.

At the front of the horde they pulled out, clear of the main force, and posted themselves on the stones. Again, there was no remonstrance from the guards. Several more of the other bands poured down to join them.

Every man looked into the north and west, and a few

minutes after, you could see the foe. At first they were only like a hurriedly moving mass, but presently it was apparent they were a mirror image, a second horde of men, jewelled with the blaze of metal, *running* towards them over the plain.

Nameless bounded across the stones. Though aware of them, he no longer, despite his promise, properly saw any of his own men. His eyes were fixed irreparably it seemed on what came to meet him.

Then something strange suggested itself about the advancing battalions.

It did not slow him, yet his brain began to work in another way, and at the same time he heard the ones following him shouting out the news, deriding and exclaiming.

'They don't bear any *weapons* . . .'

'No swords – not even *knives* . . .'

'*Shields* – that's all – see, one shield slung on each arm . . .'

'What will they do, flap them together and *clap* us to death?'

They still spoke of death, but Nameless noted their fierce laughter. He saw something else. The enemy were slowing down, stopping. They were *motionless*, and still a quarter-mile away.

That was when he experienced the unknown power, which rushed into him, from the atmosphere or the ground. It was like the strongest wine, although wine had never much affected him, he thought – had he ever been drunk? Now he was. Still running forward, he seemed suddenly to have achieved an additional, incredible speed, beyond anything possible to him in the world, and in his skull electric fires ignited, so his vision began to tinge everything with crimson . . .

At his back now he could sense that the others had been imbued with a similar genius. Growls and brayings erupted from them, like the outcry of contesting stags or elephants that charged.

Nameless, even running, stretched himself. He believed he felt himself grow much larger – every sinew, muscle, bone –

even sexually he rose up, angry, not to *enjoy*, the phallus only another weapon . . . His body was fluid, invincible – Borjiy berserker – the spell he had thought had been made for him there about him once more. Opening his jaws, he too roared.

There were lions in his voice, grey lions with beaded manes, and wolves, snarling under their silver pelts . . .

Lion – wolf—

I am—

I am *Lionwolf*—

And I will tear them all in shreds—

He was far in front of the whole Gullahammer now, and the bellowing of a beast detonated from his heart, throat and mouth. Cool above his own tumult, a diamond in his mind assessed the assault. Two minutes until he struck the enemy forward line – they could not stand against him. He, he alone, could shatter them into bits.

It had happened before.

This was when he finally saw the faces of those he was to destroy.

Had he *ever* truly seen that in the past?

Conceivably not. It shocked him, but only with delight. What did they matter? They were his to rend and splinter.

His hand that held the knife, his other hand that held the sharp stone he had picked up, combined with the long thick talons which his nails had become. Was his face that of an animal? A lionwolf?

There was one face in front of him, there in the enemy vanguard. He noticed it more than the rest. What was *that* face? It was only the face of a man . . .

The sun was low in the east, but it burned on the shields the enemy held before them. Did they intend to form a shield-wall? That would do them no service. Two shields to every man, defence not aggression: insanity.

Then the shields moved. Running full tilt Nameless – the Lionwolf – watched the shields draw in, fold out wide—

Something changed.

The forward line of the foe was breaking, lifting into the air, the *sky*—

The shields flared. They had changed their nature.

They were great wings.

Every man of the opposing force was going up into the air, and swooping now in over the racing, bestially roaring army of Shabatu.

And that face, that one face – the dark eyes had marked Lionwolf, even as Lionwolf's eyes – no longer blue, blood-red now as his hair – marked the stranger's.

Lionwolf sprang upward. It was a jump no man, however mighty, could ever have accomplished, the wrath-frenzied vault of a lion. As he did so, the winged man stooped low to seize him.

They met, between sky and land.

The impact was gargantuan, as if two mountains collided.

Lionwolf felt his talons sink through flesh, even as the talons of his enemy nailed themselves into his own. The flyer's hands were unimpeded – the wings independent.

They were eye to eye, like lovers struggling to a climax of death. But there could *be* no death now. Then what *could* there be, what invented alternative to destruction?

Like Lionwolf's the man's features had set in a rictus of fury; he might have been carved from bronze.

Lionwolf roped his adversary with his legs. This lock of limbs seemed impervious, but somehow the other dismantled it. In turn, he twined Lionwolf, and raked up one hand, clawed like that of the giant bird he had half become, to grip Lionwolf's neck.

Lionwolf instantly broke this hold, both of legs and hand. The stranger leaned away to give himself room and smote Lionwolf across the torso, a blow like that of a hammer. The stone Lionwolf had secured was gone.

They reeled apart.

The flyer, graceful as a hawk, balanced on the beating, dull-shining wings. He glanced behind and under him, searching it seemed to see how his comrades fared.

Lionwolf too looked down. His opponent and he had met some distance from the earth, then gone up higher, borne by the winged adversary's flight. Let go in nothing, Lionwolf found he did not drop, and was not astonished. Wingless, he too had the knack of withstanding gravity.

Below, he saw his own men, those first twenty-three, and many more, battling, kicking and writhing in the clasp of flying men, or crashing the flyers to the plain, rolling over them, stabbing with blades—

Lionwolf spun in air. He launched himself again straight at the one who had chosen to fight him and whom he had chosen to fight. Why procrastinate? Lionwolf thrust his knife up into the other's guts. There was slight resistance. The flyer had no armour, only leather and woollen garments like Lionwolf's own. The muscles beneath were hard enough, but not any match for steel.

The flyer showed his teeth in pain, but Lionwolf saw also he was amused.

'No death,' the flyer said, and pulled out the knife and slung it down the sky to the plain.

Lionwolf once more took hold of him then. He bent the flying man backward to snap his spine – but the flyer coiled and veered and lunged, seizing Lionwolf instead and pummelling his body so the punches rang.

'This is beguiling. You fight so nicely, like a lovely girl,' the flyer said, rocking back from the complementary blows Lionwolf slammed at his jaw.

Lionwolf kissed his lips to the flyer, grabbed his shoulders above the roots of the wings, and tore out his throat with teeth that were those of lions and wolves.

As the blood filled Lionwolf's mouth, even *then*, some memory, dank as despair, slunk through him. But he did not let go. He could feel the other weaken, toppling – and then a tilting judder as some shaft hurled from the ground went through one of the wings.

When he raised his head, face half masked in blood, hair of blood, eyes of blood, the Lionwolf saw the barely open eyes of the other watching back at him. The flyer could not speak, but somehow he swerved in the air, and, taking hold once more of Lionwolf's own neck – broke it.

Broke it. The ghastly grinding snap screamed through Lionwolf's skull and brain.

Death. There *was* death.

Deaf and unseeing, darkness like a cloud – falling now in an insulting rain of feathers shaken from the wings of what still clutched him—

Before they smashed into the stones, Lionwolf felt life come back. But it was too late. Healing, nevertheless he plummeted on rocks and on the mattressing bodies of men. He lay some minutes, only part living, and next to him the other – his *foe* – also part living, also coming back.

When he could turn his head, Lionwolf turned it. He looked again into the eyes of the other fallen man.

All that could come so far from either man's voice box was a hoarse whisper.

'I will kill you tomorrow, then,' rasped the winged one.

'And I you.'

The mantra it seemed was no longer 'No death'.

'Tell me your name, so I can be sure to find you again,' said the winged man, 'when you turn tail to run away.'

Lionwolf decided to hide his recovered name. He gave another version of it to this enemy.

'Know me. I am Vashdran. You?'

'You can know me by the name of Curjai.'

The spilled blood on his throat was already flaking off, the skin and tendons beneath were whole.

Lionwolf Vashdran lay looking up once more at the polished sky of the deathland, the bones of his spine thrumming as they knit. He thought, *If ever I doubted, now I know. I've died before.*

The other was already up and away before Lionwolf could rouse himself. But all around, beneath the lifting of the morning sun blue as an iris, countless quantities of men, winged, wingless, lay immobile.

24

It was like any battlefield. Yes, he could recall battlefields. Heaped corpses, decorated by blood, covering miles.

How could this be?

Kuul helped haul Lionwolf to his feet. Kuul said at once, 'I've remembered my name. But I don't want it, not here. I prefer Kuul.'

Lionwolf said, in a voice whose use still hurt, 'Do you remember the name of your wife?'

'Jasibbi.'

Others were moving up, the men who had been with Lionwolf – Nameless – the night before. Not all, however, not all.

'How have they died?' said Eleven, looking everywhere around. 'You can't die here. Can't be injured that will last. I had some bastard's bird claws through my eye – but it healed. Yorrin here, he got a slice in the heart – see him now.' They looked at number nine, Yorrin. The shirt and leather hung off in a stripe, all bloody, but under it the flesh was firm and closed, unscarred.

Lionwolf looked down. He saw, where he had been lying, Choy, who had been for Lionwolf a softer cushion than the stones. And how, under his healing neck, had lain the little wiry Kelp Lifli, who prayed to a shell.

'This place—' said Lionwolf. He stopped himself. He stared at them, all the ones who remained. 'We live. We will hold the rest in our memories. And we stick together like honey to a hive.'

They cheered. But all across that dreadful extensive battle-ground, aching and repaved with dead, cheers were eerily rising, for delegated leaders, for those who survived.

Lionwolf turned again to his band, now only ten in number. He said, 'My name is Vashdran.'

Going into Shabatu, the survivors of the battle stuck close, keeping to their own battalions.

The blue priests had reappeared, accompanied by the

snake-heads. A pair of phrases were spoken. Nothing about gods, death or honour. It was to do with victory, and reward.

But the men of the enemy force, the shield-wing flyers, were also encouragingly brought back towards the walls. So who had won this cutch of a battle?

The corpses were left without ceremony. In the empty sky not even any scavenger birds had gathered.

By day, the non-gleaming city walls looked only pale and unreasonable.

In through the iron gates all the men walked, Lionwolf Vashdran among them, under the silent gaping trumpet-mouth.

Within the first high wall was a space about wide enough for fourteen or fifteen men to move easily abreast. Running the far side of that lay another wall, high, opaque and toneless like the first. Both curved round together, and soon the upward-tending roadway gave on a flight of shallow stone steps. Vashdran counted the treads as they climbed. There were fifty, before another ascending roadway replaced them.

As they went on, Vashdran noted the other walls, rising and rising with them, one behind another. They were in fact continuations of the same two walls. The host climbed then on a spiral route, like that which marked the back of a sen-snail. Ah. He had remembered the name of a snail.

There had been another city too, more a big ice-glass town, effete if quite attractive. Had that also had a very long wide stair? Someone had told him of it . . . who?

Most of the men trekked up the roadways and steps without much said. There was no tiredness though many of them, so you heard, had been badly wounded, even slaughtered. Nothing remained of that.

The walls and walks were planed to a glacial uniformity, and nothing lived there, either in or on them, that Vashdran could detect. He judged their height as he would a crag. Choy had thought the city was a cliff. Why had Choy, Lifli, those others – those other hundreds spread outside on the stones – not survived?

'A long walk,' said Yorrin the heart-sliced, trudging just behind Vashdran. 'Where are we going?'

'Up there.' The voice of the one called Eleven in Jafn: Behf.

'Up *where*?'

'The top.'

Vashdran listened to them sparring, nearly good-humoured, at his back.

The sun rose with them as they wended up the city, and met them again startlingly an hour later when they came out on a high flat plateau. It was coiled in by the penultimate wall, and it supported at its centre the sky-pointing cone of the last wall of any.

The priests, who had gone ahead of them, flowed away over this space. The snake-heads still escorted the fighting force. The hair of these guards, hissing and worming about, had even here and there managed to escape by now its ties and slid down over backs and shoulders, to thrash and spit glaucous venom. The poison regularly showered both guards and warriors; the latter cursed it but seemed to suffer no harm. The jatchas had also padded up the city.

There was another gate in the central wall. This had chalk-white doors, complexly sculpted with tangled forms.

The sun had reached the zenith. Noon.

Suddenly voices sang out in a rhythmic chorus. The white gates flew wide. An imposing vista was seen inside them, a broad road lined with human-like forms which sang and danced, playing instruments. Drums beat and rattles cracked, small harps let out plinking cadences. The music burst up into the air. The words were in some tongue Vashdran did not know. Perhaps none of them could. But it bounced with feral joy, with lawless optimistic praise. *Welcome to Shabatu.*

Through the wall and along the road the victors strode and the music gyrated against them. Flowers fell on them, lush blue and purple, as if from the hothouses of a king. Vashdran caught one of these blooms. He looked into the amethyst cup of the flower, and saw there a single ice-grey eye, looking stonily back at him. He cast the flower away.

But the dancing, singing crowd was applauding them. Men were in the throng, and now women were both audible and visible, their high cajoling tones added to the chorus. Slim bangled arms shook trills from strings of bells, hair fluttered, rounded hips swayed.

Were any of them real? Or were they illusions, sprites . . .

At the end of the wide road a towering archway opened on what must be some vast palace of Shabatu.

They went in, the crowd surging and ceaselessly praising them in the unknown tongue, the unruly music.

The flowers with eyes were crushed underfoot.

A labyrinth. Hall gave on hall. Everything still stretched upwards, vaguely, coolly shining. There was no roof. The sun circled over, letting down sails of light.

Sometimes too things *dropped* from up there. Dimly seen in distance and at speed, each would strike somewhere below with a clashing thud.

There were hot springs, room after room of them. The fighters flung off garments, splashed and swam through fountains, or lay about in the long steaming pools of liquid azure water. Young men and women advanced to wait on them, bringing unguents, alcohol and sweets. When the first warrior chanced pulling a partner in with him, she swam against him in the water willingly. Soon enough, half the pools were busy with coupling. Noises of pleasure echoed through the halls.

Vashdran absented himself. After the heat of the bath, which made wet only during immersion, diminished, the cold of the labyrinth palace grew solid again. The atmosphere was visibly braided with patterns of frost. But it did not discomfort; you were unharmed.

He walked, as if idly, from pool to pool. The antics of the couples left him unaroused. The laughter and shouts were like those of children. Had they *forgotten* the morning?

For some, he supposed, to live like this – or be dead like this – was all they would ever want. War and invulnerable success,

28

sex and jollity after. Well, had he not vowed they would get these rewards?

His men – if they were his – did not follow him now. Not even Kuul, who lay out on the poolside with a fair-haired girl astride him.

Vashdran though was looking for something else. He had a purpose.

Finally he began to find groups of the enemy, the shield-wing flyers. They had not mingled with their adversaries, but their bathrooms commenced only a matter of paces off, and separated only by one more open arch.

Curjai was lying on his back in the third pool Vashdran came to. His dark hair floated round him on the water's top, his lean muscular body drifted. His eyes were closed, but the instant Vashdran stood over him the flyer spoke. 'So, you love me that much, you couldn't keep yourself away. I'm touched. Or have you only come to beg for mercy?'

Vashdran stood looking down at Curjai. Naked as the flyer, Vashdran seemed to notice similarities between them, in build, length of leg, physical stamina. Curjai too, as Vashdran did, had a skin that was tawny in colour, though the flyer's hair was a brownish-black. Neither bore scars, only the useful calluses on their hands.

Curjai's eyes opened lazily. Droplets of watered steam hung on his lashes. He smiled. 'You carry your weapon downwards. It can't be love then, can it?'

'Wake up,' said Vashdran. He was unsure why he said this.

'I'm awake. You?'

'Why did so many die?' said Vashdran. 'Answer that.'

Curjai looked aside. Men cavorted around them, in the pools or out, taking no notice either of the red-haired man standing there or of Curjai lying on the water.

'The gods know,' said Curjai. 'Why anyway is it always like that, some dying, some left alive?'

'We are not alive.'

Curjai frowned. 'You have something in that. This is an after-world. Somehow . . .'

29

Vashdran reached out into the air, and plucked one of the feathers of frost. 'This is Hell.'

Curjai came exploding from the pool, landing in front of Vashdran. Now they showed themselves to be also of equal height. And they had snarled into each other's faces not long before, were practised. 'You,' said Curjai, 'run home to your mother. I'm not done with you. Better have joy while you can.'

Vashdran pushed Curjai slowly and irresistibly away, and watched as the flyer fell back into the pool with a tidal concussion. Men swore, their sex-games disturbed.

Vashdran walked off through the arch.

'Where did you go?' asked Kuul, sprawled now eating dates and sugary things.

'Where did *you* go?'

'To a wonderful place. That girl took me there and we never moved off the spot. I must find her again in a minute.'

Vashdran sat by the smooth carapace of a wall. He thought he could feel it breathing against him. He thought it murmured, a sort of song: *Ask the snow what it is, ask ice, wind, sea and sky, ask wisely, wisely, but oh, what am I?*

A river ran through the feasthall, and away into dim caverns either side.

On each bank of it was a wide table, long as any lane, and through the middle of these two tables also two tributaries of the river went, bubbling and plashing in broad streams.

Evening was beginning, sky blue and bruising to black.

Torches burned white, like flaming snow.

Soft and easy from their bath and play the men, led by their attendants, wandered in and took their seats on the long benches. They peered into the tables' darting streams. 'Moving water! There are fish in there!'

The seating was along one side only, and on the further bank the same, so the diners would face each other, just the wider river between. The original army of Shabatu – if such it was –

sat the south side, the shield-wings to the north. You gauged
this from the compass point of sinking blue light in the west.

Music tinkled from somewhere. The unbiquitous, melli-
fluous attendants served more drink and treats.

'What will they have cooked for us? I've seen no animals
about the city.' Yorrin was uneasy.

Eighteen said, scathing, 'You ate it all up last night.'

Vashdran, sitting among them, looked for and discovered
the flyer Curjai at the opposite table over the river.

How wide was the water there? Not so wide, not wide
enough, maybe.

Then the food started to be brought in, great platters which
smoked. There was meat and pastry, vegetables which seemed
familiar, probably to all of them. Sauces were offered from long-
necked jugs like those seen in cities.

Kuul, on Vashdran's right, said, 'This is good. Better than
yesterday. Look, that gadcher of a winged thing is staring over.'

'Yes. He's raising his cup to us.' Vashdran lifted his silver
goblet, and pressed it to his lips. He did not swallow any of the
fiery Olchibe liquor he found in the cup. He would not toast
Curjai. No doubt Curjai did not down his mouthful either.

A sullen sorrow was on Vashdran. He could neither name it
– in this country of namings – nor shove it off. He bore it, like a
wound. In his mind, he saw the stony plain, and the dead who
could not die but had, sprinkled generously there as salt. What
would become of them? Tomorrow this unholy citadel must
reek from the fumes of decay.

'The water's getting up in the river,' said Yorrin.

'Along the bloody river in our table too,' added Nineteen.

They gawped. Two large fish dived high from the table-river
and arced back down, spraying everyone with water.

Nineteen, obviously believing this too succulent to pass up,
lurched forward, grabbing with both hands. He yelled.

Something else came out from the stream, attached to
Nineteen's hands.

It was like a tiny dragon, plated and sinuous. It clung on
with its claws and serrated teeth. Nineteen was screaming,

trying to pry it loose, but with no spare hand to accomplish this. Vashdran got up. He pulled one of the torches off the wall behind them and put it to the dragon-creature. Now it too shrieked and leaving go of Nineteen's bleeding fingers spurted back into the stream, was gone.

Kuul held Nineteen's shoulders as he threw up on the stone floor.

'It'll heal, fool. You can't be hurt here.'

Sobbingly Nineteen clasped Kuul like his father until Kuul pushed him off.

'Get back to the table. Eat your food.'

Already the abrasions were fading. Nervously giggling, Nineteen resumed his seat, and presently started again to dine.

'The moral of this tale,' announced Yorrin sententiously, 'is *never* pluck your dinner from running water.'

Vashdran threw the burning torch down over the bank into the black abysm of the river. He saw Curjai regarding this but pretending, like a woman, not to.

Now from the east, along the course of the river, some kind of boat was coming. Vashdran could see the soft lights at its prow, and oars dipping in the water.

His ten men had crowded round, all but Nineteen who was replacing his lost food, refusing to look up. Others from their side were also leaving the table, assembling on the bank to stare away, through the inchoately luminous arches and caverns of the labyrinth, at the boat. On the far bank too the flyer men left their places, Curjai among them.

What was slinking up the river towards them all?

Vashdran could make out the torch he had jettisoned burning there under the black surface of the tide. The water here, then, did not extinguish fire. Something to memorize.

The boat was long and low. There were no rowers, the oars worked by themselves. In the middle was a black awning, and under this were two chairs. Here sat two figures, not properly to be seen.

A priest standing in the prow blew a horn, and rounded echoes winged away from the solitary note.

'Another of those flat-faces.' Yorrin gnawed a meat bone brought from the table.

Kuul said, 'More of them, look.'

They turned and saw the priests arriving, orderly and together in their advance as things that had one brain between them. Over the river it was the same. Behind both long tables the cloud of priests assembled, raptly gazing towards the river.

'*And* from above.'

Something was drifting lightly downwards. It was a sort of broad platform, lowering itself as if weightless, on a chain which must slide from some high shelf in the walls.

There were priests on the platform, but at the front of it was positioned a slender, pale-clad shape, which as it descended folded its hands and began to sing.

'*What is it?* Is it a *child*?'

'It's a boy. It sings like the trained boys in the freakish temples of western lands,' declared Kuul, uncertainly.

Behf said, 'No, it's old. Look at its face. And the voice . . .'

The singing was alternately pure and horrible. It had rich sudden fullnesses, and a needle-fine upper register. But then the voice would stumble and change to a soulless strength-less drone.

The elderly child sang on until the platform had halted low above the river. Then it concluded, bowing its head.

Vashdran though had barely taken his eyes off the boat.

Something cold and genderless called: 'The king is here.'

The vessel had reached a spot below, just where the torch had been thrown in and still burned. The awning and its deep shadow concealed the two seated forms. But Vashdran thought one was male, and one a woman – the king then, the King of Hell, and his wife.

The unseen caller called again.

'Here are the lists of those who will fight tomorrow in the Stadionum, which privilege they have won by their prowess in battle.'

Dumbly, the men along the banks attended. Not every name by any means was called out. Vashdran heard his own, that was the name he had given himself here, and that of two of his men: Kuul, Yorrin – the very ones now beside him. And he heard as well the name of Curjai. That was enough for Vashdran. A grim satisfaction washed over his mind. Tell himself as he might that Hell had reduced him in a hundred ways, he felt settled, stimulated, very nearly at *peace*. The chosen others were the same, he saw. Only the several men not chosen were frazzled and angry. He heard rough cries – *Why not me? I fought as well as that one.*

Even this did not disturb Vashdran. He had gone back to staring down into the boat.

It was then that the male figure, presumably the King, got to its feet and walked forward into the prow.

Gradually and totally all sound ebbed from the banks.

The King of Hell, if so he was, stood taller than most and was heavily built. His bare arms showed chunks and plates of muscle, as did the column of his neck. A loose dark hood covered his head. He was the colour of Hell, bluish-grey, and the skin that covered him had cracked a little, but did not move.

'Is he . . .' whispered Kuul, 'is—'

'He's made of stone,' said Vashdran. 'That's novel.'

It was. The stone King could, unlike his skin, move fluently. His mouth had somehow looped into a thin smiling, and his eyes, black as the river and, like the river, spangled with the lights, passed across all the men clustered above and around him.

He said nothing, the Stone. Only looked at them all, in silence. Then he went back to his chair under the awning, and she, the woman who must be his consort, walked out into the prow instead.

She was not stone. She was like the liquid curving river . . . like the flight of a bird . . .

Vashdran started as if someone had stuck a red-hot dagger into him.

'What?' asked Kuul. 'Don't you like her? She's—'

'Quiet,' said Vashdran. When they obeyed him, even the other men standing near who had been murmuring over her, Vashdran merely forgot them.

He knew the woman. He did not know how, or from where. He did not know her name. Or did he?

She was slimly yet voluptuously curved, and her long hair, curling like a fleece, hung to the hem of her golden-white clothing. Her hair was black, and her eyes, but her skin blackest of all – black as night.

'Like Star Black,' Kuul risked muttering.

'Then,' said Vashdran, 'she too must have been made from snow.'

The woman did not smile as her partner had done. She appeared impassive, perhaps slightly quizzical. For a queen she had few ornaments, only the faint dust of gold across her dress and hair.

She raised her arms. They were like the stems of black irises, the kind that broke sometimes from channels in the ice fields after a harvest of dormant grains.

Vashdran paid no attention to this flicker of memory. He could not look away from the woman, not even inside his mind.

Then the moon came, the moon of Hell.

It came because the black woman summoned it. So much was obvious.

Preceded by a blazing white radiance that dulled the torches, the round orb swam into the sky above the high walls. At first it seemed to come swiftly, but once in view it grew motionless. It had a likeness to other moons Vashdran had seen, full and blinding bright. Brighter than the sun of Hell-day perhaps.

The woman lowered her arms. As she turned to go back to her chair, some small groups of the men shouted to her, surprisingly couthly, asking her to remain. If this was impertinent, or could at all matter, was unsure. But no reprimand was issued, nor did she heed the shouts. Back under the awning she went, and sat down beside her lord, the Stone.

The awful disparate singing began again from the floating platform, which now was drawn up and away. The boat rowed itself forward downriver.

Not one man did not stare after the boat. Until, as the last glimpse of it blended with distance, a whistling roar jerked them from their trance. Out of the moonlit sky something, some huge black thunderbolt, arrowed towards them. Next second it smashed into the river, sending torrents of non-wet, freezing liquid up the banks and walls. But the river closed over the missile, and it might never have been.

Vashdran, who was Nameless, and Lionwolf, roved through the labyrinth of Hell.

Far off, yet for a long while, he heard the feasthall bellowing on with drink and boasts. In his head lay a sharp-edged fragment, Kuul's murmur to Yorrin, 'Let him go. He's remembered his wife.'

Not so, Kuul. Not my wife. Or only once.

Yes, he had remembered her. He had remembered it *all*.

It had suggested itself to him that, in this edifice, you had only to wander about to find any location you ever wanted or must reach. But the palace was really like a landscape, or the inside of a mountain, mined by caves.

In just such a clandestine closet he and she – last time – had lain down.

She had made him wait for sex, but by that hour in the mountains he was ruined, half-mummified with guilt and despair. And when he put his hands on her, when he lay over her – she had drained the fire from his spirit.

Chillel.

That had been her name. But here? How did they name her, here? Because she was not quite as she had been, he believed. This version of her beauty was more sumptuous, luxurious at breast and hip. Her hair curled more, did it not? A little more . . . though it was as long and lustrous. Her face too: the same, yet – was it more *sweet*? For Chillel had been sweet *only* in her beauty, and this new version of Chillel had almost a human curiosity in her expression.

Chillel had been made of snow. She had gouged the fire out of him – but he had melted *her*.

Vashdran laughed.

The laugh cracked round the towering walls, hit the moon-struck sky.

He could remember all of his life now. It had rushed back to him, as the boat meandered away. How he had grown in ten or eleven years to the intelligence and physique of a heroic man. How he had become without any effort a magician, a lover, a leader, a *conniver* – a king indeed. He could remember the city of the world, the one that had disappointed him, with its twinkling ruby and zircon parasols and the high bastions which, to the walls of this Hell, were only toys. Lions, he remembered those, hawks and hounds, women and men, a mother, an uncle, and mortal enemies on whom he had lavished witty punishments and surcease.

He remembered also dying himself. But the actual means of death lurked behind an inner partition and was not yet to be re-experienced, let alone seen. He would come to it. But for a while – Great Gods *keep him from it.*

'Guri,' said Vashdran. 'Olchibe Uncle Guri. Peb Yuve, mighty leader of the vandal bands. Saphay, my mother.'

But his father had been a god.

Vashdran spun about and crashed his skull against one of the hard walls of Hell.

It stunned him. He slipped down to the ground, and sat propped there like some drunken idiot.

In life, if there are agonies, the escape of death is always an option. But once *dead* – what then?

As his head cleared from the battering, buzzing slightly like aggravated bees, he began to hear a different music.

Under his lids slowly he looked along the space where he had been walking. It was like a long narrow room, and gave on another through the usual soaring arch.

There sat three or four women on a glassy floor, with harps balanced over their knees. They played and sang in remote pastel voices.

At the middle of that adjacent room, beyond the musicians, was a flight of stairs, and on this the black woman who was

Chillel, and was not, poised with one hand outstretched. Down into it, from the open roof above, countless brilliant orbs were flying. They lit on her fingers, or circled round her, friendly moths that were each a tiny gleaming moon.

Their reflections danced on her, danced across the stony palace.

For a moment he did not notice she had seen him. Then he saw she had.

He sat where he was, on the floor, staring straight back at her.

After another minute, she spoke. He heard the words. 'What's there.' Not a question. She had articulated in the tongue of Olchibe. It meant: *Something of great significance is before me.* He had no urge to get up and talk to her. He rested against the wall, and soon a curtain like flexive opal dropped over the archway and hid it, even the music and the glitter of flittering moons.

THREE

Around the Stadionum of Shabatu the benches were crowded by people who excitedly shouted or laughed, waving or making gestures of contempt. They seemed physically real, but if so who were they? Where did they come from – out of the city walls? Whatever else, they had filled the thirty-odd tiers that rose up through the stadium. Snake-head sentries kept guard, set on the dividing stairways like statues, each with a single jatcha or a pair. Sometimes flowers were tossed down to the stadium's oval floor, which seemed made of marble, densely scored to prevent slipping.

Vashdran, Yorrin and Kuul stood at the oval's edge, looking about, seeing all this. For a couple of hours they had been corralled behind one of the gates of openwork metal that ringed the floor, gazing out at others who already fought. The action had been fast and violent, but with each 'kill' a bout finished. In this way and in so short a while, twenty-nine skirmishes were hatched – and terminated.

'Where does the blood go?' Kuul had asked, with reluctance.

'Soaks down through the floor,' Yorrin mumbled, his eyes glued to the current combat, by then five men – all that were left of eight – hacking each other apart. They looked perhaps like Faz warriors, having blotched their faces with blue.

'How? The floor's stone.'

'It's *all* stone. Even the gadcher of a king is stone.'

'What do you think, Vashdran?'

'It's magic,' said Vashdran. His face was stone too, had been since the previous night. Kuul and Yorrin curtailed the debate.

Ten minutes later, the last of the fighters strutting, or dragged off motionless, their gate rolled up with a snarling shriek of hinges.

Out they went, on to the blood-drinking marble floor.

Then another gate opposite went up, and three others swaggered through.

'Three to three. And *that* one. He's mine. Should have had a bet on it.'

'You knew it was him, eh, Yorrin?'

'Who else?'

Vashdran said quietly, as they began to move out over the oval arena, 'Yorrin, what do you mean?'

'We're linked, *he* and I are. I know that one. He helped sack my village in the Marginal Land. I slew him at Sham. Then I saw him again last night, at table over the river.'

So Yorrin had been of Rukarian steader stock. Vashdran considered the Marginal Land, infinities off in the world, between Ruk Kar Is and Gech. Yes, the opponent Yorrin talked of had a yellowish Olchibe cast to his skin. He might well have run with one of the vandal bands.

Names – always names – were being called by priestly voices from some upper tier. It was the normal formula that they had already heard applied to others. 'You fight for honour. Without honour you are nothing and must leave this place. Therefore fight well. Here are your matches. Kuul with Heppa and Heppa with Kuul. Ginngow with Yorrin and Yorrin with Ginngow' – Ginngow meant swan-pig: swan*swine* – 'Curjai with Vashdran and Vashdran with Curjai.'

I said I would look out for these men in war.

It was no use. Vashdran had eyes only for one.

Curjai strode forward, arrogant, grinning, lifting his arms to the enthused if unreal mob.

The high cold sun burned on Curjai, and filled his dark eyes with blue.

Vashdran found he darted forward ahead of the rest. Curjai incensed him. There was neither time nor reason to ask why.

The snake-heads had already handed every fighter weapons. There had been no choice.

Vashdran had looked in bored distrust at the apparently virgin sword they gave him, flat-bladed, the hilt ready roughened and bound in leather strips. There was now no difficulty, however. He slapped it in across Curjai's ribcage and heard the grunt of expelled breath. Curjai leaned forward, airlessly blaspheming some outlandish, never-heard-of god. But as Vashdran drove the blade back, to cripple, Curjai's own blade, a long, double-faced, notched knife, swung in and chipped the blow away.

I should have killed him at the first stroke. Why play? Some can die, but not I or he . . .

Vashdran stepped back.

'Good morning, darling,' he said.

Curjai straightened, spat on the marble, and lifted his handsome head.

'But did you slumber well, my pet?' he inquired tenderly. 'Maybe I can lullaby you off to sleep again.'

Behind him, Vashdran heard the swords and knives of Yorrin and Kuul at work on those of the other two – Heppa, Ginngow. No man had been given a shield. So *this* one would not sprout wings and take to the sky.

Curjai sliced in at him.

Vashdran felt the knife – long as any sword and square ended – unseam his forearm and drizzle over the bone.

Left-handed he struck Curjai in the face and Curjai's left hand came in turn, punching into Vashdran's throat.

Vashdran staggered back. He gagged, but his vision stayed lucid. He must end this. How to slaughter what could not be killed?

He heard Kuul singing a battle chant of the Jafn Irhon. Yorrin used slamming damning thuds of flesh and steel. But these other fights were miles away.

It was like love. Did Vashdran *know* what love was? Exclusive, immediate, augmenting or painting out the remainder of existence with its colours.

He bent, skimmed the unalive sword along the marble, its passage raising a foul shriek, brought it upwards in an arc. Curjai was leaping forward. The blade met him exactly as and where Vashdran had desired.

Vashdran felt the resistance and give of severed flesh and sinew, muscle and skeleton.

A rose-red fountain flamed into the air. The head of Curjai, so well made, dark locks swirling, tumbled away along the arena.

Vashdran straightened.

The moronic, probably unreal people on the tiers were screaming in adulation, and the filthy eye-flowers raining down.

Vashdran looked briefly over his shoulder. He saw Kuul drawing his sword from the heart of the foe called Heppa. And that Yorrin too was dead – or 'dead'.

Looking again at the head of Curjai. Vashdran could see it had bowled to the far barrier. It lay there. The eyes *blinked*. But Curjai's body was stretched out quite close, flaccid, as if resting.

Vashdran went to the body. He kicked it once, sharply in the side. And at this it spasmed.

Then he heard Curjai calling hoarsely, softly, *carryingly*, under the tumult of the tiers, 'Here – come here, you . . .'

The body flipped over. It got up on all fours, and crawled, like a bemused dog, away over the stadium.

'Here – here – hurry up. I'm *waiting*.'

Vashdran burst suddenly into laughter. Above and around those on the benches were laughing too. And Curjai's head also laughed.

The crawling dog of body reached the cut-off head. They united, without shame, and were again scarlessly one.

Curjai stood up on the oval, and raised his arms, and the crowd thundered, and the flowers fell like the snow of a winter world.

Vashdran caught one, as he had before. He looked into the petals and saw, not an eye, but a mouth fixed with pointed hungry teeth. He stamped on it.

42

Kuul was there.

'Yorrin's dead.'

'We can't die. *He* can't. It happened before on the plain, remember, and he lived.'

'No, he is dead. Some still can die.'

Vashdran looked, and Yorrin lay on the ground, bloodless. But Yorrin's opponent, the one whose name meant Swanswine, and whom Kuul had dispatched, was healing at a great rate, pulling himself up, making obscenely definite gestures at girls in the crowd. Kuul's own slain match, Heppa, was also back on his feet.

'Truly,' said Kuul, 'surely and for ever. This is Hell.'

Vashdran woke screaming. Kuul shook him fully awake.

'Sleep is still the main enemy,' said Kuul.

'So . . . you Jafn say.'

'Aren't you Jafn, Vash? I thought you were.'

'Sometimes,' said Vashdran. He sat up. They were in one of the long rambling nothing-halls of the labyrinth. It was evening. Elsewhere the feasting went on, as it did every night, apparently. Or at least as it had done for the eleven days and nights they had now been in the purlieus of this palace.

'I was dreaming,' said Vashdran absently.

Kuul looked at him again. 'Yes?'

'I dreamed of my death.'

'The death today when that cutcher Curjai finally killed you? It's the first time he has. Ten times before you've—'

'Decapitated him, impaled his heart, gutted him. I recall quite well, Kuul. He always jumps up again and his head can call his body back like his hound or hawk. It wasn't that death, today, my dream. Death here is only pain, and a handful of moments that touch oblivion with one finger. There's no such thing as death any more, for *us*.'

'No, Vash.'

'You die here too. Is it the same for you?'

He asks almost like a child, Kuul thought, surprised. *Sometimes*

43

he's like that, though so vital and shining. Who is he? I can never quite remember, though I remember a war – I remember a chariot, and riding at his back. And I must have died then, actual death, and I don't recall that either. Only my fake deaths here.

'About the same as you say. Like a faint. Like . . . sleep,' said Kuul.

Vashdran got to his feet. He had believed he and Kuul were alone in this chamber, but Kuul himself had followed him, and now Vashdran saw others must have followed Kuul. They too then had heard him cry out in terror. Anger set Vashdran's face once more like the stone face of the King.

He stalked across the space and stood glowering down on the Olchibe Ginngow, which meant Swanswine, and the other man, Heppa, who were playing some type of game with peculiar rounded dice. Curjai sat nearby, his back to the wall, carefully paring his nails with the edge of his knife.

'We meet too often,' said Vashdran. 'Why are you here?'

'Here's as favourable as anywhere,' replied Curjai temperately, not looking up.

'Tomorrow,' said Vashdran, in his beautiful voice that carried now no meaning, 'I'll think of something more challenging for you.'

'Yes, it loses its savour, all this unfruitful death.'

'Not for some,' muttered Swanswine. 'Not for Yorrin.' He threw the dice and seemingly won, though how or what was unclear. Vashdran leaned over and pulled him up anyway in mid-cackle. He lifted Swanswine high, like a boy, and slung him about sixty paces off, skidding down the room to land hard against an adjacent wall.

Heppa said stupidly, 'What was that for? We'll get enough of *that* tomorrow.'

After the first bout in the arena eleven days back, they still fought, but now two against two, since Heppa had been allocated another group. Swanswine fought Kuul. Yorrin's death had necessitated this. For Yorrin *had* died when Swanswine cut him down, and afterwards they had seen the corpse dragged away, as others had been. Where the bodies went none knew.

The indigenous population could or would not say – neither the phantasmal, brainless crowds and the automatons of snake-head guards, nor the pleasure servants. Perhaps the stadium dead went to the same graveyard as had the cadavers off the battlefield, for no stench of decay had blown up from the plain.

'Why are *you* here, Heppa, you blown-in snot-rag? You no longer fight with *them.*' Kuul was trying to keep the front united.

Heppa shook his head. He did not know, it seemed. He was a big, shaggy lout, a Vorm, though he did not much talk in their way, from the outer isles of the world, and dropped in the form-ative years on his brain, Kuul deduced.

Swanswine meanwhile was lumbering back up the hall, his braids clinking with tiny skulls, gathering speed to run at Vashdran. Vashdran shot him one withering glance, never shifted.

It was Curjai who shouted, 'Ginngow! Put your anger up your arse and come and sit down, for the love of Attajos.'

Kuul sniffed in disdain – *Attajos*, some foreign, unimportant god.

But Swanswine shook off his rage with an oath, then sat placidly down by Curjai.

'Let us talk,' said Curjai, 'like civilized men.'

'Where on the face of the world do you hail from that you think yourself civilized?' burst out Kuul.

'A beautiful upland, flowing with pretty snow and ice and galloping with herds of edible animals. I've remembered it all. You?'

Kuul shrugged. 'Similar. But you're brown-skinned. Where did you get that?'

'From my gods.' He nodded idly at Vashdran. 'As did he. And like you,' he added, now looking directly up into Vashdran's face, 'I dream of my real death. And wake up yelling for my mother, as you do.'

Vashdran bristled, grew expressionless again. 'Well. I imagine we'll meet tomorrow as usual. We can debate it then.'

'Let's meet now.' Curjai rose. He held out his right hand for

Vashdran to clasp. And Vashdran recollected how he himself had taken men's hands, and seen the current of his power course into them, seductive and total. There had been one who refused, as if guessing what would happen. *He* had been a king, but only a mortal one.

Smiling, Vashdran copied the words of Bhorth, the Rukarian king who refused. 'I will not.'

'Ah,' said Curjai softly, exactly as had Vashdran on that occasion, 'I must take *your* hand, then.'

Curjai's grip was not familiar, despite every various contact they had had when fighting – killing – each other. It was strong, nearly calming, full of a steady pulse. But what did Curjai feel? His eyes widened slightly, that was all. They were lighter in shade than Vashdran had thought, or perhaps that was only because Curjai, now, was not in combat.

And Curjai said, 'Blue eyes,' to Vashdran. 'It's the berserker scarlet I usually see on you.'

'What's this,' said Vashdran, 'a handfasting?'

'Surely. Don't warriors make that where you come from?'

'Blood-brotherhood.'

'Then certainly you and I already created that. Have we tasted enough of each other's blood, do you think?'

'The last man I swore the bond with I tricked and defeated and sent to his real death. A bad one.'

'Time then to polish the bond up again with another.'

'Not with you.'

'It's done. Too late.'

Vashdran said, in a low angry drumming voice, 'I'm royal by birth and supernatural otherwise. My father was a god.'

'Fine as sunny days,' said Curjai. 'Mine too.'

'You lie.'

Curjai laughed. He still gripped Vashdran's hand, and Vashdran had not yet pushed him off. The other three squinted at the phenomenon lamely, Kuul with his knife drawn, Heppa scratching, Swanswine wearing an uncomfortable sneer.

'How to prove my birth-line,' said Curjai. 'Tell me. I'll convince you.'

'This is the Death Place. Nothing can *convince* here. Or if it does, I'd be as great a fool as you.'

'There are none of my countrymen with me that I've seen,' said Curjai. 'I lost them all on the way. But maybe even they wouldn't have sworn to what I am – or was. Not here.'

'Curjai, I have no concern as to what you were, or are. I bother to fight you every day because, as yet, I can think of no better activity.'

'Let me suggest one.'

Vashdran dropped Curjai's hand – or it loosed itself. They stood there, still looking eye to eye.

'Well?'

'We tell them, our supposed masters here, we will no longer fight. We're matched. We can destroy each other over and over and nothing can come of it.'

'That will be the idea,' whispered Kuul. 'We're in *Hell*.'

'Then let's invent another idea,' replied Curjai, not taking his eyes off Vashdran. 'This one grows too boring.'

It was Swanswine who chuckled. Then Heppa, only taking his lead, perhaps.

Vashdran said, 'Presumably then we'll earn some punishment.'

'So what? Whatever they do can't harm us. And it might make a change.'

Startlingly maybe, Swanswine pronounced, 'They could exile us to some new spot. I heard that, in the halls: exile if you won't fight.'

'From who?'

'It just – mutters about. Haven't you heard that? Fragments of talk and music, moans, sighs – like ghosts. It comes out of the walls.' Each of the other men, even Vashdran, nodded. Yes, they had all caught these snatches of sound. The walls spoke to them, or to nothing. They trapped bits of song and vocal sorrow, and subsequently let them go, to waft through the maze of the palace. The walls were not alive, precisely, but it seemed that something *in* them was.

Vashdran thought, *In fact, that is where they come from, those*

47

men and women we encounter here – guards, slaves, mobs. Out of the walls . . .

Curjai said, 'Exile. If we're in Hell, where else is there to go or be sent?'

'Somewhere worse,' said Vashdran with distaste. 'Where the twice-dead were damned to – Choy, Yorrin. All the rest.'

But Kuul said softly, 'Or somewhere better?'

Vashdran stepped away from Curjai, turned and walked off over the floor. As if at a signal, the other men also scattered. And as they did so, a whining roar broke through the black, dull-starred sky above.

A piece of that sky now dashed down on them. It was another of the vast boulders, which every day or night inside the labyrinth they had either heard crash, or occasionally seen thundering into the river in the feasthall.

Now the howling rock hit the floor between them, a direct impact, with a sound that hurt the ears, shook the earth, made the walls sing like a harp-string.

The floor parted. As the river did, the marble received the missile, shimmered with rings and waves, settled, and was once more whole.

'Ice heals like that,' said Heppa, gaping at the unmarked ground.

Each man of the five turned as one and moved off alone, across the hall and on, into countless identical others.

FOUR

He found the Stadionum by night because he willed to do so. As Vashdran had suspected, you only had to search for a goal to locate it.

It was especially uncanny, the stadium, in the dark. Only starlight, no moons, illumined its pale, viscous-looking surfaces, the tiers of benches, the stairs and the arena. No one was there but for himself.

Slowly he descended the tiers, and sprang over the low barrier to the arena floor. He recalled, by now having seen it often, how the floor drank men's blood, just as the floors of the palace halls swallowed rushing boulders.

But, solitary in the arena, Vashdran felt himself become afraid, although he had never experienced any fear when fighting.

He thought again then of his true earthly death.

The dream tonight had shown him. It had not, in the dream, happened to him; he had *seen* it happen to a man who without doubt was himself.

There had been an ocean of the world, some huge dark mass, no ship – instead, a monster of the deep. On the back of this leviathan was Lionwolf, as he had called himself in life. Lionwolf entirely resembled Vashdran as now he was, even to the long red hair. But at once something had started to work on Lionwolf, a kind of psychic acid. He dissolved downward through breakneck periods of youth, childhood, infancy; became after this a baby, lying kicking there, mindless and shrieking. But the baby too was soon psychically eaten away. It sank into an embryo, a *seed*, a smoke . . . It disappeared.

Despite living through none of this personally in the dream, Vashdran was drenched by horror.

He thought, had the man named Curjai also dreamed of his own dying, as he had said? Very likely. All of them here perhaps must now and then do that.

But Vashdran's Lionwolf death was the product of some excessive sorcery. An Unmaking.

He knew, despite an effort to deceive himself, that several important details before this death stayed anxiously incoherent. The beast in the sea, for example, which had itself wanted to kill him and so activated his fate in such an appalling scenario.

He leaned on the barrier wall now, and sensed it shift slightly against him, like an accommodating animal. Indistinct murmurs rose from it, but he did not pay attention.

His mother too had died. He knew that. And his uncle, Guri, who had been almost better than a father to him. But the uncle was adoptive, and besides a type of ghost. Also he was an Olchibe, sinewy and braided and yellow-skinned like Swanswine, and with painted teeth.

Vashdran had recaptured their names. Yet even so – *what* had they been, these people?

The barrier walls made one of their sighing sounds, as if trying to tell him.

'Hold your noise,' he said.

The walls rustled and grew dumb.

Vashdran paced up and down the length of the arena. Overhead the large dull stars blinked as if tired.

He knew, or thought he did, no one would pursue him here until dawn. Then Kuul would arrive, and Curjai who lyingly claimed immortal blood, and all the others too. Dawn was when they assembled to fight. But the crowd – they were why Vashdran had come here. More than privacy, with a perverse and jagged curiosity he wanted to see where they emerged from, and if it was as he believed.

He slept awhile again, and the sun was rising in the unseen

east, dyeing that side of the sky-roof thinnest blue. All around, as he opened his eyes, he heard them *evolving*. Just as he had reasoned, the people of Shabatu either lived, or were constructed, in the walls.

They stepped out in strands like garlands of bodies and draperies. Shapes became women with flowers wound in their hair and bracelets on their wrists, and men dressed for a holiday. They had, as usual, every sort of clothing he had ever seen in the world, and other styles of garments too. The moment they erupted forth they formed, like bubbles from a strange white clay, and were somehow instantly coloured in and finished off, as if by invisible craftsmen.

Already they were chattering, warbling. Probably it made them, whatever unhuman golems they were, happy to be free and in bodily format, able to hurry about and flap their arms.

The guards did not come out of the walls. *They* ebbed up out of the stairs or floor, reminding Vashdran of how he had seen the first man, Choy, wade from the deadly Hell-sea by the beach of flints. The guards were at first completely dark, and lightened to their blue-grey tone, the reverse of the white clay people who had had to be tinted. Some of the guards paused to tie back their venomous snake-hair. But it was routine, they did it without fuss or any interest.

Last of all, the eyeless dogs, the jatchas, curdled into being. They came neither from walls or floors, but out of the ready-hardened bodies of the guards, one or two hounds for each figure.

Vashdran stood, and the crowd saw him and pointed and threw its flowers. But the nearest guard approached, and spoke in the group-voice of his kind. 'Why are you here?'

It was what he and others had asked earlier.

'I came to see.'

'Go in behind a gate.'

The guard's jatcha padded forward, but Vashdran had already moved to obey. As the gate lifted Vashdran retreated into the area behind it. The openwork metal dropped back. The jatcha prowled outside, tilting its lean head, seeming to peer through at Vashdran from the skin where its eyes should be.

'What?' he said to it quietly.

The dog put its nose against the mesh, snuffing up Vashdran's non-human scent.

Vashdran said, 'You know me. You're the one I named. Star-Dog. Remember? I'll be your friend.'

The dog hesitated. But only momentarily. Then it padded away after the guard who had given it life.

Curjai, when he appeared behind an arena gate, came with a shield on either arm. And behind him the other two, sloppy Heppa who no longer belonged in their group, and frowning Swanswine. They also had, each of them, two shields. No weapons.

This presumably indicated Curjai's side would fly.

Vashdran scrutinized them. No one yet had sent Heppa off or elsewhere. Did Curjai mean to stick to what he had suggested, an end to combat?

It was not, nevertheless, to be three against two. Behf now appeared inside their gate with Vashdran and Kuul. Behf seemed to be pleased to be rejoining them. He said to Vashdran, earnestly, 'The other men of our battalion ask after you. Not all of them were allowed to fight again. They resent that.'

'Poor boys,' said Vashdran.

Behf missed the irony. 'Yes, it's a pity,' he agreed.

Minutes before the gate went up and they advanced into the arena, Vashdran heard Kuul tell Behf about the confrontation of the previous night. Behf seemed shocked Vashdran and Kuul, even Curjai and his two, had not instead stayed to feast, drink and lay the willing attendants. 'The King boated by again,' Behf reminisced, impressed. 'The Queen, too. It was worth staying just to see her.'

'Did she call a moon again?'

'Oh, yes. It'll only appear if she does it. A great big moon, like before. Always at full. Like her tits.'

Then the gates hefted up and out they went.

Having seen the shields of their opponents, Vashdran asked himself if his side would now change to beasts and berserkers. This brought inspiration, and he felt the stinging heat of antici-pation, like the stirring of desire, yet quite different.

The golem-like crowd was rowdy with approval. The flower-things splattered the marble. Vashdran trod on as many as he could, going forward.

As they had now eleven, twelve times, Curjai and he stood facing each other. Curjai's face carried no memory of his earlier words.

He can't give it up. Nor can I.

Then Curjai's two shields clapped inward, outward, slanting back, becoming wings. Raising his freed arms, Curjai lifted on the wings, into the sunny grey air. But—

Vashdran, Kuul and Behf watched as Curjai swept down and along the crowd, which applauded, then shouted in make-believe or actual alarm. Curjai swooped, gifted one of the snake-heads the most dulcet tweak on the ear, and landed on the top of the barrier.

Vashdran observed him, sword ready yet passive. He wondered abstractedly what Curjai's wings really *meant*. As for the other two, Heppa and Swanswine, they had not used their shields, only put them down on the ground.

Curjai called, his voice carrying in the oval's perfect acoustic. 'We're done brawling with each other. See, I've finished with it.'

The crowd ceased its noise. It sat there, perplexed. But even the guards did not make any aggressive move.

Curjai leapt off the barrier and straight to Vashdran. He threw his left arm over Vashdran's shoulders. 'Say something, you,' he said. 'Am I to do all the work?'

Vashdran did not know if he was glad or sorry.

'Why do I need to speak, when *you* bark so loud?'

'Look out,' said Curjai, drawing aside, 'here come the bloody barking hounds.'

Dogs poured down the terraces, bounding over into the arena.

Kuul and Behf, Heppa and Swanswine, raced over. Now the men were an inseparable circle, facing out on the oval of the Stadionum.

Curjai's wings had shrivelled from him. They curled up like burnt papers and shed themselves, redundant.

The jatchas, having landed, trotted about, staying back against the gates, where other men, restrained by the mesh, were quarrelling and squalling, infuriated either by non-fighters or by authority's reaction.

'Are those dogs real?' asked Behf.

'No, they're made of mud,' said Curjai. 'Mud with teeth.'

'Wait,' said Vashdran. He called, short and sharp. 'Star-Dog! Here, my love! Come here!'

And Star-Dog, the jatcha which had thumped first into the ring, came prancing, the others – of whom there were five – running behind him.

Vashdran stood solid and let the great blue blind hound rear up. Its heavy paws, with tendons like corded brass, banged home on Vashdran's shoulders. Its rancid-smelling, white-fanged muzzle burrowed against the hollow of his throat. But it no longer stank of anything evil. Its breath was only like that of a healthy dog which had been gorging on raw meat and fish.

'My pride,' said Vashdran, rubbing the dog's pointed-up ears. 'Now you're mine.'

The jatcha whimpered. He stroked down its hard, smooth back. It too felt like stone, but stone which sinuously lived and was warm.

The rest of the pack waited a little way off, taking in the greeting of their pack leader and the new man in his life.

'Curjai,' said Vashdran. 'Do you know dogs?'

'Yes. One bit me once.'

'Forget it. Call this fellow's mate out of the pack.'

'How?' said Curjai. He sounded unconfident.

'The Great Gods know,' said Vashdran. 'But anything seems likely to happen here, if you force it to.'

Curjai paused. Then he whistled. It seemed like something

he had learned, and was piercing. At once from the clump of jatchas emerged a lean blue bitch.

She did not rear up as Vashdran's dog had. She threw herself at Curjai's feet and rolled suggestively on the ground.

'See. She likes you.'

Vashdran raised his head past the head of the hound named Star-Dog, and saw Hell's guards jumping now into the arena.

They spoke in their voice.

'You have created anew your Cesh, your Battalion, your Unit, your Band, your Squadron . . .' Other words were intoned. The men in the arena, the attractive creatures on the tiers, listened and made no comment. 'You have done well,' said the voice of the snake-heads. Imprisoned in their ties, the gold serpents disapprovingly hissed and writhed, forming a glinting web of venom. The crowd got to its feet and cried its praise. The six jatchas, turning from the six men, champed the thrown flowers.

Something was dreaming.

It bypassed Lionwolf's brain, therefore the brain of Vashdran, with a tenuous flick, half caress, half blow, both – significant.

This woke him.

It had not been his dream.

I sleep too much.

Such sleeping had happened before, in the time after the White Death at Ru Karismi, when he had cost three or four nations the best of their men.

He turned on his side, and looked at the jatcha, Star-Dog. It slept still, unruffled. How could he tell, when it had no eyes? He could.

Star-Dog had been his adoptive uncle's name. Guri: Star Dog, Dog Star.

Had Curjai named the dog's female mate?

Who – what – had dreamed and let the dream filter into Hell?

Vashdran did not know. Nor had he retained anything of the

dream. There was only the impression of some concentrated darkness, ascending.

A day had elapsed. A woman, her adorable body showing through diaphanous garb, summoned them to some further interview. She would not or could not answer questions, though she allowed Behf to have her against a wall.

All the men who had rebelled in the Stadionum followed her, individually. For each had been sitting apart from the others in the labyrinth, and to each one the same charming image, real or false, appeared.

When the limitless hallways temporarily ended at two high shut doors, patterned with the figures of men, animals and birds, the woman figure or figures silked away into a wall. This was clearly to be seen. It seemed Hell was not pretending so much to them now.

The six men hung about by the doors, as if embarrassed to meet again. Each of the six dogs though had arrived also, and now greeted one another, nosing each other's nether ends in the canine handshake. Their tails wagged.

'They become all the time more like dogs,' noted Kuul.

'They should have eyes,' said Heppa mournfully. But he had already named his dog Bony, and gave it friendly slaps on the flank.

Vashdran and Curjai eyed each other too. Neither spoke.

The doors opened with a leisurely grinding.

The dogs bounded in ahead of the men. They at least seemed relaxed and eager.

Filigreed with frost, gemmed with cold, black pillars pushed into the roof of sky.

The King of Hell was seated in a tall chair, far away. All the hounds sprinted up to him, and he lifted his stony hands and petted them as they dashed against him.

'He's in a generous mood then.'

'How would we know?'

They walked up the hall.

The dogs folded down around the chair. There were no other persons present, or none that could be seen.

Vashdran examined the King. The obsidian face had, contrary to Behf's joke about mood, no expression. Not even the cut smile displayed on the first occasion. The hood was off, and the King's head was hairless and finely shaped; sanded and burnished it appeared. Only the black eyes were like anything belonging to a mortal.

This is all a dream, Vashdran thought. His own mouth curled. *Dreams in the death-sleep. Like the dream of that other one, whoever he is, that crossed my mind last night. This is why nothing can matter.*

Just then the King got up.

Every one of the six men halted. It was intuitive. He was, seen this close, more than eight feet in height. Speech issued from him.

The guards uttered in one collective voice. Conversely Hell's King spoke in a thousand voices, and a million tongues, simultaneously. Every man there heard his own language. Vashdran alone perhaps detected and comprehended so many more. But it was only a magician's knack. Vashdran had it himself.

'You have fought well, and decided well when your contest was concluded. Now you will become leaders in my army, which is to march tomorrow over the plain to meet the ancient enemies of Shabatu. Each of you will bear this title: Saraskuld.'

It translated as *Commander*. Vashdran felt how it was different in a thousand or a million ways, delivered in the multi-faceted voice.

'Tonight,' said the King, 'you are to be rewarded for your valour by marriage to a human-born woman, or women, of your choice. This is a mark of signal honour, which you have deserved.'

Vashdran after all took an involuntary step. It was not the words. It was the face of stone. But Curjai, forgotten, out of nowhere reached and grabbed Vashdran by the shoulder.

'Hold still!'

And in that instant a curtain of white fire coruscated upward from the floor. The fire had the configuration of a huge ice-lizard, or dragon from some legend, and razor-edged heat smouldered from it.

All the men moved back, and separated from them by the fiery palisade the dogs began to whimper and some to yowl.

The voice of the Stone resumed, crushing their noise.

'You must learn your place, Lionwolf, son of Zzth. You are not king here. Only I am king here. Serve me in humility. You were told, as were all the rest, you will be flung down to a worse kingdom if you disobey.'

Vashdran bowed his head. Hell had named him correctly, even to his nightmare father. His eyes, fixed on the floor, burned crimson. He blinked – they became indigo.

'Forgive me, lord King.'

But the dragon thing lashed out even at his apology. Some white-hot coil of it raked over Vashdran's body. Scalded, he dropped, lying for several seconds in an agony beyond outcry. Then it was gone.

As his eyes unclouded, he was aware of Curjai crouched over him, one hand firmly bandaged across Vashdran's mouth.

Vashdran thrust the obstruction away. But he did not say anything.

The dragon fire died then. There was only the hall of pillars and the dogs, cheerful again, romping about. The King had left the chamber, and the other men were wandering about the deserted chair, tapping it. To this there was no opposition.

Vashdran lay on his back. Curjai sat down beside him, leaning to catch his murmuring.

'He said we're to fight enemies of Shabatu. But that was what was said before the first battle, which was between us, you and I, and all the rest. Here, war is meaningless perhaps, though absolute.'

Curjai nodded, but slowly, without definite conviction.

'How is it you grow wings?' Vashdran added. 'Or is that only some other device imposed on you by Hell?'

'I longed for wings, when I lived,' said Curjai. 'To be like a bird. Those other men too, I'd guess. Either that, or I infected

58

them with the urge and ability to fly. As you did yours with the attributes of lions and wolves.'

'Where did you live?' said Vashdran. He felt sleepy and pulled away from it, sitting up, stupefied by non-existent pain, pain's ending, and the unphysical pain that every moment pressed more near.

'Some place on the earth.'

'How did you *die*?'

Curjai glanced at him. 'Didn't I confess before? I died sobbing and half insane in my mother's arms. It was the death of straw, the death on the mattress young men dread. I wasn't slain in any battle. It was a fever. Before I went, though, the shaman came in. He said to me, don't be afraid, you've fought all your life till now. You'll find the warrior's heaven in the Afterlife. And he was right. For here I am.'

Vashdran said nothing. Presently Curjai continued. 'There are no others of my clan or people here. Among them, a man's name has two pieces. He gives only one to others, unless it is a friend, or a lover.'

Vashdran said, 'Tell me then. I am Lionwolf, as the Stone One said. It means as it sounds.'

'Escurjai,' Curjai said. 'That's spirit, heart and mind.'

They sat on the floor and watched the four men playing with their dogs. Eventually the two dogs of Vashdran and Escurjai, walking sedately side by side, came to lie down by them on the ground.

'What have you called *her*?' Vashdran asked, indicating the bitch-hound.

'Atjosa,' said Curjai, 'which is the feminine mode of Attajos.'

'Your god?'

'My god. And my father.'

Milk-white hands reached from the living walls, and caught him.

'Stay . . . Listen . . . Vassh-drann . . .'

They held him fast against the pulsing alabaster. He could

tell which genders they were without looking at them. The female hands were placating, urgent, the male hands rough and desperate.

'. . . listen . . .'

They held his hair, his arms. They circled his ribcage, beat on it lightly as if he were a drum.

'Say it then.'

'Ah . . .' they sighed. 'Ahhh . . .'

He remembered his mother Saphay, rocking his newborn self in the midst of a blizzard, shielding him with her body. He thought of Guri, dying impaled on some sort of spike. And of his father who, like Curjai's sire, was a god, and more cruel than any man.

Then, only then, Vashdran recollected the little toy animal he had found on the beach of flints that was the shore of Hell. He tried to take hold of it inside his garments, no longer sure it was still there. The hands would not let him. The female hands gentled him then slapped. The male hands were harsh, then sorry.

'. . . wait.'

The wall grew softer now. It was like an upright bed, mattressed not with straw like the deathbed Curjai had mentioned, more like some couch of the effete western cities, Ru Karismi, or Thase Jyr, which he had ruined, or which, through ruining him, had also perished.

Vashdran wept, chained by the hands of the wall. Then they wiped away his tears.

And finally they let him go.

He had learned nothing. Or—

'Who is Curjai?' he said, kneeling on the ground, head hanging.

'Curjai . . . is your shadow. You . . . are his light. Without you he cannot be. Without him none can see what you are.'

Vashdran did not understand. He kneeled on the wintry floor crying. He tried again to search for the toy his uncle had given him at birth, but could not unearth it from his clothing. He supposed he had lost it.

He had lost all of them – all the ones he should have loved, cared for and protected. All were swept away. Only he was here, lost also.

Again he was being returned into childhood, reduced to his essence. Broken.

He broke. He lay there. A silence came . . . out of which, along the shining floor, a small wooden toy on wheels was trundling. It was quite artistically carved, an ice-mammoth, complete with striated hair and curved, winding tusks, the trunk also humorously somewhat curving. Normally it required a couple of basic magic words to make it go. Guri had taught him. What were they? The toy batted along, without the words, independent. Its two bright eyes, made from tiny chips of quartz, beamed at Vashdran. When it reached him he picked it up. 'Forgive me,' he said. To the toy, to his kindred, to his warriors, to the dead lions of his chariot. To the Gullahammer, to the cities of the Ruk. To the world.

The wooden mammoth was light brown in tone. It quickly darkened from his tears.

In the walls, the hands of women and men slid over each other, in futile consoling gesticulations.

Once more they were outside the city. They stood on the plain of stones, the soaring walls, which from inside looked only like alabaster or marble, glowing in the outer darkness of Hell's night. The men had been kitted out, all six Saraskulds of the stone King's army, in black armourings inlaid with gold and cold jewels, grey topaz, speckled serpentine. It was fancy stuff, as Swanswine had remarked. He had been aggrieved at the dress armour. Swanswine, who was in fact only half Olchibe, got on an enslaved girl of the Marginal Land and reared by his father, wanted to lumber into battle as he always had in life, astride a mammoth, clad in Olchibe gear, his teeth freshly painted and with a decaying human head as a banner. Heppa however was foolishly proud of his new clothes. What sort of commander would he make?

The plain gave way to the long, sharded shore, and they tramped down it, the dogs padding among them, and the cloud of priests drifting before with their incense. Tonight, no fog bank occluded the view.

In the dark the sea was as sticky and non-oceanic as any of them recalled.

At the head of the procession, the weird elderly child who had fluted above the river gave his unnerving solo.

'I would smother that brat,' remarked Behf.

'In Ru Karismi,' said Kuul knowingly and inaccurately, 'they would have shot it dead with bow and arrow.'

Reaching the brink of the sea, where the pebbles and flints seemed wet, everyone stopped.

Vashdran thought, *What if I wade out, walking on water as I can still walk in sky, here. Or sink. Sink to the bottom.*

But who could say what lay under the sea's turgid skin? They had come *up* from there.

The wavery song ended.

Miles out at sea, something became visible.

The once-living men were quickened.

Spectral on darkness, rank on rank of sails were appearing, over the rim of the water.

There seemed to be at least a hundred vessels, maybe more. As they drew closer, the sea was crowded by them as if by a flock of gulls or kadi.

Behf said, 'I've the long-sight. I can tell you, it's worth a look.'

From where did Behf come? He had kept the Jafn name of Eleven, but he was surely no Jafn warrior, no westerner or northerner either.

Vashdran stared, indifferent, towards the phantom ships.

They were rafts, flat assemblies of defrosted logs, each with a single sail. They moved, blown by some unfelt, unseen wind, towards the barren coast.

I too can see with long-sight.

On every raft was a solitary female figure. Some stood upright, holding to the thin mast, gazing shorewards. Others were huddled, or lay along the raft's surface, sleeping or insensible.

These women were all young, all, so far as could be made out, well formed and alluring.

Vashdran passed his extended glance over their faces. Some of them might have put on masks, devoid of anything. Others wore an aspect of bewilderment and some of fear. A very few looked joyful. They were of several races, and once more not all were known to him.

The six Saraskulds were to choose from this multitude of wives, one or more per man.

The priests were actually urging this now, insistently calling back to them, like pimps.

The men shoved forward, and the priests gave way. The men stood with their feet in the sea, elatedly pointing out this one's virtues or that one's.

Curjai even had moved away along the beach, scanning the rafts, also deciding.

Human-born the stone thing had said to them. Dead women then. Dead women banished to the War-Hell, subserviently to companion warriors.

Vashdran could see nothing in any of them, nothing in them at all that he wanted. Between him and these undead brides, *she* floated, like a flaw in his sight. Chillel . . .

It was not he wanted *her*. When he had at last possessed her, had been despoiled by her and burned her up in turn, even then he had no longer wanted her. It had been only that he must have her. And curiously, depressingly, even now it seemed he must, whether in her original cool persona, or that of the moon-bringing queen of Hell.

But the other men were busy choosing.

Vashdran watched, neutral.

Kuul selected two, and Behf four. *He* boasted he could keep them all happy. Heppa was shy. Swanswine mocked him till Heppa conceded, 'That one then, her, with the malt-colour hair.' Swanswine opted for a herd of six. It was common enough, among the sluht-camps of his people. Not true wives either, only slaves, for none of these were good enough, not being yellow-skinned.

Curjai by now must have chosen also.

A priest mewed at Vashdran.

'None,' Vashdran said. He had the wish to swat the flat-featured priest away.

'You must select a wife.'

'No.'

But the priest, face like that of some ice-locust unlocked from a socket of frozen grain, pointed out to sea, and Vashdran found he looked again, where the priest indicated.

Vashdran saw then one he almost recalled. Who was she? Through his brain fluttered the wraiths of the women he had delved, in the ice-village of Ranjalla, in the garth of the Kree, on the march north and the Gullahammer ride to the west and south.

The woman on the raft had disagreeable hair. It was a sort of green, like grass he found once in other circumstances. The witches of North Gech sometimes gave themselves such hair. Her skin was sallow more than yellow. She clasped the mast with one hand, and with the other fumbled over a string of beads she held, thaumaturgic doubtless, though just now of no use to her. Her face was shut up, unwilling to display her thoughts, but her eyes were frightened.

'Tell me her name,' said Vashdran. 'If she's mine.'

'Taeb.'

Taeb . . .

'How did she die?'

'Before her time. An animal slew and ate her.'

Taeb. Yes, he knew Taeb. The northern witch who had assisted in the killing of Saphay's Jafn husband, and who had helped cast Lionwolf and Saphay out of the Klowan-garth, to sure death in the ice waste. Taeb, who had been also foul Rothger's bedfreh; she had absented herself before Lionwolf sacked the garth. And now she was here.

'Very well,' Vashdran said. 'But she can expect no kindness.'

Perhaps fate, even now, permitted him one more soupçon of

revenge. But he no longer cared about any of that. Ah then, vengeance without meaning. What else, in Hell?

The Saraskulds had chosen fifteen women. The youngest, who was Heppa's, looked barely nubile, but she was one of the few who did not seem afraid.

Shockingly, back along the beach, the trumpet-mouth mooed from the city gate.

Before it had been the motivation for grim gathering and war. Now its statement provoked only the sea.

All the men shouted in horror and affront – all but Vashdran. It appeared the choosing was some malevolent tease. For, from the depths of that gluey ocean, something was rising, rising, more dense and intransigent even than the water.

A giant whale – I dreamed of it – now I recall the dream – the whale – its back . . .

Nothing, nevertheless, was to be *seen*, only the sea thrashing in waves – and something *in* the waves, wheeling, *severing*, like an enormous scythe.

In ones and twos, tens and twenties, the rafts of the brides were overturned, *snapped* away. The women went down screaming. White arms flashed like sea-spume, flying hair meshed with water. Here and there, a Jet of dark red sprayed against the stars, but fell away again, back into the deep.

As the hubbub settled, the sea sluggishly thickened. Nothing at all might have gone on. Generally, the surface was empty, but over the water fifteen intact rafts were still speeding in to land. Almost every woman left on her raft stared terrified behind and about her. Some wept and shrieked. But they were the chosen wives, and had been spared the tumult of second death. And of them all, now, only Taeb was serene, her face secretive, pensive.

Once the rafts had bumped home on the shore, the cloud of priests enveloped them. There was a droning, wasps tutoring newcomers to the waspery. What the priests said to the brides none of the six men heard.

There was no formal marriage, not even an abbreviated Jafn handfasting.

The women were sent along the beach away from the city in a straggling unspeaking group. And the men were next encouraged to follow.

Behf, Swanswine and then Kuul set off galloping, Behf whooping in a manner that soon made the leading female group increase its speed. These three men at least seemed already forgetful of the cull they had just witnessed.

Heppa went slowly, though, with a long, worried face. Curjai kept pace with him, ignoring Heppa and also Vashdran. Curjai too was stern and preoccupied. He had chosen a tall, slender young woman, dark-haired, her eyes bright with panic.

The jatcha hounds meanwhile ran enthusiastically everywhere; they even darted into the unsea, like dogs.

Vashdran walked along the beach last of all, and up into the plain of stones. There was, apparently, some building outside and beyond the walls of Shabatu, in which the merry nuptials would take place. Gradually all the others dwindled into distance.

When Vashdran reached the building, it was a travesty of his memories.

Stone blocks had built a type of lodge. In their translucent bricks cryogenized fish were sealed. The lodge rose from a grove of trees neither leafed nor cryogenic. These trees were of twisted petrified stone.

The fifteen women and five men were already presumably inside the lodge. The dogs too had either entered or found other pastimes.

Vashdran, who did not care, went in at an open doorway. The floor was glassy, like floors in the city. Ahead lay one of the wide arches, and then a downward slope of frost-feathered stairs. It was dark here. As he descended it grew darker still. A small light then drifted towards him, waxing as it came. It was a miniature floating moon, about the diameter of a crait's egg. Sheer radiance blazed from it. It hovered in front of him, determined, he could see, and whether he was compliant or not, to light his path.

He assumed he was being led ritualistically towards his 'wife', the witch Taeb. And he was curious, a little. Only that. An irony had addressed itself to him. He had asked forgiveness of so many, even of a surreal wooden toy, yet this woman, who had assisted in his babyhood ill-treatment, he had declared must expect from him no kindness.

I am two beings. Of course. Lion, wolf. Mortal, god.

Where had the others been led?

He stepped off the flight into a grotto, far beneath the lodge and the plain of stones.

There were swart hollow caves, and on the ribs of them frozen ferns that might have been pure ice, and slim frozen streams like platinum veins. But there was fluid water too. Coming from a live world of snow and winter, even now fluid water could never leave him quite unmoved. He looked at it, how it wavered over a toothed pyramid of rock cascading away to one side and into some only-imaginable void beyond the light.

Then Taeb came skulking out around the pyramid.

When she saw him, she grew motionless. She had a clever face. He recalled how he had been told that she helped in Athluan's murder, Athluan who would have been, perhaps, Lionwolf's surrogate father, if the Jafn Chaiord had lived.

'You fled once,' Vashdran said to Taeb. 'But it seems you didn't get far enough.'

'Everything must be paid, in the end.' She was pragmatic.

He said, almost intrigued for a minute, 'So you know you're dead.'

'Yes. How else all this?'

'How did you die, Greenhair?'

'In the ice swamps near the Copper Gate. I left my house at the wrong hour and met a wolverine.' She added, without any feeling, 'It tore me in pieces.'

'Then you must be glad to find yourself together again.'

'Yes. But for how long?'

'Oh,' he said, 'don't fret. I won't harm you. I won't even trouble you to open your legs. I don't want you, and if I kill you for your past offences against me, I suppose you'll only revive, or go elsewhere like the rest of Hell's twice-dead.'

'There is one,' she said. She hooded her eyes. 'There is one who has come after you. Who chose to seek you here, in anger.'

'Who?' Alarm coursed painfully through him. In his mind was the sudden image, a man with fiery hair and a blue stripe like a Fazion's across his brows – Zeth Zezeth – Zzth, the god who had sired him and had so wanted this son dead.

But I am dead.

Death, of course, for such as Zzth the Sun Wolf, might not be sufficient.

'It is,' said the witch, 'one you have never met in life. From the big city in the Ruk, Ru Karis.'

'Ru Karismi? Who then from there?'

Relief made him stupid, he thought. For she said after a second, 'I can't see who it is. But only human, once, though gifted with magic.'

'Why are you telling me?'

'You chose me and spared me the churning second death in the deadsea.'

'I didn't choose you, Taeb, girl. I was given you.'

She shrugged her slight shoulders. 'Even here,' she said, 'I have some powers. I can tell you things.'

'Like this tale of some man of the Rukar who is in pursuit of me.'

She lowered her eyes.

Around the rock with flowing water, on the other inner side to the fall, he began to make out a chamber with a couch. It looked so ordinary and inappropriate he reckoned it sinister.

No, he would not lie down with a witch there.

'Taeb,' he said, 'you can go where you want, or where they'll let you. This is all the couching we'll have, you and I.'

She nodded. Not meek, he thought, only cunning.

'If any ask me about this,' she said, 'what do you wish I shall say?'

'Say whatever you want.'

She bowed her head and slunk across the space and up the first of the stairs. When she had gone out of his sight, he walked through carelessly into the room with the low couch. A kind of membrane hung across it that he had not seen but which parted before him, rather like the web of some huge ice-spider giving way.

Turning back to see what it was, he put his hand against something that now closed the opening off from him, transparent and hard, like crystal.

Vashdran looked back into the room. He saw that after all a woman was on the bed, who had been quite invisible from the barrier's other side. She lay on one elbow, her black hair falling over and along the floor as the fountain fell from the rock into the shadow. Her naked body was as black. It stretched there perfect and complete on the couch's paleness, high yet heavy breasted, narrow of waist, wrist and ankle, the half ellipse of the polished ebony hip like the ripe curve of a black plum.

Vashdran forgot Taeb, forgot his insane and vicious paranormal father. Forgot the unknown man from Ru Karismi who might vengefully seek him here. Forgot he was in Hell.

Oh no, desire was not over in him, or not for her. He stood still, gazing at her.

'Are you Chillel?' Would she answer this naive question? He had never, in this incarnation, heard her speak.

The woman who was queen of Hell smiled. The midnight stars of her eyes had diamonds in their centres from the reflection of the little moon, which now balanced lovingly in the air above her head.

'My name is,' she said, in the *voice* of Chillel, from the *body* of Chillel – yet all not *quite* Chillel, not now, not here – 'Winsome.'

Vashdran stared at her.

The polyglot language available to all in this afterworld, where anything spoken in whatever original mother tongue was somehow instantly translatable to every man, threw the delicate, appealing and somehow scornful word at him like one more stone.

But 'Winsome?' he said lightly. 'Well, so you are.'

'Lie down with me,' she said. 'This bed is softer than the floors of Shabatu.'

Vashdran said, 'You're his wife. The stone King. Not that this frightens me much.'

'No, I am not his wife, he is my husband. I am the moon of Hell. I am the dark moon who gives light.' Her voice was honey. It dripped through his bones, turning to hot wine in the core of his loins. 'It's from me he takes that power, all the powers of light which fill the city. Lie down.'

Vashdran said, playful he thought, perhaps not only that, 'If you're the moon, you'll burn me, maybe.'

'Not you,' she said.

In the worldly Chillel there had been only a vast empty landscape of night. But in *this* Chillel, who was called Winsome for her own beauty, some other expanse lay there dormant, welcoming perhaps, yet also indecipherable.

'The last time,' he said, 'we did each other harm.'

'This is not the last time.'

He moved towards her, and when he reached the couch her arms rose like snakes and coiled about his legs and buttocks, pulling him in against her, while her hair spilled all around them.

Yes. She burned. And his garments, all that armour, had evaporated.

He thought, astonished, *I am alive after all.*

Then he slid down into her arms, upon her body, her breasts, her mouth, no longer concerned with anything but to have her and to be had.

Curjai, who had spent his living life engaged in endless battle, and died of fever on the straw mattress, had never had an interval to lie there or anywhere with a woman. Confronted by the girl he had picked from the rafts, he was uneasy. It was a fact, some premonition had made him aware that to choose her would be to save her from something worse. Had he foreseen the extent of the massacre on the sea, he would have picked every woman left out there unselected.

'Don't be afraid,' he said at first, noting how she pressed her hands together, and the skitter of what he took for fear in her dark eyes. But then she looked him full in the face, and he saw she had been shocked, but only that. She was not fearful. Something else tensed her and made her eyes so stabbingly bright.

'I know where I am,' she said to him then. 'In a hell. I've travelled a great distance, through many horrible and partly seen dead lands, to reach this one. I will tell you why.'

Curjai waited.

They were in a cave-like small cubicle inside the lodge of fish-stones, with one white torch flaming on the wall. There was a mattress on the ground. An unaesthetic and uninspiring love-nest. He had always, Curjai, preferred to look at pleasing objects, and in this room she was by far the best thing to be seen.

'I will,' she said, 'if you insist, perform with you the sexual act. Aside from that, my business is with the one called Vashdran. My name is Ruxendra. I was an apprentice of the highest Maxamitan Level, in the Insularia of the Magikoy at Ru Karismi, City of the Kings. This city Vashdran, through his war, brought to destruction. When our ultimate weapons had been loosed on his horde of savages, death fell out of the skies also on us. Of this plague I perished. I was fifteen. When you're done with me, barbarian, go to Vashdran, your brother. Tell him Ruxendra is here, Ruxendra who is not a woman but *Magikoy*. Whatever enemy he must otherwise face, he is my foe for ever, or till time *itself* is dead and rotting in some hell.'

Fourth Intervolumen

Sometimes flowers open in darkness; they are generally the thorned kind.

Proverb: Ruk Kar Is

Compared to Lionwolf's hell, the largest island of the Vormland was warm, encased in centuries' frozen shores of ice and hills of snow, over which snow-plastered mountains craned. The day was sunny, too. A fierce earthly sun leisurely crossed a steep blue sky. Out on the distant liquid sea, icebergs sunned themselves like huge seals, and steam lifted from them in long trails resembling smoke.

The god-house had been built beyond the shore village, on the side of a hill. It was a temple in the Vormish, Faz or Kelpish style: a box covered with ancient fossils and shells dug over years out of the undersnow cliff. Inside it had the usual wooden roof, made from an upturned boat. An altar of stonewood carved with fish, whales, porpoises, sharks and so on supported a mass of yellowish candles. When the goddess came out of her inner apartment, she would light them by breathing on them. Men had journeyed for miles to watch this sacred act.

'She is Our Lady Saftri. She rose from the sea on a wave.' This was what her priesthood told all visitors. They had seen the miracle in person. Naked and saffron-haired in a spurl of spindrift, she had landed at their feet. Then they had dropped at hers in worship.

Majord, the bard, composed a hymn on the spot. Two years on, it was still carolled about the islands, along with the others made since.

He stood now, Saftri's priest-bard, by the doorway of her temple.

Inside it was dark. She did not sit in presence then.

She was a goddess, but Majord suspected her of sulking. She grew bored easily, and sometimes lost her temper. Once she had drowned a fishing fleet. But then she wept and rescued the men, sweeping them ashore. None of them grumbled at having to rebuild their boats. Irrational divine wrath was what you must expect, sometimes.

In the first months she had been all misery, mourning the loss of a son, also obviously a god. Women throughout the Vormland were mourning too in just that fashion.

Perhaps a tenth of the men of the north seas had gone to join a war far in the south, on the great continent there. For the first time in known history, Vorm, Kelp and Fazion had allied with the continent's Jafn clans, the yellow Olchibe and crazy Gech. There had been a leader, a hero of extraordinary powers. All had followed him in a battle Gullahammer against the luxurious cities of the Rukar. But the mages of the Ruk deployed some supernatural weapon of colossal force. Not one man of the Gullahammer, they said, had survived. The Jafn clans suffered the worst, having invested every warrior of fighting age in the conflict. Olchibe and Gech fared little better. Only women and some of the ignorant tribes of northernmost Gech remained.

But the Rukar themselves had not done so well either. They had lost their smaller cities to the war. Unleashing their sorcerous death-strike, they caught the backlash of it on the capital, Ru Karis. The metropolis now stood defunct, abandoned save by the dead, snow-drifts drizzling over it.

During that year of mourning, almost every reiver of the north sea who had not joined the war and so survived threw himself into a new pact. Kelp and Faz and Vorm prepared their jalees, their scaled fish-horses, their fat Mother Ships. Their shamans raved in groves of ice, calling home the spirits of the local dead to swell their fleet.

Before, they had usually only raided along the Jafn coasts. But now the whole table of the continent's upper lands lay unprotected, defended only by ancients and girls. The Ruk had been a living myth for ever of wealth and plenty. Once the poison-plague had rinsed itself away, all the unguarded treasures of the Rukar lay there for the taking.

The reiver ships set off. Those that returned months after, in the second year, told tales of easy fights and limitless gains. And they brought with them proof: curious foods and beverages, materials, ornaments and weapons, slaves. Even the stonewood altar in Saftri's god-house had come as a trunk from Jafn lands, while the candles were the tribute of a Rukar village.

Majord cleared his throat. He warbled a flattering line. '*Fount of grace, as morning is sun-haired.*'

In the core of the temple he heard a sort of hiss.

Ah, she was not in a happy frame of mind.

Next second she manifested on the other side of the altar. Not a single candle did she light. A pity, for then the bits of Ruk gold hammered in there gleamed satisfactorily. Nevertheless her golden necklaces sparkled, her earrings and rings. She herself seemed made of pearl and topaz.

'Our Lady.' Majord went to his knees.

'Oh, get up. What use is that?' Up he got. 'Why are you disturbing me?'

'I come to beg on the new fleet your blessing. The fleet of Krandif's men, two jalees and—'

'*Another* fleet.'

'Bound for the south, Our Lady.'

'Yes, yes,' impatiently. 'Where else do you ever go? There are other countries, I've told you this. Northwards and west.'

Dubiously Majord nodded. 'Yes, Our Lady.'

'But you don't believe me. You dare to disbelieve your goddess.'

'No – no – but such tasty pickings there are to the south, and the other way would be a long, difficult voyage—'

'Oh, a hail of fire on it,' spat Saftri, using one of the – to her – inadequate curses of the Vormland. 'Very well. I'll come and bless your cutch of a fleet.'

Majord was accustomed to his goddess's foul mouth. He had

learned ages ago what *cutch* meant, and that it was fairly cutching useless to entreat her not to say it.

Saftri herself, who had been known in her former life as the Princess Saphay, progressed with a walk like music to the temple door.

She looked down with disfavour on the large village below the hill, the houses that were huts with sharkskin shutters, the one narrow hothouse for fruit, the nets and drying fish strung up, and the forlorn reddish cows that ambled about the streets, allowed to do anything, even eat hung-out washing, they were so scarce and precious. A stand of ice-poplars blocked off the view of the cliff's lower edge and the bay below. But she had flown out there last night, unable to rest, and seen the assembled two jalees, one of which had sixteen ships, drawn up on the shore. Men had enhanced the cow or whale horns on the prows, and old human skulls had been cleaned and decked with coloured wool and unsuitable jewels pilfered from the Ruk. The two Mother Ships wallowed at anchor further out on the wet sea.

Saftri-Saphay had flown about a great deal over these past two years, getting her bearings – less geographically than personally. Being a goddess had many perks. Also a downside. For one, she could rarely sleep, exactly like, she exasperatedly thought, the Jafn peoples to one of whose chiefs she had once been married. The Vorms too did not sleep. Vorm, Faz and Kelp could go six or seven days and nights without slumber. This, as with the sleep-deprived Jafn, made them either psychic or deranged, she had still not decided which. Besides, as a goddess, she herself could now see Jafn sprites and spirits in the atmosphere – hovors and vrixes, glers, corrits, all sorts. She perceived they kept well clear of *her*.

Flying – not that she *flew* precisely, only swirled through the air as she had seen Guri do in her previous past – Saphay had found the landmasses further north and west. But, if she were honest, which generally she felt it best not to be, they alarmed her. She had never gone close. These continents were anyway like all the rest of this winter-shrouded world, cloaked in white, sea-edged with ice floes and bergs. If she ever supposed she caught the glint of lamps, she ignored it. She preferred the insane configurations of Vormland's northern lights, which fluked across the night skies at irregular seasons. Their spasms and colours pleased her, flickering, beaming, fawn and bronze, hothouse rose and iridescent turquoise.

Flying was her hobby.

She had though never returned to the Southern Continent. The idea of Jafn lands depressed her, partly from having heard of the wreck her son's war had brought them to, and partly from her bad memories. Ruk Kar Is held no allure. Her own country had been nothing to her ever, as she had never been anything to it.

Majord had now backed away, genuflecting, and was off at a trot to tell the ships their goddess was coming.

Saftri meant first to visit the village bath.

This was a hot spring about two miles further inland. Fogs of steam sometimes went up there, at others the spring shrank away into the earth. Brown grass grew lustily round its brink, and a single short tree that bore uneatable but pretty yellow fruit. Here the women of the village would congregate to bathe once or twice a month. They took their babies and younger children with them.

If Saftri was there, the women were always thrilled. They loved her and loaded her with garlands of the grass threaded with shells and bone trinkets they had made. Sometimes they told stories, glancing shyly at her. Saftri too told *them* stories, suitably translated from the Rukarian. Mostly she looked at their children, at the boys who were now all the ages Lionwolf had been, when she had borne him and seen him grow. Half god, in ten years he had become a man of twenty or more. These everyday infants took their time. She could gaze on them, sometimes hold them in her arms or stare into their eyes, for up to twelve years before she must let go. The mothers did not mind. The benign involvement of a goddess was also a blessing. And they remembered her lament for her dead son at the time they too were lamenting their own dead sons of fighting age.

Not aware, of course, it was her son who had drawn theirs to annihilation under the walls of Ru Karismi.

The women at the spring exclaimed as Saftri appeared out of the air – one more perk of goddessdom was this knack of manifestation.

Saftri found their adulation gratifying. She could not help herself. She had been so often discounted and ignored in her mortal life.

Soon she was seated near the steamy well, her hair garlanded and her favourite child, a male of seven years, positioned on her lap.

His name was Best Bear. His mother looked fondly at him sitting with the goddess. His mother opined there must be great things due for Best Bear.

He was a sturdy child, good-mannered and good-looking, with long brown hair bound back in a whale ivory clip. He lay quietly against Saftri, who intrigued him. He was conscious also of his exalted status in being chosen.

'Tell to me a story,' he demanded.

Saftri smiled, and the women nodded.

'Once there was a mighty hero,' said Saftri.

'What name was his?'

'His name . . . why ever do you ask?' Both of them were coy.

'Was his name – anything to do with bears?'

Saftri smiled again, mysterious. A glorious scent came from her, and from her hair, at all times now. The boy was in love with her, as a boy may be with his mother, at first. But neither his physiological mother nor his peers were jealous. They too had piously accepted his destined importance.

Saftri told the story of a hero who grew to manhood and won great riches and three wives of surpassing loveliness.

Best Bear sat thoughtful, as always, entranced.

He was not Lionwolf. Only Lionwolf could be that. But he was wholesome and handsome. He let her hold him and there would be at least five more years before he was a man and she must release him.

Sometimes she vaguely wondered how it was that Lionwolf, himself half immortal, had *died*, when she who had only, she believed, had *dealings* with the gods became one herself. But her grief still lay deep within her like a sleeping stone, and had never allowed her hope of Lionwolf's return. She had *felt* his death. As if her womb itself had been plucked away and flung under the ice of the sea. She knew also she would never again bear any child. Nor did she want to.

Out along the bluff that marked off the bay, an iron gong clanged into noise. It was the summons to the men, the women too.

Irked, Saftri relinquished her maternal clutch on Best Bear, who was in fact the first of everyone preparing to run to the shore.

There were always these duties. Once a princess, Saftri was well schooled, if mutinous. No prowess could be had without some concomitant task.

She too got up, and de-manifested. It was time to bless Krandif's pestilential ships.

Horsazin were being persuaded out of the open sea after a swim. The fish-horses shook themselves, their glassy manes and tails. Greyish in ordinary tone, they had already been striped over with waterproofed magenta dye by the Vormish reivers, ready for raiding and battle.

Saftri sniffed. The air reeked of fishy horse. But she must bless them also before they went up the ramps into the lower decks of the two Mother Ships.

She did her duty solemnly, and looking very young herself, a virtuous royal child.

Touched, her people – for hers they were – clustered in reverent silence. Even the horses kept still, and now and then nodded their single-horned heads.

Krandif the ship-lord moved among his men, hanging on

them fresh luck-charms for the voyage. Though the continent was now so easy to burgle, the seas between were always liable to problems. Last, Krandif came to the goddess, put his head down on his fists respectfully, and kneeled in front of her on the ground.

'Go with my blessing, Krandif Wild-Heart. Go and kind weather go with you, and vast riches await you, ripe as fruit on a hotshed vine. Amen,' she added, in the Olchibe way. She had not spent all those years with Guri without picking up the odd mannerism. Guri too had died. She had often wished to attack him herself he had so irritated her. But he had been loyal to her son, and his death unfair.

The goddess now seemed sorrowful.

Worried, Krandif gained his feet.

'Do you have for me a warning of something, Our Lady?'

Saftri said, 'All will be well with you. There's no warning necessary.'

Krandif, a Vormish warrior in the prime of youth, was not seriously unnerved. Nevertheless he thought he had better look for omens and read them sensibly when once at sea.

They were packing the horsazin, whinnying and boisterous, into the deck holds. Men rolled their slimmer boats down on runners to the liquid sea of the harbour.

Heavy with stores, horses, and travelling war shamans who would undertake to harm any foe by magical means, the Mother Ships rode low in deeper water. One had nine masts and one had eleven, all clotted with canvas.

Saftri had viewed similar events many times during the last year, and the victorious returns.

There had even been some slaves brought from Ruk Kar Is. But none of them had survived more than a month on the uncivilized Vormland shore.

Above the sky was purely blue. Saftri yawned with impending ennui. Best Bear was diving about among the men, asking to go with them, and laughingly praised and denied. It seemed to her suddenly he was becoming too male, too fast. Perhaps she would not have him to console her more than another couple of years.

By noon, Krandif's fleet, sailing due south, had made fine headway. All land was by then out of sight, save for the occasional islet or tower of ice. A weightless wind puffed from the northeast. The oars churned the water. Men sang, glad to be at work.

There was nothing untoward anywhere.

Once a small whale breached about ten ship-lengths away. Its horned head shot high, but it was less in size than one of the Mother Ships, and went down again smoothly, with no bother.

During the afternoon, they passed among a herd of emerald-tinged bergs, and on the far side clouds strayed over the sky. But these too slid away. The sky generally stayed clear – unreadable.

Krandif patrolled the narrow upper deck, when not taking his turn on the row-bench. He had not been able to rid himself of the instinct that something unusual might happen.

The day ended in a soft dusk.

Fit and keen, the men elected to row on through the night.

Darkness began, just the horizon retaining a greenish luminescence, as often it did. Above, no flickers of lights appeared, merely stars, but they were enough, and then two moons came up, one full and the other a slender bow.

It was about an hour into full night that the sound started ahead of them.

One by one the crews rested their oars, and perched silent, looking away into the south, from where the sound seemed to come.

There were several and various peculiar noises to be heard out on the moving seas of the north. Whales mooed or ululated. Ice split like the blast of magicians' cannon. Weather too spoke eerie or threatening. And the wind, they knew, carried the voices of the drowned, which would sometimes tell you things.

None of these ocean-accustomed men had ever heard a

sound like the one now penetrating the sky and drawing every second nearer.

It was a kind of bestial scream, but compressed to the width of a needle, and stretching over the whole arch of the sky. It pierced not only the night, but the ears, so men put their fingers in them. Brave faces filled with a murky uncertain look.

On the decks of both the Mother Ships the shamans had come out. Chants drifted in a sizzle of mage-fires. A rumbling woke from the underdecks among the agitated horsazin. They did not like this new noise either.

Then fire burst out across the sky, one extended streamer of it. It was golden-red, with a central vein of blackest blue, and like no northern light any of them had ever seen. In a breath it was miles off – then *overhead*.

As the fire coursed over they felt the *freeze* of it scorch them. Men flung themselves down. The sea heaved. The ships bucked dangerously.

Krandif, the leader, kept his station at the horned prow. He stared up into the fire and saw it was like a flaming rope, spitting and sparking, pulled now on and away at great speed into the north.

Behind it followed simple darkness. The moons shone out again, seeming less vital than they had.

Krandif looked about. A few men had toppled or sprung off into the sea. They were being hauled out and wrapped in furs. Skins of grog went round. The shamans had ended their sorcery, perhaps convinced they had sent the fire-rope packing.

The leader called, pitching his voice to all twenty-seven of the long ships.

'A star-stone tumbling out of heaven. I've heard of these. My grandfather saw one. It will mean for us much luck.'

His message was accepted. He was the ship-lord.

He himself was not so sure. But he had had the warning he anticipated, had only to think how to judge it. For if it was a *fall*, then whose? The Rukar had already fallen, and the Jafn. Maybe it was their anger then, all those dead, blown away from the south in fire-breath, delayed for some reason, an afterthought.

They always brought her supper when the sun went down, from what was cooked for their men's evening meal. Sometimes Saftri would eat what they brought. She never needed to, and the food was, to her Ruk-educated tastes, frequently unpalatable. Another measure of her boredom was whether or not she ate dinner.

Tonight she picked at some type of porpoise stew, then pushed the bowl away. The little apple she consumed slowly, devouring even its core and pips. There was a dearth of fruit normally, the village hotshed meagre and constantly getting cold.

Saftri went out of her temple, and waited on the hill for moonrise.

How strange these luminous nights. She was never used to them. She had earlier dropped asleep too, and dreamed of love-making. First her companion was her Jafn husband Athluan, who had been a very pleasing lover. Then *he* was there, the god, Zeth Zezeth Zzth. He, of course, had been a lover beyond all compare or scope. In the dream she had dissolved in ecstasy, but then woken in fright. The god had always wanted to murder her for her impertinence in becoming pregnant with his child. She thought now she had, in some esoteric way, inadvertently robbed Zzth of some of his mightiness, when she had done this, for though he had haunted her in her human sleep, terrorizing and in dreams harming her, once Lionwolf was born she had not seen Zzth anywhere for a great while. In the end he had returned with threats. But that too might not have been reality, only some sort of hallucination. At the time she was in the comfortless care of Yyrot, the second of her three personal gods.

In any case, Zzth *had*, she assumed, eventually caused the death of her son, and of Guri, and of herself.

Two years had gone by since then. Perhaps, as it had seemed before, Zzth could no longer find her.

Was it her boredom made her think of him?

Was horrible terror then preferable to dullness?

Despite the deliciously lascivious dream, Saftri must enduringly hope Zzth would avoid her.

The moons danced over the horizon. The first was full and the other a bow.

She might make one of her wingless flights. She was a goddess now. She could, if she truly wished, fly right up to the moons.

Saftri was still poised before her doorway musing, and the moons just over an hour up the sky, when a shattering bang shook the air and the island, and out on the horizon to the south a plume of scarlet fire cancelled darkness.

What was *this*? A storm – some eruption of an ice-volcano far off in the sea?

Below, people were surging out of their houses. A hundred hands superfluously pointed towards the south.

This had been the direction Krandif's fleet had taken. Had something gone wrong with his adventure?

Speculation ended with an answer.

The red fire-line hurtled straight at the Vormland, straight as a spear flung at the bay.

Saftri gave an ungoddess-like squeak. She had deduced the aerial missile was aimed at *her*.

She did not need to inform herself who had sent it or – as she could now see – was a *part* of it.

Much worse than any nightmare, the flame sprayed open like an aspirated boil in the skies above the harbour. A blazing gout, it roiled there, and in the midst of it was the image of a gigantic snarling wolf, blue, a blue almost black, and its eyes like molten, bleeding gold.

It glared right down at her. Into her gaze.

Saftri, goddess of the Vormland, felt herself wither with infantile fear.

Why he had waited she did not know. Some further game?

Now he was here. 'Your punishment I keep for you . . .' this was what he had said last, '. . . we shall savour it, you and I. I shall flay the skin off your soul's blood . . . Into eternity I will take you . . . It is owed.'

Her impulse was to bolt for cover, but there was no such chance. He was – *omnipotent*.

They were shouting below. The entire village, the bluff, the ice and snow, were lit to a lurid daylight.

The wolf that was Zeth Zezeth leaned from his fire-cloud and blew fire also out of his jaws.

In the bay, with an explosion, three remaining anchored Mother Ships died. Columns of fire hit the walls of night. Flinders, ivory pieces, bits of oars and masts and planks spouted in all directions, striking on the bluff in a clinketing rain. Nearer the shore a scatter of jalee ships and fishing boats were alight too.

Some of the men left in the village had begun to pelt harbourwards to try to save their vessels. But they turned and sprang back the other way as the wolf-god breathed again, almost mildly now, in across the shambling village.

Fifty roofs, made of old boats and covered by snow-slabs and oiled skins, crackled into ignition.

The calling and screaming was agony to hear. People, reduced by evil radiance to silhouetted fiendish shapes, gushed to and fro. Children shrilled. The side of a house caved inwards, another detonated outward. The choked air was full of whirling objects and the cacophony of panic.

Saftri slunk to hide herself inside her fragile shrine.

But blue-black was spilling swiftly from the fire-cloud. It circled down, spinning, and contacted the island. Saftri had not even got in at her door. She saw *him*, indistinct for a moment, wolf or man or neither, poured upward to describe the form of a god. He was only a few strides from her. As in her dream, her recollection, Zeth Zezeth was as beautiful as only a god could be, maned with hot silver, his eyes like solar discs. And in that place, all this beauty had become the most repulsive obscenity ever to exist.

Her bones were water. She must throw herself at his feet and beg for mercy. It would make no difference to his sadism. Yet she could not help it.

Behind him, behind the figure of Zeth Sun Wolf, a woman with her hair on fire was stumbling up the hill. She carried something. She was crying Saftri's title, *Our Lady! Our Lady!*

But I am powerless, now.

Zeth smiled. 'Good evening,' he said, '*Saftri.*'

His voice was like a glacial wire and full of mockery – the endless scorn of a god.

How could she have dreamed of love with him? How could she ever have accused herself in the past of only loving her *son* because he had reminded her of this devil?

Saftri backed stiltedly away from Zeth Zezeth. He did not take a step but yet kept pace with her retreat, staying where he had been: only a foot or so from her. She put her hands behind her against the uprights of the door of her temple. What use was the temple? It could never shield her from *him*.

'Is there,' she whispered, as she had before, 'no other recourse? What have I done to anger you? It was *you*—'

'*Silent*,' he said. That was all. His voice was barely audible yet tremored the hill. In the incineration of the village further house-frames cracked. 'I have allowed you this interval,' murmured Zzth, 'to spread your insignificant wings. To believe yourself safe from me. But now we are done with that, you and I, Sa*phay.*'

Despite the rest, Saftri blinked at his use of her former name.

As she blinked, the vista beyond the god cleared in an unanticipated way. And she saw that the woman who struggled up the hill in the smoulder and sparks of her burning hair was one of the village mothers. What she held, with some awkwardness, was a dead child. Saftri-Saphay took in, even in that infinitesimal blink, the boy's own unburnt hair, lustrous and brown and caught in a whale ivory clip. His head hung to one side, spineless, the neck snapped. It was Best Bear.

Tears filled the eyes of Saphay and dropped from her. Before they reached the ground they changed. They too became gleaming fire.

She was weeping flames.

Saphay raised her head and looked through her incendiary tears at Zzth.

'You killed my son.'

'So I did,' he said.

She did not hear.

Saphay, who had become Saftri and the goddess of the Vormland, was also now metamorphosing.

Her hair exploded to a stiff flambeau of gold, her face became at once both that of a woman and that of a lioness. She *was* a lion, standing upright. She was a woman, leaping forward on all fours – and where her metallic pads met the snow, bubbling rents appeared.

She reached Zzth in one heartbeat more. Her mouth undid itself on a river of laval notes, between a lament and a guttural roar. Her entire body was in flux, an entity of pale flame and brilliant flesh, each able to be the other.

Long claws of adamant struck home in the flawlessness of Zeth Zezeth. With her other forepaw she smashed his body backwards.

He was a god, Zzth. One of the least amenable.

But *she* was not Saphay, not now.

He tipped off the side of the hill, floundered and went down like any earth-born creature. The lion-faced goddess landed on him and, cat-like, shook him by the throat.

Zzth howled. He tried to slam her from him. Golden bolts dashed upward, but she beat his hands off her without effort and sank her fangs into his etheric body. He was no longer beautiful. She had ruined his looks inside a few minutes. He flopped in the snow, gurgling, struggling, impotent. What must be his blood – dark and silvery – was coiling down the hill.

From all sides men and women had by now come staggering. They balanced on the hill's edges, with their burning world at their back, and watched as Saftri gnawed and ripped the demon which had come at them from the sea.

They watched in awe, in stunned pride, despite the evisceration of their security and their hearts.

The goddess finally seemed to be trying to tear the god apart, limb from limb. This she could not quite do. Nevertheless, he appeared lifeless as a rag, unconscious perhaps; certainly he no longer attempted to fight her off.

Saftri rose from him. She stamped on his belly, in his spangled blood. The lion aspect of her went out then like a strong light, yet still she was sheathed in a gold glow.

In the sky meanwhile all trace of the fire-cloud had dispersed. Only the village lit the night.

Saftri turned that way, and as her enemy had done she breathed, this time towards the sea. Icy mist flowed from her lips and covered the coast, blooming over the arson of the houses. Their redness dimmed to black. Smoke drifted, smelling of soot and ice.

Saftri stepped off her lover, the father of her dead son. 'You will have other spare lives for your use,' she said, 'a closet full. I will do this to all of them if you come back. Like you, I have eternity now.' The wolf-god's apparent corpse sagged into the snow, crumbling like wet bread. There was, over the smog of smoke, some other aroma, holy and bewitching – the pheromones perhaps of an ethereal argument.

Seventh Volume

LET THE LION ROAR

The ourth may trumpet,
And grumble may the bear;
The wolf will howl –
But let the Lion roar.

Children's song: Olchibe

ONE

Pale sky met white land. Between the two, still, lay the city.

No road any more led to it. It was surrounded by a feature-less waste. There had been dust, curious dust, but winds had spread it or shovelled it away. New snows flaked down and frosts hardened. The city itself had kept its likeness to these snows and frosts. Occasionally, despite everything, from the heights above the walls a splinter of crystal might glitter, ruby or diamond. From far off you could even now, at certain times of day, mistake Ru Karismi, City of the Kings, for something populated and alive.

A wind brushed the evening along. It was not any wind that had risen after the White Death. Yet it had an unsettling music. Through keyholes of window-empty towers it piped, and down the streeted slopes.

On the Stair of a thousand marble steps a band of men paused.

The treads were broad, but on every one was set a steel statue, each confronting the next diagonally. The statues were generally of persons straightforwardly recognizable: swords-men, crowned kings and queens, hooded mages of both genders, priests. One or two defied analysis, however.

'What can that be?' Krandif's brother Mozdif inquired.

The Vormish men considered the statue.

'It is a woman, is it? A man?'

'No. A beast it is.'

'A woman,' said Krandif, making a leaderly decision, 'who's a beast also. You'll all have been meeting a few of those.'

It had turned out a fair crossing after the fire-star omen. And riding inland the country was deserted, no opposition anywhere. Perhaps a fight would have been more cheering.

They went on, mountain-climbing the Stair.

Healthy, strong men, used to husbandry and rowing, they yet found the steps difficult. There were not many staircases in the Vormland.

Further down, in the long intervals of silence, the discontented neighs of horsazin might be heard. Other parties from the fleet rummaged there through abandoned stately houses whose roofs had sometimes collapsed, and most of whose coloured windows had been stormed out and now littered the roadways like jewels.

They had come across old funeral burning places, still black under two years of ice. They found skeletons too, the grinning balls of skulls. Once or twice there was a corpse the cold had entirely preserved, but even these had given up their humanity, and were like carved, painted things which had faded.

There were plenty of treasures left in Ru Karis. But more than gold and silver, the sea-peoples valued the unusual and nutritious foods and drinks, and foreign armaments, and of most of those the city had been despoiled. Either that or its own citizens had taken them away to the west. The Rukar had some town of tents there now, it was said, ruled by the last King Paramount, a coward who had run from the final battle and so lived.

Of course, there were supposedly mechanical wonders in the city, but none of these were ever located. They had had, these Rukar, magical servants made of brass and iron. And also they had been served by the greatest magicians of the known world, the Magikoy. But all the Magikoy, so the story went, died, either at the loosing of the fatal weapons or in the months that succeeded. The Magikoy were no more.

At the top of the Stair was a high wall, but part of it had given way. The entrance into the parks and palaces of Ru Karismi's royalty was uncomplicated.

They picked their way in over the stones. They peered along

twilight avenues of ice statues, shattered glass parasols, latticed and pillared pavilions.

'There are ghosts in this garden.'

'In all spots. With us came our own ghosts from this very war. They will take care of all such.'

The wind whined. Stars showered on the sky like the broken glass of the city's windows.

For a moment Mozdif, turning, caught sight of a shining shadow, man-like but sculpted, and much taller than a man, with the head of an animal.

He drew his long knife and moved stealthily after it, where it had seemed to slip back among the architecture.

After a fruitless search of some twenty minutes, he gave it up. The apparition too must be a ghost, or the spirit of the beast-woman-man off the stairs.

Although he, along with the rest, had heard of the Magikoy and their mechanical golems, Mozdif did not identify what he had seen.

Long after the reiver band had forged on through the gardens, the great Gargolem of Ru Karismi stalked from its alcove in a section of wall which no longer existed, passing indeed – and obviously – from its own other dimension.

It stood, looking down on the darkening city. Its head was elongate and fanged, but was the head of an obscure creature none had ever dared to classify.

In the aftermath of war the Gargolem had vanished. Those remaining had not known if it too was destroyed, or if it had only abandoned them in their fall.

Unreadable now, the visage of the Gargolem. But it had always been so.

From isolated man-made caves, the little lamps of the Vorms flowered up. They washed their horsazin with stale seawater, then feasted in the halls and houses, and sometimes sang there. But they were not the vandals they had been, or had been said to be. Ru Karis, where they would spend the night in order to tell the tale properly in the future at their hearths, commanded veneration. They offered wine and titbits to the dead; their songs were low and slow and sad.

Westward, where the night hung totally black with overcast, Bhorth the king, who was no coward and had not run from battle, walked his own city.

It had a title. It was called Kol Cataar, from the Rukarian firefex, sometimes named Ctar, that was *Risen From Ashes*.

Bhorth was a big man, but he lost fat after the White Death. He had regained, not entirely unwillingly, the bulky muscular physique he possessed in former years. His blond hair was thicker too, where his waistline had lessened. This had been the secondary benison of that which somehow saved him from the Death, a side effect of magic.

He had not known, to begin with, what it was. But there were other survivors. He dreamed often of Armageddon and its epilogue. How they sat in a circle in the desert of dust – which was all that was left of arms and armour, chariots and armies, nations, men. And how those in the circle had only survived through being *proofed*. Bhorth remembered Ipeyek the tribesman too, who had explained: 'Through wife. Wife of me.' And, later, 'Whoever lay on her.'

True enough. Any man it seemed who had dighted that irresistible woman, blacker even than this night, lovelier even than life, had survived the Death.

'See there, lord king. The third storehouse is done.'

'That's good,' said Bhorth, marshalling his thoughts, gruffly encouraging.

'And one whole extra street.'

'Yes. A fine job. Very straight.'

The new houses were built of forest logs tough as rock. Bhorth had forbidden the use of ice-brick except for temporary shelters. Mostly the town – city – of Kol Cataar was still made of ice. And where not of ice, of skin tents and leaning bothies of branches and snow.

Five hundred odd, those were all the citizens and steaders he had been able to establish here. For even once they left the poisoned Ru Karismi, his subjects fell dead on the journey. Not all of them perished from the weapon-plague. Some only gave up. The weather had been bad. Snowstorms, hail and wind like swords from the east – as if it would never stop blowing over them the dregs of the Death, the *dust*.

The Magikoy had done their share of dying as well. When the survivors stabilized in the first year to approximately five hundred, only three of these were Magikoy. Two women, one man. The women maguses were young, but the man very old – two centuries old he looked to Bhorth. How long, even with his arts, could *he* last?

Bhorth had often considered too what had become of the city's own guardian mage, Thryfe. He had not apparently been present when the weapons were used, though there were reports of his being noted in the city afterwards, attempting to ease the sick. Too late. It would always perplex Bhorth, Thryfe's derogation from duty. Before that, the tall striding magus had if anything been over-immaculate and harsh in his service.

'There is the third hothouse, lord king. Unfortunately the sheets of quartz in the outer wall cracked.'

'I see it.'

'We'll start again tomorrow.'

'Yes, better start again.'

The king and his architect, planted on the straight narrow street, looked mournfully at the slightly leaning mess of the third hothouse. Already the men had been ten months over it. Probably it would never be completed satisfactorily. One and two were not so efficient either. They might have to go the way of the Jafn barbarians, using stonewood and ice again, and magecraft, if the three maguses could rise to it.

Bhorth patted the architect on the arm.

'You've done well. Don't be concerned. It will come right. Maybe you should get home now, to your wife and fireside.'

Thankful, the man and his assistants went off through the town.

No, you could not dignify it with the word *city*. Even razed

Kandexa to the north, even razed Or Tash and Sofora, had been greater than this shambles.

But Bhorth was not pessimistic, and he too turned back for his 'palace', his three guards ambling along with him.

Bhorth liked the informality of this pioneer project. He *liked* the fact he had supernaturally been enabled to live through the blast of hell. Also, he liked his present queen, and the son she had given him the previous year, about the time of the Garland Festival.

Something remarkable there. Something more to cogitate over, when otherwise fate seemed set against his people of the Ruk.

The 'palace' had been put on a terrace of snow-blocks, and was built of snow. Bhorth had stipulated that a palace proper, one of stone or at least logs, would be the last building in the new city to go up.

This was a big house, though, with a wide wood door braced by steel and guarded by two more men in the dilapidated mail of Ru Karismi.

Bhorth hove inside.

Torches blazed on walls, and little wet rivulets of melted ice wiggled down from them. The entry broadened into a hall. It was a sight. Rare screens of ivory and gold stood about in it, and candles burned in silver sconces. When it was dinnertime, the cooked game and frost-bitten fruit would be brought in on plates of glass, the excellent wine served in goblets patterned by gems. All this inside an ice-box! Besides these everyday souvenirs of the Ruk, there were the velvets and silks and tapestries locked in chests to save them from the cold. Bhorth and his queen wore deer leather and bear fur.

There she was, Tireh, Bhorth's queen, among her four women by the big iron-clad hearth. The boy, just a year and a half in age, was sitting by them on the warm hearthstone, reading – yes, reading – from a little scroll with coloured pictures.

Bhorth gazed at this, not startled, for he had seen it before, from the boy's ninth month.

Tireh was not royal. All the royal women had died, save the

two queens of the former King Paramount, both of whom had retired from the city a while before the war, and did not reappear. Tireh was merely a young woman who had, during the awful trek here, trudged along in the snow, allowing her grandmother and aunts – her mother being dead – to sit in the lashdeer-drawn carriage-slee.

Bhorth had noticed her bravado. One night, when he was doing the rounds of the bivouac to see how his people had fared, which usually was not well, he had complimented Tireh on her care of her folk. An hour later she and he were coupling in the 'royal' tent.

They had six or seven nights together. Then the business of the exodus drew him away.

He saw her next when she arrived with one of her elegant aunts. The aunt announced Tireh was with child.

'Well,' Bhorth had said then, 'but may I ask if it's mine?'

Tireh only said, 'No other, lord King. I was virgin, as you know.'

'So you were.' Yet, he thought, there could have been others subsequently. Whatever, poor girl, he had better look after her anyway. He put her in a private slee, and sometimes rode by in his own sleekar to visit her. Three or four more times they made love. It was friendly rather than passionate.

By the day they reached the western Ruk village Bhorth had decreed would be the root of a new city, Tireh was swelling very fast. She gave birth not long after the 'palace' was erected, but several tent lanes away from it.

He heard the outcry and thought something had caught fire, the barely started metropolis melting. He rushed through Kol Cataar, his men at his heels, and found instead of fire an element black as night. Blacker. As black as the woman he had lain with before the White Death, the woman who had somehow inoculated him, by the sexual act, against dying.

Among the Jafn, Bhorth had learned, such a child was reckoned a hero, constructed directly by God. Bhorth did not believe in God. He believed in *gods*. Only a plethora of such personalities could create the bloody mayhem everywhere demonstrated in the physical world. Despite that, Bhorth was impressed. Everyone was. To the refugees of the Ruk this uncanny baby represented a miracle – a sign of renewed reward and faith.

Bhorth therefore married Tireh. She was crowned with an ancient crown of gold, his queen. They got along famously.

But the boy.

Gazing over at him now, Bhorth felt as always a kind of jumping in his veins. It was a question – and an answer.

Never before had Bhorth come across the notion that a man might lie with a woman, and *she* get *him* with child. But that, plainly, was what the black woman had done. Bhorth, escaping death, had been gravid with the offspring of their union. Having himself no womb he had needed to pass on the seed. This he soon accomplished by the mundane biological means. But Tireh's baby was undeniably also the baby of the woman whom Ipeyek had called Chillel.

Now the little boy saw Bhorth.

The child put down his scroll and bounded sure-footedly forward, arms held out.

He was black as a fossil-coal in the fire, and superlative. Besides he looked older than his months. A child of three or four perhaps would be his match.

Bhorth caught him and swung him high.

'Father!' he cried, staring up in joy at the dripping ugly ceiling.

Bhorth hugged his son. He loved the child. He had had to name him too, that was the custom. Sallusdon had been the name Bhorth elected to give. It was the name of the last King Paramount, before pernicious vile Vuldir had assumed the throne. Sallusdon had been inept and selfish but that did not matter now. His was a king's name without stigma, and the boy must bear it.

'Sallus – what have you been at today, while I was busy?'

The child smiled into his eyes. Tenderly he said, 'I missed you, Father.'

They ate supper by the fire with the old Magikoy, something

that would never have happened in Ru Karismi. Bhorth squinted at the old fellow now and then, afraid to catch him out in some senility.

A poet came and spoke an ode over the twanging of a narrow harp.

The evening ended. Everyone went to bed.

Bhorth and Tireh had sex in their comfortable greedy fashion. They were well suited.

Sleep filled the palace and the city-town, prerogative for the western peoples, for whom more than one insomniac night was an affliction.

Bhorth dreamed, and Tireh also. She dreamed she was standing in the midst of a waste of snow, calling and calling in fear for her son. Bhorth dreamed he hunted an unseen, unknown beast, running it down, always almost taking it, but always it got away.

The chaze, a snow-snake about the length of a woman's arm, came in through a torch-licked hole in the terrace side, and slithered awhile in the understores among casks of bear meat and jars of oil. Able to resist, as all its kind now could, the freezing winter of the world, the snake still enjoyed heat. When a chaze would happen on some village or camp, fire-wary it avoided the direct rays of the hearth, preferring to snuggle up with men and women in their toasty bed-places. Being virulently poisonous it must often have been disappointed that the ones bitten by it so quickly lost all warmth.

The prince, the son of Bhorth, Tireh and Chillel, lay sleeping under his rugs with the utter peace of childhood.

As the white, grey-barred snake slid fluidly in beside him he did not wake, and in a short time the snake slept too.

It was the moons which half woke Sallus.

There were three of them in a group, but all only a crescent. Nevertheless they gave a permeating light, which crossed over the high skin-glazed window slowly, throwing lit panes down on the floor.

Sallus stirred, his eyes almost opening as the moonlight

infiltrated his dreams. Sensing a companion, he took it for the known body of a favourite toy, and gathered it in his arms.

The chaze thrashed fully alert. Its riot roused the boy. Surprised, it was not until the venomous teeth closed in his shoulder that Sallus cried out – and then only at the pain.

Bhorth leapt from his mattress. Tireh surged upright, her hands to her mouth. Down the corridor there came the noise of a woman's shrieks and the thudding rattle of armed guards running.

Thrusting through his men, Bhorth ran into the room the first.

Sallusdon's nurse, her hair standing on end, posed in a screaming moonlight tableau. Bhorth pushed her aside.

The boy sat there, continuing to seem surprised, holding the dead rope of the chaze in both his hands, which together were just big enough to encircle it.

'Look, Father,' said the child.

Bhorth *looked*.

He saw the snake had had the life wrung out of it by his son of less than two years, and also that before dying the chaze had bitten the boy in the left shoulder above the heart.

'Stop that fool screeching,' Bhorth advised. One of the guards took hold of the nurse and dragged her outside, where there came the sound of a slap and sobbing. Bhorth leaned over his son. 'You've been very brave and clever. Keep very still now.'

'But it's dead, Daddy,' said Sallus, letting go of etiquette in puzzlement.

'Yes, but we must see to that bite.' Bhorth knelt on the bed-rugs. He saw a scarf with the imperial crimson and silver of Ru Karismi, and the favourite toy, a black woollen seal, and nearly began to rant in anguish and sorrow. He thrust the clamour down. The boy would die, in horrible agony. Bhorth had even seen such deaths here and there among the steads of his own estate. The only chance, and it was slim, was to suck the filth out of the bite-holes.

'Do you trust your father?'

'Yes, Daddy.'

'I need to clean your wound, my warrior. Hold quiet.'

Bhorth put his arm round the child, bent his head and fixed his mouth on the mark. He had watched a mageia do this once. Though she swallowed none of it she had been sick for a year from contact with the poison, and only her magecraft saved her. But the victim lived.

Bhorth understood something was quite wrong, however, the instant his lips and tongue met the bite.

The taste of the infected blood, he knew, should be bitter, and the edge of the wound metallic. They were not like that. The blood of Sallus had the meaty taste of health, with something else spiced inside it. The cut skin was clean.

Notwithstanding, Bhorth siphoned up the blood from the bite, turned and spat it on the ground, put back his head to suck and spit again.

Around him Bhorth's men had stayed immobile as statues. Tireh, unlike most mothers at such a juncture, was equally motionless. A splendour of a girl, a born queen. And the boy was a royal prince. Not one whimper or plea, and this must have hurt, maybe worse than the bite.

Exhausted, Bhorth sat back. He wiped his mouth. He felt dizzy. Was that the poison? But the vertigo went off. Sallusdon looked sleepily up at him.

Perhaps, perhaps I was in time. He'll live – he must live.

'It's all right, Father,' said Sallusdon. 'Thank you.'

Bhorth got up presently and went out. Before he made himself precautionarily throw up off the terrace into the moony dark, he flung the dead snake on to the bare street below.

In the morning, those who looked for it saw it had gone. No doubt someone had taken it to peel its skin for gloves, not realizing yet what ill-omened harm it had done.

Some days later when Bhorth, strong as an ox, was out hunting, and the young prince running laughing and shouting through the palace's back corridors ahead of his still-shaken nurse – who had expected only death for her negligence – the chaze reappeared. It crept out on the rough-laid tiles and gazed with first one then the other grey sidelong eye at the boy.

The nurse, always resourceful, fainted in a heap.

Sallus asked sternly, 'Is it you?'

The snake seemed to think that it was. It turned round like a legless cat. Then laid its head flat on the floor for Sallusdon, son of Bhorth, Tireh and Chillel, to put his foot upon. An uneven black ring went round its fully alive body, the reminder of how and where the child had crushed it to death, this boy of less than two who looked only four, yet had employed the strength of a man of sixteen.

'Very well,' said Sallusdon.

He put his foot on the snake's neck. The snake allowed this, even vibrating slightly, as if pleased.

Across almost the length of the continent, eastwards, in Jafn country, the Holas House was celebrating the Feast of Embers. The two years since the calamity in the Ruk had seen an improvement for this clan whose emblem was a roaring seal. Youths thought too immature or weak to join the Lionwolf's Rukar war had by now mostly grown into adequate men. Even some of the greybeards worked with a will. Willing work also took place on the mattresses. Twelve daughters and twenty sons had been the result, all yet living and hale. One of these was the Chaiord's son, that every one of them knew must become a hero.

Arok had not been idle in other ways. He had secured the defences of his garth, then ridden over the seaboard ice fields and inland territories suggesting alliance with every other clan that would. Not all wanted to comply, and some never had. But against a background of constant reiver raids from the north, for the most part the good sense of Arok swayed the Jafn, even the hot-headed Kree and the conniving Shaiy. At Thing meets along the coast, under frozen pylons, giant ships and other curiosities, handfuls of men quibbled, debated, and truce was made. Not one of the clans had not been pared to the quick by the White Death. Every Chaiord who met with Arok was, as Arok was, some kin, close or obscure, of a previous leader who had died under Ru Karismi. But at the meets Arok saw the face first of one man, then of three more, he had met before after the Death, there in the mystic circle. Fighters who, as he had, had possessed the black woman, and over whom the white flash of annihilation had gained no power.

He had sped away from the circle and from them all that night, loping off through the unspeakable dust, turning east against his will. He had felt then separate even from these brother survivors, because of them all Chillel had picked him out. Him she had *wed* in the Jafn manner. When Nirri bore Arok's son, and the child was black as starry night, Arok had thought that must be why Chillel had chosen and married him – that he was the only man capable of becoming – why mince words – knocked up from *her* seed.

But when he saw, here in the homeland, the faces of four others from the circle, Arok had needed to think again. For it was always the same. 'Here is so-and-so, son of so-and-so. He, like you, Chaiord, lived through the Rukar curse. And his woman has borne a son – a son black as Star Black Made-By-God.' Many of them had been promoted to Chaiord too, of course, even if they were no relative at all to the former king's line. For what else should you do with a warrior who sired a phenomenon?

Nirri pulled a face each time she heard the news. She had been so vainglorious about their baby, their precious Dayadin named for the constellation of the Hawk. And now she was only one more mother amid a rash of heroes, as Arok was only one more father.

There must be others, he knew. How many men had sat there in that circle? Thirty? More? They had been of all races and climes – Rukar, Olchibe, Gech, as well as Jafn – even the alliance-breaking reiver Vorms and other outland scum. All had lain with Chillel. Some had even – erroneously – called her 'wife', though only Arok could legally have claimed that.

Chillel had said she was a wine cup; any might drink from her who would. Each who sought her she lay with, and each no doubt she impregnated. Yet and again, only one had *she* solicited – himself. Why?

Why?

The joyhall boomed to cheers.

Arok pulled out of his reverie and politely nodded round. The hall was packed with Holas men, and Chaiords and warriors from all the neighbouring allies, Irhon and Shaiy, Kree, Arbo and Banjaf. Even a couple of absentees had sent gifts of meat and black wine for this Holas feast.

Presently Arok would give the sign, and every fire in the House and throughout the garth be doused. Then they must sit speechless and wait to see what communication, if any, came to them from the vulnerable dark.

Last year a swarm of vrixes had invaded the Holas House and only the skill of the House Mage had seen them off. Tonight, Arok and some of his guests had seen seefs spiralling along in the fresh snow near the gate, while a corrit had soured all the milk in the garth. But you could not avoid these pests. They clustered about any Jafn festival like hothouse flies on a split orange.

In a way too Arok quite *liked* to see them. He had mislaid them after the Death, and pondered if, for all his new vigour and luck, he had gone psychically blind.

The company drank, and on the rafters hawks rustled their feathers. The chariot-lions still left to them, some elderly and as gap-toothed as some of the older men, padded round the tables on the off chance of treats.

The hour had come and Arok gave the signal. Three garth mages rose from their benches and stretched out their hands across the space. Every torch-flame and lamp, every glowing hearth, closed to black. Outside, taking the signal from the House, the lesser mages performed their task, and the external firelight died too in the high House windows. Darkness had all.

Troubling moment. It was always like that.

Arok could recall when he had been a child himself, and almost afraid, if he had allowed it.

They sat like wooden things. At the perimeter of the room the women did the same. In the upper room Nirri, who had stayed playing with their son, would do this also. She had said the first year Dayadin would be frightened when the lamplight went. But she reported afterwards he had not seemed so. And when she told him he must keep motionless until the fires were again lighted, he did. For an infant he had already a real grasp of concepts, and had spoken fluently since about nine months.

Conceivably this year nothing would occur.

Then Arok glimpsed, by dimmest starshine, the House Mage standing, pointing up into the roof.

No, it was not the stars at the window he had seen by. A cold blueness had begun in the black hollow above. As it solidified, every hawk positioned there took off with a sharp clap of wings. Down to the tables and the wrists of men they cascaded. The lions growled and lowered themselves on their bellies.

Whatever it was that came then was more significant than any other supernatural relay Arok had witnessed at a Feast of Embers.

In the cryopathic light a man hung upside down. He clasped a long sword against his body, which wore Jafn clothing. His hair fell loosely in a curtain. In the blue light it seemed brownish-mauve. And then they saw that it was red.

None must speak or move. A wise stricture. Otherwise there might have been pandemonium.

Most knew the vision by description. Some had watched him in the flesh as he rode across the land. A few like Arok had seen him day in and out.

Lionwolf.

It was the Lionwolf. The god-king who had drawn the Jafn people to obliteration.

There was an awesome extreme coldness in the hall. A subtraction of fires alone could not have caused it. It was like a wave from the depths of a sea of ice, and colder even that that.

Gradually, as they looked on transfixed, the image of the

hanging man changed. It melded into the sword, became all a sword pointing upwards, which in turn altered its appearance. Now a blue sun levitated in the roof, and white flames tangled from it, and then, like the shutting of an eye, it all disappeared.

After the briefest instant natural warmth gushed back into the room.

The House Mage spoke out rather hastily and the fires were reborn in their places.

Men shifted, glancing at each other. Not one of them voiced his thoughts, which were generally the same: such an augur could not be optimistic.

Upstairs in the bedchamber, as a lamp rekindled, Nirri picked up her unbelievably-not-unique boy. He was handsome, already heavy with young muscle, more like a child of six, she thought.

'How cold it was,' she said. 'Cold as some say Hell must be.'

The black child Dayadin, seeing she was uneasy as she had been the year before, stroked her cheek with a comforting hand.

These reiver raiders did not, as in former days, issue from the sea into the east. They rode out of the south of the continent, loaded with pillage already, but hungry for a proper scrap.

The weather and the going were undemanding. Transparent skies produced sleek hard veldts of snow.

Krandif's fleet had unevenly divided. About three hundred warriors had cantered off on their horsazin for those desolate ruins previously bypassed – Thase Jyr, Kandexa. The move was decided in Vorm Assembly, where each man's vote counted. Mozdif had led that band. Krandif thought it was a waste of time and energy. Thase and Kand were nothing now, but to the north-east the familiar Jafn lands, where settlements were resurrecting after the catastrophe, were worth a visit. Two hundred and thirty-three men agreed with his plan.

True, many men of the Vorms had been allied with the Jafn,

under the blue-sun banner of the Lionwolf. But they were dead and that past was cancelled.

It would be a bonus too to get back to the sea – any sea. The horsazin were fractious for a swim, and the barrels of flat sea-water kept for them by now stank. The men wanted the coast for more emotive reasons. They were of the sea-peoples, and on the Vormland you could always smell the sea, unless you had, insanely, trekked to the mountains.

On the evening when they sighted the coastal ice in the distance, with a dark line of liquid ocean beyond, Krandif's band rejoiced, and dug deep into the snow to make a hidden camp. Here they took a sleep night, the first for nine days. Unlike the Jafn, who slept a few hours every three or four nights, the Vorms, Kelps and Fazions, when they did sleep, would indulge in twelve or fourteen hours of blissful oblivion. As their sage, Gunri, had once declared, 'Like a man who only samples his wife but once a year, when he does it he is entitled to make a pig of himself.'

They slept like logs.

The horsazin were restless at their pickets in the snow cave, but resigned, scenting the sea, shuddering and frisky with longing. Finally they slept too, on their feet.

Day came and shone over the hump of the camp, gave up and went away.

In the second night the camp woke, drunk with slumber, and blundered about heavy-headed. But by the following dawn they were actively refreshed and rode on.

Krandif had undergone a weird dream in his thirteen-hour coma. He wished Mozdif had been there, to discuss it with him. Instead he sought the chief shaman who accompanied them. The shaman did not ride. He bounced alongside the horses. A lean scarecrow, he cawed like an ice-crow in answer to any query – then showed you his meaning by conjuring a symbol in the air.

'This I dreamed,' had said Krandif. 'There was a red star, like that we saw sea over. This fell on the earth. To see it I went, and when there I got it had turned to black. I picked it up. Cooled it was – and smooth. I held it. In the dream I thought these words: I will gift to Our Lady Saftri this fallen black star.'

The shaman barked, an innovation perhaps, but all that ran up on the air was a little twiddly pattern, such as a child might doodle in stolen octopus ink on the snow.

He was a war shaman, however. One took no risks.

'Many thanks,' Krandif said. 'I'm much obliged.' He led them on into the north-east.

'They're coming.'

Arok nodded. His face was set in grim familiar lines. 'Sir,' he said to the House Mage.

The Mage had risen. 'I'll go send the tidings to the neighbouring clans.'

The other mages had by now gathered and together they all went into the Thaumary behind the joyhall. A dull sizzling filled the air as the sorcerous sending winged away in three directions.

This would be the first reiver attack for some while, but they were always a possibility. It would seem these raiders had already beached their jalees up on the western coast and gone to try the wreckage of the Ruk before travelling here.

Soon the sword, kept horizontal in peacetime, was anointed with animal blood, and fixed upright on the Holas House above the door.

Men stared at it. Arok knew their thought and thought it too. The vision of the Lionwolf on Embers Night must have predicted a raid, for the accursed hero had hung upside down and the sword in his clutch therefore had pointed upright for war.

This would be then a special fight.

A Holas hunting party had spotted the reiver band about fifteen miles off – Vorms, striped purple and charging about the shore, pausing only to allow their horned fish-horses to swim. Despite their horseplay, if left unchecked they would be on the garth before nightfall. That must not happen. Arok and his men were kitted out in mail, the chariots stood in the yard on burnished runners, with the youngest chariot-lions positioned to draw them. The beasts had been dressed in their war collars. Everything was in order.

Arok's charioteer, a boy of sixteen, sprang up ahead of him, breastplate wobbling a little; it had been the boy's great-uncle's and he had not yet quite grown into it. It should have been Arok's younger brother who drove him. But none of Arok's brothers lived.

Yes. Everything in order: a Jafn host of forty men, nine of them each old enough to be someone's grandsire, and the rest, aside from Arok, barely out of boyhood. And the reivers? Oh, just two hundred or so. A snack for any hungry warrior.

If only they had come in along the north-eastern sea, as normally they did. Then the strategically placed watchtowers would have given warning sooner.

How much time before Arok's cunningly attached allies – Arbo, Banjaf and Kree being the nearest – could catch up to him? Some hours . . . a day . . .

'Face of God,' Arok muttered. 'Prick of God,' he augmented. His charioteer shuddered at the blasphemy.

'It's well, my boy. God understands.'

The three remaining war mages had come out and climbed in their vehicle, stony-mouthed. As well they might be. The House Mage, who must stay behind to protect the garth, came out too, his sending done.

'We will hold the Thought of Victory for you, by all our craft.'

Arok expressed thanks.

Women drooped over the yard, trying to seem fierce and resolute, some holding their babies. A couple of the older ones were tearful, but the very oldest not, putting a brave face on for the honour of their elderly husbands in the battle chariots. Nirri walked out now. He had told her she must set an example, and was glad to see she did. Her head was held high; she wore all her necklaces, and was confidently smiling, and by the hand she led the boy.

Seeing *him*, a susurrus of intuitive relief wafted across the yard. And by the gate others pressed closer.

'Dayadin!' Arok theatrically and gladly cried. He lifted the boy up so everyone there should behold him. This garth had a hero. They were blessed. How could any harm befall them?

Dayadin smiled too. He looked at his father and said, 'Take me with you.'

Arok almost choked. Where the idea of defeat and perhaps death only depressed him, this now filled him with terror.

He tried to laugh it off.

Great God – with all the garth practically watching.

'No, son. You stay here with our Mage to guard your mother and the women.'

Dayadin frowned. He seldom wept, but frowning was sometimes a prelude to it.

God – forgive my bloody blasphemy – don't let him cry – not now!

In fact Dayadin was not upset. He was thinking. Already nearly two, he had begun to learn that adults must now and then be outwitted.

A hovor flicked abruptly in over the House wall.

Foul abomination. But at such moments one must have a care for everything, as Arok well knew.

'Look!' said the child. He stretched out his hand and the hovor, swimming down on some current of air, flipped something into his palm. Then it flitted away.

'Let me see.'

Dayadin showed his father, and everyone else, a single smooth chip, probably the shed tooth of a small whale, with which the hovor had gifted him.

Arok heard the murmurs around them. 'A good sign.' 'Even the spirits honour Dayadin.'

Arok kissed his son on the forehead and lowered him from the chariot to the yard. Dayadin seemed content. Did he even fully grasp where Arok was going – or that he might not be back?

I shall come back. Didn't I live through the White Death?

But Arok was not sure. To Arok, the blade of a knife or sword was a more certain and different matter from any Rukar magic.

Besides, he had served Chillel's purpose now. Perhaps invulnerability had worn off.

Nirri, when she had seen to her queen's duties about the beleaguered hold, trod up the ladder-stair to the upper room of the house.

In her belly was a cold weight. She was afraid Arok would die, and also that the whole garth would be overrun by bloodthirsty reivers. The notion of being murdered frightened her. But so did that of being taken off as a slave to northern lands. She had spent so much of her life living in affectionless, unvalued poverty before Arok found her. She did not want to return to it.

The room was cheering enough. Rainbow hangings and polished weapons on the walls, a mattress heaped with furs, and a fire-dancing brazier. Two of her women were there, trying as she had to seem buoyant and assured.

'The gates are shut fast,' Nirri announced. 'And soon enough the Banjaf at least will be with Arok. Over fifty warriors. Ours too is a vigorous garth, and we still have twelve young men to defend us.'

This was mere ritual, and the 'young men' were aged between seven and fourteen, but the women brightly agreed.

Nirri looked for her son. Something had perplexed her slightly. It was the whale tooth the hovor had given him. Surely, Dayadin already had a tooth just like it? One of the garth boys had found and carved it for him . . .

'Where's my boy?'

'Oh, he went back to hall, Nirri lady.'

Nirri turned involuntarily, aware instantly Dayadin had not been in the hall.

She now felt, along with all the rest, a gripe of fear in her stomach, and told herself not to. Dayadin was always off about some business of his own. He had been like that since he was one year old.

And Nirri was quite right. Dayadin was off about his own business.

That particular hovor had been a pet of his for months. He had told it therefore, using only words in his mind, that it must come, lift the whale tooth from the ledge where it lay and present it to him in the yard. Faultless parent-fooling distraction. Once Arok and his men had ridden off, Dayadin waited briefly. Then, evading everyone, he made his way down the lanes between the many vacant houses of the Holasan-garth. If the garth had not been so unpeopled it was doubtful no one would have seen him, for he was unique to them and caused a loving prideful interest wherever he went.

He again met the hovor which, as instructed, awaited him by one of the high outer walls. Below the terrace dropped steeply for three man-heights to the ground. But Dayadin, though unusually mature in intellect and body, was still a child, and the hovor raised him over the wall and safely over the platform to the snow with enormous ease. Thereafter Dayadin broke into a firm indefatigable run in pursuit of his father and Arok's tiny army.

All the clumps of little villages gave the clue. Deserted and dilapidated, they carried the emblem of a parading seal – a Jafn marker. One of the garths would be close.

Krandif's men were in high glee, their horses sea-washed, newly striped and up for anything.

Then came some cliffs, and the way through conducted them into ice-forests of glassy cedar and blanched, knotted tamarisk trees tufted with raw silver. Huge boulders of ancient snow, with translucent icy eyes, watched their progress. Jafn sprites whiffled in the winds. But the Vorms were not nervous of any of these elementals, who anyway they could rarely see – and then barely. They had their own more immediate and concrete divinity at home.

Descending the tumulus of a snow hill, they looked at a scoop of open land several miles across. At the western end of it a hint of organized smoke showed on the sky – too much for any village. That must be the garth.

Then they saw a Jafn pack coursing out of the distance towards them. Lion chariots raced, sending up a haze of sprayed top-snow.

Dismayed, Krandif controlled his jinking horse.

'Is that *all* of them, Krandif?'

Someone called, 'A mistake they've made – they thought only their own kind had come against them, so didn't bother.'

'*No*. That's all there *are* of them *left*.'

'Then excuse me that speaks, but it's no fight.'

'Courage,' said Krandif. 'Perhaps when we get over the bodies of these ones, their women in the house will give us a better combat.'

The antique scores were always ready to be considered. The Jafn nation and the outland peoples had always fought, as Olchibe and Gech had always harried and wished for vengeance on the Ruk.

But – were only skirmishes possible now?

Krandif's band made up their minds and souls. They would settle for simply killing these Jafn, as a man killed a scrat in his grain store.

Off and down the slope they thundered in a panoply of loose snow, Krandif's two hundred and thirty-three reivers, towards the lion chariots and Arok's forty men.

We will die.

Then let us die in glory.

Arok met the first line of the Vormish charge with a swinge-ing series of axe-swipes that took off enough heads to line one of their soints of ships. A few hands and arms went too.

Horsazin shrieked and neighed, filling the air with kicks and the reek of gamy mackerel.

Peripherally Arok noted that, though only a lad, his charioteer was collected and canny. As one of the barbarian's long knives sheered inwards, the boy ducked and struck up with a dagger, punching a tidy hole.

The chariot careered in circles, the lions letting out gusty snarling snortings. Where they could, well trained, they raked with their long, amber-ringed claws. One Vorm leaned in too near and learned, yelling, his chin had become the prize of Arok's younger lion.

Arok felt his axe break on the breaking back of a man. He let it go and drew out the sword. One, two, three, four, five, six. The corpses showered like hail.

Already the snow was carpeted over with red. Glancing, Arok saw that he had personally contributed. Though he could feel no wound, something had nipped him; he was scarlet on the left side, the side of the heart, which was not ideal. It proved anyway he was no immortal, no longer invulnerable, and had better fight properly now and no more like a silly girl.

Through every corner and chink of sight, beyond his own sphere of battle, he saw his warriors going down. Young and old, clever and weak.

In God's Name. There had only been forty to start with—

Arok bit his mental tongue. At least they had fathered children. But – these Vorms would have those. The children would die too, or become slaves.

Rage lit him. Arok reared, snarling like his lions, and clove a man in two bits.

Then the chariot tilted.

It was unexpected. You never reckoned it could happen in the thick of war—

Down he fell. He was on the coloured snow, which crinkled and crunched beneath him. A dead lion lay over him and he had to push it off – it was his, the best – but at least it had a Vormlander's separated chin in its jaws to take to the Other Place.

The young charioteer was dead. *God – where is justice?* He had been fine and valiant – so young—

Be quiet, heart. Let the mind think.

Arok lay as if slain under the wheel of his chariot, with the inert lion still partly on him, and looked with one eye to see what could be done.

Nothing, it would seem.

The Jafn force was engulfed.

Over there, the three mages, not even defended, were working up rays that wobbled into the mêlée – but the wretched Vorms had their shaman, and the mage-rays kept going out.

Nevertheless, the sparkle of Holas blades continued.

One of the oldest of the men, ninety years he always claimed, but others said he was only seventy, lashed about him with a beautiful accurate abandon. Vorms dropped like smashed plates.

They will sing of this.

But who could survive now of the Jafn Holas to sing?

And if their allies even came to join them, that must be too late.

And nor would *they* sing.

The Jafn peoples had always been chancy in their own alliances. Only that man-god, Lionwolf, only he had brought them together and made all one, even with the stinking Vorms and Kelps and riffraff. Only Lionwolf, and look what had become of them, under his banner.

Arok erupted bawling like a bear from the pile of dead lying over him, and slapped his sword through a reiver's guts.

It was then he saw, across the shoulder of the battle, something very dark bowling over the whiter snow beyond. It seemed winged with a frothy opalescent wind – sprites, were they? Seefs maybe, sihpps, things that liked to drink blood by proxy through observing the feeding of fleer wolves or kindred vampires.

Arok experienced a strange softness that sponged along his skull. It rang. He turned over and went down and men on foot ran across him, and a horsaz leapt to clear his body.

Now I finish.

He could not move, yet he could still see.

What he saw was his son, Dayadin, dashing suddenly over the vista.

Illusion.

Arok remembered what his son had said. *Take me with you.*

Nirri was forever remarking that Dayadin nearly always got his own way—

Arok floundered. Judging by the blood which covered him he *must* be near death, but he had to reach his child—

He saw the child spring high in the air – a hovor was lifting him, and three others attended, flapping into the faces of the Vorms who, ignorantly blind to Jafn spirits, rubbed their eyes and swore and doubtless thought the weather was getting up.

It was Krandif who glimpsed the boy and did not believe it. Then, seeing him again and again, it was Krandif who disengaged from a dying man at least seventy who had almost split his torso with an axe, leaned over and grabbed the child from the way of a toppling horsaz.

The boy writhed. He had seemed to be able to fly. He was perfectly black: skin, hair, the centres of his eyes.

Krandif recognized him instantly.

'It is.'

The boy seemed to understand the Vormish language. He glared at Krandif in fury, and replied, 'I it is. Where is my father?'

'Who,' said Krandif, idiotic, 'is your father?'

'He is *king*.'

'Ah. Then a Jafn, is he?'

'*He is king.*'

Krandif knew, whatever the father was, this boy was the being he had dreamed of, the fallen star, flame to darkness.

'You are god-given.'

The boy shot him a look of unadulterated vitriol, and writhed all the way about.

'Daddy!' shrilled the child.

Then he recollected himself. Although the man he loved most in any world was crawling on the slush of pink snow, his body running with blood as if he had bathed in it, before an enemy you stayed formal. 'My father,' said Dayadin. Dry-eyed

118

and fearsome he added, 'Hear me that says this: spare him, or I'll see you dead.'

Krandif held the child and answered, 'Come with me to Our Lady. That's where you must go. Do that, and we leave your people be. Say it, and all's done.'

Dayadin closed his eyes. Krandif did not see this gesture, that of a grown man who can bear no more.

'I will.'

When Krandif belled his lungs and sounded the hoot of retreat, every one of his men that could obeyed. You did not quarrel with your own in a fight.

However, it would take some explanation, for the garth was just down the valley and these Jafn were at their end.

As for the Jafn themselves they stared in amazement as their outnumbering foe turned tail and galloped away.

The snow was laid with blood and bodies.

Seventeen Jafn men stood or leaned there, some badly hurt, gazing at the reiver retreat.

Only Arok, who was to find he had no wound, had only been laved unknowingly in the gore of others, kneeled on the snow, his head still ringing from the blow of an iron knife-haft, his heart, that he had bade be silent, torn in two. One half, black as night, had been carried away with the reivers. One half, the lesser, stayed in his chest. This with the rest of him he must take home, to tell the remains of his people and the boy's mother what had befallen them.

TWO

On the tenth day the landscape altered. Until then the plain of stones had persisted, deadly in its sameness, causing a sense of enervation, desolation, or near panic. Occasionally crags went up miles off to either side, one or two with boiling indigo plumes. The smoke of these volcanoes, if that was what they were, unravelled on the grisaille of the sky. Sometimes forests of stone rambled over the scene. The tree-like forms of these were tall, and top-heavy with formations of boulders or huge flattish piled stones, resembling frozen foliage only in the distance. The men marched or rode in the black chariots. The vehicles were hauled forward by fauna that were most like enormous grey weasels. Portions of the army had even laughed at these animals on first seeing them. But their fast, creeping, muscular gait was sinister and disturbing. Like so much else, they had evolved from their surroundings, in this case out of the plain itself. And once on the move the troops of the Hell King often spotted similar life-forms, oozing up out of the ground or down from the columns of the stone trees.

But on the tenth day a lake appeared. It was a lake of creamy fire, crackling and spitting, from which black burnt particles were constantly fired off into the air.

There was no way across the lake, which filled in the view from one side of vision to the other.

The Gullahammer of Hell halted its advance.

It sat or stood eyeing the lake.

Bird things winged by high up, calling in skeletal voices. They had seen these only now and then before.

120

'What next? Do we swim?'

Vashdran glanced back. Who had spoken? Any of them. Though he had been made a Saraskuld commander, like Curjai and the others, he gave no orders to this force. Rather, they and he acted – at least physically – like one coherent whole. They paused at sunfall, made their bivouac, resumed at sunrise, trundled on. The direction they had been pointed in was west-ward, and they maintained it. Was this arbitrary?

Vashdran said, 'Swim? Can't you fly?'

A frisson of alertness energized the lines of men behind his chariot.

Before the chariot, the two weasel things stayed immobile. They had no curiosity. They had no *smell*. No persona. Did any of them, here, aside from men?

And this war they had been sent on, this conquering of ancient 'enemies' and liberating of captured cities – was any of it real?

Vashdran considered Hell's queen. That night lay eleven days behind him. In some other world, he would have revelled in the recollection. But here – here he was not sure. Every delight he had contrived with her – although he was now uncertain if he had actually *had* her – still left an unsatisfied memory of *Chillel* uncoiling in him. The midnight eyes of Winsome had shown him, too, what he had woken in *her*. Her body wrapped his in an embrace of fire more searing than the white lake. But with the rising of the cold blue sun she had been gone, and only Taeb the Gech witch lurked outside in the grotto. She said guards had sent her back below to wait for him. He asked himself if *she* had been the one he lay on, her perhaps Hell-augmented powers leading him to believe in all ways she was another.

After all, was *Winsome* even real? How could she be? She was Chillel – a Chillel who had sought him and taken him. A Chillel whose orgasmic pleasure had only engendered fresh desire – not cored his soul of its light.

Each morning of the war march – if it *was* morning, or a march – he asked himself if any of this place or any of these shapes, these creatures and plodding men, were what they seemed.

But what else was there but to go on?

It was, Hell, like life in that.

The men of the Gullahammer were springing up into the air, *flying*. Vashdran could see, over on the left flank, Curjai's men also ascending, beating their shields into wings.

The distressing birds above hurtled off, not happy at rivals.

Vashdran sprang upwards also. He arced, with countless others, above the army that so far remained on the ground, over the abandoned chariots and weasel things, which did not even raise their heads to watch the flying charioteers.

It did not astound him when, one by one, vacated cars sank into the grey-white earth, which for less than a minute was darkly stained by them. The creatures curled down too, seeping away.

This place . . .

Vashdran turned his head resolutely for the farther shore of the lake. Having risen high, partly to avoid the black spittings of the fire, he could just make out the perimeter, another stone forest bundled at its edge.

When they alighted over there, Vashdran was convinced the black metal chariots – or identical chariots – would come up again from the ground. The trees would spawn more weasel-ings.

Everything came and went – and came back.

Even the glamorous armour the Saraskulds had been awarded, that they had carefully been dressed in by the attendants at Shabatu, *melted* off when unneeded or inappropriate. When he had reached out for Winsome, the armour had dissolved. When he got off the couch the following day, yes even as he hesitated there, staring round the empty chamber, the armour had formed again on his body in exact order.

Had he exchanged any words with any other man here, since that night?

Vashdran could not recall. He had been thinking so much it seemed to have cancelled recent memories.

Taeb, he knew, had been guided into the city by the priests, along with the other brides – all but one, that thin girl with very long dark hair, Curjai's choice. She had protested, shouting she wished to go with the army. She said she could fight psychically, had been trained to it, and been more than a mere witch or mageia when she lived.

He remembered this because it had momentarily fascinated him, her logical angry protest, her *reasoning*, and the incongruous, now inevitable words, 'I had respected abilities, when alive.'

Curjai must have won her love during their night, to make her cling so.

Then Vashdran had lost interest. He did not see the outcome of the argument. Probably she would be punished for protesting, as he and others had been before. Or maybe instead they let her accompany the march.

Curjai had said nothing to Vashdran. Besotted too? Curjai had seemed to mean something, as Choy had, and Kuul also. But quickly that decreased, melted from Vashdran like the armour.

No doubt all human preoccupations seeped away into the ground or the stones like everything else.

All, that was, except sex, and aggression.

Vashdran spun on over the lake. He looked into it a couple of times, but it seemed the same from above as from in front, seething and laval. It gave off however no heat. If anything it gave off even greater cold.

He thought, *I can fly without wings. Presumably I can walk up walls and trees here, as I did . . . elsewhere. What abilities have I lost? None? I've gained some, maybe, and not found them yet. But any man can do as I do. And nothing is of any use. If everything is limitless, I am limited by it. I am in chains.*

This was why he felt only dreariness at the idea of combat. This was why Winsome, who was Chillel, had rendered him no true satisfaction, no proper victory.

Of *course* he could cutch her here. *Here* he could do anything, providing it had no value . . .

Vashdran skimmed the end of the lake. Boulders, semi-molten, lay bubbling below. He landed on the forest's roof of stone foliage.

In the distance now he could see something different.

'Hey! Hey!' Heppa landed by Vashdran, ungainly and still unwisely tickled at his accomplishment of flight.

'Look,' said Vashdran.

'What?'

'Another city.'

Heppa screwed up his eyes to see. His eyesight stayed faulty. He made something out.

Other men were raining down on the forest tops. The army pointed and squinted all one way.

A desert expanse of what seemed to be frosty sand, rather like the fine-sifted grains of the Uaarb of northern Gech, stretched for miles. The blue sun was travelling on the same route, westward, and shone on a mass of escalated, manufactured walls. The structure was pale, like Shabatu. Shabatu's instructive priests, sending them to this metropolis, had given it no name. It was only the city held by ancient enemies.

Curjai dropped neatly down on Vashdran's tree. Vashdran observed, bored with it now, how Curjai's wings folded at his back.

'A word with you.'

Vashdran was irritated by this play-acting of normality. Surely they must give it up?

'What do you want?'

'I tried to tell you – five times I've tried. You walk off.'

'You sound like some girl.'

'It's about some girl. Do you know of a high order of magicians – Magikoy?'

'Rukarian. In the world of life.'

'One's here. She's sought you through the geography of this underworld, and wants your blood.'

124

'Well, she can have it. It isn't going to matter, is it, either way. Besides, *she*? This mage is only a woman.'

'She demanded to attend the army. To be, she said, our mageia. She said it was common for an army to have battle mages. Plenty of the men shouted out that this was a fact. My people too, where I . . . lived. We used such magic.'

Vashdran thought, *I missed all that – the woman saying she was a mage. How did I miss it when I was standing there? Or did I only forget? Nothing has any meaning. Or did it never happen at all, and only happens now because Curjai tells me it has?*

'Be quiet,' Vashdran said loudly.

Curjai stepped swiftly over the treetop and slapped Vashdran backhanded across the face.

Vashdran reeled, pulled up, swung to return the blow – and stopped himself before he could deliver it.

All around men became an audience, enjoying the little tiff between their irrelevant commanders.

'I gave you my true name,' said Curjai, very low. 'Don't talk to me like your dog.'

'I speak more nicely to a dog.'

'So you do. But those dogs were left in Shabatu, and I am a man and now you can speak nicely to me instead.'

Vashdran looked away at the city.

'None of this has any substance. How I speak to you or if we quarrel or are vow-brothers. Whatever glory or disgrace we incur. Whether we die or live or lie face down on the rocks. *Nothing.*'

The men had been distracted by another thing. They started cheering and waving at a colour in the sky.

Vashdran and the others looked up.

'This,' said Curjai, 'is *her*.'

The woman flew in swirlings of her long hair. If they all had magic powers here, then she had chosen to use also some imagination. Great scarlet wings supported her, like those of the legendary firefex. Her clothing was the deeper red of blood. As she soared over, she sang to them in a wild high voice, smiling and beckoning them on, on to the city and the war. She was able it seemed to imbue them with a fierce lust for battle. Their cheers rose to bellows, and the clang of fists on shields. But passing over Vashdran's head she, like the lake, spat full in his face.

Something made him fling up his arm to protect himself. The spittle of the Magikoy mageia Ruxendra flamed as it flew. And as it scattered along Vashdran's forearm he saw it form letters – in the alphabet of Ruk Kar Is, that Saphay his mother had shown him. *I am the payment*, read the message Ruxendra had written on him. It would fade. It was not real. But it did not fade . . . perhaps it was.

Their Magikoy mageia rode, as was not the custom, at the forefront of the advance, in one of the recreated black chariots. Unlike the flying men she did not slough her wings when they were unneeded, but kept them on display.

Curjai, you became aware, stayed well away from her.

As they neared the second city over the ice-sand of the plain, somehow she urged her chariot and slink-striding weaselings to a gallop.

It seemed she could not wait to sink in her teeth.

The sun was at the zenith now. It clearly showed when the gates of the city opened and the fighting force spilled out, gathering in a great pond of darkness and glitter under the walls.

Vashdran felt nothing. He was indifferent, even to the words scorched on his arm. And yet he did not jump down and walk away, but rode the chariot on. All the chariots began to race now, though no order had been given and Vashdran certainly had not made any signal to his running beasts. Only the war-mad mageia apparently prompted this headlong rush.

The dark battalions facing them were forming into an arrowhead, its point aiming straight at the galloping Gullahammer.

The enemy also had black chariots, grey weasel beasts, armour which caught the blue sun. Men with wings were rising up there, circling, diving in along the sky. The ones who flew on the Gullahammer side put on their shield-wings and went up too, line on line of them, like craits rising from an ice floe. And now the enemy chariots were racing.

Everything would meet with a clash and rumble. Everything would collide, explode, like mirrors shattering, and jets of fiery blood go up to hit the sun.

Ruxendra, as Vashdran glimpsed in the seconds before the opposing chariots struck each other, had also taken to the air again. He watched her flapping scarlet cross high above the airborne men who were already at grips, hacking and ripping each other on the wing. She screamed with viciousness or excitement, and sorcerous rays spread from her like burning cirrus, feathering earthwards on all of them.

The chariots met.

Vashdran saw a face – unknown, unknowable— He killed the face and his beasts trampled over the beasts of the fallen chariot, trampling on into the thrust and clamour of the fight.

The sword swung. The knife. Sometimes there was the Olchibe bow Guri had taught him how to use. Five arrows veering away at a single twang of the string, the dead dying, falling under the runners and feet, lying there till death-life should come back to them – and, as before, some not returning, the twice-dead sprinkled like pebbles on the shore of Hell.

Vashdran's chariot, rammed from the left side, splintered and gave way.

Vashdran too fell under the runners, the pads of the grey beasts. He should lie here. Why flounder about? It would not affect him, or only with pain at least.

But he found he had grabbed the runner of another car, pulled himself abreast the bodywork and over into the black shell of it. He slashed the charioteer in the neck and heart and pushed him out.

This is why I can't die. This in me can't die. This irreducible immortal dross. This brilliant rottenness of self . . .

Fighting, he heard the cheering gush up again. Who was winning? *They? Or us?* But it was irrelevant, for they were all the same.

Vashdran rode among the first into the open city gate, above which an iron mouth was now mooing just as one had at Shabatu.

This city . . . was identical. The broad, winding roadway, undefended, unpeopled, led to a citadel high above.

Welcome to Uashtab sang the crowd inside the carven white gates.

Rattles cracked, harps let out plinking cadences.

The men and women who, it seemed, they had liberated from the ancient enemy danced, singing with feral joy their lawless, optimistic praises. Flowers made the path blue and purple, and in the lush petal cups of amethyst and azure, cold eyes regarded the boots of warriors which smashed them.

At the end of the wide road a towering archway gave on what must be the vast palace of . . . Uashtab, city of Hell.

In they went to a labyrinth, hall giving on hall. Walls stretched upwards, vaguely coolly shining. There was no roof. The sun sliced down with swords of light. Somewhere a boulder dropped with a whistling scream, a dull deep thud.

Curjai stood over Vashdran.

'There are hot springs here too. Those baths with the girls. Why not come and wash off her spit?'

Vashdran glanced at the scald of letters on his arm. They were still readable. *I am the payment.*

'You should,' said Vashdran, 'have treated her better in bed. Then she'd have less interest in me.'

Curjai said, 'I didn't take her. She didn't want me.'

'You should have made her want. Or taken her anyway.'

'I never had a woman.'

Vashdran said, without interest, 'What have you had, then?'

'Nothing that way. Only a never-ending fight.'

'This is the same city,' Vashdran said.

'I know it,' said Curjai, 'and the name—'

'A play on the letters of the first name: Shabatu Uashtab. Like a Rukar word game. Probably there is a king here made of stone. And a black woman who is queen and calls the moon.'

'We're trapped in a circle. Perhaps we can break out. Even she – the red mageia – might help us do that.'

'No. We're to be punished. There can be no breaking out. No help.'

Vashdran put his hand inside his shirt, searching for something – the toy mammoth – but again it was not there. Curjai stood gazing at him for a little while, but Vashdran only stared into his own thoughts. Curjai went away.

In one of the corridors, some of the snake-head guards went by, dragging in chains a prisoner from the battle. Here, thought Curjai, was one difference from the last time. Those they had overcome had not been welcomed to the city equally with the conquerors. The defeated enemy were driven along, naked and in shackles, and beaten as they went with whips. Curjai had seen such events in his former life. But something in these groups of prisoners unsettled him, and also unsettled many of the men of the Shabatu army, some of whom had seemed actually afraid when prisoners were hauled by.

Curjai moved back to allow the single captive and his wardens past. The captive appeared genuinely hurt. Curjai noted this, and then saw the face of the man, matted over though it was with blood and ragged dark hair. With a horrifying sensation of rightness, Curjai leaned there on the wall, staring after the procession until it rounded the curve of the passage, and was gone. The man beaten and in chains had also been himself. Had also been – *Curjai*.

THREE

At first the children had cried all the time, for their fathers, their uncles and brothers, just as the very old men cried, if quite tearlessly, for their sons. But with the arrival and departure of the months the old men and the children came to accept that the women, who were many of them young, and some of indisputable power, must rule. If not for ever, at least for another decade.

Naturally, some younger men had missed the war and lived. But they were all unsuitable to lead the bands or govern the sluhtins, being severely lame or not whole of mind, or physically too feeble. Three men had returned to their homes, or so the story went. But those sluht-camps were far off, isolated by many miles from this large one here under the frozen fig trees and pineapples.

Piamtak sat with her coven in one of the great sluht halls that was her husband's castle, when he lived. Peb Yuve had been old, but still a strong warrior. Now he was dust. As for her children, they had all been sons and all grown men; they had gone with Peb, and so were dust too.

Piamtak had not only lived as one of Peb's wives, but was the crone or Crax of her coven.

This coven comprised a virgin girl of eleven, a young woman of sixteen, and a woman who had borne children, though all the men she had favoured were dead as well in the war, and perhaps she would not bear again.

Piamtak was swathed in a mantle of white fur. It had been gifted to her by the wondrous god-being, Lionwolf – just before he mesmerized all the Olchibe men and led them off to their deaths.

That day, that death-day, Piamtak's coven, and several others across the Marginal Land and southern Gech, picked up the psychic broadcast of catastrophe. It had marked all of the women, even the youngest.

Some of the old men subsequently reproached Piamtak, though she was Crarrow, about continuing to wear her white fur. Had not the demon-get given it her? Was not her man, the leader of thirteen vandal bands, destroyed – and had she not seen it in her coven fire?

That evening of the reproach, Piamtak had told a parable to the sluhtin, a thing women did not do, standing there in her mantle, her forehead clasped with gold and green stones braided in her grey-black hair.

'In the beginning, the God of the Great Gods, He who made woman first that she might bear the first man, created too the animal world, to please, intrigue and assist her.'

Piamtak told the gathering, all the women who were left and the impaired males and the children – who were still crying then almost all the while – how God gave each creature his shape and covering, his abilities and his voice.

'The youngest among us know the song,' said Piamtak. 'Come then, for the sake of your perfect fathers and brothers that we will never forget, sing out to me that song.'

And the children, most of them, choked off their weeping and sang the song, because she was Yuve's widow, Yuve once their leader and priest, and she was a Crax of the Crarrowin, the wisest witch-women, so the Olchibe claimed, on earth.

Piamtak then repeated the last words of the song, which had been antique time out of mind. 'And so the God decreed as follows: the ourth may trumpet, and grumble may the bear; the wolf will howl – but let the lion roar.'

A stillness hung on the crowd, dense as the nectarine-coloured smokes which had stained all the inner roofs.

Old men, and the company of women, thought of loss. They thought too of the ourths, their beauteous and mighty blond mammoths, turned to dust along with their men. The children sobbed and snuffled, drowning the breasts of their mothers in tears.

'Who knows,' said Piamtak, 'the meaning of this song?'

An old man shouted from the crowd, 'It means the woman must know her place, under the jurisdiction of the male. And what if she be Crax, and what if I am bent and old, nevertheless I tell her to burn that fur of a white bear.'

Piamtak waited. Then she said, 'I will explain to you the song. The God of the Great Gods allowed each animal his authentic music. The mammoth is a warlike beast, and so he has the note of a trumpet, and the bear is sullen so he rumbles and grumbles. The wolf makes a serenade to the moons, and he has three pipes in his throat, the moon number, to howl with. But the lion is greater than these. He is the grey shadow that moves through the snows, and men see him at dawn or twilight, and they do not trouble him, for he is lordly. And among the lionkind are females too, strong and maned like the males.' The sluhtin listened. Even the children only wept softly now while the Crax spoke. 'It counts for nothing,' said Piamtak, 'what any tell you, or what is done to you. If you are a lion, you will roar. Olchibe is a lion. A lion wounded and lessened. But we live. We live and we will roar, as God made us to do and the Great Gods endorse, amen. Who here then believes that of you all, I am not a lion? What do I care that *he*, that demon-get as you named him, gave me this coat of mine? Am I to fling it off because of *him*? Was *he* the white bear? We are more than that pettiness. We are the lion. He that tricked and sullied us is gone. And here we are. Roar, my lions of Olchibe. And I and all your women shall roar with you.'

Hevonhib, the sixteen-year-old, sitting beside the Crax today, was remembering all this. She mentioned it quietly. The coven duly recollected. Only the nubile woman who had borne three children sighed – for those perhaps she would never make.

'There have been raiders along the coast,' said Piamtak, after they had recalled for long enough. 'And inland, too. That pile of

ruins, the Rukar city, they have been there, and next met the
Jafn, who are also our enemies again. All these allies once under
that banner of a blue sun. No more. We must arm ourselves and
prepare.'

Hevonhib said, 'I heard of one of the Olchibe warriors who
returned – he sired a kiddle. It was black as night.'

'Get up,' said Piamtak, doing so herself. 'We will go and
make our own fire, and see.'

They went through the jungle-forest, walking on the track of
cut logs. Deer were among the glades, white ghosts behind the
crystal stems of trees. They did not shy away from the
Crarrowin coven, sensing its preoccupied passivity.

In the usual spot, the women formed their four-cornered
circle, facing inwards. They called the sheer amber fire up out
of their abdomens. It rose into the air, collected together, poured
down and became a burning bush of flames.

'Cast in the blood.'

'Weed-of-light and kiss-grass . . .'

'Sweet honey, berry beer . . .'

'Iron ice.'

They gazed into the fire. A disc appeared. Inside the disc
they saw a sluht, a small one by the side of a frozen waterfall,
off which women were chipping pieces for drink or cooking. As
in all other sluhts now, only a scatter of men were visible,
mending things. A hunting party was setting out – women
again. As with the great sluhtin of Peb Yuve, it was mostly
women who braved the jungles and the wastes, armed with
male bows, in search of deer, hares and icenvels, or traipsed
along the white shore with seal-spears.

They had learned these skills from their men in the past,
fathers, brothers, husbands. Those who knew currently taught
others.

The image in the witch-fire circled round and flipped like a
coin.

The four Crarrowin saw directly into one of the dwellings.
A potted fire glowed on the ground. A boy sat on a rug
alone, playing a game with painted mammoth teeth. He was

important. Only a special child would receive such toys, particularly now almost all the mammoths were gone.

He was black, as the rumour had it. But he looked in age about five; too mature then to have been conceived after the war.

Hevonhib, however, when she beheld the boy, felt a peculiar tug within her body. She had never borne a child, had not yet lain down with a man. Like the older nubile Crarrow, she had resigned herself to the fact that now very likely she never would – at least not with one of her own kind.

The black child raised his head. There in the disc inside the fire, he looked back at them intently.

What was *this*?

The boy spoke, seeming nearly amused. 'I see you!'

'Yes, he sees us,' said the Crax.

She slapped her hands together with a crack, and the picture went out; the fire bush became four spirals and lifted again up in the air, hovering protectively above them.

'What is he? Is he a mage?'

'So young to be empowered – he is a miracle worked for Olchibe.'

'Why,' said the nubile woman, 'have *we* not received such a miracle *here*? Our sluhtin was among the largest and best, our leader shining, like a night of three full moons.'

But the Crax Piamtak had turned right round.

The other three women turned more slowly.

He had come from the west.

Men generally, even the lackwits of the camp, did not trespass on the work of the Crarrowin. But this one anyway was not of their camp. Or . . . no longer.

Piamtak knew him. Long ago, he and she had made love and a child themselves. Because she was Crarrowin she was permitted sexual freedom, and later on this man's son had been lauded as hers, along with two others by other men, and lastly the tribe of sons she had produced for Peb.

This man however must be dead, for although he seemed quite real and solid, standing there with a tired face and carefully braided and adorned hair, he was young. He was as young as when she had seen him last – about twenty-eight years of age.

The dead man offered a solemn show of respect in the correct Olchibe fashion. As yet he said nothing.

Piamtak said to him, 'From where have you come?'

Then he did speak.

'From some place behind the moons – or below the seas. The places of the unalive.'

'Will you tell us then about the other world?'

'Best not,' he humbly said.

'What do you want?'

'To bring you something. That is, bring the sluhtin something.'

'Your name is Guri,' said the Crax, remembering. It was his voice perhaps, this young voice stalled for ever in eternity. 'You were with the Great One's first band.'

'Yes, Mother,' he answered, awarding her her social title.

She thought, *He doesn't recall me. Well, now I'm old.* And was a second startled at this inappropriate vanity.

She said, 'Well, what have you brought?'

'A man,' he said. 'From the war under the city – a man who carries that seed like black pearls, from the night-woman Chillel.'

'Ah? Is that how it happens . . . a woman's seed inside a man. Is she a goddess?'

'God-made, Mother. Not our gods, whom anyway I've given up, if you'll forgive me.'

'More about the man. He is Olchibe?'

'From Northland Gech – the desert over the mountains. The other men she canoodled with took other women and passed on the seed. But this man, Ipeyek he's called, was the first with her. He's done nothing with it since. He wanders about, half crazy. But he survived the Death in the Ruk, and he carries the seed. The next woman he has, she'll swell with it and birth you a hero. I've been driving him here, the way I used to drive the deer along before my second death. It's taken me a time, Mother. Normally I have to be somewhere else.'

All out of turn, Hevonhib whispered, *'Where?'*

Guri glanced at her. 'That place,' he said. 'Don't ask me. You wouldn't care to hear of it.'

'Is it where we all must go?' cried the youngest girl of eleven.

The Crax turned her head, but did not chide either of them.

'You?' he said. 'No. *You'll* never be where I am. None of you.'

His face was riven now.

One must be tactful with the dead. You saw they already had enough to put up with.

'Guri, I thank you for your gift of this man. We'll watch for him. The Urrowiy of the far north are not our people, but near enough to Olchibe. What in return, Guri?'

'Keep my name,' he said. His eyes were blazing with desperate unhappiness and hope. 'Keep my name in Olchibe.'

'Whoever is the mother,' said the Crax, 'this son shall bear your name, Guri. Great Gods witness me.'

'Amen,' they said. All of them.

In the air the fire fluttered as Guri winked out of the world like a morning star.

Ipeyek who had been the first, if unofficial, husband of Chillel staggered into the sluhtin the next day.

He had tried in a futile way to live life after the White Death as he had in his hirdiy in the Uaarb desert. Lacking dogs or transport he still roamed in oval treks over the same terrain, only wandering out of the areas after fresh game. He met no one human, and if ever he came on a village or stead, kept clear of it. Men had been heavily weeded from the south-east region in any case.

Ipeyek was profoundly affected by his recent experiences. He had no true means of expression for this profundity. Sometimes he drew strange abstract shapes in the snow, or saw others inscribed on the face of the moon by clouds.

When two years had almost ended, Ipeyek began to be plagued by a spirit.

He knew what it was, and attempted to see it off – but though he had been thought priestly among his priestless hirdiy, he was no match for this thing. Also, the bones of his ancestors were a quarter of the continent away in the Uaarb, with the wives and children whom he had deserted.

Ipeyek's ploys and snares did not disperse the spirit.

One evening it sat down at his fire.

It did not have the appearance of a man, and yet something was there in it, something masculine and of humanity. To this, despite his aversion, Ipeyek was susceptible.

A white blob, it lurked across the fire. Then it seized a bit of the meat off the botched skewer and slurped it. The meat declined, repellently, *through* the non-substance of the spirit, and landed on the snow – and who could eat it now? But the spirit seemed to have enjoyed the repast.

Then it vocalized.

'You've come from the Rukar city. You lived through the Death and the dust. You're Gech. I've seen you about the Gullahammer – you brought the black woman, Chillel.'

Ipeyek sat gaping and dismayed.

The spirit went on, 'You haven't screwed a girl since.' Ipeyek started – the verb offended him almost as much as the crudity. But 'No,' went on the spirit, 'I can discover it in you like a dark jewel. Go north then. Go into Olchibe. You're not theirs, but you'll do.'

Ipeyek threw a chunk of hard kindling at the spirit. Like the meat it sailed straight through.

Even so, the apparition faded. Next day it was back.

The spirit overtly chased Ipeyek across the snow, uphill and down, over frozen waters and under ice-locked boughs where fruits hung in pods of coldness. Around the outer boundary of the Rukar calamity the spirit herded Ipeyek. Always north.

Ipeyek knew this was his penance for survival.

Then he stumbled into the sluht camp, and beheld they expected him – or someone.

Five days he lay, mostly unconscious and reasonably at peace, under a sloping roof of tent and snow and tree boughs, tinted orange and cerise from measureless smokes.

Then food came, water and alcohol. And then a lovely butter-coloured girl, her hair unbound and scented with spice.

She lay beside him and fed him slivers of thawed roasted pineapple. It was full of fibres which gently she prised from his lips and teeth.

In the end he was soothed. The spice, and the incense she had flung on the fire-pot, roused him.

'I on you?' he inquired, in the honourable manner of the Uaarb.

'Do all you will,' said she.

She was Hevonhib, sixteen years and a virgin, and a Crarrow, longing for a child of night.

Ipeyek obeyed. At the end, he simply murmured, 'Wife.'

They were married. And *she* was pregnant.

Fundamentally, that was how it stood, near the end of the second year. The lands above the barrier of the southern mountains of Kraagparia were emptied. As the capital of the Ruk, such as it now was, moved into the far west and became Kol Cataar, the south-eastern villages, towns and estates dwindled. In the tracts of snow you might come on a deserted stead or towered mansion, caked in ice and blind with cold, its surrounding fields of dormant grain long since rotted black, and wild deer and elephant feeding in the last of the hump-backed orchards.

Where everyone had gone was something of a mystery. Though many had died at Ru Karismi, or in surrounding places that the White Death enveloped, outlying villages that the Death had not touched even so lay vacant, the lairs often for packs of pale wolves.

South and west, the village of Stones had also been entirely vacated. Or almost entirely.

A woman lived on there, at first with two aggrieved servants, but they finally ran off. Then she lived there by herself.

Each day she would wend her way to the village ice-grove, and shake down or snap off icicles for water. She would take a turn round the houses built of tree trunks and ice-brick, observing how they deteriorated. Her own, which had been the lodging-house of the village, was too by then in poor repair.

When wolves meandered through the village, she took shelter indoors. But they were timid enough, and kind to each other, unlike the lean solitary black wolves of the upper west and north.

There was a store of food. It kept, of course, in the endless winter. The villagers had brought her this provender, and voyaged away over the snow on their slederies drawn by long-necked sheep. They even left her one of these lamasceps, which was in milk. They knew she would not have to soil her white hands with milking it, but could employ magecraft, being a witch as well as royal.

She had asked them with slight concern where they were going. They told her north-eastward, perhaps even to the Marginal.

Although she had not informed them of anything she might have witnessed in her scrying mirror, still they seemed to know some horrible event had overtaken the capital, that it must be avoided, and that this part of the world was now worth nothing.

The woman put back her long black tresses and they acknowledged her as very beautiful and completely useless to them, both of which she was. But not only was she a witch, she had been a queen in Ru Karismi, so they bowed as they went away.

A bizarre thing happened that night. The woman who had been a queen woke up weeping – not for herself, but for the villagers and the Ruk.

Maybe it was the only time in her life this far that Jemhara had felt another's pain or loss. She seemed to have learned it through her own.

Now and then, if there were no wolves, Jemhara would go to visit the eldritch Stones themselves. She would pause awhile, watching them gleam with their internal lighting, turquoise, rosy, ashen, one burning up like a candle, then the next, the next, until all fifty of them flamed and the bleak dusk was coloured over. They seemed to have grown bigger.

Perhaps only in her personal perception.

By that savage light, and in her shape-changed form of a black hare, he had caught her, her lover, the magician Thryfe.

Never before had either of them truly desired or loved. Overwhelmed, they coupled for some incalculable time inside Thryfe's southern house, until time itself had coalesced and blocked them in. When the sorcerous stasis gave way he had loathed and hated her, for during the days and nights of their sexual trance Ru Karismi had let loose its psychic arsenal and thousands of lives had been smashed.

He had cast her out, and she had gone. When she dared to wander back in the darkness, his house was again sealed, now only by impassable magic, and Thryfe had ridden towards the city.

Jemhara saw what he found there. She saw it in blurred and shaking images that bubbled over her scry-glass and eventually broke it in fragments. But for all the horror and despair she had seen, Thryfe she could never locate. He was Magikoy, a Master, and her enemy: naturally therefore she would never see him, either in any mirror, or ever again in life.

At last she stopped going up to his house. Its towers by then were webbed in spun ice. Some weird noise rang inside it on and on, now loud, now vague, possibly the echo of his rage and grief.

All her days she had been a schemer, even a murderess. But these deeds had really come about through the actions and wants of others. Thryfe, however, wrongly believed she had set out to trap him. It was a fact, he of all the Magikoy might have prevented Armageddon in the Ruk. And by discovering him, by loving him, she had kept him from it.

Late in the second year, Jemhara dreamed of Thryfe. It was

not the occasional repeating dream she had in which he came towards her with a sword to kill her, and she stood her ground in dread and misery to let him. In this new dream she saw him suspended – hanging upside down in the claws of long steel chains. His eyes were open wide, brutish with agony. All around him was a limbo of incoherent dimness. She woke with a jump, unable to breathe and gasping. When she had recovered herself, still she did not know what had happened to him, or where he was, or whether even his plight were literal or a cipher of his mental state – let alone if the nightmare showed *anything* actual. Yet somehow it seemed to her he had allowed her to receive this dream.

Until then she had understood he was forbidden to her. She apprehended this not only as a woman but as a sorcerous sensitive, for his overruling must be supreme – he was by far the greater mage. But, following the dream, something flowed back into her like clean blood into a bloodless heart.

That day Jemhara made magic, there in the moaning, snow-leaking guest-house.

As she would not be able, even by witchcraft, to see him with her waking eyes, instead she conjured a creature out of the air.

It was a rat-spirit, intelligent and quite eloquent in its own tongue. Jemhara had enough skill to translate its phrases. She offered it a dish of meat cooking on a brazier, and for a while it pranced about in the smoke, drawing in sustenance or only nasal enjoyment.

But when she made her demand, it listened couthly, its rat hands folded.

'Him to find? Him is mage. Is easy not.'

'You have partaken of the meat. Do as I say.'

The rat vanished in a trail of the smoke it had dragged with it to devour.

Such beings came of some spillage of the entity-consciousness of all their kind. It could therefore detect any of the findings of that kind. Rats ran everywhere and in many guises, big rats and small, icenvels and scrats.

It reappeared in the twilight.

'City,' said the rat-spirit.

'Which?' prudently inquired Jemhara.

'How I know? Walls is there and runnels. Ground have little wink things as colours is.'

Jemhara drew breath.

She had seen in her scryer, before it exploded, the tinted glass of Ru Karismi dewing the streets.

'High up in the city or low?'

'See not.'

'*Beneath* the city?' Her voice was *less* than a breath.

The rat-spirit considered judicially. Then it spoke a name it could not know, yet did, so powerful was the name, and now so awful. '*Insularia.*'

Free of the upsetting ghost, Ipeyek soon established himself among the people of the sluhtin.

He had learned to speak all languages as part of the boon – or trauma – of surviving the White Death. He correctly treated the elders, was good to the kiddles, and seemed appreciative of the women, especially Hevonhib.

Ipeyek was also a hunter of consummate ability.

Definitely, twice-dead Guri had done the sluhtin some favours, and no doubt Ipeyek too. For Ipeyek had not wished to go home to the Uaarb, having become another person than the one he had been there. Olchibe suited him.

Hevonhib grew very large very fast. In her third month she was like a woman in her eighth, and in the fourth month her time came. It was as if this child, having been delayed so long by Ipeyek's continence, meant to hurry now.

Hevonhib was a Crarrow. She did not shriek. With the help of Piamtak and her coven sisters she left her body, and only sat astride it, assisting it and the baby to separate. This was safely accomplished in the pre-dawn hour.

A perfect boy, black as iron against fire, he undid his eyes and plainly saw them all, and everything.

A month after, as this year of never-ending winter drew to a

close, unheralded as always now by anything other than some
markers on a calendar of stone kept by the Crarrowin, the boy
was already crawling and sometimes trying to walk, nor so
unsuccessfully. He could already say a few words, and when he
was told he was called Guri, that was *Star Dog*, he smiled and
said the name over and over. Despite that, as the next months
passed and he got up and strode around, read the words woven
on the blankets and rugs in the sluhtin, laughed and leapt like
a boy of ten, a finish was, almost inadvertently, added to his
name. Guriyuve became his ultimate cognomen. Piamtak said,
'I don't believe he will mind it, that undead warrior, to have his
own name wedded to that of the Great One my husband, whom
Guri loved so.'

The journey was to be extensive. Jemhara prepared for it as the
year concluded. In the city there would have been a festival, but
she was here and on her own. She would not even waste a
candle on the dying year – after all, each year was precisely like
all others, a slab of winter leading to another such slab. Yet it
occurred to her she was twenty-one. Time had gone by.

She found a slederie and attached the female lamascep to it
in the way the villagers had done. Jemhara was light in build,
but with provisions it would be a hard haul for a single sheep.
Jemhara thought she would let it go at any reasonable settlement they came to.

On the morning of departure the sky was a thin clear blue.

She had noticed the night before, in her agitation unable to
sleep, a vivid constellation in the sky. A decided shape was
picked out in bright clusters of stars, presumably by the god
Ddir, the Star-Placer. It was like an ice-iris, the petals folded
open. It reminded her too of some other thing. She did not
know what. Perhaps it boded well.

The land-raft of the slederi jounced along, the female lamascep gamely pulling. Often Jemhara got out to walk, leading the
sheep. Coming here at the order of King Vuldir, her evil genius,
the ride had been quite swift, even if she thought it was not. But

she had then been riding in a lashdeer-drawn slee, with every comfort.

They went on, and on. The days were blue and transparent, the nights lighted with stars, and at evening with the starry iris.

If I can reach him, she thought, *there in the totally inaccessible Insularia of the Magikoy beneath Ru Karismi – he will spurn me. I can be no help to him. Perhaps we shall both die.* An old song of her childhood rippled through her brain: *By all the winds that never blew, I sing of you.*

His anger made no odds. On she went.

Whenever she stopped, Jemhara melted ice for water with a silent flicker of her will, and created fire. She and the sheep stayed near it. She was sorry for the sheep, but it was healthy and its milk had finished. Probably it did not mind some exercise, or the warmed grains she put out for it to eat.

One night a tribe of elephant roamed near, some twenty or so beasts. They paid no attention to firelit Jemhara and the sheep, but moved in all around them. Woolly, grey-white animals, they puffed and snorted like pigs, she thought. The smell of them, dungy, grassy from the dormant plants they could, with their tusks and long trunks, unearth, gave a curious solace. How terrible it was, she who had been heartless and shallow, to leave her callousness behind. To become what she must.

By her reckoning it was forty days later when she saw the ramshackle village, planked in against the roots of an ice-crag. Forest statically tumbled from the top, porcelain-white plantains and eucalypts that clung all down the cliff. The village surrounded a tiny hot spring, fringed with stunningly green ferns. No wonder they had not run away like the rest.

The men who came out had the mottled skins of the eastern Ruk, and they brought a single sibull with them, a woman of middle years, who took one look at Jemhara and declared, 'Give she what her wants.'

Jemhara slept that night in a snowhouse heated by a stove, having bathed in hot, *hot* water. She had realized she had strayed too far to the east. Tomorrow she must regain her bearings. However, they familiarly knew of Ru Karismi here. They spoke of it in awe and distrust.

In the morning she gave them the lamascep and they were pleased, as was the sheep, whose milk had already come back during the cosy night.

The sibull appeared at Jemhara's door.

'How will her get on, undrawn?'

Jemhara said she had other means of mobility.

The witch nodded and said she had seen Jemhara was one of the mage caste. Then she invited Jemhara to meet the village goddess.

Jemhara did not want to waste the time, but politely she agreed. Partly she thought she was secretly glad of these excuses for delay – her gods knew what she would have to confront in the doomed city. Besides, she had made up her mind on how she would travel the rest of the route. It was cunning, and dangerous. Half an hour more before she must do it was welcome.

There was a bothy of frozen wood, and in it – nothing.

'She away,' said the sibull, smugly.

Jemhara, still polite, asked what she should offer the absent goddess.

'Nothing,' said the sibull, 'nothing, like all-nothing in here.' She cackled. 'But offer it genteel, lady, her like neat service.'

Jemhara elegantly scattered nothing on the floor of the bothy.

The sibull grinned, her mottles flushing a rich gravy red. 'Her the goddess of wood. Take this.'

Jemhara saw the sibull had given her a little dry branch. Did it have any power? Doubtless not. Never mind. They parted the best of friends.

Over the snow, away from the crag and the village, a slim black hare went bounding.

Since puberty Jemhara had been capable of this. But *he* had taught her, cruelly and surely, that she must not lose herself in her shape-change, must keep always at least one iota of herself as guide.

To do it now was like her proof to Thryfe. She had been an apt pupil. She had earned the right – had she? – to save him alive.

Travelling in this manner, how swiftly she moved. Yet how *huge*, threatening and forbidding the terrain.

She foraged in the dusk through cracks in topsnow and ice, dredging up what she could. She skated through deer herds, who lifted their hooves over her, and only tried to kick her when she attempted to eat what they had already uprooted.

Unerringly now, the right direction drew her like a magnet. She ran flawlessly west and north towards the ruined city.

Lacy snow sprayed back from her, the stars burst like fruits of light, she dived uncatchable – more human witch than hare – between the paws of an astonished wolf, and fled on.

There was anyway no chance she could forget her human self, not now. She was only for him. Always for him. All caution mislaid, all doubts erased.

Thryfe – Thryfe – lover – lord . . .

FOUR

Vashdran entered the feasthall of Uashtab. It was very much as he recalled from Shabatu. A river divided it, black and deep under the high banks. Caverns yawned away on either side in white torch-flume.

The difference was specific. One table, vast enough to seat hundreds, had been spread on this near bank. It contained the remembered bisecting tributary, which splashed along, stocked no doubt as the other had been with fish and small vicious dragons. All the men filled up the one table, now sitting both sides of it. They were drinking and eating the dainties that gauze-clad women brought them.

On the river's other side there was no similar table.

Nothing was there, only a cave of darkness.

The men of the army or Gullahammer or whatever it was supposed to be banged goblets on the table to welcome him. Vashdran, the Saraskuld. He must, apparently, receive this tribute, though he had issued no orders and done nothing spectacular by his own assessment. He was no king here. He was no commander here. Empty show, like some echo from another place.

Heppa and Kuul came up to him, dressed in their glamorous armour.

'Vash! Come eat.'

He sat down among them.

He had a sense of dire immanence, some bad extraordinary thing which drew close.

But it seemed he was alone in that. Or maybe it was only for him.

Certainly he had come to the hall to face it. For it was no use hiding. Not here, not now, never ever again.

The chat, the food and wine went round him, and the black rivers went along the table, and below. The men became very noisy. Huge roasts and cakes appeared. The women attendants, most likely made in the walls of Uashtab as the other women had been in Shabatu's walls, permitted themselves to be fondled, pulled down. Vashdran scanned the table's length. Of the mageia Ruxendra there was no sign, but he had expected none, not here. No free woman, even if dead, would sit alone in such male company.

One tense, shadowed expression there was. Curjai's.

He looked at Vashdran, then away.

Vashdran got up. Heppa protested, and Vashdran patted Vormish Heppa, who never spoke like a Vorm, on the metal shoulder. Vashdran walked along the table to Curjai's place.

'What now?'

'None of the enemies we beat are here. Do you see?'

'No. How perceptive you are, Curjai.'

'Yet they *are*.'

'A riddle,' said Vashdran. He leaned smiling over Curjai.

Curjai raised his head. 'Don't you know yet? The same city, the same palace. The same war – and the ones we fought, also the same. They were *us*. They were ourselves. Oh, not every man,' said Curjai in a quick hoarse voice, 'fought and killed *himself* out there on the ice-sand. We killed others we never had the space to recognize in the heat of the battle. And some anyway – some *lived*.'

Vashdran understood he had already thought this, *known* it, but – *not* known.

Slowly he said, 'That's their table, then, across the river. Invisible. But our table still.'

'No. They – *we* – are captives. Vash – *I saw my own self*. They dragged me – I was broken and I bled. No healing, no springing back to health and wholeness.'

Vashdran said, 'Stand up. You and I. We at least will confront it. Leave these drunken sots to their trough. We'll cross this sewer of a river, and see.'

Curjai swung at once off the bench and stood up.

Now none of the other men paid any attention.

But at that instant a wide sonorous bell-like note pulsed through the feasthall. To that, no one could avoid responding.

The diners looked up, startled, their hands full of meat and drink and the fluent flesh of women. The men with their backs to the river turned round.

Over the water, light was rising like a pale unblue sun.

It lit the cave there like a stage.

A fearsome groaning and whining sound began to issue from the feasters. In droves they were staggering upright. Some fell forward and some on their knees. Many wept in the harsh ragged stammer of those who have never in adult life shed tears before. Many rushed from the hall, screaming, howling, calling on gods or for comrades they had trusted when living.

Across the black river, on the far bank, was piled the offal all war leaves behind it. The dead.

They sprawled, some on their backs, some on their faces, layered under and over each other like slaughtered carcasses flung down on the ground. It was all told a mountain of men. It went up high. And out of the mountain poked and hung feet and heads and hair, and hands that held nothing now, no food or wine, not even a blade.

Vashdran picked his way through the living dead who crouched and knelt on the floor. He was aware that, in some impossible supernatural fashion, every one of them had looked into his own dead face across the river. Every one had seen his own corpse.

They reached the near bank's edge, Curjai and he.

'How do we cross?'

'Fly. How else?'

Curjai lifted his arms. 'The shields that make the wings are gone.'

'Then fly without wings.'

They sprang together off the brink. For a moment Curjai seemed battered by gravity or by some contrary air current. Then he too had aimed himself over the divide as Vashdran did.

The mound of corpses peered at them from myriad dull-glinting eyes. They were naked. The stink of corruption was all over them.

Curjai gagged, braced himself. He pointed. 'There. They've finished with me now.'

At the top of the heap Curjai's own body had been draped, loose-limbed, boneless. The head hung down, the darker skin defining him among the other men who were speckled or white or yellow of complexion. The hair was a torn flag, and the eyes open too, glacial and pitiless. *What should I care for you?* the eyes said. *I am done with you all.*

'Who brought me down, I wonder? I never met myself when we fought with – them. And who killed me in this palace?'

Vashdran dived straight upward. He seized Curjai's body from the corpse mountain, standing on the faces and legs of other men.

At Ru Karismi, the omnipresent dust had obliterated all this. But elsewhere he had looked at it, moved among it. Even here, among the twice-dead.

He dropped back down and laid Curjai's body on the bank. The body, as they all were, was without clothing, and gouged and striped with wounds and the toothed tongues of whips.

'This,' Vashdran said, 'is not yourself. *You* are *here*.'

'Yes – no. A part of me is *there*. Don't you feel that, Vash?'

'No,' Vashdran said.

He thought, *But my body isn't here.*

And Curjai said roughly, 'You are not among the dead.'

Over the river, the last men were crawling or running away. The sweet attentive servants had vanished. Overturned wine dripped into black water.

On this side the ground was now shifting, rising up in lumps and pillars that promptly became guards, all in their black and gold, their snake-hair fully unbound, exhilarated and hissing

150

and striking out. The smell of the venom infiltrated the stench of death and was one with it.

Jatchas shouldered and nosed around the corpses.

Vashdran and Curjai stood above Curjai's corpse, and watched wordlessly and thoughtlessly as the guards of Uashtab, aided by their eyeless dogs, dismembered the mountain and pushed its components into the river. A torrent of men guttered down. The water parted itself for each and knit together again above him.

None of the guards so far approached Curjai or Vashdran or attempted to grab and sling away the solitary rescued corpse.

As the hideous mountain decreased, Vashdran again picked up Curjai's body. He did not know what could be done with it other than what was being done with the rest. But it was Curjai who said, 'Throw it over too. Throw it away.'

Vashdran said nothing. He walked to the lip of the bank, and let go his burden. He, but not Curjai, watched as this body also entered the river and was swallowed. Turning again he found Curjai had gone, but ten of the guards had left their work and closed about him.

'You will not resist,' they said, in their amalgamated voice.

Vashdran did not resist.

They took him somewhere in the labyrinth. Hall led into hall, into hall, into hall. Once he heard one of the boulders descend quite near them, to the right. The ground trembled at the impact and steadied again to vitreous.

His mind crawled about sluggishly as the men had crawled around and away from the banquet.

You are not among the dead.

I have died, he thought. *I am dead.*

An archway gave on a chamber whose floor seemed oddly tilted. Vashdran could not decide how to place his feet, to walk. He fell without warning.

Looking up, he saw why.

The Lionwolf hung headfirst in chains from one long beam which straddled the roofless upper walls. He was as Vashdran, and a million or more separate others, had known him, unmistakable. His hair was the shade of sunsets, his tanned skin alone clothed a body of exact proportions, wide at the shoulder, narrow-hipped, legs long and strong, held there in the clasp of silvery shackles. Even the male weapon was on display, large, quiescent and kempt. It slept, but he held his arms rigidly upright against his sides. His eyes were not blue, but also red, as they had become in war. The red eyes moved in the upside-down face that was yet beautiful, sightless and *living*, searching the chamber, the air, the world of Hell, for something. They found it then. They found their doubles. They found Vashdran.

Vashdran stared. He pulled himself back to his feet, still staring.

The figure hung high up, but given Vashdran's everyday power of flight could be reached at once.

Vashdran did not attempt to reach it.

His forearm burned sullenly. He did not need to look at it to know that the words scorched there by Ruxendra's spit were flaring. *I am the payment.*

All ten guards grouped against an archway, small in distance as children, unconnected to this scene. Soon, maybe, they would slide again into the floor.

Blood trickled like the table wine on the river bank, from Lionwolf's ears and from the corner of one crimson-pupilled eye. It was a torture of the sophisticated western cities of the Ruk, this method, to depend a man by his feet and leave him there. In the end he would go mad, or die. But it was not a rapid end.

Vashdran stood swaying, glaring at his image, and as he did a woman moved out along the chamber. She too was all in red to match the occasion of hair and blood.

Ruxendra regarded her quarry, *both* of him. Vashdran, unable to look away from himself, did not see her face. But he heard and felt the melody of her *hatred*, playing for him, like a rusty scratching nail.

Fifth Intervolumen

The apprentice, who had been given many hard tasks, said to the mage, 'Sir, it seems you wish me to be in two places at once.'

The mage replied: 'I simply wish you to work until you are exhausted. For being in two places at once, only the gods can do that.'

Padgish story: Simisey

The sheep, though not lamasceps, had lion faces and the long necks known all over the Ruk. Their fleece was very thick and soft. In temperate weather, the shepherds led them up to the creases of dormant grass in the southern mountain snows, among the green beryl of caves and milk-glass of centuries' static waterfalls. When a black sheep was born, they said they would take it to the Woman. It must be hers, because of its colour.

Kraagparia lay over the mountains, or so they had heard and believed. It was no less real to them than any other myth, and they had assumed the Woman came from Kraagparia, for it was a land of wonders, where people could dance *Summer* back into the world for days on end, and pass knives through their necks without harm.

The Woman, though, had never done anything like that. Nor had they requested she should. Sometimes she told them stories, that was all. She would go to their fires on the mountains, or to the communal fire in the centre of the sheep-village, and beguile them with her tales and her voice.

She was always gentle, fragrant as flowers they had seldom seen, lovely as the deep nights she resembled.

She had been with them by their reckoning, which was not like that of the Ruk, seven years. Her name, she said, was Chillel.

*

Just before the evening when the black sheep was born, a new constellation had been put up on the sky by a god the shepherds called Didri.

Higher, the biggest shepherd, admired the stars courteously, making the proper appreciative gestures to them, as he climbed up to Chillel's hut carrying the gift.

The hut was exactly like all the others, except that no smoke issued from its smoke-hole, and instead Chillel's scent breathed about the doorway.

When he called to her, she came out at once. She never seemed, like other women, to be now and then in the middle of some task she could not instantly leave off. Chillel perhaps did nothing when she was in the hut, save sit or lie on the bed of fleeces. Sometimes the village did not see her for days, or else they saw her walking over the slopes, even up on the mountains, not seeking their company. They let her be at such times. To themselves they had named her Story Maker. This gave her an official function, and added sense to the idea that she be fed, housed, clothed, and respected. Frankly though her stories were not always clear to them. Possibly they liked them the better for that.

'Here,' said Higher, extending the young sheep to Chillel.

'A lamb,' said Chillel mildly.

'*Black* lamb. Yours,' explained Higher, feasting his eyes on her.

The shepherds did not use many words. Neither did she, even in her tale-telling.

Now she put out her slender hands and took hold of the sheep, which gazed at her just as Higher was doing.

'Thank you,' said Chillel. 'I will care for her.'

The sheep was female, altogether a good present, since she could later be bred on and would give milk.

Higher felt he should go now, but he did not want to quite yet. So he said, 'Much grass up on pasture. Awake brown grass. Weather warmer. The sun shone on the glacier and I see flowers in it.'

'Flowers?' asked Chillel.

He pondered, did she know about flowers? Even though she smelled of them, perhaps she did not.

'In the ice,' said Higher, 'trapped long, long out of memory. Blue and yellow. Too dangerous to try take them.'

She turned her head on the exquisite slender neck, looking at the mountains above. Like the black curling fleece of the little sheep, her hair. She did not speak. So Higher said, 'Will you come tell a story at moonrise?'

Her eyes returned to him. Such eyes . . . 'Yes, then.'

'Have you seen the star-burst there?'

'Yes, I have seen it.'

'*That's* like a flower. The dark blue flower in the ice.'

When he got back to the village, the evening meal was being brought out to the large fire, with beakers of fermented milk. Higher, to the surprise of many, for he had a fine appetite, strode by and up to the hut of the village magio.

He, wrapped in his wool and hair, was chomping busily and did not care to be disturbed. Despite that, Higher felt he must be made privy to the news before anyone else, and did not trust himself to sit on it until later.

'Father, I have taken the sheep to the Woman.' The magio scowled and bit pointedly into his meal. 'It's that, when I was by her, I see her belly.' The magio stopped chewing. He nodded, *Go on*. 'It gets round, Father. Like she's in teem.'

The magio's gulp was audible.

'*Baby* in her?'

'So it looks, Father.'

'Whose?'

Higher spread his hands and lifted his brows, offering the guess to the whole of the universe.

'No man been in with her?' The magio considered; he answered himself. 'No. No man.'

'Seven years she's here,' said Higher gravely. 'She could never bring it with her.' He was right in this, for even by Ruk standards, over two years had elapsed since Chillel appeared among them.

'On her wanders in the mountains, then,' decided the magio.

'But Father – always we can see where she goes there. Any man would know if other was up on the heights or anywhere about. And dogs would yell too.'

'True, you're true. A spell then. She's not like other women. But it must bode well. *Two* such creatures.'

'She'll tell story tonight,' said Higher. 'Then you see too.'

The magio nodded. 'Then I see.'

A duo of moons rose. One was full, the other at half, and they glittered light all over the mountains and the village.

Chillel came to the fire in her woollen gown, and not one of them could not make out that her stomach was suddenly big and round as a ball. To Higher, oddly, it seemed even more pronounced than when he had noticed it earlier.

The star-burst of Didri was by now moving over to the west, but it too still offered light. Chillel gleamed unearthly in the moon and star rays, and sat down.

'The sun,' said Chillel. She was obsessed by the sun, nearly always making her stories concern it. 'It shone so bright that it scorched the world. Things died in droves. Men and beasts withered to dust. Then the sun was sorry and cast himself down through the west into the world under the world, which is Cold Hell. There the sun is blue and can burn only like ice.' They waited. Chillel then told them some adventures of the sun before it fell, how it was also a male god and a hero, very handsome and strong, who fought men and monsters, and rode a great whale, but in Hell he was put, for his sins, into chains, and hung upside down helpless for all to curse and deride.

The children listened wide-eyed, and the adults too. They had never heard this tale before.

After Chillel had spoken about all this for quite a while she merely ceased speaking. She sat and looked round at them. The story, ultimately, seemed as obscure as most of her others.

Several children jostled. Another called out what would happen now that the sun lay in chains in Hell.

'Who can say?' replied Chillel. The next inquisitive child was shushed by his mother.

They offered to the Woman dishes kept from the evening meal, and Chillel ate a mouthful and drank a mouthful of the milk-alcohol.

As she was leaving the fire, the magio beckoned her aside.

He too was consistently respectful to her, as she was to him. Although not mightily blessed with powers, he had the knack, and was well aware of her uniqueness if unsure what it amounted to.

'Woman Chillel, are you with young?'

'Yes,' said Chillel, without inflexion.

The magio asserted himself. The father figure of the village, he had some authority. If any other unattached woman had been pregnant he would have questioned her thoroughly. As with the sheep and dogs, breeding mattered.

'Who have paired with you?'

Chillel looked long at him. He found he could not stand the lustrous intensity of her calm gaze, and brooded down at his feet, abashed.

'I have lain,' said Chillel, 'with countless men. None of these is the maker of my child.'

'One here then? Will you hand-tie to him?'

'It is no one here.'

He shot her after all a sidelong optic question mark. 'By *no* man then?'

Chillel smiled. Surely none could be unmoved by that. As she had with the boy at the fire she said, 'Who can say?'

She walked away up the slope to her hut, and everyone on the street watched her go. Her long hair brushed the icy track.

Chillel entered the hut. She glanced about her as if there were a hundred interesting objects there – but there was nothing much, only bare walls of ice-brick and sheepskin, the woven door and bed of fleece, and two pots in the corner, one for unfrozen drinking water and one for functions she need never attend to, unless on a whim.

Ddir, Didri to the shepherds, he who placed the stars or,

more accurately, shined up certain ones to show patterns, had made Chillel also. And when he created the pattern of the star iris a handful of nights earlier, it was because, apparently, he was conscious of Chillel's fecund state. It was not really an iris, either, there in the sky, but a flawlessly formed female vulva. Maybe he had even done this to boastfully celebrate his own cleverness in remembering to give her both vagina and womb. After all, he had nearly forgotten her navel.

Even fey Ddir, however, did not know the *mind* of Chillel.

Did she know it herself?

As the third moon was rising, she left the hut. It was often her habit, as they had noted, to walk on the mountains.

Some few days after, having briefly caressed the lamb, Chillel left the hut again. This time she did not do it in the accepted physical way. Or by means of the door.

It was, if any had seen it, an alarming excursion. Chillel poised there by the hut's unlit fireplace. Then – she poured *inward*. This was like water running into and down through some tiny aperture or drain. Through some central part of herself, positioned roughly between her middle ribs, all the physical presence of Chillel swirled in and away. Her fluttering mantle of hair vanished last of all, sucked out – or in – from the world of mankind.

Nothing living was there now in the hut, but for the little slumbering sheep, which had not stirred.

Chillel descended, or flew upward – it could not be quite certain, the tendency of this medium she rapidly travelled through. In the medium also there was no *substance* even, yet perhaps a faint encouraging light. The journey was indescribable, yet actual, and lasted only a split second split again and again to a final splinter thinner than the strand of a spider's web.

Elsewhere a point of scintillant dark appeared, and out she flowed once more, out and all around herself.

Chillel stood entire and intact and in another place.

Now, however, she was no longer quite . . . Chillel.

More voluptuous, softer, the midnight hair more curling, her eyes with another luminosity, less cool, more coolly warm.

Instead of the coarse wool gown she wore a dress of sheerest white, dusted with golden particles that shimmered. Gold was on her hair too.

She smiled that smile of hers, and even this smile, always so wonderful, was subtly unlike itself. It had, here, a hint of connivance, even of flirtation.

Winsome, queen of Cold Hell, moved across the glassy floor of her chamber, where women servants stretched out to her appealingly, half formed from the walls. There was a flight of steps that led up high into the roofless top of the palace. Winsome went up them, up and up, as high as the stair itself stretched.

How high now she is. Winds from a night sky unlike all skies of any earth play with her hair, unfolding coils of it, sensually draping it back across her body.

She stares at the opaque stars of Hell, none of which have any pattern. One thing though there is which has stayed with Winsome that formerly had been Chillel's. It is the swollen belly of pregnancy.

Winsome holds up her arms, and from nowhere at all scores of the small moons and the greater drift towards her down the dark.

They sing, these moons, in high tinsel voices, a wordless song. They swarm around Winsome, laving her in light. The moons are company, in a way all the company she has here or has engendered anywhere. Because *what* she is she too does not know, nor is she urgent to learn. Neither Chillel nor Winsome cares about her identities, either or any of them. And even when surrounded by persons, even when, in the past, lying on or beneath her succession of mortal, passionate, adoring or jealously violent lovers, she is and was indifferent to herself in that aspect, and so has gained no more of herself from having looked in the mirror of their eyes.

But Lionwolf, who is not mortal, is unique to her. Lionwolf is fire. In *his* eyes, when they lay together, Chillel or Winsome saw herself as never elsewhere. She saw his father too, Zzth the Sun Wolf. Zzth's release from the body of Lionwolf at their first congress destroyed her – but during destruction she had known it did not matter. Spread as meltwater on the floor of a green cave, Chillel had remained as much herself as she ever had been. And when she rose again from the ice she, of all things, was unamazed.

The Lionwolf is now in Hell. For this reason she too comes here.

Her memory is fully documented for her, encompassing additionally events she has never seen or heard of, and she forgets nothing, even if she may say she does, even when she is another woman, among shepherds, or with singing moons. Lionwolf, to Chillel or Winsome, is what life is, as total, as alien, as unavoidable. As desired.

Winsome lets moons perch on her fingertips. Others dip into her hair. One sits on her risen belly intrigued, maybe, by the thrum of the second life inside.

After a long while, she sends the moons away, tolerantly, like children she is fond of, and since she has something else to do.

Winsome entered the hall which contained Lionwolf. In the Uashtab labyrinth, where so much was duplicated not only from itself but from the previous city of Shabatu, anywhere he was would be easy enough for her to find. He glowed like the flame he was through all the endless stone barriers and tiresome repeating architecture.

Besides, like herself, he too had now been doubled.

Although it was not the same, not at all.

It seemed to her she should name the one hanging from the beam across the sky with the familiar name: Lionwolf. And *he*, the one who in this world had again been her lover, she would give the name he had chosen here, the Rukarian name which *meant* Lionwolf: Vashdran.

Vashdran leaned on the air. Somehow it was keeping him

upright. He stared at the live prisoner who was himself hanging in chains.

And nearby waited, like a preying tiger, the astral thread known as Ruxendra.

Neither of them seemed to be aware of Winsome.

'You see,' said Ruxendra to Vashdran – but as if the unregistered Winsome's arrival had kindled dialogue – 'how things are. I had powers when alive. Now too. I asked for this and earned it in the battle. You're mine – or *that* is mine.'

Vashdran said nothing. Had he heard her?

Ruxendra did not like his reticence.

She went over to him, to Vashdran, and struck him, using her hand but also a shaft of lightning that punched out from it.

Vashdran partly turned. He caught her wrist and stared down into her face.

'Does it hurt you,' Ruxendra said, 'seeing that live carcass hung there?'

He let go her wrist. Again he said nothing.

Winsome saw that he was at this moment like an infant. Not his strength nor any male arrogance kept him tight-lipped. It was that he did not, lost on this sea, know what to answer, or even to ask.

But Ruxendra again misinterpreted. She showed her teeth and snapped, 'I will take that *thing*, that thing in *chains*, I will take it and pull it apart. And you – you will have to search for it, for all the bits I shall carve it into. And do you think it can die? Can *you*? *Have* you? You live and *it* lives. It is you. I'll make this filthy doppelgänger suffer for ever, for I have for ever, here. And you'll feel every drop of its pain, every bumpy mile of its anguish. It's *you*.'

'Do it then,' he said. 'I shan't prevent you.'

'Yes, I'll do it. How *could* you prevent me, now?'

Briefly deflated by his blankness, the vengeful Magikoy apprentice, fifteen when she died of the White Death, gabbled some litany of malevolence, though the Magikoy, despite the ancient armament they had unleashed, did not use such baleful formulas. Their remit had been always to help, and for self-protection, even vengeful justice – if ever needful – they prescribed other behaviours.

Winsome did not intervene.

All things had their correct times. To such as she, what must be done by her was consistently evident.

Like Ruxendra, like Vashdran and his simulacrum, she waited.

For what did they *wait*?

It was as if they must pause, to maintain the tempo . . .

Yes. From the sky, gusting, wailing, casting its black shadow, one more boulder rushed towards the hall.

Winsome was beyond the range of it. Between the three other figures, two standing, one hung upside down, it crashed.

Something happened that was not as either Vashdran or Ruxendra at least had seen before.

That area of the stone floor smashed into a million fragments. They flew upwards and everywhere, shards like needles, larger pieces like quartz bricks or blades or axes, and some slivers like narrow daggers honed ready for injury.

Both the man and the mageia-girl were cut; one missile spun her and she went down with a furious cry. The hanged man too bled all over again, his whole body striped like that of a warrior of the Vorms or Kelps.

Vashdran said to himself, as if he were an idiot for whom things must be spelled out, 'Thoughts then. The notions we send before us or think up when here. They break into the pool of Hell like stones through water, and fracture the ice.'

Ruxendra crawled over to the hanging man. She struggled to her feet and propped herself in front of him, as if she would have to hold Vashdran off.

Vashdran did nothing.

Still reeling, Ruxendra opened from her shoulder blades the huge red wings she had selected, and flared them wide. Into the air she went, over the floor that was now just like the shore of the Hell sea, stones and shards, flints and flinders.

She smote the chains that held Lionwolf. As they gave in a

welter of white sparks, slight as a snake she took hold of his naked and bleeding body.

Her arms she had about it, her legs, as if, memory of his first battle here, in a parody of the sexual act. Last she sank her teeth into his neck.

Tears of blood rolled from his eyes. He shut them.

So perhaps he did not see as Vashdran, standing watching, shut also his.

Ruxendra's wings bore her skyward, into the high darkness and over the top of the palace. She flew heavily, like a lammergeyer made of rubies holding a victim also made of rubies.

Vashdran opened his eyelids. He trod across the shattered floor. He came to Winsome when he reached the unscarred stone beyond.

He saw her now, did he? 'You're not real,' he said. 'Don't speak to me.'

She was real, but she did not speak.

Flecks of his blood, showered off from his hair, flittered over her and settled, like the gold and the moons, on her own hair and her dress, and on the globe of the child within.

It was his child after all, conceived in Hell at their initial couching, and possibly it felt the blood, through all her supernatural flesh.

Higher sat with the magio on the ground. They gaped gloomily into a large bowl of water on the hut floor between them. Only the magio thought he could make out anything in this primitive scrying glass.

At last he raised his head.

Higher reverently kept quiet.

'She's away,' said the magio.

Higher nodded. He already knew this, having not seen the Woman for two days, and so having gone up to the hut to take the lamb some warm milk. The lamb had been in good condition, as if well nourished. But the Woman was nowhere to be found.

'She goes off,' said Higher. 'But not through door. One or other down here is always looking that way, at her house. Even at night, on the sheep-watch.'

The magio shrugged. But he said, 'You go up and stay by hut. When she comes back, look how she is.'

Higher agreed.

Three days ago, they had *all* seen her, and some of the women exclaimed. Higher, who had ten small children from his own wives, knew well enough how long a baby took to bake in the heat of the female womb. From the start he had thought Chillel showed suddenly and large. And just before this absence of hers – of which maybe there had been others, missed by the village as they never normally approached her house – Chillel had walked along the slopes, and then she was *very* big. From a woman who seemed midway through her term, abruptly, in a pair of days, she had become like one close to parturition.

'Perhaps she go to birth it somewhere else?' he suggested now.

'Yes. You men must look about for her.'

So, while a party of shepherds and dogs set off to seek the strayed and magically invaluable wonder of Chillel, Higher went up the slope and sat down by her doorway.

For some reason he could not fathom, occasionally he pushed at the edge of the woven door frame and peered into her empty hut.

He decided he was checking on the lamb, but he was not. It was the way you might look again in the same spot for something you know must be there, but is missing.

Because of this, though no one had ever so far seen Chillel's departures to and returns from Lionwolf's Hell, that evening someone did.

When the glimmering sable point appeared inside the hut in midair, Higher thought it was his eyes, and rubbed them. When he stopped that, there she was, the Woman, petal-opening out of herself and out of nothing at all, in a broadening black nimbus of being.

Higher stuck his head, mouth undone, eyes on stalks, right in through the gap between door frame and wall.

There was Chillel, now burstingly heavy as a lambent tree with her fruit.

She glanced at him.

She spoke.

'What comes soon you must not see. It may frighten you.'

Already frightened out of his wits, Higher mechanically retreated and went on hands and knees away from the hut and down the slope, forgetting to stand up until he reached the street below.

So he missed the second, far less common, marvel of the night.

She had carried for nine days. Nine days that was by a Rukarian calendar.

Now Chillel was conscious the hour had come to bring forth.

She touched the black lamb, which unlike Higher was staring at her now with unperturbed approval. Obedient and calm, the lamb lay down on the floor. Chillel stretched herself out on the fleece.

Women screamed with some cause in the agony and horror and panic of labour. Chillel's labour was devoid of all three elements. She did not scream.

She had raised her skirt and spread her legs wide, and now a soft earthquake moved through both her belly and her female parts below. Beautiful and easy as a lovely mouth which opened to yawn, the birth canal visibly and entirely expanded. Perhaps the sensation was even pleasant – *like* a yawn. She had closed her eyes, but her expression slightly curved into a smile.

From the divine intimate tightness of a young and perfectly made woman, Chillel's vaginal corridor had now smoothly enlarged until it resembled a small, rose-pale cave. There was no blood, and no prenatal waters spilled.

Something though moved deep inside the pulsing entrance. Then a form, with no preamble, *swam* outward. In fact, this was more of a slow diving than a swimming motion. First emerged the hands and arms, held forward, the head tucked neatly between, the body then with the legs pressed together. Out upon the fleece the dark image slid, and lay unfolding itself like a flower and showing itself to be a well-made baby, black of skin like the mother, eyes shut, loose and relaxed, unstigmatized, unweeping.

The smooth core of Chillel's loins instantly drew inward.

The yawn of birth was done. In a minute she was again like other flawless young women who had never borne a child, and had the firm, shapely vulva of an iris.

She sat up without haste or discomfort, and touched her newborn lying on the fleece, rather as she had touched the lamb which lay nearby. Both were female.

As there was no distress, illness, tiredness or pain on the face of Chillel, so there was no tenderness – no *mother-love*. She looked at the child as if at the not uninteresting progeny of another.

There had been no blood, there was no birth-matter. Nor was there any afterbirth. And to the baby there attached no umbilical cord.

She lay there, this brand new female offspring, on her back, her arms over her head, slowly breathing and gazing up now at Chillel with just-opened black eyes. Plainly she could see.

The lamb was nosy. It got to its feet and came to the fleece. It sniffed the baby, which carried neither the taint nor the intrinsic odour of arrival. The lamb nuzzled into the child, and the child, turning a little, put out a tiny hand, already equipped in the usual wondrous way with all its fingers, against the curly coat. Perhaps the lamb had decided this was a sibling, and one a little younger, which it must therefore instruct, care for, and boss about.

The baby had at least one distinct difference from her mother – even from the lamb. Across her head a down of hair lay like shavings of red-gold. But this was all she had brought into the world, that you could see, of her father the Lionwolf.

After a while, Chillel again lay back. If she slept was not apparent. Perhaps she did. The event had been after all, even if not uncomfortable, physically significant for her.

The baby cuddled with the lamb and vice versa.

Ddir entered the hut a short while later, like a fall of dust.

He was nondescript and colourless, as always, and his feet were bare. A genius artisan, he spared no margin to concern himself with his own appearance.

He was a god even so – one of the three given to Saphay, Lionwolf's mother. Yyrot and Zeth, the other two, were cosmic distances off, and meant it seemed nothing to Ddir, who was a part of them. But despite that, he had created Chillel, and now, in mythically honourable tradition, had come to regard her baby.

What he thought was not obvious.

He pottered above the infant, scarcely alerting the lamb which gave him only one sleepy glance.

Then, abruptly, the god bent closer. He looked with a sudden sharpening of attention at the more or less un-flawed body of the child.

Like some elderly nurse Ddir, Placer of Stars, clicked his tongue – exactly what he had done before, confronting his own similar oversight.

Leaning right down he dipped his finger quickly, neatly, into the belly of the child.

She too had woken, and gazed back at him, quizzical but not alarmed. Clearly the god had not hurt her, though his uncanny pressure had implanted a miniature round *hole* in her stomach. Lacking an umbilical cord, it was the navel she could not other-wise possess.

Like father like daughter. Chillel had forgotten.

Along the south-east plate of the continent, the variable beach ice had been disturbed.

Cracked and broken fragments floated on black pools of liquid sea. An ice-cliff, a mile inland and running parallel for four or five miles, had received some blow that had fissured it in long inky veins.

Now and then the cause of the damage became discernible.

A gigantic creature was cavorting out on the horizon, where the sea was mostly fluid.

Evening light played silkily over a tall black hump, over the scimitar flash of a colossal tail that raked the ocean, sending, both as it rose and as it went down, squalls of water insane distances into the sky. Often small tidal waves also resulted. They smacked the landmass in the mouth, breaking up the floes, hammering the barriers of cliffs. Earlier a chunk of forest had been dislodged. Massive trees, still in their casings of ice, lay nearby along the tideline as if waiting for the gargantuan vandal to apologize.

It was a horned whale. But much more than that. Even if any had lived thereabouts to stand, unwisely, on the shore and assess the beast, the size of it would have defeated them. Two strong men, neither particularly human, had taken more than two days to cross its back. The horn was a palatial mountain of a tower ringed with spurs that were also towers. Here were meshed the bones of some of those who had died in the environment of its back. Other skeletons creaked and clanked among the rank gardens, filth-hills and foul woods that grew about its hide. Occasionally the whale, diving to the depths, would allow some of this architecture to be washed or wiped away. But much was by now so established it clung on, indomitable.

The head of the whale ballooned out of the water, showing off the mountain towers of spurs and horns to a single pale and nervous moon.

The eyes of the whale, even after dark had come, blazed like tiny golden suns.

Brightshade had been resting on his laurels.

For two years, which to him were short, he had gone about his whale business in the sea, enjoying his feeding and fighting and copulation. All this while his brain sang with the memory of how he had, finally, ended the jealously abhorred life of his half-brother Lionwolf, the part-*human* child of Zeth Zezeth, also father to the whale. Lionwolf's demise had pleased their father too. Zeth had wanted Lionwolf eradicated and had aided the process in supernormal, effective ways.

Yet now . . .

Seeing in *shapes* of thought, the whale had lolled in the deep, beginning to learn, as always by a sort of osmotic wordless telepathy, that Lionwolf – though crushed into non-being – still left his footprints on the mortal earth.

At the start there had been a dream of rising from the ocean, up – yet also *downward* – and dredging out into some vague and pallid nothingness, where a blue light dimly shone. The dream recurred in Brightshade's intermittent sleep, warning him of problems he did not then suspect.

For what Lionwolf had conjured in the world, Brightshade had no idea, until the night when he made out the group of stars like an iris cast from diamonds glittering in the east. Even then the whale formulated no concept of the type of revival of Lionwolf which was now current. That was, the whale had no concept of a *child* – let alone her gender or her worth. Brightshade understood only that some burning drop of his hated brother had *returned*.

With inordinate blind rage, up from the bottom of the continent's south-eastern sea he came, breaching like an avalanche in reverse, showering the sky and the land with wet fury.

This area was largely unpopulated, at least by men. Deer feeding in the injured forest had fled to safety at the first intimation of the whale.

The mysterious people of the Kraag perhaps knew what took place. These were their lands, but reality was unreal to them, and by disbelieving in Brightshade's insane wrath very likely they were spared it.

Dead fish littered the shores, smashed in the whale's upsurge. Birds who had hurried over to feed soon regretted it as the blasts of water continued.

The night became black, only the solitary moon, growing always whiter in dismay, and the iris stars moving over.

Near midnight, Brightshade lay in against the upset shore.

171

He lay *thinking*. But the thought process of Brightshade was *not* thought.

Mirages of vengeance and denial wove through his mind. Once or twice, with his forelimbs, he pawed the ice and ripped it apart some more.

In a strange fashion, the red-haired child born that night was herself doubly related to Brightshade. Daughter of his half-brother Lionwolf, she was also Chillel's; Chillel who had been constructed by Ddir – who, in the way of such triads, was one being with Yyrot and Zeth.

Gradually the image of the child began to appear in the mind of the whale. He puzzled over it, though he had seen children before, generally after shipwrecks caused by himself.

How to react, then, how to undo this procreation as Lionwolf had been undone.

Near dawn a *thing* manifested on the shore, moving along towards Brightshade's horn-crowned head.

Brightshade watched it through one fiery eye.

The thing was tattered, mostly visually animal, limping, yet – shining? Something blue sponged over the muzzle and around the eyes, which were ruddy. A sick wolf?

Brightshade who might, if he wished, have ingested such a wolf with one small snap of his chasmic jaw knew already he could not.

He had never seen his father. But the imprint of Zeth was there in the whale's mixed and marvellous genes. Brightshade grasped in two or three seconds that this was he.

Smoke smouldered off the apparition's ruffled pelt. It sank down close to Brightshade and snarled at him feebly.

Brightshade was surprised.

Anyone reasonably might have been.

This was a god, golden and crimson and terrible in his own right.

'Yes,' said a voice, or the equivalent of a voice, inside the vaults of Brightshade's mind. But *Yes* was only another *shape*, like the words which followed.

'I have been harmed. Outside this paltry world I am as

always. But to come here and find you, I have had to put on this *corpse*.' The wolf paused, panting. It put its head on its front legs. Had it assumed a human masculine form, it would in fact have looked much worse. Dull trails of a substance once sparkling trickled away from it here and there.

Ichor?

'You served me well,' said the vocal *shapes*, presently. 'Now you must complete another task.'

Brightshade's terrifying eye fixed like a gold arrow-head. An autonomous *shape* from Brightshade's brain questioned, *Kill child?*

A wolf paw, scarred yet not unvigorous, swept the question off the snow like a fly.

'Leave your dreaming. *This* is your work: what *I* tell you to do.'

Brightshade received a transmission of vast open waters – the north – and of a stretch of land, and ships massing there, jalees. One more gold thing was gleaming on a rise.

'An old enemy of yours,' said Zeth Zezeth the wounded wolf, in patterns, to his son the giant whale. 'Twice you tried with *her*. She is much stronger now – but so are you.'

Brightshade was disappointed.

It was not that he ever minded killing anything, but he had lost interest in this woman, the one with saffron hair. There had been two of her last time. Both were tipped in the sea. If either version had bobbed up again, surely she did not matter now? Only Lionwolf and the deeds of Lionwolf could matter, or would need to be cancelled.

Sensing all this prevarication, the god-wolf was angry. He struck Brightshade sidelong, in the brain. Though so wrecked in person and persona, Zeth still packed the punch of any god, and Brightshade collapsed.

When he unsealed his eyes again, and blew water out of his blowhole, where shock had made him inadvertently inhale it, the wolf had left the shore. Only some marks were there like those from the slime of a freakishly large sen-snail.

Of course there was no choice. Brightshade eased himself

away from the land and out towards the eastern ocean. Before he turned due north, he fought with and slew several of his own kind, practice perhaps, or only temper. He was not his father's son for nothing.

In a scorchingly gilded landscape, orichalc crags belched madder plumes, orchards of topaz fruit crowded to a flaming hub. The wounded god lay there, by a stream like honey, staring through it, back at something in another world.

Zeth Zezeth had been truly hurt in his brawl with Saphay.

He had not expected it of her, not understanding that the third member of the triad, Yyrot, Winter's Lover, had seen to it Saphay too became not only immortal but empowered.

Zeth glared through the stream. He was nearly as thoughtless as the whale, for being created a god from his inception his intellect was severely limited to the sublime. Now he barely recalled any details of finding Saphay that first time, when she was drifting and drowning under the deep sea ice. All he retained were facts. He had sated and possessed her in an act of immeasurable yet momentary stupendous sexual love. And during that moment she had dragged into herself not only his potent seed, but a third of the essence of himself, his god-fire, and used both to make her son.

Zeth was a minor sun god, reportedly the god of the legend of a lost sun below the sea – the formerly hot sun of the world's long-ago, when there had been *Summer* as well as cold. He was, like all such gods, a symbol.

He had derived most of his character from mortal belief. Rukarian in origin, he had been thought to have two natures, a benign and a cruel side, and so these evolved in him. His benign side was also passionate and supremely selfish. His cruel side was evil.

Saphay, who had become Saftri of the Vorms, would be punished. If Zeth could be harmed then so could she. Her death by now was another item and not overly important. Actually, it would delight him more to inflict horror on her forever, and if she could not *physically* die and so escape him – all the better.

He was not, however, gazing at the world of Saphay in the honey of the stream.

What Zeth was viewing was a world that substantially stayed bolted and barred against him. It was the world of Lionwolf's Hell. Not much was ever clear there. How could it be, such hells being as they were? But something Zeth had sponsored did have for him a great ruby clarity as it flapped across an achromatic sky, starred with that huge blue sun of Lionwolf's war guilt. Zeth observed it, then lay down, an invalid on the burnished grass.

If that was Hell, this place of flame and warmth was Zeth's own paradise. It came from him and was his. Here only could he heal. His wounds were not real but they had almost incapacitated him. The philosophy of the Kraagparians would have reviewed his plight, but Zeth knew nothing of *them*. He was a god of the Ruk. They were humans, and *foreigners*.

Sixth Intervolumen

It is best I pay for what I have had, with my own blood.

Song of Lalt: Simisey

Each day he would do what he had done in the past. Each night the others would come, and to him it would in turn be done.

Soon he did not know which he dreaded most, the nights or the days, his own chastisement or the inflictions he forged, unable not to, aware as he did so that they would next be inflicted upon him.

There seemed no end to it. It never could end. There was no route by which to get away.

Before, when he had been dead, he had lived pretty well, charging about between the physical world – where he could in that identity perform miraculous feats – and the twilight 'tween-world, where he had partaken of full-blooded-seeming wars, feasted, and diddled mermaids.

Always too there had been a promise of some even more wonderful place – at the back of the stars, perhaps. He had never reached it. He had stayed behind to help rear Lionwolf. And then to be with him, loving him like a son.

When, after all the epic dreadfulness of the last unbattle and the White Death, he had met up again with Lionwolf, Guri had no longer loved him. Yet they were bound to each other. Together they crossed the dirty garbage pail of the whale's back, and confronted there inevitable fate.

Learning of the particular death-destiny reserved for Lionwolf, Guri had wept, and turned his shoulder to the gods of his people. It was that bad. It went that deep. Deeper.

So now, once more spitted and undead, Guri did not even have a god to cry out to.

Only his people themselves, his geographically unsecured land, did Guri keep. Olchibe. And that despite the war customs of Olchibe which had brought him at last to this.

He had sometimes too the weirdest notion that he need not, yet, have suffered any torment. One day certainly there would have been, since hell existed, a reckoning. But it had been his brush with Lionwolf, after which he had lived part in and part out of reality, that pushed him early towards atonement.

Day was ending now in Guri's hell.

It was like earth, like the ice-locked Marginal. Ice-jungles massed the distances; somewhere lay sea.

Today he had fought among his vandal band, whose leader was neither a friend nor Peb Yuve. Hell had none of Guri's companions in it, only those *others*.

The terracotta sun went under the world's edge as Guri and his accomplices impaled their male captives, and left them shrieking to die the leisurely death. There had been women too. Guri had raped three. One, who had begged him not to, he had cuffed. She was a woman of the Marginal, peasant Rukar maybe. Since she was not good enough to sell in the slave-market at Sham, when he was finished he held her by the hair and cut her throat. The children, of course, in the Olchibe manner, they spared up to the age of twelve. A boy who claimed to be twelve, however, Guri killed. He was obviously older.

Now they went in to feast at a tented sluht which, as night grew in the earthly hell, looked flimsy to Guri as an assemblage built of smoke.

And as always, no sooner did he duck in at the doorway than all changed.

The first time it happened, he had stumbled, fallen by the little open hearth that was no longer the enclosed potted fire of an Olchibe dwelling or camp. He did not know what was wrong. And then – oh, then – he did.

He . . . was she. That mundane. Guri, picking himself up, found he was picking herself up.

Whether he was a comely or skilful woman he did not know, no more than she. But breasts she had, and strong young *female*

arms, and the feet of a woman, and her long hair had no braid-
ings or skulls. Her skin was fair-sallow.

As soon as the alteration claimed him, he – she – knew why,
and for what purpose. He felt her womb inside himself, and her
undefended entry.

Only then did she hear the yelling and yowling, the crackle
of fires and clout of blades, the tingling hiss of arrows. One
arrow slewed in at the door and struck her through the forearm.
Her flesh was softer than Guri's and it scalded. She gave a cry.
He gave it in her voice.

Then, at the low hut door, three or more Olchibe men slunk
through, grim-faced and dedicated.

'She's not much.'

'Useless for the markets of Sham.'

Outside, albino phantoms, the mammoths trampled and
snorted. Running figures were speared about a central fire.

The first time, Guri had tried to speak Olchibe to the
invaders, to brave it out. But the woman's voice that jagged
from him or her had no words of Olchibe or anywhere in Gech.
It was some Rukar dialect. And like the speech he had heard in
the village town of Ranjalla, though he understood its meaning
it was as unlike Rukarian as anything he had ever heard.

The three or five men wore fur caps. Their hair was twined
with little skulls, and their skin leopardine yellow. They *stank*.
It was worse than any bodily odour. It was the effluent of
unempathic wickedness.

They raped her. Guri thought the first time she must have
been virgin, to be hurt so much. But no, it transpired the men
were dissatisfied. The bitch had borne children and was not
succulent enough. They brought a club then, from the outer
darkness, explaining to her in words she could understand if
not replicate that the *club* was the right fit for her, as she was so
slovenly and big.

Guri, the woman Guri was, died each night from these and
other attentions. But always she *woke* – then on and on it went,
one session and death after another.

He, or she, he supposed, recognized none of the men, and

sometimes too they were different more or less, though always Olchibe.

At least none of them, he thought, had been *himself*, when living.

In dawns lily-like or coraline over the snow, she would once more revive, and find that she was he.

After the initial experience he thought that was to be the only occasion. But he was wrong.

Frequently his trials as a woman were alternated by male sufferings. A village man then, he was anally staked, or burned one limb at a time, to screaming death. He always guessed now what was coming, having watched or personally done it that morning.

Tonight, stooping through the doorway in the sluht, which quickly would transform to the hut-place door of a Marginal settlement, Guri felt the nauseous leaden pangs of true fear sweep through him.

Suffering did not strengthen him, or accustom him to itself. Once you knew to be afraid, you became, he saw, afraid of *everything*. He was a coward now.

Morning broke, *that* morning. He went out and, as sometimes happened, threw up on the snow. His unknown Olchibe comrades, ready for the day's pillage and horror, mocked him, saying he had 'drunk too much' the previous night.

Guri had found he could not resist the raids they went on. His body, even his thoughts, would not obey him. Only his *inner* thought stood back, shivering in stress. Struggling, still he would swing himself on to the kneeling mammoth – which always, during the course of the fight, would die, sobbing, breaking his heart. Nevertheless he could only give in and let all again occur.

Yet today, *that* day, something different.

Up on the slope above the Olchibe camp, a spiky object pierced from the snow. The snow had sprinkled over its swathed form, with its unsettling bunches of arms or hands.

The rough hair was sugared white, striped like that of a badger from the darker jungles.

Guri gazed up at the object. It turned and, with a hand fingered by long knotted twiggy branches, beckoned him.

None of the daytime others paid heed. Guri climbed the slope. It was a novelty. Besides, *her* he remembered from the world. Ranjal, goddess of wood, *made* of wood.

But there had been an old woman too – Narnifa, Ranjal's deceased priestess. Narnifa had been, by the cataclysm of the White Death, incorporated in the broomstick goddess, both of them coming fantastically alive. *Ranjal-Narnifa, I.* That was what she had said, before flying off over the dust plains beneath Ru Karismi.

Guri balanced on the snow, looking at her.

Her eyes were bright and black. She seemed confident and hearty.

'Bow me,' she said. Then, '*Give* me.'

Ranjal had always liked to be given nothing, save by Lionwolf, who had spoiled her, bringing her citrine crystal leaves or wild icy flowers from the forests.

Guri did not move. What point in it, now?

From nowhere, a psychic bolt swiped him. He rolled down the little hill. No one took any notice, and when he raised his face from the snow again the goddess beckoned.

Guri toiled up the hill a second time and stood there.

'*Bow* me.'

Guri shrugged. He bowed low. Then he set down before her handfuls of nothing, one after another, on and on, until she exclaimed in her young sportive voice, 'Enough. *Excessive!*' In, of all things, an aristocratic Rukarian accent.

'Are you in hell too?'

'I? This hell? Why I be in any hell?' She was back to her normal outlandish tongue.

'No reason, only you're here, old lady.'

Now her striking him was quite gentle. He only staggered. And he saw she grinned.

'Old not now. All me young. God, I.'

'Yes,' he said, 'you're another god.'

'Ask me,' she said, 'what is you want.'

She had always been like that, even when stuck in her solely wooden form. Men went to her in troops, praying for prophecies, and everything she said was without exception of the best. She never predicted any bad event, even for those you saw after cut to pieces or fried to dust.

'You tell lies.' He anticipated she would hit him again.

But she did not. She said, 'Never.'

'Yes. You lied to the men in the war camp, saying they'd get all they fancied.'

'Some of them do get it,' she responded with asperity.

Guri looked down at his booted feet, toeing the snow about.

Ranjal said, 'Make glad them.'

'With lies,' he could not resist repeating.

'Make happy by promise is not to be lying. In end-of-all, all men get all ever wanted.'

Guri squinted at her. He thought she probably knew, being now properly deified. But end-of-all was a soint-muck of a way off.

'Ask,' she said benevolently again.

Guri glanced over his shoulder at the Olchibe men, spectral or concrete, getting ready for their jolly day of mayhem prior to the torture of night.

'Have me released from that. From this.'

Ranjal frowned. 'Cannot.'

'Then you're no bloody use to me, wooden lady. Why are you here?'

'You,' she said, 'kind to me. Back before, never ask for anything.'

Astounded, Guri said, 'I never was kind to you. You were just an ugly bit of wood.'

Curiously unoffended, Ranjal insisted, 'To me that was sibull, to Narnifa, kind. Before she I and I she.'

Guri laughed. It was the first he had ever laughed in his hell. It tasted bitter, like bad wine. 'No.'

Ranjal said, 'You speak they words to her, and she all alone.

You make her angry, keep her hopping mad and in world by me. So when the white breath comes we join. Thank you, I. Both of I.'

'Ah? All right,' Guri reluctantly said. 'You're welcome.'

'Ask,' said Ranjal.

Guri glared into her face. In her rough and sturdy way she was not now unattractive, for a badger-woman with branched multi-hands.

'Let me see Olchibe again – the real Olchibe. Let me go back once in the world – let me make some change for them. The best Olchibe warriors died at Ru Karismi. All the beasts died. Great Gods know what can be done—'

Ranjal smiled widely. She had no teeth, he thought, only a row of wooden pegs in there. What could the rest of her be like?

Then she was gone. *Hell* – was gone.

Guri found himself alone on a white plain of the real ice-world, under a blue aerial ceiling strafed by cloud. He could *smell* the sky.

For him, the episode that followed was all one extended jumbled day, sunset and night, which happened in random order over and over. Time in the world was not like time in Guri's hell.

He quickly came across Ipeyek wandering stupidly about and soon conned Chillel's gem-dark seed in Ipeyek's mating equipment, primed, ready and unfired. He haunted Ipeyek, drove him crazy, and herded him towards the north and east, towards the sluhtin of dead Peb Yuve – if anything should be left of it.

Guri gloried in what he did. The fleet impossible running, the near flight, the invisibility or manifests of his ghostliness were irrelevant at last save where they assisted this one task.

When Guri had delivered Ipeyek home to the Crarrowin and the sluhtin, he knew he must report back from his holiday, to hell. He could not shirk it, nor did he try.

The Crarrowin had sobered him too. The Crax he had slept with, infinities ago. She was old now, though still an arresting woman. But he had thought these wise women *so* wise. Yet even they said nothing against unprovoked war and thievery, the slaughter of non-Olchibe men or children above the age of twelve, or the rape of un-Olchibe women. If they had ever protested he had never heard it. Despite all this, the love of his own kind, the need to make them powerful and favoured, did not leave him. The Crax had contracted with him that the black child would bear his name. And even as he was hurled again from the world to the inner prison of that place of damnation, he could hear the reborn echo of his name, and was for a moment energized, and cleansed of all blame, all terror and all sadness. But the moment ended, and night was there in Guri's hell, and into the hut they came, nine men now, with a red-hot brand.

Eighth Volume

THE WINDS THAT NEVER BLEW

Hell lies colder than the Here and Now, But if the Here and Now be cold enough – Perhaps the Here and Now Are Hell.

Gech saying: Sham

ONE

Jemhara entered Ru Karismi naked as her day of birth – aside from a single twig caught in her hair.

She had run the final laps in her shape-change of a hare. No clothing could survive that, only hard things such as certain jewels and metals. The twig though had been given her by the peasant sibull in the hot spring village. It must have properties because, wound in a tress and so in her hare's pelt, it came through.

From her magic she had learned that the gates of the lost city were both undone and undefended. Even the reiver bands which had flocked there to maraud currently left the ruin alone, superstitious, or sick of it. Jemhara had reasoned that some apparel, or merely even odd furs or cloth, would linger among the houses. Otherwise, she trusted her sorcery to protect her flesh, and her youthful, adapted endurance.

But – O gods – the shock of the cold sliced into her and nearly knocked her down. When she stood against it, muttering her protections, the weather sneered and the sky clouded. Snow began to cascade earthwards.

I am a fool. He would tell me that, she thought. Considering Thryfe, his pictured reprimand, even if contemptuous, warmed her slightly.

She went in at the hole which was mostly what remained of Southgate.

Jemhara, who first came to Ru Karismi poor and wide-eyed, knew the city well. She had lived variously in its sectors before achieving the palaces on its heights. Even when royal,

Sallusdon's second queen, Jemhara had quite often gone back to the lower city on forays, carried by slaves in her litter. The Great Markets, the lesser markets, the temple-town with its daunting milieu of Rukarian gods, little pleasure gardens and fine buildings where esoteric books might be read, all these were familiar to her.

The snows of previous years had covered much, hardened, *baked* to permanence by the coldness of the earth. Trees frozen in their armour had still extended roots beneath the ground to tilt columns, crumble steps and walls. Even the disintegrated stained glass had now died beneath the frosts. There was nowhere any hint of heat or light, an absence of colour as of movement, scent and sound.

Beautiful Jemhara looked vivid against the monochrome. It seemed to make her a target for the wind now rising. She shuddered and hastened up a slope of street towards a block of just recognizable houses.

An hour after, she huddled still naked inside a mansion below the Stair of one thousand steps. All garments or soft materials had been removed from the city – looted or simply made unusable by weather. She had instead found closets of coins, some jewelry, and a store of wine – breached and sampled by robbers but mostly left intact; perhaps they had not liked it. Scrolls and bound books she found too, their unprotected sheets and leaves often fallen away. And there were the dead. The skeleton sitting bolt upright in his chair of carven ivory, with the rotted paper in front of him from which she could still read the words *Upon all magicians may the sky fall*; or the small dog, perfectly preserved, his coat like pale brass, lying as if asleep at the foot of a bed of human bones.

By now Jemhara experienced the cold like a covering. Also she spontaneously shook, her feet were numb, her hands ached, and the points of her fingers had become desensitized. The nipples of her breasts stayed erect and sore as if bitten. Another would have moaned in pain and fear. She was silent. She focused inflamed eyes on the marble Stair. Snow caked across it too, and more was coming down. She could barely see the steel statues, let alone the top of the flight. She must go up, she had decided. Among the palaces she might detect some remnant of protective wear.

Without this essential she felt she could not dare the Insularia, which lay under the thick ice of the River Palest. The immodesty of a nude female might provoke some psychic attack.

Jemhara forced herself out of the shelter of the house. The bladed wind was sheering round to the south. Snow filled her eyes and mouth, melting tardily. Over the Stair whirling whiteness danced like Jafn air spirits she had heard of. It came to her, unbelievably, she might after all die if her dilemma could not soon be resolved.

And what was this now? Did she hallucinate?

There inside the spiralling storm something was descending the Stair, solid, gleaming yet shadowy – and very tall.

For one heart-stopped instant Jemhara thought it was Thryfe the Magus, walking down the Stair towards her.

But the form was in fact *too* tall even for tall Thryfe.

Jemhara stared, freezing where she stood, briefly not noticing this.

Then the snow parted like curtains.

Through them stepped the impressive figure of Ru Karismi's Gargolem.

The Gargolem moved with impeccable mechanical coordination. Its metallic hide, golden-bronze, burned like a lamp through the snow, and the great expressionless head, maned, fanged, noble, appalling, faced towards her, so eyes of unfathomable intelligence could meet her own.

Jemhara screamed. So hypothermically reduced was she, the shriek was pathetic, more like the mew of a tiny bird.

Although it was the guardian of the kings of the city and of the city itself, few had seen the Gargolem except far off. The Magikoy made it, perhaps aeons before, and they could speak to it familiarly. But otherwise such messages as it sent among men were carried via magic, by mirrors, oculums, or by lesser gargolems. Kings supposedly had irregularly conversed with the Gargolem. It was always addressed as a man and named Gargo.

'Gargo,' croaked Jemhara, trying to recover. She blurted, 'I've done nothing to offend you—'

'Yes,' said the Gargolem. The voice of it was neither robotic nor at all human. 'Sallusdon, King Paramount, was poisoned by you at the will of Vuldir, then King Accessorate.'

Jemhara breathed, 'I had no choice.'

'There is always choice.'

'Shall I make amends?'

'You will do so. But not here, nor at this time.'

Jemhara looked away from the Gargolem. It stung her eyes worse than the cold. She had seen from her own magecraft at Stones that when the White Death was unleashed, this enigmatic servant of the city had vanished without trace. If a guardian, it had proved a dismal one. But then, she had never grasped its real function or the real nature of its imposed vocation.

Jemhara gibbered and tried not to. The Gargolem stalked towards her, something unfurling darkly from its almost manlike hands. This *must* be death. But she had space for no pleas or quavering outcry. Death swooped on her and smothered her up. Death was warm, soft. She found she grappled it to her. Death, as it turned out, was really a loose velvet gown dropped over her head, a cloak of fur wrapped round her.

The Gargolem, bending from its dominant height, slipped boots of tenderized leather on to her feet, which fitted her like gloves. The gloves it slid on to her hands also fitted her – like gloves.

'Drink,' said the Gargolem, putting a flask against her mouth.

'Is it . . . what is it?'

The Gargolem did not bother to reply. Jemhara drank the brew, which had in it wine and spice and some restoring medicine she herself, long since, had mixed for others.

*

192

The graves lay in the floor, all along the inner chamber. It was the Morsonesta of the Insularia, where the Magikoy dead were laid to decay under stone. There were other historic burial places about Ru Karismi, and sometimes even a Magikoy cadaver had been interred elsewhere. In the city's final days, only a minimum of bodies were brought down here. Many dropped at their posts while tending the sick and dying, or performing such manual offices as digging death pits and tending funeral pyres. By then, with no ceremony, they were chucked in on the corpses of ordinary men, women, children and animals. The Magikoy, not long after the White Death, had largely been stripped of respect or specialness. And they had not by that date argued. These graves here therefore were an uneven combination of ancient and modern. Each bore a name, some well known and some by now obscure. Jemhara looked down as she walked over. She did not like to tread on them but had no option. Herself, she recognized no name. At the room's edge she noted four or five small graves set apart. These were of apprentices of High Level, it seemed, who had died helping the afflicted populace in the short days before no one troubled with burial any more. *Flazis*, Jemhara read, *His future bright has ended in this darkness. Vrain*, she read, *Death is not the end*. On the last grave Jemhara paused. She stopped as if listening, for a strange vibration seemed to sound beneath it. Looking down again, unwillingly, Jemhara read: *Ruxendra. Fifteen years of age. Beloved daughter of good family and talented in the Great Magics. Now in Paradise.*

But the Gargolem strode by, and through a huge doorway Jemhara followed, as she had followed it down the city and in under the river by secret ways.

It had been the Gargolem's ability to undo all doors that enabled Jemhara to enter here and to proceed.

She was astonished to be helped. But she had not attempted to ask why.

The Insularia was not as once or twice she had heard it described. It was bigger by far. Yet also it was desolate. If any sorcerous vitality remained in these hollow caverns and lightless, untinted, towering rooms, it was not apparent to her sensitivity. All true power seemed to have been leached away.

They were in a tunnel corridor then, and a metal sledge with a vitreous sail stood on the ground.

'A wind will come,' said the Gargolem. 'Call it.'

'I? Can I, *here*?'

'It is a simple thing.'

Jemhara rifled through her witch's memory. She thought of the song of her Soforan steader childhood, 'By all the winds that never blew'. It meant all those things one had never been able to achieve, all those opportunities missed and blessings withheld. As a girl she had never known the meaning. Now she knew.

Jemhara whistled.

The wind came bowling along the tunnel. When she and the Gargolem stepped on to the sledge it rose about four feet off the ground, and bore them away.

After a while the sledge sailed through another chamber, where stone heads, none human, gazed into empty air. A pair of gates, high as the high arched roof, leaned wide. On the floor lay a huge inanimate thing, like a snake all made of metal too, silent.

The next chamber was black as pitch.

Intimidated though she was, Jemhara was curious. Curiosity had often led her to knowledge.

'Did they do this?' she asked. When the Gargolem did not reply, even when they flew out again into another tunnel, this one twisting and turning, Jemhara said, 'The Magikoy destroyed their own work here?'

The Gargolem spoke. 'No, Jemhara. It died when they did.'

This perplexed her. 'Then even their artefacts – were a part of the Magikoy themselves?'

'In a way.'

'But you,' she said, 'great Gargo, *you* persist.' The Gargolem did not answer. She thought perhaps now this was only because what she had stated was self-evident. 'Are there others of your kind – other lesser gargolems still active?'

'They too are gone.'

Just then the tunnel was amplified and they sailed out into an enormous underrock hall, wide as a volcanic caldera and high as twenty or thirty storeys of an average building. Although situated beneath the River Palest, the Insularia complex must extend miles into the city on each side.

Obsidian bridges crossed the cavern. Below ran paved roads lined with plain stone apartment stacks. The scene was both awesome and modest. But the desolate atmosphere that overlaid it now, the absence of any warmth or lighting, gave it too a mood of sinister depression.

Jemhara gripped her hands together. 'Gargo, will you answer me one more question?' The Gargolem did not speak. 'I believe you are taking me to the Magus Thryfe. Is this so?'

'It is so.'

Jemhara breathed. She said, 'If they're dead, and all this is – dead, does Thryfe live? Or are we visiting his grave?'

The Gargolem said, 'He is not in any grave, except that of his own body.'

'Tell me plainly, Gargo. You know what I ask you.'

'He lives.' The Gargolem added, 'Yet he is dead too.'

Jemhara's face flushed with a scared fury. She knew enough to know that the Gargolem did not sadistically tease her. It uttered absolutes. But she could not think how to make it respond directly in the human way, and could not bear any more. She bit her tongue, literally, as sometimes she had when afraid in her youth. That was an inspired precaution. The sledge rode over the cavern, and presently the Gargolem told her what next she must go through, in order to reach her goal.

I am here. I am trapped for eternity. May some god help me. But I believe in no gods, save only those weak entities that assist, superfluously, the vanity of men. And these devils are not mine.

She heard a voice – his? – but only in her head.

Thryfe. It was Thryfe.

Perhaps she imagined his censure and his despair.

The way was unguarded. Jemhara guessed several lesser gargolems had formerly monitored the passage, and who travelled it.

On the walls, emblems demonstrated old questions and answers, the successful circumnavigation of significant tests. But perhaps only she, or one like her, could have read it.

The Gargolem had brought her here. Left her here.

Before her, a shaft plunged into some abyss.

She knew, Jemhara, she must leap. For him. Only for him.

She leapt.

It was a well of black glass, plunging to an unknown depth. Balanced on air she tumbled swiftly and in terror, by means of the shaft's own surviving mechanism. To the place below.

The Telumultuan Chamber.

As always, to any who fell here, and you could only enter by falling through the shaft, it seemed you were thrown into a narrow cubicle barely big enough to contain a living creature. It was made of stone and blind of windows. It had no door, either in or out. Meanwhile the entry-aperture of the shaft disappeared.

Jemhara saw this, and that she remained alone.

The fall she pushed from her mind. Incarceration she knew from what the Gargolem had said was temporary. Yet this was one of the cardinal sanctums of the Magikoy, the outpost of that terrible chamber of weaponry which had released the White Death. The Gargolem had also notified her that she – untrained and uninitiate of the Magikoy – must undergo here some awful examination of body and will.

'What?' she had asked.

The Gargolem did not precisely reply. 'It is never discussed. But it is demanding. And, too, it may be survived.'

For a while there in the enclosure, nothing else. She waited in trepidation. But, well trained in her own amateur's ways, her not inconsiderable self-control persisted.

Then from the walls, another gargolem, that of the Telumultuan Chamber – presumably surviving where other lesser servants had not – spoke unseen. The phrases were not specific to her, for it challenged any who ever came into this room. And Jemhara now knew as much.

'What are you doing here?'

What could she say? She knew at least she must tell the truth.

'Thryfe,' she said. 'I am here for Thryfe, Magikoy Master.'

'Do you know the price?'

She did not. She replied, truthful, 'No.'

'It is high. Will you pay?'

'For him – I will pay.'

'Pay then.'

Love secretly rules all worlds. Love is the only element which will do such things, for itself or another.

The chamber being what it was, safeguards had been fixed on it centuries before. No mage could enter there and lightly unlock the weapon store.

From the wall in front of her a sword snaked out. It danced, whippy and silver, and sliced through Jemhara. She screamed again, then shut her lips together. The Gargolem had not instructed her – maybe had trusted her to be, herself, mageia enough to know – she must keep still under this onslaught.

Jemhara kept still as a rock. She knew she could not die for she must find Thryfe.

The sword went into her like a thin knife through snow. The snow turned scarlet. Her blood lay on the walls and floor. The world was red.

When the razorous cuts ended, the walls and floor had analysed all that she was from her blood. Which must have been sufficent.

A door appeared, filled by icy light.

Jemhara crept through and as she did so her lacerations entirely healed.

Beyond the door lay the full scope of the Telumultuan.

Before Lionwolf's war, no living thing had entered here through countless centuries. Apart from during nightmares.

Then seven Magikoy had come in, to wake Hell on earth. After them, one other.

Now Jemhara was here.

The space is high and far, and on all sides slides into a misty dimness and an elongated perspective.

Things have stood here, once. Faintly glimmeringly grey and countless, tall as a forest – taller; featureless and unique. *They* are gone. They have sped upward at one unknowable word, utilized openings made for them in a frozen river, arced invisible and unseen, touched the ground again at the pre-scribed areas. After which – whiteness, stasis, salt pillars, *dust*.

Jemhara looks all about. She seems to see the *shades* of the weapons hanging there yet, ground to air. The sourceless light trembles. The floor of polished granite, if it is, stays pure.

Jemhara walks forward, dwarfed by the expellation of any-thing else.

The chamber is empty save for its own aura and the ghosts of Death. Jemhara is only . . . an afterthought.

She moved ahead for perhaps an hour, glancing always about her. Then something twitched in her hair. It was startling, as if a beetle had flown in there, the sort that laired in old wooden furnishing. Jemhara put up her hand, and into it fell the twig the sibull had given her in the village with the hot spring. Jemhara halted, and looked at the twig lying on the palm of her glove. A strange shape it had, rather like a doll's skinny hand with too many thin fingers.

Then, on her palm the twig shifted. All its fingers pointed now one way, which was across the limitless chamber to Jemhara's right. Nothing was different there. Everything dwindled in perspective, everything was empty.

A little sharp tapping came from the twig. After a moment it ceased.

Jemhara, beyond thought, fixated solely on one idea, turned herself and walked in the direction the talisman had shown.

Almost instantly a barrier was before her.

It was a sheet of material of such transparency it was like glass. She could see through it, but only now she stood in front of it – before that it had faithfully mirrored the enormous featureless spaces of the chamber. On the far side of the glassy surface Jemhara beheld a place of darkness, full of a kind of smoke. And in the smoke a figure hung suspended. She could not quite make it out. She did not need to, having already looked at this scene when dreaming.

The barrier however must be magical, impenetrable.

Instinctually, nearly tranced, Jemhara put one finger to the wall. It was cold as ice. It *was* ice.

A low cry came from her.

Since childhood she had had the gift of melting ice to water.

Was it possible such a village witchery could work even in the Insularia of the Magikoy? She stood in doubt, forgetting the hidden aptness of the world, how minor atoms might change monoliths and insignificant events catapult prodigious ones into being. As if the earth, building its own harsh and insurmountable walls, left in them tiny keys, ready for turning.

She had after all melted the ice of Thyrfe's chastity. She had, after all, melted the ice that had locked her into a vicious, paltry life.

Jemhara made the spell with a neurasthenic calm. Nothing occurred, and then a piece was wept, in a great gush like milk, out of the barrier. As the liquid ran foaming and sparkling along the floor, Jemhara stepped through into the room of smoke and darkness.

Two years, two centuries ago, Thryfe the Magician had driven his sleekar back across the plains where the snow was brown as excrement, and entered dying Ru Karismi. Climbing to the top of the city he had watched the vacancy of gardens and palaces. Below he saw the dead put out for crematory wagons.

A few days after, the dead were simply tossed from doors and windows, down on the fine streets. By then he was helping to collect and burn them. And, too, he went into the city's homes. He held the hands of dying women and children and men of all ages, told them they would live beyond the body's end. He believed not a word of it. But where life betrayed, only an afterlife could offer recompense. Most of the priests were also dead. Someone had to do it.

Later he told himself he should not have lied. This was when he realized he, very likely, would not die himself. He had thought he must, coming back among the poisons and the sorrow. Just as he knew – or reckoned that he knew – the brown sandy snow that ran for miles beyond the walls would harden with cold and finally return as a bleached, sere-grained ice, also like sand – as had the ice desert of the Great Uaarb of northernmost Gech, where, the books said, a test of similar weaponry had once been played out before.

When he did not die Thryfe felt a new disgust. He had prevented nothing. He had helped not at all. Useless, into the dustbin of the world he should go. But instead golden children went there, and innocent kind old men. And here he was, this apostate of magecraft, moving and breathing and mouthing commonplace reassurance.

One girl died in his arms.

She was herself nearly a Magikoy, one of the apprentices who had reached the Maxamitan Level. He had never really noticed her – as he had failed to see so much, even the danger of the mindless bitch who came to him in her glowing magic and wound him in her web – Jemhara.

The dying girl though, in her dirty smelly dress, her hands worn from tending the dying, the dead and their fires, had turned her head on his arm and gazed long at him from overbright dark eyes. Some went mad from the poison and she was somewhat like that, if not very much.

Outside the windows of the well-to-do house that had been hers before she became a Magikoy apprentice, pyre-smokes still rose like a black-trunked forest. The air was murky ochre. The stench of roast meat and bone would make you choke if, by now, you had not become so accustomed that it was the only atmosphere you could recall.

'I shan't live,' she told him. A decision – as if she alone had made up her mind.

'No.'

'What lies beyond . . . here?'

He had said so often to others that something much better did. Now the phrases stuck in his gullet as the smoke and stink of the city did not. She was only fifteen. 'What would you like to find there?'

'Oh,' she said. She smiled sleepily. 'Vengeance.'

Mechanical he said, 'But you're Magikoy. There's no teaching which—'

'*Revenge*,' she said, her smile and sleepiness gone. 'I know who caused this.'

'There were many causes.'

'Hush,' she said gently, as if comforting a younger child, 'don't concern yourself. Whatever is there, I'll meet *him* there.'

'Who?'

'*Vashdran*,' she said.

Thryfe felt the Rukarian version of the name of that superbeing, half god, half mortal, and having the worst of both, strike through his ribs like a spear. When he had cleansed his brain enough to speak, and turned to look back into her eyes, he saw they had fixed for ever.

Then her parents cornered him. It had been the way of it: sometimes the older ones or the less strong survived, while the fresh and fit and young died in droves.

'We had four sons,' said the woman. She still wore her jewels, or had put them on to show him her prestige. 'All dead,' she announced. It was the husband who began to sob. 'But our daughter, she was Magikoy.'

'I know she was.'

'Yes, Highness Thryfe, of course you do. Please – take her down to the burial yard under the River Palest. Where you Magikoy lay your own dead. Other apprentices of High Level were taken there – Flazis was, and he was only from the minor city of Or Tash. But our Ruxendra, she was by us much loved, and talented in magery. And we – why, my husband has a distant relationship to the royal family.' The woman's face clouded. She added quickly, 'I mean to the last king, Sallusdon. Not – not that other, Vuldir.'

What did it matter and what was there to lose? Most of the Magikoy had perished too.

Thryfe said, 'Wash and dress your daughter in her best. I'll take her down and myself see to her interment.'

Their profusion of thanks embarrassed him, humiliated and horrified him. But he said nothing against it, and did not inform them that the only means by which their girl would now get into an Insularian grave was with Thryfe himself wielding hack-blade and spade.

He carried her there in his arms. She was light, and no other suitable transport was available.

For a while he had stood looking at the river, the huge fissures which had been created in the ice to let out the weapons as they flew.

Once through the esoteric entrances, which still responded to passwords, rather surprising him, Thryfe was in the Insularia. Reaching the yard of tombs he broke the paving in a spare position and lowered the girl into her bed. Her mother had put on her a dress of scarlet velvet trimmed with silver, for the colours of Ru Karismi. Also she wore a pearl necklace he had seen the mother wearing, and gold rings obviously kept for Ruxendra alone – they would have been too small for her mother. Stitched into the skirt of the dress – he had heard them rustling as he carried her – were wishes for happiness, benign mantras and, so he reasoned, a page or two of Magikoy sayings.

When she was in the grave he threw a swath of silk her parents also supplied over her face. Then he flung in the earth and laid back the stones. Fusing them with his power, he also cut an inscription there. They had begged him for one. It told any who might ever find her that she had been of good family and loved, talented with the magic of mages. 'Say too,' had whispered her father, 'she is in Paradise.' Thryfe did so.

Annihilation, to this world, is Paradise enough.

After the burying, he wandered about the regions of the Insularia. All were, like the city, dead or dying. Here and there a wan-coloured iridescence stirred; now and then a failing gargolem spoke. By the great gates of the Nonagesmian Chamber the serpent-worm lay exhausted.

'Who comes?' it asked in the voice of death.

'Sleep,' he said. It slept, and did not again wake.

Finally and inevitably, Thryfe descended to the Chamber of the Weapons.

This would have been allotted to him, had he been both present in the city and quite unable to prevent their deployment. Seven Magikoy had gone down. One of these had been a substitute, for Thryfe, despite his steely modesty, was one of the Highest Order and that echelon alone was authorized.

The drop through the shaft, the slicing swords, meant nothing now.

As Jemhara would do, after these two years, that were – to some – centuries, had gone by, Thryfe moved out through the empty Telumultuan.

Naturally he was versed in its tricks and concealments.

For a time he walked there and then, without warning, the full edifice of despair crashed down about his head. Presumably until then he had generally held it off by trying to render some assistance. But here at last, with all in ruins and the symbolic child-girl with her mission of astral vengeance laid to rest, the structure of resistance gave way.

It had been the father who wept. Men were weaker. Thryfe had often thought so. Women, with their legacy of childbirth and, often, subservience, must endure. Their tears were more illustrative than profound, or *if* profound, then unnegotiable.

But when Thryfe had wept, there in the Telumultuan Chamber, he knew it was only the weeping of a fool staggering under his debt.

Pay it then. Pay the damnable thing.

He raised some barrier – glass, ice – went through and closed it. And in that place the smoulder of the funeral pyres came flocking immediately, and all the reek of them, more repulsive and again original than when in the city, for here the air had been clean.

These vestiges massed out of his memory, his thoughts. He

welcomed them with an awful sense of rightness. Night settled too. Welcome, night.

When the paroxysm of grief was spent, he slept for some hours lying on the ground, in the familiar miasma and dark of world and self-criticism.

Rousing, he had been stripped of anything he supposed he was. And so he shouted for release.

An antique torture of Ruk Kar Is was to hang a man alive and upside down. In Thryfe's smouldering sleep the image had come to him, though it had not been himself but some emblematic fiery male writhing in chains. By now no intellectual connection was made for him with emblems he had read in the past concerning a man who was half god, half human.

From an unseen ceiling chains rolled down and picked Thryfe up. As they seized him he in turn seized them, in an exuberant frenzy of abnegation. Until they curtailed all autonomous acts.

Swung over and depended, he was aware of the blood of a viable vascular system thumping into his head. It stunned him, and when he revived gradually altered him.

With a sort of bitter pleasure he felt his mind give way. Fragments scattered his consciousness like broken shells. No birds fluttered from them. He was immeasurably glad.

Time now became nothing.

Back to his babyhood and his beginnings he spun. It was that morning when he was two years old, and foresaw the killing of his mother by a black wolf. Again he must go through it all, shrieking and put aside, standing to see her fly apart under the tree of ice.

Eagles whirled him upward, as the forgotten chains now did. He was fifteen. He flew in their taloned grip, revelling in the bemusement of his village. Then he was sent away. He was in town after town, next in cities of the Ruk. He was examined, proved. He suffered all the trials of the Order that now appropriated him. He felt the teeth of whips, the bite of beasts and fires. He fought off fear and lust and longing and loneliness. He closed himself for the first behind a barrier of invisible glassy ice, this one mental and, he believed, never to be penetrated.

Worse than all else then, through the humming of his bruising brain, *she* stole.

A black hare ran. Thryfe the Eagle brought it down.

Jemhara. Lovely as stars at sunset. Sweet-mouthed, sweet-breasted, clothed in her black hair, her cream skin just blushed with her blood – blood that smelled, since the eagle had spilled it, of pristine water.

Shape-changer. *Mind*-changer. Destroyer of ice and barriers and the ramifications of the forged and adamant heart.

A beautiful and shallow face, until he saw the depths within her eyes. Until she looked at him, saw *him*, her own heart springing open like a bud.

Some sorcery was on them both – yes, now he glimpsed as much, hung here to die slowly for his sins of non-attendance and inadequacy. Perhaps not all her fault then, that timeless year or month or hour of their lovemaking.

Sweet, so sweet. So good, so *nourishing*.

Like food to one starved, drink to the thirsty, warmth to the frozen cold – all these. But then, replete, warmed through and all the protective iron of the ice gone to liquid, *then*, waking out of the dream to find he had lost the world. Worse, he had lost that world not only for himself, who deserved nothing else, but for so many thousands more.

All the dead stand now in the limitless empty chamber of Thryfe's mind, whose scope is larger by far even than the Telumultuan. They stand, fixed in their unheard screaming, in the moments of *white* below the walls of Ru Karismi. On and on their scream, bleeding to the colours of silver, ebony and carmine, and back again to the blank of snow.

Let me die. God help me and let me free . . .

But there is for him no God, no gods, not even those fallible malicious demons worshipped in the Ruk. No, Thryfe sees the void before him, empty also of everything. He aches and yearns towards it as once towards the joys of the flesh he renounced.

Yet it is miles away, oblivion. It will be a journey of millennia to reach it.

And now he is an infant again, and he too is screaming as the wolf rips his mother into bits under the tree.

His eyes were open, but he did not see with them.

All of him hung there like the captive body of an eagle, a lammergeyer, its wings trailing downward, feathers of bronze and black raggedly torn.

The surrounding fog was very thick. It had the taint of old burning.

Jemhara had hurried through it and stood beside him now. Thryfe's face floated in the murk just above her – all of him by a small amount out of her reach. Sometimes a galvanic shudder would race through his frame and he would swing like any criminal confined on a gibbet. But the mask of the face never altered. The eyes were always blind.

For a long while she remained there, gazing at him.

She did not try to reach up to him, or even touch a trail of one unravelled sleeve that hung temptingly near enough for her fingertips to brush it. Perhaps a quarter of an hour eroded. Jemhara sat down on the floor below the living dying body of her lover. She never took her eyes from him. She began to murmur. Was it a prayer? Some cunning spell? It was the song from her childhood. *By all the winds that never blew* . . . She spoke the words to the shroud of smoke and the deaf quiet, and to his intermittently convulsing flesh, and to his unseeing eyes. *I sing of you.*

Once before they had been condensed in timelessness. Timelessness returned to them in the darkness. Soon all sound ended, even the whispers of her breathing and her words. Jemhara, not really knowing what she did, began to pierce, in slow awkward stages, the outer casing of Thryfe. That was, her awareness pushed like a remorseless needle in through the skin, the muscle and the bone, in and further in, to the essence of him.

There she located the eagle. Not that she saw it, or even imagined it. By other unlike senses, she discovered this animal genius of his psyche.

It perched on some bleak high crag of his soul, wings folded, staring into a type of vacancy. For a very long while nothing had alerted it. It was inanimate and void, though it had not so far lost its etheric non-visual outline, or its paraphrase of might and flight.

And as Jemhara came to it, the eagle suddenly swerved its hook-beaked head, as if at an unforeseen noise or flick of brilliance.

Gems of light appeared too in its eyes. Very fearsome it looked, described in that unseen iconography by which Jemhara now saw. Pitiless it looked, and blood-hungry, and still vital. There was no remnant of humanity now, no restraint. But life there was.

Maybe she had known all along, unconsciously. Even so she had come here, and had she not said to him before, 'Let *me* die for you. Kill me, if you like.'

She rose, there in the physical room of darkness. Then she was gone. On the ground poised the black hare of her witch's shape-change, with one jewelled spark of *Jemhara* still flaming in its brain.

And on the mind-crag of soul and thought, near where the dusty wicked eagle perched, a black hare loped from a crevice. Next instant it sped away.

The eagle, glaring from its sideways eye, lifted with a heavy slap of wings. Over some symbolic plain it soared, and the black hare fled below. The bird stooped. A screech burst from its throat.

In the outer dark the form of the hanging man grew translucent. From the body of Thryfe the eagle of his aura flowed like fire out of lit coals. Upward it dashed, and the whole of the foggy space expanded at its coming to make room for it.

Here too the hare ran, pathetic and small, across a vista that

207

was both plain and floor – but also neither. Again the eagle gave its hunting cry. It wheeled, clapped shut the sweeping wings and fell downward like a lightning bolt from a black sky.

Hooks of bronze, the talons seized the little hare. The very crash of the hammer of the fall must have broken her back. Down on the ground he pinned her, and rent her with his beak till all her velvet sable was red.

Deep within herself Jemhara held her psychic core intact, distant from the agony of the blows. She felt them, they were real and terminal, enough to kill her, surely, but it seemed her powers were greater, had been made so by former dealings with Thryfe. She did not die, she did not give way. And when abruptly the eagle let her go, standing there above her, Jemhara too flowed upward out of herself, on this occasion the human flowing outward from the animal genius of the hare.

Naked she came, and unmarked, speckled only fractionally by the unstopped blood she had passed through, her hair flying around her.

With both hands she grasped the terrifying eagle by its neck. Clash its beak and twist as it might, she would not let go. The wings spread like lethal fans. Jemhara took no notice.

Up from the floor or earth the great bird rushed, dragging her with it. It beat towards the shape of the hanging magician, seeking its eyrie of flesh.

What hung there had also begun to move, to struggle. The eagle lashed against it, unable to access return, while the body swung and contorted, mindlessly at first like some corpse animated only by magic.

Then something flared inside the eyes, something *live*, something mortal and aware, but neither sane nor gentle.

High above an incendiary explosion shook the incorporeal walls of the room. Smoke and dark fell in disintegrations, and a briary of chains splashed down with them. Thryfe fell. As he fell the eagle altered to a stream like molten metal, broke free of captivity and gushed over him, back *into* him, vanishing, leaving no clue save in the laval insanity of his eyes.

With these madman's eyes Thryfe watched Jemhara as she

crouched on all fours. She too had been dropped from the eagle's supernatural talons. Quickly she propelled herself to her feet. Then he surged up from the ground.

Thryfe, in all his tatters, filthy and damaged, his brain in loose rattling sections bruised blacker than any smoke by upturned blood, dizzy at being gravitationally upright, reeling and slavering, retching, coughing, cursing in a backlands slobber no one had ever heard from him since his sixteenth year.

'Thryfe,' Jemhara said. Her voice was thin, like a cobweb.

His voice was like a cracked knife.

'I am no longer Thryfe. This is not Thryfe, you bitch.'

All her dreams of him then had been true. The dream of his hanging, but also the previous dreams in which he came towards her to slay her.

He staggered at her like a drunken man on the deck of a storm-battered ship. She stood immobile as a slender rock. And he foundered on her, he and the ship of his murderer's intention, foundered as he had before in the spider-silk of her love. Down he went, unconscious at her feet. But bending over him Jemhara heard him breathe, and under her hand felt the gallop of his heart.

The Gargolem had waited elsewhere. Possibly it had even retired into that other unnamed dimension it utilized. Now it was present in the Telumultuan Chamber.

How it had got there went unanswered. Certainly it had not come through the descending shaft, as men must. Nor did it, in any apparent way, evolve out of the air.

Whatever, it had divined unerringly the moment of Thryfe's release, Jemhara's second triumph.

The woman, straightening from the prone body of the magus, turned reflexively and saw the Gargolem through the hole she had made in the barrier of ice-glass. As earlier, even now the sight of the Gargolem astonished and frightened her.

She began to shake with fear of it, where through all the other terrors she had more than managed.

The Gargolem however nodded to her. An unusually urbane gesture.

'You must leave this place,' the Gargolem said.

'Yes – but how?'

'I will show you a route from the Chamber.'

Jemhara looked at Thryfe. She had learned that tears when genuinely cried hurt her, so pushed them away. 'He . . .' she said. Then again, 'He.'

'I will carry Highness Thryfe.'

With no effort, the Gargolem did as it had said.

It led her then through the awful Chamber to a spot where there was a narrow door. Had it been there from the start? Jemhara neither knew nor cared.

The Gargolem, bearing Thryfe as easily as the mage himself, two years ago, had borne the dead apprentice Ruxendra, climbed ahead of Jemhara up slopes and flights of steps, in semi-blackness, lighted only by some mysterious occult glow – which was itself perhaps imagined.

Through the last doors and exits they went. They emerged finally on a bank of the River Palest. The snowstorm had ended, and the sun was sinking with hardly any colour. Jemhara did not know if this was the sun of the same day she had gone down into the Insularia, or that of several days later. She did not ask.

In the grey sky the heights of the city sparsely glittered, faded.

Twilight sponged Ru Karismi melancholy blue.

A sleekar stood on the street beyond the ornamental broken lamp-standards, with a team of lashdeer waiting quietly in the shafts. From where had they come? Again, Jemhara did not bother the Gargolem. Instead she asked it, 'Where must I take him?'

'Go to his southern house at Stones.'

'But the house is sealed. I won't have the skill—'

'You have the skill. Think what you have done.'

Jemhara gaped like a small girl told without warning she is now all grown up.

Then, dubiously, she set her attention on the ice-chariot and team. Normally only a strong man could control such a vehicle.

The Gargolem this time presumably read her thought from her body language.

'You will find no problems.'

'The deer—'

'They are swift and obedient. Though you are of light build, and also the car will contain the magus, you have only to trust what I tell you.'

Jemhara said, 'The lessons of the Kraag. Nothing is real, only unreality. So all is achievable.' She had not read theosophical books for nothing.

Surprisingly perhaps, as the Gargolem laid Thryfe down on the mattress within the sleekar it volunteered: 'The Kraag are an elder people, their knowledge cleverly concealed by innocence and a perceived semblance of naivety.'

'I've met none of them.'

'Few persons of Ruk Kar Is ever have.'

Jemhara paused. Her mind on all things else, and yet nervous of the Gargolem, still she inquired, 'Have *you*?'

'I have met them. But I am not human.'

Some bundles of food, carefully wrapped, and three flasks had been secured to the sides of the chariot. Thryfe the Gargolem proceeded to strap down, either for the magician's safety or Jemhara's. Maybe both.

She mounted the sleekar. She took the reins and felt instantly the vast pull, even while static, of the lashdeer against her.

'What is real is unreal,' she said softly. 'What is unreal is real. I am strong enough. We'll run like the wind. Like all the winds that never blew, and lingered to blow now.'

'Highness Jemhara,' said the Gargolem, 'drive well.'

In utter amazement, the young woman craned her neck to stare back at it – for it had accorded her the title only rendered a Magikoy Master.

But the Gargolem was gone. Not a trace. And on the snow-bound street night frost formed, hiding any footprint.

Jemhara glanced at Thryfe. 'Stay sleeping, love. Till you're home.'

She cracked the reins as she had seen so many drivers do. The deer leapt forward. She braced against them, and understood it was possible to her. They were sorcerous probably. But they would do the work.

As two moons emerged from the east, little faint bent bows, and a third one rose an hour or so after, shining big and proud to mock them, the sleekar bounded over the freezing land, away into the western south.

TWO

Curled like an embryo in the womb, that was how he lay.

How else? It was as if he had never been born.

Besides, the wall had taken him in. It had offered itself, a blanched cave, yet smooth and gelatinous in texture. He had crawled inside.

Other creatures were regularly ejected from these walls and bounced alive, clothed and garlanded. *He* went inward, hoping to be expunged – was not.

The tragedy of too vibrant an individual. Some went out like snuffed candles. Some it might take a detonating sun to wipe away.

Curjai, who had been searching for him, found him, the way regions and people could be found in the cities of Hell through *wanting* to find them. Curjai sat down by the wall in which he had detected the coiled form of Vashdran, now like a fossil.

The remaining commanders – all but Behf, who was missing – were grouped in one of the other areas. Heppa was crying because he had seen his own dead face. Swanswine was raging, slamming his fists against the architecture because he had seen not only his own corpse, but himself when living tortured by terrible processes. Heppa's bride, the very young girl, posed meekly nearby. She kept her optimistic serenity even in this extreme. Taeb, who was the wise woman or witch, combed her green hair, her sly eyes cast down. Kuul was mournful. He continually recited bardic poems of the Jafn featuring the death of heroes, one named Star Black, and one strangely titled Kind Heart. Men coped as they could with the fact of death, just as when alive they had had to. Uashtab, city of Hell, was full that day of comparable scenes.

At first Curjai had been transfixed by terror like all of them at sight of his own body. He had told Vash to shove the remnant into the river where the others were going. Then Curjai took himself off. In one of the innumerable halls of Hell he strode round and round, his thoughts labouring over what he had seen, until he had remoulded it into a negotiable form.

For dying did not *count* here. He was dead – and alive. More, Curjai, *Es*curjai to his friends, knew that along with these macabre penalties *he* at least had been favoured and rewarded for his courage and his battles in the living world.

When he came across the others of their band, he patted Kuul on his pale-haired head, slapped Swanswine on the back, kissed Heppa smackingly on the forehead, remarked Behf's absence, drew two flowers from a handy wall – greenish for green-haired Taeb, white for Heppa's patient partner – and went to find Vashdran.

He predicted that Vash, his dead skin not having been hung out with the rest, had been selected for a worse show – worse even than Swanswine's harrowing personal account. Curjai already grasped that Vash had both earned this and also must undergo it. Curjai remembered the smelting of steel for swords. Through fire and water and beating it went, and so was made perfect.

Vashdran was after all a god. That was laughably obvious.

Having discovered Vash there in the wall, Curjai too began to speak a bardic lay of his own people.

'So then says Lalt, bleeding, I have paid enough. Get up then says the other, for only your misapprehension keeps you here.'

Curjai told the story of Lalt, the god-hero of Curjai's native land, the great country of Simisey. How he was conceived when a woman was striking a flint for fire, a boy *ignited* into being in this woman's womb. He told of Lalt's youthful adventures and how, eventually, he went down into the depths of the deadland to rescue his friend and blood-brother Tilan.

The road was so black he tried to light a torch but the torch wouldn't light. 'Lalt exclaims, So dark it is, how shall I see to find my way? And the unlit torch replies, You'll find your way better if you're blind. Because then you'll *have* to.'

Lalt roamed through pits and underpasses of the under-world. Here and there he had to pay a toll – a kiss to a maiden made of bones, a snip of his unshaven beard to a shadow, a cup-ful of his blood to a scaled worm thing that had given him fruit and water.

'At length he comes on his friend, lying on his side in a stupor in a box of stone. Lalt says, Wake up, brother, morning's broken. But Tilan won't wake up. Lazy in death he lies there. Lalt shakes him, spits on him, pulls his hair, insults him – nothing.'

Curjai paused. He waited, and waited, and his eyes were sly at that moment as the untrustworthy eyes of Taeb.

Behind him at last in the wall, a voice, deadly dull, is still asking: 'So what did he do?'

Curjai, his back to the embryo-fossil which had just addressed him, smiled unseen.

You're only a boy, thought Curjai. *Like I was. And you've been told stories before.*

'Well, what can a man do when his brother and the man he loves best among men lies curled in a tomb of his own devis-ing?'

'I don't know.'

'Let me show you, dear heart,' said Curjai, leaping up and dancing round, a sword like a cleaver in his hand, come from nowhere, for this was Hell and inventive. 'Let me *show* you what Lalt did. *He smashed the fucking grave.*'

With a concussion resembling a localized earthquake, the blade stormed through the wall. Particles and slivers of the milky quartzine stuff hurtled through the air; huge chunks met the floor and disintegrated. Out of these unfolded amorphous parts of physiognomies and physiques – elegantly quarter-made ears, toes and eyes, jewels and wisps of clothing.

Vashdran too plummeted out of the wall.

He sat up on the floor, glanced round him and bellowed – at

which the tiny atomies rushed away, even the eyes gliding on miniature unseeable runners.

Curjai stood over him.

'I was born like that,' said Curjai. The cleaving sword was sheathed and gone.

'Out of a wall,' said Vashdran, his eyes, despite the shout, dull as his speaking voice had been and was.

'No, from a struck flint. My mother was barren – five years. The king turned to other women for his sons. Then an ember off the hearth – her gown caught alight. They beat it out – and she was with child. She bore scars on her left ankle and calf, which she showed me after, where the god had caressed her before seeding her. Attajos. I was his son.'

Lionwolf got up. 'Why didn't you leave me be?'

'Does the son of a god leave another son of a god – and both flaming fire gods at that – cribbed up in a wall?'

Vashdran advanced. He flung his arms round Curjai. He held him close for a few seconds, then thrust him away. 'We're done. Now let me alone.'

As Vashdran moved off, Curjai sprang at him like a lion. Both of them crashed down headlong.

'*What did they make you see?*'

'Enough. Get off me.'

'Make me.'

'Oh, it's this again – this never to be ended futile war—'

'*No.* Tell me what they showed you, Vash, these ones here – were you dead?'

Vashdran said, pushing Curjai aside and once more getting to his feet, 'Alive.'

'Torture then? Unspeakable humiliation and pain, just as Swanswine was forced to witness for himself?'

'Alive and upside down in chains.'

'*Where?*'

'Gone now. That red Magikoy witch – she took me – she took – what I had become. You were right about her. She has considerable powers in Hell.'

Curjai too got to his feet. 'And?'

216

'And nothing. Let it go. Let *me* go. I'm over, Curjai, like a book some fool has read and failed to understand.'

'*Es*curjai,' said Curjai. 'Listen. Lalt broke the box of stone and Tilan stumbled out dazed—'

'It's a story.'

'*We* are a story. *You. You*, you say, are a *book*. Listen, Vash. We'll go and—'

'No.' Vashdran looked away through the vistas of Hell. 'The weight of too much is on me and I'm *sick* of myself, I am *poisoned* by what I've been. And still – still – I don't *know* what I am, or how I caused it all, or why I've come down – to *this*.'

Curjai glanced idly at the dismembered wall, back into which ejected atomies were still busily crowding.

'Wine!' he called, imperious.

It seemed he had learned the system here rather well. For out of the same wall at once, in a flurry, were hatched two girls with rounded arms and alabaster vases of booze.

Vashdran stood, thinking nothing, knowing himself lost, staring into a golden cup which had a pattern of jet black snakes, and was full of a rich yellowish wine.

'If you won't hear the tale of Lalt, maybe I'll tell you *my* story. *My* book,' said Curjai.

'You're the son of a fire god.'

'So I was. He made a mistake.'

'Do they? Yes. Perhaps they do. The god who fathered me made a very great mistake.'

Curjai raised his goblet and drank. Vashdran copied him. The wine was good, as always.

They began to walk, slowly, as if just getting the knack of walking, along the hall, through an arch into another hall, through another arch and on.

'My father was a king,' said Curjai, 'by which I mean the husband of my mother. He had seventeen sons when I was delivered, the gift of Attajos, into the royal bed. Out I came, and my mother – she heard a silence. And then she heard one of her women give a wavering squeal. I know. My mother told me this.'

'Such a remarkable baby,' said Vashdran, 'too beautiful to keep quiet over.'

'Ah.'

Still walking, Vashdran looked aside at Curjai. Handsome and fine, he paced at Vashdran's side, smiling even now a very little.

'I was a monster.'

They walked.

The story of Curjai exerted its fascination over Vashdran. Gaps appeared in his agony of ego-absorbed pessimism.

He resisted, attempting to preserve a firm hold on his misery – but kept mislaying it, amnesiac for seconds at a time of self.

And Curjai read aloud from his book.

Simisey began at a sea as usual frozen for miles, and went inland in hilly snowfields that everywhere were uplifted into cliffs. Ice-forest clung on the sides, flashing like zircons when the winds funnelled through defiles.

A dark-haired, tawny people, the Simese wedged their villages and towns in the snow rockery of the land, and rode over the terrain in sleds and chariots drawn by tall sheep-like long-necked beasts thatched in brown pelt, whose backs also went up like a small mountain, or a pair of them. The capital was at Padgish, and here Curjai's nominative father ruled as king, as his own father and grandfather had ruled before him. The palace was built of whole tree trunks, and throughout they stood like pillars to hold up the roofs of latticed stone. Curjai's earliest memories, after his mother, were of these towering pitted black columns, and of the enormous pawed feet of the hump-backed dromazi. Later he saw the horses kept in the royal yard. Sometimes they were ridden, usually in war, or when hunting deer and snow-tigers.

Curjai yearned after the horses, their care, their riding, as he longed to see the battle banners and hear the accounts of fights with marauding neighbours from land and sea.

Placed on his colourfully woven rug before the courtyard

door, he watched everything, all eyes, yearning and longing, and soon sad.

He had learned swiftly, perhaps by the age of three, none of that could ever be for him, though he was the legal son of a king by his foremost queen, and through fire the son of Attajos the god.

Curjai had been born this way. Both his legs ended at the knee, his right arm at the elbow. His short left arm was equipped with a hand, with one finger and a thumb – a blessing, some crone of the house had remarked in his earshot, for otherwise surely he must have been destroyed like a deformed kitten. Curjai knew these facets of himself familiarly. However, he had never seen inside a mirror, though his mother, being royal, had one of silvered glass. In the end, inevitably, Curjai did see himself, by an accident of his mother's women, probably not malign, for by then they were quite fond of him.

His face was no face. It was the rudiments of a face before features had been carefully applied. He possessed an apparatus to breathe through, if with a degree of difficulty. His mouth was shapeless, and had a limited selection of long teeth – just enough to eat with. Ears he did not have. Only his eyes were there, one rather cloudy, and both of a colour that was too pale, like dilute beer. He had been dressed sumptuously as befitted his rank. Otherwise he had not a single hair on him. At that hour of the mirror he was about six, and he floundered away, afraid. He did not know, until people came running and he saw their reflections too, it was *himself* he had been shocked by.

'Break the mirror.'

His mother said this.

'But lady – it's of *glass*—'

'Break it! In a millon pieces.'

The mirror was broken. Something broke also in Curjai. He did not reveal any evidence of it. How could he, when all he was must be taken now for evidence of *prenatal* breakage.

Though he still loved and yearned after the glory of the warriors, he had long ago given up the dream of becoming a man.

Now he began to notice the birds. If he had *been* a bird, the child reasoned, his physical deficiencies would not so limit him. The abbreviated arm and hand would be incorporated in wings and bear him up. And he would need then no legs, for he thought had he been a bird, he would never have come back to earth.

In the palace they were all tender enough to him. They liked him. They made sure he heard the stories and the songs and legends of Padgish and Simisey, and was instructed, to a certain extent, in the role and duties of male royalty.

One day a favourite warrior brought him a small carved bow – not to be learned on, of course, merely to have – and he cried out with joy at seeing it. That very afternoon Curjai, who had no external ears but heard too well without them, detected the voice of this warrior, laughing and saying over the courtyard wall, 'But Curjai can't live, can he, not for long? A blessing' – that word again – 'for the King.'

Curjai could crawl on his stumps if he had to. He put the bow, which he had been nursing, under a loose tile in the main room of his mother's apartments. He did not want to hurt the bow; it was not its fault. That was the year he was thirteen. Also it was the year he was to bless his father the King by dying.

Many caught the fever. It was nothing much; even the old mostly recovered.

Curjai was watching the birds sailing over the world of the sky when he felt the first intimation of it. It astounded him, for suddenly he found he no longer cared about the birds, and he could not think why not.

They carried him to his pallet and he thought that was all he wanted. But the pallet could not make him comfortable. Then his mother arrived. She picked him up, able to because he was so small and so much of him not physically present, and bore him to her bed. She got in with him and held him, and spooned liquid water into his mouth when he sobbed for drink.

Her hair was tan, between brown and red. His sharp ears had heard the King wed her for her hair. Fire in her hair, Curjai thought. She talked too of fire.

'You can't be sick much longer,' she tutored him, sensibly, 'you are my only son. You're the son of the fire. Look, see where he kissed me, Attajos, before he made you in my body.' That was when she showed him the scars on her ankle and her lower leg. It struck him chaotically in the spinning of the fever that perhaps the god had withheld his own legs for that very cause. But why both legs, and also an arm, fingers, ears and nose? His mother had not been burned there.

In the end agony infused Curjai. He knew nothing much of that time. Only her tears on his face, her rocking arms. By then both of them lay on a straw mattress at the will of the physician. He heard it rustle through all his tumult. A straw death, the death of illness and weakness any warrior shunned.

The king's mages never visited the room.

The clan shaman came in near dawn. Curjai was having his last lucid moment.

Curjai's mother spoke to the holy man.

'Is this all? Why are the gods so wicked?'

'Tainted by us, lady. It goes up, our muck, with the offering smokes.'

'Then all's hopeless.'

'He,' said the shaman, staring at Curjai with an old hot gaze, 'death will be the gate for *him*. Don't hold him back. You wouldn't from a war.'

'Death . . .' she said.

Death, Curjai heard, over and over in his scrambled brain.

But then the shaman's litany entered there.

'Don't be afraid. You've fought all your life, harder than any warrior, to stay in this world. How else could you have done it thirteen years? In the Afterlife you'll find the warrior's haven. I see it, and will mark it on a scroll.'

The sun rose, and Curjai died. The last he had of earth was the savage threnody of his mother, tugging on him, still trying to keep him with her. Then dark. Then light. Then – this.

'I woke up here a man, formed and complete, as you see. A dazzling figure. I'm quite enamoured of myself, Vash, I can tell you. And here I fight as a warrior and I win. And death and sickness are nothing. Even seeing the death of this man I had also become. What died? Only my reflection again in my mother's mirror. But I was a boy. As were you? Perhaps. And now I have everything I longed for, including, when I like, wings made from shields. Oh, Vash, pardon me, but this Hell – it isn't Hell for me. This is my Heaven.'

Today the blue sun was roped by blue cirrus. Ruxendra flew beneath, intransigently holding Vashdran's other self.

When night had come yesterday she alighted with her burden on a block of stone, one of many in a shingled valley by one of the lakes of pointless white fire. She sat there all night, watching him. He did not try to get away. But then, she had nearly drained him of blood – not drinking it, she would not wish to, merely letting it out of him through bites, and stabs she gave him with a paring knife. The knife belonged on an attirement table of her mother's and was used for cleaning the nails. Ruxendra had not seen it since she went to the Insularia, yet here in Hell she found it usefully fastened in her sleeve.

The moment she was dead, Ruxendra had begun to travel. She had come to herself in fact walking firmly along a wide paved road, like those in the city of Ru Karismi, save there were no buildings to be seen, and no funeral pyres.

She was glad she felt better, and clear-headed, but rather uneasy after all knowing she was dead.

On either side of the road stretched something she had never beheld in her life. A kind of grass or grain was growing in vast quantities, very pallid and feathery, and running away to left and right and behind and in front for miles, she thought, towards horizons of swag-bellied cloud. There was slight colour to anything and this had disturbed Ruxendra too, but after a while a change came over things. The sky soaked bluer and the grass-grain of every steader's wish-fulfilment, the subject of many homilies on the delights of the next world, more greenish.

She was glad to be alone. But as the miles went on she did

not like to be totally alone. After that sometimes she glimpsed peasants working in the fields, and a few birds flew overhead. In the end, no doubt because she felt the day had lasted too long, a sunset happened, scald-red. Any stars? Yes, out they trooped, even some in constellations that she knew.

But this was not Ruk Kar Is. This was not the world. And during the next day, which started with a sunrise gaudy as trumpet blasts, Ruxendra found she distrusted the landscape. At which, in soft blurrings, it melted away.

She lost her bearings rather after this. There seemed to be smogs and twilights, and sometimes rivers she journeyed on, raft-borne and solitary, or in a type of half-seen company. She seemed sleepy, dull, no longer unnerved. That all these incoherences might be due to her own lack of flexibility never occurred to her. Besides, her purpose stayed fixed. It shut off other elements from her, whatever they were or might be. She wanted to seek the god-demon Vashdran who had ended her world. She thought he too was dead, was sure he was – she had been given some reason to think so. But what area did half-gods frequent in death? Hell, it would seem.

So Ruxendra was convinced she travelled towards Hell, and thus with time – or perhaps without it – she identified the deadly, wide lands she traversed as outposts of nastier confines – those he would be consigned to.

Like Lalt of Simisey, had she but guessed, Ruxendra was now presented with myth and story challenges. A herd of large grey animals stampeded towards her through the mist – bossy brave little girl, she halted them with a loud shout and Magikoy symbols summoned from the air. A table lay before her, set with tempting food, fruit and pastries, and she spurned them and then saw they were only cleverly painted stones. A liquid sea appeared across the land, impassable, but Ruxendra sang out a Magikoy sentence and the sea froze over and she walked across it.

She had always wanted power. Not power to harm, it was true, power to do good. But she was opinionated and had died too young. All these tests of her seemed to spring from her own unconscious mind, but her soul, if such it was, revelled in them, making up for what it had never had the space to do on earth.

If she had outlined her adventures while travelling, Ruxendra would have embroidered, but factually she forgot much of them or never really saw or attended to them. *I travelled for years*, she would, and virtually had, said. *I was offered this or that and I turned away from all, wanting only one reward.*

At last she found herself on another night sea, riding another raft with a sail, one of the contingent of undead 'brides' blown towards the shore of Shabatu.

That someone had chosen her and so saved her from the fate of most of the other women, abruptly engulfed by some ghastly mechanism of the deep, Ruxendra did not guess. The experience left her shaken, but already she had spotted Vashdran on the shore. She knew him solely from description. None of the fully fledged Magikoy had ever been able properly to coax his image in an oculum. But the city had been flooded by second-hand reports: his burning hair, his eyes blue as sapphire that turned red as ruby during battle.

His beauty left Ruxendra, rather than unmoved, more angry. The beauty of the other one – Curjai – enraged her too.

By her remaining and mostly Hell-augmented astral powers, Ruxendra determined some link, closer than brotherhood or loverhood, between shadowy Curjai and fiery Vashdran.

So she would damage both of them. But Vashdran *first*.

Over the battle-mad men in Hell she knew how to exert fascination. In life she had always been able to tame men, other than the abstemious and studious Magikoy Masters. Her father had been the proverbial putty in her hands, her brothers too. As for the apprentices, one had thrown himself out of a high window at the lack of her returned affection. He lived but was banished from the Insularia. Ruxendra did not even remember him. But in Hell she had more than girlish charm to her armoury. She had the stature of a talented witch. It was no longer necessary to flirt or flatter. Now she could put her foot down. Down it went.

Despite what she had said, Ruxendra had asked no one's permission to abscond with Vashdran's double. She had not frankly thought she need apply to anyone, for once more most of the beings here seemed misty, not quite real – yes, even the warriors she had goaded and entranced.

All the success, bubbling in the cauldron of her hatred, boiled over in a paroxysm.

When she sank her teeth and claws in Vashdran the Lionwolf, and soared with him on her scarlet wings – leaving him also abject and shatter-spirited below – Ruxendra reached the highest peak. It was not however as high as she had anticipated. It was a little less.

And all this after, this flying about, was not so wonderful either. She meant to secure some fastness here, and to take him there for her – what else – *pleasure*. But a sort of tiredness was coming on.

He did not respond as she had wanted, *neither* of him.

Under blue sun and blue cirrus, Ruxendra quartered the sky and eventually flapped eastward. Some mountains had appeared, amazingly high, with cloud wreaths round their pinnacles and actual snow flaming white.

When she threw him across the flank of one of these heights, Ruxendra decided she must build there a tower. That should be easy. It was.

She drew it up out of the rock with the snow still glinting on its shoulders. It was rough-hewn; her abilities did not stretch to those of the artisan. Lopsided even, slightly, the tower, with unmatching windows of too-excellent shape, and stained glass in them because of the casements she recalled from home.

He lay as if dead. But he *was* dead, so had nowhere else to go.

Except of course the mirror images of the men had died, completely, all but this one. Really though, it was *not* this one who truly concerned her. He was her hostage, and hurting him was more demonstration than achievement. It was the *other* she wanted, the original, Vashdran. Would he follow her captive? He must.

Inside, the tower had no stairs. It hardly inconvenienced winged Ruxendra.

She lugged her plaything up into the head of the tower with the artistic windows, created a floor of transparent vitreous, and dropped him on it, thump.

The Lionwolf Vashdran looked at her. Had this mirror-man ever spoken? No. He shed blood, that was all.

'Speak to me,' said Ruxendra, 'or I shall increase your suffering.'

'What,' he said, 'shall I say?'

Ruxendra grimaced. She settled on a spur of un-smoothed rock above him. 'Say what you are.'

'Lionwolf.'

'*Vashdran*. Can you die?'

'That is all I can do.'

The sun was moving over. Bars of shadow drifted from the windows, dark viridian and magenta.

'What do you mean? I won't kill you – not yet. You have some worth.'

'My worth is my death.'

'I'll harm you instantly if you persist in your silliness.'

No reply.

Ruxendra turned and gazed through the coloured glass. She sighed. A tiny figment of her plucked at her heart, whispering it wanted to be five years old now and tucked up in bed with its doll, and Mother and the slave girl bringing hot milk with cinnamon, and only nice things in the morning. Only nice straightforward things.

They had come to the black river. Neither meant to, or thought he meant to.

The feasthall was gone, the tables with their streams were removed or dissolved. Two or three torches burned, their light less hard.

Vashdran and Curjai stood on the bank, and saw one more curious sight. The stone King of Death was stationed there farther along, with a pack of six dogs bounding round him, sometimes feeding them morsels of what seemed to be only meat.

King Death was as ever bald stone with cracks and lines running up through his bluish-greyishness. Then he looked over, and he smiled. The stone moved, ponderous yet willing, about his mouth.

'Approach,' said the King of Hell.

Curjai and Vashdran exchanged a look. They walked towards the King.

As they went, the six jatchas came flying at them, their pack from Shabatu – Star-Dog and Atjosa, the hounds of Behf, Swanswine and Kuul, and Heppa's preposterously happy Bony.

Frisking, they thoroughly licked the hands of the two men. Like dogs, like dogs.

'Do you see—' Curjai was awed.

'I see. Where their eyes should have been.'

'Something – *is*.'

From slits in their jatcha hide, the gleaming beginnings of bright dog eyes looked up at Curjai and at Vashdran.

But the King was waiting. Best not to annoy, going on previous occasions, especially as he continued to smile. He loomed over them. He was not a man. Had he ever been?

He read their minds.

'No,' he said, in his voice of a thousand voices. 'I am Hell. I am the cause of all you see.'

Neither man understood him.

Vashdran said, 'Forgive us, lord King.'

'That is over,' said the King. 'You have learned how to be humble, if not humility itself. You have learned fear, but not how to deal with it.'

'You are wise, lord King.'

'And to flatter very poorly. You must do better, Lionwolf, son of Zzth.'

The King placed himself between them and let down his heavy stony hands like lead weights on their shoulders. He was like a regal yet amenable father with sons, and all round ran the family dogs, winking new eyes and wagging tails.

'Your men, the other Saraskulds, are approaching this chamber. Some of your bride-wives are with them, those who play a part in this. But not Ruxendra, who is ahead of you.'

'Another war?' Vashdran asked tonelessly. 'Another combat in a stadionum?'

'To your kind, so much is war and combat and a stadium. But you will go after the red witch. I believe you have discussed it.'

'Sir,' said Curjai, 'heroes go to rescue their friends. Sometimes even their enemies.'

'And which of those is the Lionwolf to Vashdran?' asked the King.

Vashdran said, incongruous, 'I never said I'll go.'

Just then Heppa, Swanswine and Kuul appeared along the bank. Behf had turned up too and come with them, solemnly downcast. All four men fell prudently on their knees to the King. But their own dogs rushed at them. Heppa was the first to give in. 'Bony! Bony! You bad hound!' In the background stood Taeb and Heppa's bride, but none of the other numerous women the men had accumulated.

And Winsome? Vashdran dismissed the question from his mind. He believed he was done with her. She had seen, while Ruxendra taunted and the body hung in its chains and the boulder of thought crashed through the floor. That time, he had barely noticed Winsome. She was not real, not in this place. If she had ever been.

Yet she had said she was the well-spring of one facet of the power of the stone King . . . had she? She alone could call the moon, or light the cities.

'Yes, come forward,' said the King, over their head.

Vashdran saw Taeb was creeping up, suspiciously timid.

She did not speak but pointed at Vashdran's forearm. He glanced, having forgotten the words written there in Ruxendra's saliva, and used to the gnawing scorch of them. *I am the payment.*

228

'Let me take her curse off you,' said Taeb.

Vashdran held out the arm to her – and looked away as if afraid. He did not reckon she could do it.

But Taeb bent over his arm and he felt her cat's tongue rough on his skin, licking up the words.

'It's gone, Vash,' Curjai said.

Vashdran looked back. The words were no longer on him. Instead he glimpsed Taeb's tongue glinting with them. She spat them out three times on the floor, where they shone and dried to nothing.

'I have magic to match hers,' said Taeb.

The stone King had withdrawn, as before. Either he had disappeared, or curiously melded with the cavernous hall. Perhaps that was him still, standing there – that man-like looming stone among stones. Or there? Or . . . there?

The others were all gathering round Vashdran, seeming more cheerful now, telling him they must get ready for the journey, acting out again this semblance of mortal life, or heroic legend.

Something came to Vashdran's attention, jolting him, *astonishing* him.

The little malt-haired wife of Heppa was also before him, her hands folded. They, and the woven girdle, had lifted at her waist over her swollen stomach.

'Heppa—'

Heppa grinned, proud. 'Credit he that says this. What you see is true. She's got my brat cooking in her oven there.' It was the first time Vashdran had heard him talk even partially in the vernacular of the Vormland.

Vashdran's eyes travelled to the demure face of Heppa's wife.

Heppa said, 'We heard it can happen here. Some other woman, got with child she was. I – never managed it – in the world. Who'd think it, eh, Vash?'

Indeed, who would think it, pregnancy here among the legions of the dead and damned.

THREE

Leaders and warriors, when dead, they burned. Long in the past enamoured wives had sometimes climbed up on the pyre to die too. Otherwise men and women of ordinary rank were buried under the nearer mountains in the snow. Children were buried there, too. It was always thought best to discourage the attendance of parents and friends, so that the death itself might be forgotten, only the *life* recalled. And with this in mind, mourners were not encouraged to tend towards the graveyard, once the snow was pushed back over a mound. Nor were the mounds marked in any way. In fact the graveyard seldom looked like what it was, the one or two fresh graves soon snowed under. But there had been clear freezing weather, and so many dead, almost a hundred and fifty of them. Large mounds and small ones were picked out like diligent sculptings from the ice, there under the frowning embankments of the mountains with their white combers. Despite this, the burial place was deliberately many miles inland. Who anyway could find the time?

Two did.

The mother with her incinerated hair shorn to stubble, and the lioness-goddess Saftri.

There had been no jealousy before. Horribly now there *was*, a little, fermented from grief. '*He* was her favourite.' 'She never though saved that boy.' 'Carries her, she does. To make fast the going.'

Saftri did carry the mother of Best Bear, otherwise it would have been a distended and impossible trek. Saftri had been

230

carried through the air by Guri, and she politely asked the mother initially if to air-carry her was acceptable. It was. They did it out of sight of the village, but some saw. Some always see what is not meant for them. It is a law.

Yet Saftri had ultimately saved the village, perhaps all Vormland, from the fire wolf who unseamed the sky. In the end, they were dumb about these grave visits.

Saftri-Saphay sat on the ice of the graveyard facing Best Bear's mother.

In the beginning, the mother had asked if the goddess might raise Best Bear from the dead.

This had petrified Saftri. She was an inexperienced deity still, doubted such an act was in her range, and feared it besides, for in what state would the poor child emerge?

'No,' she had answered. The woman accepted this with a stricken quietness. 'I might however draw out your hair and grow new for you—'

'No, no. Let it be as it is. If you allow.'

By now they only came and sat here, or sometimes wandered around, staring at other identical graves, the mother trying to recollect whose they had been.

There was no longer any purpose in coming here. Neither Best Bear's mother nor the goddess believed he was in the graveyard. He was in Paradise, or in the sky, somewhere delightful with an improved climate.

'Is there warmth there?'

'Once I glimpsed a land of warmth,' Saftri said. 'Golden trees and mountains.' But she suspected that geography had something to do with Zeth.

What had become of *him*? Had she definitely vanquished him? After her seizure of power and vainglory, when she had beaten him, as much as was feasible among gods, to a pulp, Saftri entertained a couple of doubts. Suppose he recovered and returned? Would he always be doing this? There would be no Vormland left . . .

A plan had commenced then, within her mind. She had not yet voiced it and, for a plan, it had actually undergone little planning.

Saftri heard Best Bear's mother give a sound like cold water falling on a hot stone, and turned her head sharply to stare in the same direction.

About twelve feet away a male figure sat, as they did, on a grave mound. But *his* mound had taken on a shape which was like an ice-carving of a huge cat. He had come from nowhere.

'*You.*' Saftri's tone struck neatly between alarm and disgust.

'I.'

Best Bear's mother, no fool, had got on to her knees and, fists to forehead, was bowing over and over down on the ice.

Saftri ignored her.

'What do you want, Yyrot?'

The god, second of Saftri-Saphay's birth-given pantheon, was just as she recalled, greyly smooth of skin, exactly like the dog he sometimes turned into, black-haired and rimed by icicles. He wore an inelastic agate robe that resembled a sheet of permafrost. This was not his angry side, in which he laughed and gave off heat. No, he was in a benign state of mind, and loaded the chill atmosphere with planks of extra coldness.

'I have not visited you, Saphay, since you lived among the ripe wheat inside my icebergs. You will be pleased to know your cat is well, has grown to a large size, and also borne me, or my canine aspect, thirteen children.'

'*Stop* it,' Saftri snapped at the bowing woman. 'My cat can do as she likes. Her repulsive offspring I saw when I was enmeshed in another's dream.'

'Just before,' Yyrot tactlessly went on, 'the great whale got hold of you and flung you to your second death in a freezing sea.'

Haughty, Saftri said, 'Death is an experience you have missed.'

'If you say so. For yourself it was necessary as a fixative. It sloughed off the last of your untidy mortal crumbs, and let you become what I, simply by my attention, had taught you to become, a goddess. *He* did not realize. Zeth. Curious, if he is supposed to be one with me and I with him. But then there is Ddir, maundering about in the sky. He too is supposed to be part of both Zeth and myself, but who can make head or tail of his doings? Have you seen his latest effort? An artistic cunt of two hundred lighted stars. Curious also.'

Yyrot did not look as if he were curious. He only sat there as if trapped by courteous manners at some lacklustre function. Best Bear's mother had given over her genuflecting, but stayed face down before him. Saftri stood up.

'Zeth I chastised.'

'Yes, the ether rang with the blows. But he too is now up and about again.'

Saftri, despite all resolve, whitened.

'What does he mean to do?'

'Oh, some bad-tempered thing.'

'Let him come back,' blustered Saftri. 'The snow by my door still shows the sludgy unwisdom of his last visit. I'll hang him upside down next from one of the ice-trees on the bluff.'

When she said this, pictured it, Saftri felt move inside her a sickening quake of the heart. She did not know why. Did she still fancy Zeth Zezeth? The image of a man, glorious yet almost extinguished, hung up in that old Rukarian fashion of which a chattering court had once told her . . .

Saftri shook off the pang.

But it was Best Bear's mother who sat up and said to Yyrot, 'Exalted sky-one, do you know how my son does?'

'Your son? Oh. He is dead.'

Saftri flinched. The mother did not. She anticipated, as Saftri saw, nothing better of gods, even in the light of Saftri's patronizing kindness.

However, the woman explained, 'Exalted, I mean *after* death?'

Yyrot now stood up. How odd. The mound he had sat on, which had taken first the form of a cat – Saphay's? – had surreptitiously altered to the outline of a horned whale. Doubly insulting. But she too, Saftri concluded, expected nothing better of gods.

'Mortals have a spirit creature inside them,' announced Yyrot, waves of refrigeration beaming about his lecture. 'They always persist, somewhere. Only deities are immortal and therefore finally burn out like suns.'

If the mother understood him at all, still she said and did nothing more, lowering her eyes and her head meekly.

Saftri crossed to her and pulled her on to her feet quite roughly. 'We must be going. It'll be dark as the inside of a piss-pot in an hour.'

As she spoke, some supernatural aptitude of her ears brought her the far-off ringing of the iron gong above the harbour.

A warning?

Had the fiend Zeth already returned?

Yyrot was standing, scanning the mountains, intrigued per-haps by potential glaciers. Above the sky was indeed clamming up towards night.

Saftri lifted herself and the mother of Best Bear into the air about twenty feet over the god's head.

He observed them idly.

Saftri shouted back over her shoulder, 'Tell my cat she is a slut!'

But Yyrot, Winter's Lover, had already vanished from the spot.

Miles out, miles off, the indigo soup of sea depths was brushed vividly aside. The mobile fish that lived there swarmed like bees from the way of a comet. Those frozen to objects in clouds of ice stared indifferently, lit to gold, fading back to iron.

Zeth Zezeth passed.

He was Sun Wolf, and Sun Beneath the Sea. According to the unwieldy legend, the hot sun of former millennia submerged there and left the world to a ghost sun, an impostor that gave insufficient incandescence and so started five centuries of winter. Maybe this fable was true, but more likely it was not. It was the same sun up there, itself burning out as Yyrot had predicted for his own fellowship of gods. And if Zeth had ever been the sun's prince, or its cipher, this did not really now show on him or in his deeds. He was soulless as only his kind could be. An intelligent and brilliant moron, clothed in beauty and unreasonable power.

As he sped along he was aware, vaguely, of others who worshipped him – all were Rukarian, of course. Since three gods were given to everyone born in the central Ruk, Zeth had often been dispensed along with two others, in those cases *not* Yyrot or Ddir. Zeth had been, for example, one of King Sallusdon's gods, in company with Preht and Yuvis. If he cared to, Zeth could manifest to all and any worshippers even while he was doing other things. Gods could be, naturally, not only in two but in myriad places at once.

Now his main focus was on the lump of matter cruising ahead.

Brightshade, giant of the deep, felt the first intimation of his father in a sizzling sting across his skin and brain.

It revolved him, sending him crashing into undersea floes, breaking columns and drifts of ice, the water bubbling bright blue.

When he recovered, Brightshade settled to the floor of a trench. Here he lay, waiting.

He, this leviathan, was apprehensive.

Zeth shot by him, gilding darkness, and dazzled before Brightshade's right eye.

'Imbecile! Why do you dawdle? I showed you where to go. Months you take over it. I should smash you in pieces, split you, you stinking malformation.'

There was in Brightshade's vocabulary of mind-*shapes* no word for sorry. Now he coined one and produced it copiously.

'Silence, drek. You will speed yourself up. Leave off this fornicating and skirmishing. You have enough to do, as I told you, when you reach that scab on the sea called Vorm.'

Brightshade stiffly grovelled. In *shapes*.

Which stung him afresh. He was not used to it.

And too he had always been perfect. No reprimand, let alone insult, had come his way.

Zeth viciously smote him again before spearing off into the ink blots of night-falling ocean.

Brightshade lay on the floor of the trench, blinking at prehistoric evidence ancient as his planet's babyhood. It had no allure for him.

Shape-thought occupied the whale. He seethed with resentment and never-before-known fear.

The gong had been ringing on the headland to signal the return, not of Zeth, but of the jalees of Krandif and his men.

They had been gone months. Now, both Mother Ships and long vessels laden with cargoes, the warriors came back, buoyant with success and tales of fights and reiver scams and cities and torrid homesickness – to find the leftovers of the burnt village, a charred stump above a harbour devoid of any other shipping.

A thick groan had risen out on the water when they saw. They believed the Faz or Kelps, always uneasy neighbours, had visited.

Krandif leapt ashore.

He seized Majord, Saftri's bard-priest, by the arms. 'What went on here?'

Majord told him the horror story in ten or so poetic sentences.

By then all the men were off and on the shore. The shamans were ranging from the Mother Ships, the horsazin, noticing nothing changed, splashing in the sea.

'Did Best Bear die?' Krandif sensitively asked. He was not considering the boy's mother.

'Yes. Neck-broken. Laid to rest by the mountains now. She goes there nearly every day.'

Mozdif came up, with a wonder walking grave and dead tired beside him.

Krandif squared his square muscular shoulders.

'Moz! Ah. Here is one. Let her see this.'

Majord had already been gaping. Now he made over himself an antique religious wave.

'He's been a talisman for us,' went on Krandif, encircling the figure of wonder with one arm, possessive and supportive. 'He gave himself in exchange for his father, a Jafn chief. We let the man live and brought the boy with us. He's not more than six, but speaks often like a warrior of eighteen. And when sharks came, what to do he told us. We *sang* to them, soft, and they went to sleep and sank away.'

'But – what is he? Not human? What's he made out of? Midnight?'

Krandif smiled. 'A hero he is. A Jafn hero. But now he's ours. And *she*' – he raised his hand to salute the god-house up the hill – 'he's for her. I dreamed of it. And if her favourite's dead—'

'Best Bear. Yes.'

'Best Bear was fine as silk, but only a boy.'

Majord looked down at the midnight child.

Calm sad eyes looked back. But Majord could not see the human sorrow for the marvel.

'By what name?'

The boy spoke, in faultless dialectic Vormish. 'This one is Dayadin, son of Arok, Chaiord of the Jafn Holas.'

Having established the village was not under attack, Saftri landed behind the hill. She and the mother of Best Bear walked home.

Krandif's jalees had voyaged in, only one vessel missing, leaving twenty-six long ships and two Mother Ships, and besides just a handful of men lost. Saftri was glad. Her unplanned plan was firming up and becoming promising.

They would need more ships. But messengers could now be sent across the Vormland and to outlying islands. Before, no one could be spared.

Saftri walked up the hill to her temple with shells on the

walls and candles on the altar. Night was down by now, moon-
less for another hour at least and very dark.

Hearing boots crunch on the snow behind her, she turned in
the doorway.

There were Krandif and Mozdif, and Jord and Majord and
the other seven of her priests.

With exasperation she assumed they all wanted congratula-
tions.

Then she saw the night had become a child and waited on
the path about ten paces from her.

Saftri was amazed. Only her own Lionwolf had been so
extraordinary, so flawless. She did not see that even her
Lionwolf had not possessed some elusive quality that this one
had.

'Our Lady, *look*.'

'Our Lady, he was brought for you.'

'He is Dayadin of the Jafn. He is like the star we saw which
fell – that fell here and killed so many – but altered to gentle
darkness.'

'From sharks he saved us all.'

'From a storm, from that he saved us, saying how we should
breathe and then the wind would breathe as we did – and the
wind did breathe that way and the sea was flat. Flat as this hand
of him that says it.'

Saftri looked on at the boy.

Star Black.

She knew the legend. It was one of the first Jafn myths she
ever heard from her husband Athluan, who had drawn her
from the iceberg.

'Why do you call the hero Star Black?' she had lamely asked.

'His hair and skin were black as coal.'

'Are you a phantom?' she demanded of the child.

'No. I am Dayadin, son of Arok.'

Arok . . . that name too seemed familiar to her.

'You were stolen,' she said. Something shifted in her. She did
not, after all this while, know what.

The men were thrusting him forward, and he obeyed them,

plainly not afraid, only worn out and steeped in emptiness. He would not waste himself on protest.

Saftri watched.

She did not think what she made of this.

Then the men had ebbed away from the hill and she and the child were there by the doorway, against the wall of shells, where she had pulverized Zeth.

'You're Saftri,' said the child, 'a goddess of these people.'

'They shouldn't have brought you here. You're nothing to me. My son died. They think you can make that up to me?'

'They're stupid,' he said. But without either rancour or aggression. Stupidity was just a fact. 'My mother,' he said, 'she'll cry. No one can make *me* up to *her.*'

Saftri glanced and lit the candles in the temple by a blink, not even a breath. She was improving.

'Go down to the village,' she said. 'There are lots of women there who are without their sons.'

The child frowned at her.

He said, 'My mother hasn't a hair's breadth of your goddessness. But she's more a queen than you.'

This was not said with a child's rudeness. It was an adult footnote, and it went through Saftri like a lash.

She would have struck him, but he was too small. Six? He was not so old. She could sense he was not. Yet he spoke, as they said, like a young man.

'I have no concern with your mother.'

'No.'

'And I don't want you. Go to the village.'

'Send me back then,' said the boy simply, 'send me back to my father.'

'You are impudent and our – their – prisoner. And your tongue is too sharp. You're cruel, as he was.'

'Who was cruel?'

To her own distress she seemed to have no control of her words, which spilled out, and now tears ran from her eyes. Unlike the fire-tears of the battle, these were only water, symptoms of femaleness and lack of choice.

'My son,' she said.

She turned from the child who was Dayadin, or Star Black, and marched into the shrine.

She recaptured, not wishing to, in a tidal wave, Lionwolf, his colours of fire and sky, flying through the snow-forest and the costive village of Ranjalla, waking everything. She saw him in firelight in Nabnish's chimney of a house, leaning on her, smiling, as she told him stories. In ten years he became a man.

'How shall I live,' she had cried, *'if you leave me—'*

The shame of her words. Her shame. Her love.

'Go then. What are you to me . . . To leave me here . . .'

And leave her he did. He left her to the mercy of the cold world and ignorant men, and the skittishness of gods, and to her own cracked heart.

My son. Who is dead. My son.

'Don't cry,' said the child in the doorway. 'My mother will cry because of me. But you don't have to cry.'

Saftri moved into the dark beyond the candles, weeping. Only when she heard the child begin to cry too was she riven out of herself. Her first instinct was go to him. A second instinct intervened, more harsh and practical. Grief had spurred her mind. She smeared the wet from her face, and being now a goddess was instantly pristine and ready for new action.

FOUR

Sometimes they flew, or levitated. Sometimes they ran. The dogs would not go up in the sky, but bounded below, or alongside on the ground, barking now and then as if to say, 'See, we're *dogs!*' The two women strolled. All the men but Curjai and Kuul had been disapproving. Heppa's girl was in the family way, and chariots were so easy to come by here. But she did not like, the girl, who was named Wasfa, Hell's animals, except the dogs who were now so dog-like. She preferred therefore to walk. And after all, like all the rest, Taeb and she could travel in the air if they wished to rest their feet.

The Red Witch who had abducted Vashdran's mirror-body had flown generally east of Uashtab by the sun. They could see her sky-trail, fading only slowly, like a rusty scratch.

As always, the armour had fallen from them, not being appropriate. They wore random clothing of many lands and styles, formed by thought.

Night was the time they really talked to each other; as they sat unsleeping under the underlit stars, and the narrow new eyes of the jatchas glinted in firelight. And then conversation or monologue was always of home. That was, of life, who and what they had been and done. Curjai did not say much about this. Vashdran said nothing.

Kuul praised his wife Jasibbi. He said neither of the brides he took here had matched up to her, and seeing his lack of affection they had both carelessly wandered off. Swanswine knew no ordinary woman was worth a woman of Olchibe. Heppa, resuming their speech patterns, talked of the Vorm Isles, the mountains and sea voyaging, mentioning no woman of any kind. Behf's provenance remained unclear, though his community seemed to have been of a fisher-warrior sort. He muttered *only* of women. The current two, Wasfa and Taeb, waited on the men and did not reminisce. Both already knew how to summon food from the earth. Wasfa did not object to the pale shoots that sprang out, or the loaves of bread from stones. Joints of meat would come too, but those bloody and convincing dinners Wasfa did not touch, and neither would Taeb eat them, even after roasting them on witch-invented fires. 'Some food always comes out of the ground,' Wasfa said. 'But not ready-butchered dead animals.'

Taeb called water, wine or beer from the sky. That was probably only her sense of theatre; it could have come from anywhere. It poured into a big round cup made out of the ground of Hell, and they would scoop off goblets-full, and later the goblets, cast aside, would return to shards.

Some nights Wasfa began to tell stories: heroes, deeds, riches.

They liked this. Even Vashdran liked it, though it pierced him to the quick. He had always felt isolated, as indeed he was, but never so much as now.

He began to wonder, as perhaps he already had, if any of the others were real or only more inventions of Hell. All but Curjai. Curjai was real enough.

Curjai had suffered in the world where Lionwolf had flourished. Now in Hell Lionwolf-Vashdran suffered and Curjai found Heaven. Vashdran hated Curjai. Or loved him. And was not sure which. Such had been the life – and death – of the Lionwolf, that now he could hardly tell the difference.

The square of packed-down snow at the village's centre was bigger than it had been, since the burned houses were cleared away. Torches flamed on poles. The shamans had tinged them with mauve. This was Assembly.

Krandif the ship-lord and his crews stood on the men's side.

The women had gathered on the other, where at last the first moon of the night was rising.

Her priests brought out the goddess's chair, too, which had been filched from the Ruk a year ago. Saftri sat in it, looking round, and Dayadin sat on a stool by her knee.

He did not seem uneasy, was used to being gazed at as a paragon. All trace of his tears, like hers, was gone.

They had discussed things anyway in her temple. They had made a bargain.

'But Our Lady,' said Jord, 'we'd all die.'

'One thing it is for the men who brave the waters,' said Krandif. 'But what you moot – our women are mortal, Our Lady. They can't, with the best will the world allows us, do what you can.'

'Listen to me,' said Saftri, rising with her snake-like hiss of impatience, the one her priests had overheard so often inside the god-house, 'if you remain here, you'll die for *sure*.'

'But, Our Lady, you protected us, and killed the wolf-demon—'

'Kill? How could I kill him? He's a god, as I am. Meanwhile one hundred and six women died during his attack, and twenty-one of your men, and twenty-one of your children too, among whom was Best Bear.'

'Lady,' said Krandif with diffident sternness, 'look at the lad we brought you instead.'

'Children aren't a commodity, Krandif, to exchange one with another. Say it to the mothers of the dead. Say it to the wives who cry and the men with no wife and no son – and no house left either, after the filthy fire-breath of the wolf. What he *is*, this boy, is your amulet for a voyage.'

The men rumbled. They surged there, coming forward one by one, or in groups, haranguing the goddess. During Assembly the word of all and any was equal. The village refuse-picker ranked with the leaders and the warriors, and a goddess too, though always treated respectfully, must attend to them.

Saftri sat scowling.

She looked, Dayadin noticed, like a furious girl of about four, who had been told she would not get her way and must go to the sleep-house.

'You are fools!' she shouted at them suddenly.

And from her hand a flash of light peeled off over the square, struck the wall of a cattle hut and exploded. Two or three logs clattered down, and three of the surviving precious cows came blundering out mooing.

'Our Lady – take care! Spare us our lovely cattle – only ten remain since the night of the wolf—'

Saftri snarled, 'I do it to educate you. I'm your goddess and look what you provoke me to. But if *he* comes back, and I've heard he will, do you think one stone here will stand on another, or one cow not have been roasted alive?'

Over on the square's east side, a woman shouted, 'It's the men who are cowards here. And they blame it on us, saying we're the weak ones who can't be risked.'

'Krandif Shiver-Heart!' called another.

Out over the square the women came pouring then like melted snow. They had plainly been reining in their anger as Saftri had not.

'Must we be made to stay and die, because the menfolk are scared of open sea to the north?'

'Our Lady says there's land there. Let's go and see it.'

'*This* land is spoiled,' screamed one higher anguished voice, 'by the bodies of our dead blighted.'

At Assembly even women might have an equal say. It was Vormish law.

They had stung the men, too. Krandif had gone red then pale. Others were arguing and grumbling.

Some hundred women stood firmly in the middle of the square in the purplish torchlight, and others grouped ready at the square's eastern edge.

'Let's us take the jalees,' called the woman who had led the assault. 'Let's leave these ones who tremble, and go us, and Our Lady, and find another country. Weaklings are we, Krandif Knock-Knees? Let you go and get yourself with child and labour to push it out, and then see who's the stronger, we or you!'

An hour later Saftri waited in the doorway of her temple, watching the huffy hearth fires burning behind village shutters. Women were banging pots, scorching food, sacrosanct this one night since it was their right to have an opinion in and *after* Assembly.

Saftri saw another movement. Dayadin was returning up the hill, and behind him something skittered on the night wind like a ripple of transparent washing.

'A hovor,' said Saftri.

'They can't see him,' said Dayadin, 'or not properly.'

'I lived among the Jafn,' said Saftri. She omitted to confess that when only human she had never seen any of the Jafn sprites, or not enough to be sure.

Dayadin had already told the goddess of the Vorms how, when he was abducted by Krandif's men, the hovor had first defended him, then fled. It had been his pet for some while, but obviously barbarians unnerved it. Dayadin did not hold its flight against it. It was only one more family friend he had lost.

'Then he came back.'

Dayadin called the hovor 'he', and had ages before given it or him a male name, Hilth, which apparently it or he had agreed to accept.

The hovor, Hilth, followed the reivers' two jalees back out to sea. Hilth blew in on a wind, and wrapped himself round Dayadin's body, mostly not spotted by the crew. Or, *if* spotted, not as anything real.

Dayadin had been very glad to have this creature beside him again. He was touched by its loyalty and persistence, which were unusual, if not unheard of, in Jafn tales.

About fourteen days on, when they were far out on the leaping black seas, sharks had come up out of the water. They were large examples of their kind, each more than fifteen feet in length, sea-black, with narrow horns for ice-breaking set in above their grey dead eyes. The water quickly grew choked with them. They thudded in again and again, whacking the sides of the vessels, nosing and bumping. Oars bashed, braining a few. Other oars snapped. Snouts with snaggle-pointed teeth nosed up the timbers. Even the Mother Ships rolled around while the shamans on the decks staggered, looking as if any moment the tide of sharks would capsize them.

Men used long knives, bows, arrows and spears. But the sharks were uninterested that night in the blood of their own. They could smell man-meat.

Krandif had lurched over the tilting walkway to Dayadin. 'See there, the Mother Ship with the blue decoration? If this vessel goes down, get on my back. I'll swim and fight you across. The shamans will see you safe.'

'Your shamans are crazy,' said Dayadin. 'They can't do a thing.'

Krandif was offended, but another buck of his ship put that from him. It was Dayadin, and oddly another something, operating out of thin air, that grabbed the ship-lord back from falling over into a shark-maw.

As he righted himself, he heard Dayadin say, 'Tell your shamans to shut their mouths. Their wailing is making these things eager. Even worse than the noise of those four-legged cod down belowdecks.' Now the horsazin were insulted. 'What you must do is sing.'

'. . . sing . . .'

An abrupt lull occurred.

Dayadin, standing there small and collected among the angry horrified men and sea of starving sharks, began himself to do what he had suggested. His voice was high and carrying, with the purity some boys' voices had until about the age of eleven or twelve. It was a Jafn lullaby.

Hearing him, astonished, the men fell quiet and an attendant silence filled the jalees. Even the shamans left off their excited chants.

As for the sharks, they too were suddenly immobile.

The sea rocked. Boats and ships and sharks rocked with it.

'Sing,' Dayadin said, between one verse and the next.

Krandif took the chance. He yelled the order towards all the ships.

The men began to sing along, wordless, to the Jafn cradle song, which generally they did not understand.

After about five minutes, great watery omissions undid the sea. The shark pack had started to sink and float away under the water. Their eyes were wide, but it was evident they slept. Down they went.

When the water was all open again, Dayadin ended the song, and so did the Vormlanders.

'Will they die?' Krandif asked. 'We must make offering if so to the shark god. There were ninety of his people here if there was one. He won't like to lose so many.'

'Sleep won't kill them,' said Dayadin with scorn. 'Sleep only kills men if practised too often.'

'Right. You have the right of it.'

This story Dayadin had told Saftri. Next he told her how the storm came after. The fleet was soon lying over on its side, and one vessel had been smashed.

It was Mozdif who roared across the walls of sea and storm: 'Hero-boy, will you sing again?'

Dayadin shouted that the wind was world's breath. The hovor, as he also informed Saftri, had somehow taught him as much.

'I said they must keep still and breathe deeply and quietly, in and out.' Rationally he added, 'Because the song worked with the sharks, they did the breathing.'

Glassy-eyed, the men inhaled, exhaled. On the shaman ships the shamans gazed from thin jealous faces. None of their spells had worked.

The hovor though dashed up into the teeth of the gale, where Dayadin saw it brutally tossed about. It came to him that Hilth was brave, as well as loyal, but he went on breathing.

And in the end, perhaps a quarter of an hour later, when everyone was all but tranced, the wind slumped and dropped in the lap of the sea.

Hilth sprang out of its toppling folds and gave to Dayadin a tiny white pebble of ice. The boy wondered if this were the wind's heart, which Hilth had valiantly torn out. But although he could communicate with the sprite by speaking to it aloud or in his mind, Hilth could not convey words, and seldom concepts, only its willingness or reluctance to obey.

'And so you saved his jalees,' said Saftri. 'Will you take part in this next voyaging for me?'

'I'll do my best, if you keep to your half of the bargain.'

Saftri said, 'I don't break my word. I'm not a man.'

Dayadin had nodded, and looked away. But after the Assembly he said he would call the hovor to show her. Perhaps it was to show her to the hovor as well, and also he was testing to make sure she really could see such things and was therefore a proper goddess who had lived among the Jafn.

'He has a gift for you,' said Dayadin. 'I know you expect one.'

Saftri saw the hovor bore a little carved whale tooth.

She held out her hand, and the wind-being let go the tooth into her palm.

Then she stood perplexed, forgetting Dayadin and the village. She had been once more reminded of whales.

In her past, Ruxendra had moved about Ru Karismi some days before she fell ill. She had been trying, by means of her Magikoy training and her youthful confidence, to heal the sick. When she was five she had healed her kitten by a laying on of hands – that was how it had been first seen she had magic potential. However, after the White Death, her optimistic efforts were useless. Then she could only help burn the bodies. That was bad enough, but she never supposed she too could die. She had early on thrown the hideous idea out of her head and barred all doors to it. But death got in at every pore instead.

In the initial phase she refused to accept and still wandered about the emptied thoroughfares till she collapsed. Someone brought her home to the fine house of her rich parents and its cloud of fear and mourning. Ruxendra, once she regained her senses, could not believe that any of this had happened to her.

She fought death off then, sitting bolt upright, sometimes spewing in a bowl, determined to get better.

Next morning just after sunrise, a stranger walked in at her bedroom door.

Ruxendra thought he was a physician and told herself he would make her well. He was young and wonderfully handsome, in a marvellous way that was nearly familiar even though she had never met him. Was his hair blond? That must be so, and he had also powdered it with shining silver. His complexion had a golden cast she had never seen except on statues which had been gilded.

Zeth Zezeth was one of the three gods given to Ruxendra at her birth. He had come from her mother, who in turn had him from her own father. All three of these gods stood, each in double aspect, as a small jewelled sextet in one corner of the chamber, but Ruxendra had not troubled with them for some while.

To start with then she did not know him. But when he leaned over her and his hair brushed her face, she did.

She said at once, offended and frightened, 'Have you come to take me away?'

'Not at all,' he said. 'Only to look at you. What a lovely girl you must have been,' he added, callously, 'before you began to die.'

'I beg you – save my life. I have – things to do.'

'Oh, dying will never stop that.'

Ruxendra opened wide her eyes.

'Won't it?'

'You must do something for me, and for your city, when you go down to the shadowlands,' said Zeth winningly, seating himself like a human friend on the side of her bed. Anyone but himself, or someone near death, would have hallmarked this pose as ridiculous. Perhaps even certain dying persons would have. 'He that destroyed Ru Karismi, Vashdran as you call him, is my enemy too. I shall kill him – or, going on the curious time of mortals which is so consecutive, I may already have done so. Go seek him therefore in Hell. You shall be my pretty hound and track him. There, your powers will equal his. And he too will be only a shadow you may worry at and tear apart for your little personal vengeance, my greater one.'

Ruxendra was confused. The room swam and she lost consciousness, and through her internal dark moved a silver-golden light, constant as a lamp.

Waking because a man's footfall sounded in the smoky room, she anticipated – what? She could not recall. And anyway, it was now a Magikoy of the Highest Rank who entered, Thryfe, who attended the city's kings.

'Revenge,' Ruxendra had told Thryfe, arrogant again and sure in her final moments.

But it was the geas of Zzth on her that had made her certain. And by the time she reached the proper Hell, as promised, Lionwolf was indeed already there.

He lay there now before her, Ruxendra the Sun Wolf's vengeful hound.

She sat up on her ledge below the stained glass windows, looking while the multi-coloured dapple crossed his body. It had nearly mesmerized her, though she did not know it, how his red hair became fluted with magenta and tawny green, and his skin, on which the stripes and cuts stayed always open and ready to bleed, was resurfaced now with a beautiful changeful leprosy.

All the way to Hell she thought her revenge had blazed before her golden and silver, like the lamp of the god.

Yet now—

Now.

What was it best for her to do, either to Vashdran or about him?

Her vicious loathing of him was withering on the vine of her heart. She had not been brought up by either her parents or the

Order of the Magikoy to harbour resentment, let alone to maim and slaughter.

Improvisations of torture were deserting her. Worse, her wish to use them.

Besides in the end he could only presumably die, like the other mirror images. He had seemed to say so.

Nevertheless she had brought him to hold hostage, wanting the other, the *true* Vashdran. And what would she do about that true Vashdran then? *He* must suffer.

Ruxendra upbraided herself. She should be as she had been when she swore to the barbarian man Curjai that Vashdran was her foe for ever, or till time itself was dead and rotting in some hell.

He did not stir, there on the floor. Seen clearly through the vitreous, the rest of the tower descended back into the crook of the mountain. Nothing moved below. Nothing, but for the windows' coloured reflection, altered.

FIVE

White snow contained or decorated the mountain pinnacles. Swags of bluish cloud hung low around them. The hyacinth sun was going down in a sea of distance.

'Now I go on alone.'

His companions and fellow Saraskulds looked at him dubiously. Above was the stronghold, a raggedly hewn tower inhabited by a dangerous witch.

Each of the men said something. Swanswine even vaunted a Crarrow lover, who had taught him a spell or two – entirely inadmissible, since the Crarrowin shared no knowledge of that sort with any man, let alone lover or son. Yet it was Taeb who said, 'Let me walk behind you. I'll cast some power around the place.'

And Vashdran turned on her, lion and wolf, his crimson mane flaring like the live snake-hair of the guards of Hell. *'Keep here.* Only *I.'*

Kuul commented, 'You said you didn't even say you'd follow her.'

'Nor did I. Now I have. *Stay.'*

Curjai stepped forward and warded them off, shaking his head. In his brief earthly life, about which only Vashdran knew anything, Curjai had spent most of his days with women. He had learned something, not knowing he did, of their necessary mild placation, their needful flirtatious wiles, lies and interventions.

Vashdran was changeable. As if differently tinted lights passed over and over his mood. Now an anxious child, now a

252

raging hero, now a god who feared nothing and could accomplish anything. And now a man near death, full of grief and guilt, and bitter as a gall.

Vashdran climbed the steep mountains. He *walked* up their sides, leaning out horizontal to the ground – his old habit. Either flight had not suggested itself to him, or he found it by now samey. Or was he pretending to be only a hero?

The men stood watching him. Heppa sat down and let Wasfa braid his hair and deck it with beads she drew out of the stones – an Olchibe fashion Vorms did not utilize. The dogs sat too, panting, exercising their eyes. Only Taeb and Curjai stepped apart, though in different directions. She roved along the landscape about a hundred yards behind the others, muttering, concocting some sorcery after all. Probably only, Curjai thought, to safeguard herself.

Otherwise Curjai observed Vashdran and the mountains exclusively. Up there something sparked suddenly, as the last sun licked off the light to take away with it.

Hell's palette did not have many colours unless you made them. It would seem therefore Ruxendra had formed those slivers of raspberry and green crystal. Were they windows? The palace at Padgish had had one such, above the god-hall.

Vashdran himself did not look back. He was glad to slough them all; they were nothing to him. He could not care for them, nor behave honourably to them. Their still-human needs, conflicting constantly with his, often exacerbated him beyond bearing. As when he had witnessed Heppa pissing neatly against a rock, when no natural functions were valid any more. Even Heppa's baby in the girl's womb was an absurdity, and doubtless an imaginary pregnancy. Swanswine, with his physical similarities and nearly total unlikeness to Guri, irritated like a pin in the boot. Jafn Kuul, and Behf whose origin, if known, Vashdran had mislaid, perturbed him with their memories of things Vashdran himself had experienced when alive. Curjai angered him more badly, like a brother. In some way linked, he could never be shot of him. Taeb annoyed maybe the least. She was untrustworthy and her efforts to hide it laughable. You knew where you were and *she* knew she was dead. He had seen her one evening as they came here, working some curse on the animal which had eaten her alive. Like Ruxendra then in that, she wanted retribution on her murderer.

The mountains were clean of intellectual clutter. They held only voracious and primal emotions, and his own captive body.

He dreaded reaching it so much that now he was running towards it, straight up. He did not know what he would do. Had never known. He remembered how he had said to Guri that time when the true human Gullahammer marched towards the Ruk, 'This road I'm on – sometimes I look back and see the distance I've come. Or forward, and I see a light as if the world burned – I wonder what choice I have.' And Guri had answered quietly, pragmatically, 'No choice. Your kind – none.'

Balanced on her spur, the Magikoy apprentice slept. She had dreamed or believed she had of the city, bright and whole, like her own future once. As she opened her eyes, longing swamped Ruxendra. Then she heard Vashdran coming in at some portal in the rock below.

It was not that he made a sound. The noise was psychic. Her undead brain or her soul heard him.

From her shoulder blades the blood-red wings unfurled. A slim scarlet crait, she clung to the ledge, staring down through the last of Hell's daylight.

Vashdran appeared. He lifted his head and stared back at her through the transparent floor. At the body lying there he did not look at all.

Then he jumped upward, a sort of dive, and Ruxendra too sprang into the air, up into the head of the tower, shocked from her perch as his upraised fists and his skull hit the vitreous. It splintered in an eruption of needles at the impact, and like a nail hammered through plaster he rose on through it, his hair glittered by glass, otherwise unmarked, and his face a mask like gold—

In that instant did she recall the god she had, in all but

essence, forgotten? Vashdran was his image. Save – Vashdran was more like the god Zeth now than Zeth Zezeth himself had ever been.

If she did recall in any case it was not obvious.

She closed her wings and dived in her turn straight down at him.

Vashdran caught her. He held her round the body, her arms trapped by his, her feet kicking at him, while he seemed not to notice her struggles and her blows, which were made weak by proximity, and he gazed into her face. Behind her the wings flapped strenuously, impotently, sluggishly.

Vashdran said, his mouth almost against her lips, an icy kiss, 'What did you want done to him? Do you think your fury with the Lionwolf can match mine, you *child*?' She tried to speak, to shout and spit at him, but now her psychic force was impaired by his own. Zeth had been wrong. She was not this being's equal, even here. He pressed his face against hers entirely, brow to brow, her slender features allowing his some margin. Into her very mouth he spoke.

'The Lionwolf – you know nothing of him. I will tell you. He put men to use like beasts – less than beasts, for of animals he was quite fond, and when he killed *them* he was tender. But men and women and children too – little girls like Ruxendra – those he gave to savagery and to rape and to a hundred deaths. But then, both his enemies and his friends Lionwolf gave to the steel and stink and treachery of dying. Because he was a god, and what does a god care for human things? No more, my girl, than for the meat or the fruit he carves with his knife. Yes then, to your effete metropolis, your toy city of Ru Karismi, he brought his multitude of warriors. Had they got in, that pearl of the south would have been spattered to ten million bricks, ten million million bones. And such as you would have bled out your lives on your backs or your faces, speared over and over by the other sword men wield between their legs like wolves that rut. Don't shudder,' he said, soft now, worse now, 'don't close your eyes. Look into mine and through mine and see what's in the refuse pit of my brain. *Do* you see, Ruxendra? A crawling thing that's less than any man and calls itself a god. *Lionwolf*. There he is. And when your Magikoy masters let loose their ultimate weapon on us, that too, as you so sensibly understood, was my singular sin, not theirs. I stood alone in a desert of dust that was all the men I had brought there, all the beasts, all the world I carved with my knife and tried to eat alive. Yes. I should be made to pay, Ruxendra. But you, you whining pathetic ignoramus, aren't capable of the task of harming and destroying such a monster. Better then, girl, let the monster do it himself.'

When he dumped her back on the remains of the floor she simply lay there. She was stunned by the non-human physicality of his astral self, by the boiling lava of his self-hatred and his seething immortal rage.

Dizzy as at her death, she turned to see what he would do next.

Dense blue darkness was coming. Yet a hollow radiance persisted, unable to escape and trapped in the tower.

She saw Vashdran lean over the prostrate form that was also his.

The eyes of the prone Lionwolf, if so he was, were open. Vashdran and he looked at each other, coolly, almost with indifference.

'Are you prepared?' Vashdran said.

'Yes, prepared.'

'For the world then. For all the world—'

The great blade that swung upward in both Vashdran's hands descended too fast for the girl to see. It was like a lightning flash. But in its wake soared a crescendo of blood.

Lionwolf screamed. The scream went on for ever because here, in this place of stones, there was no need to draw breath.

Ruxendra pulled herself to her feet.

She gaped, not realizing what she beheld. For perhaps a minute she watched the intricacy of the gleaming blade, the surgery it performed, the flags of flesh and burnish of strange shapes suddenly revealed beneath and between.

Vashdran too was screaming now, bellowing, never drawing breath.

Again and again the lightning flash, the crescendo.

It came to Ruxendra what she saw, as if blindness left her vision.

As her city was dying, she had witnessed much. Nothing like this. Nothing in all her universe ever, like *this*.

His eyes were fire. All the rest was blood. The sword was blood, his body and hair, the second body – blood – blood and offal, and all of this framed in a long double crying without pause to breathe—

Ruxendra, who had travelled such a way to exact payment, leapt through the hole in the floor, her wings beating inaccurately against the sides of the rock, and stumbling out from the tower, falling and bruised on the night flank of the mountain, she too began to scream, yet breathing, *breathing deeply*, between each shriek.

A shadow inked over Ruxendra. Night was in full bloom, yet oddly a single round moon had come up.

Ruxendra sat. She looked at the newcomer in terror.

As once before he said, 'Don't be afraid.'

At that she threw her hands over her face and wailed. 'Mother – where's Mother? I want her – I want my mother . . .'

Curjai seated himself beside her. Her wings were gone and her dress was tattered and grey in the spiky moonlight.

'Your mother isn't here,' he said, flatly but not unkindly.

Ruxendra sobbed. Presently, when he slid an arm about her, she bowed into him and wept on his shoulder.

Curjai had flown up the mountain towards the glint of windows. Then he had made an interval, during which his own shield wings dispersed. By the hour he had arrived all sounds were over in the tower, and outside too. Yet they had been recorded there on tablets of granite. So he heard it still, the screaming.

As Ruxendra drained herself to calm, he found a fleece cloak by them on the rock, rolled it ready and laid her down there. 'I won't be long.' He thought she would cling but, already exhausted, she was asleep. Asleep in Hell. The moon showed him only the face of a sad young girl, vacant now of anything but loss.

Curjai walked up the last of the mountain and went into the jerry-built tower.

A peculiar light was burning there – but no, it was the moonlight angling through a trio of windows.

Had Hell's queen sent this moon? If so, why?

Not bothering with the re-creation of wings, Curjai merely levitated to the broken floor and went through. He positioned himself, and began to realize the two dark blots he had spotted from below were a pair of bodies, each apparently quite dead.

Both were Vash.

Both were – not.

One lay in separated joints, hacked, eviscerated and butchered, like the meats that rose up from the ground for cooking. There was therefore not much by which to identify the mirror-body they had composed. It too now was totally deceased.

The other body was face down, sprawled. A huge sword lay by it – or rather a sword that seemed to dwarf the figure. Curjai began to reason that this was because the second form of Vashdran was no longer that of a man, but of a boy not much more than twelve years in age.

'Vash?'

Curjai touched the boy on the arm and felt 'life' there, under the surrogate flesh of one undead.

Gradually Curjai turned him over.

He had been copiously bleeding too, but all the wounds had closed and vanished scarlessly away. Only the blood stayed, hard and dry, describing the areas of assault so obvious on the other disjointed body. They were the same injuries, of course mirrored. Yet even now the dried blood flaked off. *This* body surely could not die in Hell, only suffer and endure. But it had changed, for without doubt now he was a child – just past the age of twelve: too old for Olchibe mercy.

'Vash . . .'

The eyes of the child opened. They were piercing rich blue as the last of Hell's sunset.

'Guri,' said the boy, 'I'll die. Don't make me die here. Not like this.'

'You can't die.'

'I'm half mortal. The mortal half . . . can die. Uncle, don't make me die *here*.'

Curjai bent down and picked the boy up in his arms and carried him to the break in the floor, jumped through with him, and took him out on to the night mountain.

As he did this, Curjai thought, *I never could have had a son.*

Below, far off, there was the sequin of a fire on the plain. Heppa and the rest were there. How easy it was to persuade oneself all this was factual.

Curjai sat down by Ruxendra, who was still fast asleep. He held the boy in his arms until the child too seemed to drift asleep.

The moon did not cross the sky. It stayed fixed above, a steady candle in the dark.

Looking at it, Curjai seemed sometimes to glimpse the ghostly outline of a woman's face, ebony in opal.

Eventually he too slept.

Below, round the fire, the others, even the dogs, were sleeping also, all but Taeb who, out on the plain of stones, was fighting with the conjure of a wolverine. Occasionally she called it by a Jafn name – *Rothger*. The violence went on and on.

Vashdran, who was Lionwolf, descended or ascended or walked a level invisible path in utter darkness beyond all nights, to a tiny place darker yet, and colder than any Hell.

Here he stopped, for there was nowhere else to go.

He had reached the metaphorical basement of existence.

For a long while he sat, his back to nothing, resting on nothing, his arms and his head on his knees.

Where he had been, each blow he struck against his mirror-self had rained also on him; he felt everything he did, even as he viewed it happen. Finally the other was vanquished. Then he too dropped headlong into oblivion. But oblivion it was not. His consciousness continued, his sense if not of body, then of being. In this state, once – twice? – he heard himself mumble words. But it was as if another spoke, and miles away. He was only *here*. Curiously though his guilt and panic, which had followed him here, were separate at last. They went with him as companions now – but no longer as internal foes. He saw them clearly, and their faces – despite the fact they were faceless and formless – were composed and nearly dignified. They did not lash out at him. They had been completely recognized and so relaxed their grip.

I am in the place where I was first made.

Within his brain, if it was now only a brain, he saw a smith hammering out a piece of metal on an anvil. Sparks ricocheted like jasper beetles. The metal was first dull, then brown, then like new-minted bronze.

Like that, he thought. He knew faint wonder at the miracle of his life. And at the waste he had made of it only regret and sorrow. Anger had burned away.

The picture faded.

Sleep was coming in soft waves. Gratefully he let it come, thinking it to be at last genuine death – extinction.

But sleep took him in its arms and swam strongly with him through all time, all dimension, all actuality and all nothingness – that too – but it was only like a journey under a midnight sun.

Clouds of solid ice passed him, glimmering, and armoured fish, and other oceanic creatures. But they were symbols, as the sea was. He was inside his own deeper mind.

Yet the travel soothed him. He had no fear of self, not any more, nor of what he had done. And if at any unnoticed second he had ever been timid at life or death or the world, that too was done with.

This melodious progress went on for an indefinite space, until eventually he grew aware of a kind of anchor. A warm opening was there, and something set in it, like a red gem inside a flower. He stared at it, waking in the dream to sudden fascination. The gem was for him. It was his. For now he must wait, but soon the gift would be ready to claim.

Swimming, he spiralled round this ultimate of symbols, astonished and glad, eager, and also diffident – and *patient*, as never had he been in all his godlike days on earth.

When the blue sun dawned, the round moon was still fixed to the sky. Although the moon dimmed, it did not disappear, but Curjai thought now it had moved a little towards the west. The boy lay heavy on him and Curjai was unnerved, remembering what slumber had made him forget. He turned his head and Ruxendra knelt at a basin of water called out of the mountain, washing her face and hands and combing her hair.

As she realized Curjai had woken and looked at her she said, frosty with nervousness, 'Don't let him see me.'

Curjai glanced at the boy, then back at her.

'He's younger than you are, now. You shouldn't be afraid of him. He can't hurt you.'

She said nothing. She began to cry again, then gave it up. Vigorously she laved her face once more in the water, which had a pleasant perfumed smell, an unguent no doubt from the Ruk. She said, drying herself on a silk cloth that had also manifested, 'Will he start again – will he – to wound himself—'

'I don't know. Maybe not. Maybe that was enough.'

She shivered.

'It is my fault,' she said, solemn and miserable. 'I've soiled my training. I was Maxamitan Level. They would have cast me out of the Order.'

'Never mind that,' he said. 'There's no Magikoy rule book here.'

Wanting to stand up now he shifted, to test how the boy he clasped would respond.

But the boy lay unresponding, and heavy and stiff as wood.

His face was Lionwolf's – Vashdran's. Just so he must have looked at twelve or thirteen.

'Vash? Wake up now.'

As he said the words Curjai heard his mother howling in memory, grabbing on to him. But he, Curjai, had already been gone.

'What is it?' Ruxendra whispered.

'This too,' Curjai said.

'What? What?'

'He's dead. Real death. Second death.'

'No,' she said.

'Yes. Look.'

'No, I won't look.'

Curjai stood up, then bent and laid the boy's body down on the mountain.

The head, too stiff, did not loll; the torso and limbs were immovable. He had died and frozen in that position of being supported and held.

Ruxendra tilted her face to the sun and moon and started to wail.

Curjai took hold of her. He drew her in against him and found as he comforted her noise into silence that he smoothed her hair, which smelled sweet, like young lilies, with his lips. He did not mind she clung to him now. 'Ssh,' he said. 'Hush, sweetheart.'

When she raised her child-woman's face, he kissed her mouth, unintrusively but with the demanding passion of any fraught moment in Hell. And Ruxendra kissed him in return, and when they drew apart she was flushed and altered and no longer hysterical. In their lives, he thought, she had been two years his senior. She would never have let him kiss her then.

But be damned to that. Why live in yesterday when today was here, sufficiently laden with tragedy and hope?

He carried the second body of Vashdran back into the tower, went up and laid it by the other, the raw meat body, on the vitreous floor. Then he took the cloak he had found for Ruxendra and spread it over them.

A terrible grieving ripped at Curjai and yet he gave it no attention. He did not believe in this or any death. A sort of unseen, unheard, unknown, inexplicable assurance was on him. Do this and this, and *this* will not matter. Denial was all. Then let denial reign supreme.

They walked unnecessarily carefully down the mountain, taking only a short while over it even so.

When they reached the camp the men, Kuul, Behf, Swanswine and Heppa, were sitting uneasily, watching green-haired Taeb prancing round the cadaver of some big striped hairy animal out on the plain. Heppa's bride Wasfa was placidly cooking porridge in a pot over the fire.

'Do you see that?' asked Swanswine, pointing at Taeb. 'All night over killing it. Never trust women, unless Olchibe and Crarrow.'

'What type of beast is it?' asked Behf.

'I told you. Wolverine. From the ice swamps of north Gech.'

Kuul said, 'She was squealing it had eaten her alive. She called it by the name of a bastard soint of the Jafn Klow, Rothger.' Kuul spat. 'She was *his* witch long ago. I seem to have recalled that much.'

Heppa peered at Ruxendra. 'Who's she?'

Curjai said, 'Up on the mountain, Vashdran died the second death.'

One by one their heads rotated on the columns of strong necks. Only Wasfa did not turn, but instead made in the air a lilting gesture, to some god of the dead most likely.

How normal she looked, with her swollen fecund belly and the bubbling pot of porridge, the dogs sitting anxiously by, wanting breakfast.

How unnormal, everything else.

'Who's leader then, who's chief Saraskuld?' asked Behf.

'I,' said Curjai, with a prince's authority. 'Who did you think?'

They grunted. No one argued.

They had not recognized Ruxendra. That was not so odd. Persons came and went here in an incorrigible manner. Besides, she did not look at all as she had.

Taeb was stalking in over the plain. She bore in one hand a large bloody bone torn out of the huge left foreleg of the wolverine.

'I can read it in the fire,' she said, 'Lionwolf is no more.'

That was all.

As the sun slid up the sky, cutting its way with a razor edge, they kept to the hearth and ate Wasfa's porridge, which was good, salty and spicy.

There was beer too. They drank it, mostly unspeaking. Only Swanswine said in the end, 'What next?'

'Wait for night,' said Curjai. 'Then we'll cremate them. His two corpses.'

'That moon's going down,' said Kuul. 'Only the Queen here can call the moon.'

'She called the moon to mark Vashdran's death.'

Heppa peered again at Ruxendra, sheltering small, seen-and-not-heard under Curjai's non-literal wing. 'Who *is* she?'

'Mine.'

And then Ruxendra added for herself, very low, subservient or cunning, 'My mother called me Dawn. After the sunrise when I was delivered.'

'An adorable name,' said Kuul. 'In Jafn that would be *Ushah*.'

The others, where applicable, generously donated extra names for a dawn in their own former tongues.

Ruxendra gave a small smile, a girl who was flattered by big brave men.

But Taeb spun about three times on the spot, then flung the wolverine leg bone up at the sun. So far as they could see it did not *hit* the sun, but her action wrecked the atmosphere rather. The dogs bolted out on the plain and pretended to hunt invisible things.

At day's end, they lit torches and went up the mountain. The five men walked at the front, Wasfa and Ushah the Dawn and Taeb and the six dogs at the procession's back.

None of them employed flight. It was only again the speed and great ease with which they scaled the peak's sheeny side that gave the strategy away.

The tower was wilting. Abandoned by Ruxendra-Ushah's will the rock of it was crumbling, subsiding into the parent crag.

Curjai alone entered it. No one else wanted to. Had they in the end felt connection to Vashdran, or loyalty to him, or anything at all? Probably not. Certainly Kuul, who had attached to him in the beginning as if Vashdran were a battle-standard, had lost faith. Kuul's life-memories, even though impaired, had not helped the process either. They had all run with Vashdran to this area because it was something else to do.

In true life, Vashdran's charisma had drawn men and women, even beasts. They had raced towards him, in love with all he was.

In death he was only one more outcast spirit.

And even in second death, solely Curjai seemed compelled to organize a funeral rite. And it was in the nocturnal style of his own country.

Inside the tower he uttered prayers he had heard said for warriors of Simisey. He offered a couplet or two from the Song of Lalt, Lalt's elegy for dead Tilan, his hand-fast brother. Above, under the cloak on the transparent floor, a carcass lay red and black, and by it the body of a boy of twelve years, curled up on his long red hair.

Curjai slung his torch into the melting structure of the tower.

'I never knew till we met I had a brother, born not of my mother's womb but of the same metal that forged me.' Lalt had said this. Curjai said it over. 'Sleep a while, brother, and then return. Or half of myself for ever wanders in your underworld, and here in the lands of men I stumble, lame in one foot, sightless in one eye, old as winter like an old man. Attajos: consume flesh, and let the spirit free.'

Before the fire caught hold of either body, Curjai stepped out of the tower.

The others threw in their torches, haphazard, Behf and

Heppa looking nearly embarrassed, Kuul grim and Swanswine blank.

Vashdran's jatcha, which he had named Star-Dog, began abruptly to howl. Either it had fathomed its owner was dead, or it smelled something alien in the pyre.

Kuul dragged it away.

They all trailed down the mountain, and the firelight flamed over and reflected ahead of them, drawing their shadows too on the pale ground, doubling their number, threatening omens of the gods knew what. Behind them blocks of the tower cascaded with awful cracks and thuds. Pieces of the stained glass hailed around. Nothing harmed the funeral party. Despite all appearance and sound, the debris was weightless and incorporeal. Once they reached the plain, to those that looked back – Curjai and Ushah, Taeb and Kuul – the last of the tower offered a concluding burst of fireworks. Then it sank in a rush and was absorbed instantly by the mountain's snowy crown.

A year, almost that, elapsed on the plain. Or it seemed to.

They did not unremember what they were or *where* they were, but nevertheless they – *lived*.

A small settlement became built about them, more camp than stead let alone town. Its population was consistent: five men, three women, six dogs. They had raised the tented structures, having found trees locally that were a sort of familiar icy wood, and later animals had spontaneously shown themselves – or materialized – and these, being earthly, were hunted with the jatchas for meat and skins. Even the bones and pelt of Taeb's wolverine they put to use in various domestic ways, Swanswine having first asked Taeb if they might.

While the months or seeming months lagged by, Swanswine began to court Taeb in an unfriendly yet dogged fashion. He said to Heppa she was the nearest he would get to an Olchibe woman, the Gech being quarter kindred to his own people.

Taeb let Swanswine woo her. Eventually she took him into

the shelter he had made for her and they did not come out for most of a day.

The other men were at first celibate, even Heppa soon, for Wasfa grew enormous. Her pregnancy went slowly, despite her size, yet she was unconcerned.

'How many are in there?' Heppa had asked Taeb, between greedy glee and disconcertment.

But Taeb shook her head. 'I have no power here to scry.'

Heppa believed she lied, but did not challenge her. She was a witch.

Kuul and Curjai and Behf excavated their native games from the landscape and taught each other moves and counter-moves with dice and clay figures and boards that had squares or circles on them.

Curjai and Ushah made no arrangement. Since the moment on the mountain they had been circumspect, courteous and distant. Now and then something happened between them, hand brushing hand, the scent of each other causing a swift chemical reaction in brain and blood. But Curjai was really far off, locked into the intensity of a *life* he had never been able to have before, not wanting to muddy the issue yet with any woman, let alone one he had claimed with a kiss and the public word 'Mine'. For her part Ushah-Ruxendra was in love with him, and too much a Rukarian minor aristocrat to display it. That he was a barbarian she had erased but her own pride she wore as a mantle. All else was gone, but for Curjai and lusting love and pride.

Kuul and Behf formed a male bond after several months, in the honoured tradition of Jafn fighters who might be without women for the duration of a war.

How much time *did* go by? There *was* no time. *No* time went by. Yet . . . almost a year.

The sun by then looked less blue, brighter. At sunrise and sunfall the sky blushed at its extreme horizons, east or west. Even the stars polished themselves up, and often the moon came, only one it was true, but much better than no moon at all.

All around the campstead they had found icy forests, and

sometimes, in certain lights, the earth was so white there might have been snow and ice down. The wells they created stayed. One, pouring from a slanted rock, would freeze over in the night, sweating back to liquid only at noon so morning ice would have to be chipped from it as the women had done at home in the world.

Then a water-freezing night came, and Heppa thundered yelling out of his tent. 'Taeb! Taeb!'

Taeb emerged from the cover of her tent and Swanswine.

Ushah said, primly, 'Wasfa's in labour.'

Wasfa did not cry out. She said she had no pain, only the great urge to push as if to turn herself inside out. She did not seem frightened, and explained she had never seen a child born; it had not been allowed her, *before*. Possibly she did not know childbirth *did* hurt, and had only heard epic tales of pushing.

The men, thankfully barred from the tent, went some way off, gazing at the night through which deer herds occasionally wafted, phantasmal until studied closely.

Swanswine whittled a minuscule skull for hairdressing, Behf and Kuul diced vulgarly for colossal heaps of gold coins, Curjai suffered a weird inexplicable shame.

The sky lightened with Ushah's dawn.

As the blue-pink sword tip of the sun unsheathed itself, Wasfa gave her first and only cry. It was loud enough to startle the men, but was a signal of triumph. The child had left the womb in a gush of crystalline and odourless liquid – somewhere someone must have told the living Wasfa also about a woman's waters breaking. She had simply got them in the wrong order.

Heppa stole into the tent, pink as the morning.

'A boy,' revealed Taeb, adding, 'as I said.'

Ushah-Ruxendra, who from her Magikoy instruction accurately knew about the business of births, had hidden her surprise at the peculiarities of this one and assisted ably. Now she put the baby, duly washed and wrapped in a woollen shawl, into the mother's arms.

Neither Ushah or Wasfa said a word.

Nor did the others, now.

Only Taeb, the clever one, had missed what was under her nose.

Sensing she had blundered, she turned on Swanswine. 'The blame is *yours*.' At which Swanswine struck her. With this fanfare then, the sun returned to Hell.

'. . . my hell may not be the same as yours.'

Guri heard his own voice, speaking over unknown distances.

And what had Lionwolf replied? He wished Guri a better hell than his own.

Not long after, the god-whale killed them.

Is your hell lovelier than mine, Lion, or more hellish?

Guri lay in the hut. He was not female, so it must be close to sun-up when he would be an Olchibe man and go out to slay and ruin. Once or twice he had woken early like this, after the female or male abysm and deaths of the night. Not often.

Something too – not like other times.

He could hear still a voice, calling to him. The voice was not his own, nor the mesmeric voice of Lionwolf. It was—

Was—

It is the voice of an embryo and a soul, joined by a fiery cord to the womb that houses the infant it is due to be, and meanwhile the spirit running wild, playing truant, coming and going as it wants, glad to look in at its maturing self, or about at the approaching world.

'Guri – Olchibe Uncle Guri!'

Yes, not the voice of Lionwolf when a man. This is the boy's voice, a child's voice, back at the commencement.

Call out my name, Guri had said, promising rescue.

Lionwolf had called it, and Guri had answered the call.

If he had kept his gods, the Great Gods, now Guri would blaspheme them royally. But what is the point in shitting on the non-existent?

Guri puts his head to the ground, and in that fraction of a

second the side of the hut gives way, and something bounds through, shining and flaming, lit like the morning sun that here in Guri's hell is not yet rising.

'Guriguriguri!'

The boy, about eleven or twelve, throws his arms round Guri's neck and hauls him off the ground to hug him more thoroughly.

Guri cannot speak. Cannot think. Dies in some form and in some form comes back to life.

'How – are you here—'

'It's me! Uncle, it's me!'

'Yes – I know you. I know you.' Something splits Guri's heart and rears out in an insane expression: 'Great Gods witness. Amen.'

'It reeks here, Uncle. Putrid.'

'I – know.'

'Tell me about the whale.'

'The – whale—'

'How you rode on his back to the bottom of the sea, and saved me from the stink-god, old Blue-face.'

'Did I? Are you – saved?'

'*Yes!*' cries the boy.

Guri looks at him and sees he is.

Guri throws off his personal feebleness and says, 'You mustn't stay here, Lion. No, it's no place for you.'

'That doesn't matter, Uncle. All places are for me.'

'Not – this one.'

'Look,' says the boy. A spangling red jewel slides from his hair and smashes on the floor of the hut, becoming there a hundred jewels. 'Mine now,' says the boy, '*only* mine.'

Guri binds himself in iron.

'In a while I must go. I have things I must do – foul things. But I get no choice. And by night – *never come here by night.*'

The boy's beautiful face is troubled only a moment.

He puts his hand on Guri's hair.

How gloriously hot the touch. Like sunlight after chill.

'Only call out my name,' says Lionwolf, as Guri had to him so many millennia ago. 'And what is my name?'

'Lion – Lionwolf.'

'Yes. When the night comes, call me. I know a trick or two.'

Guri lowers his head.

When he looks again the boy is gone. The jewels too are only bits of flint.

A dream. A dream in hell.

Outside, bleak hellish sunrise. Notes of men and mammoths, the day's vileness in preparation.

The dream has done nothing to counteract such stuff; how can it? And as for today's night of punishment and despair, Guri would no more draw that child, dream or boy, into it than he would try to evade its justice.

Going out however Guri finds Ranjal, goddess of wood, parading about on the snow, unnoticed by the Olchibe men. Even the mammoths fail to detect her, trampling through her, as she grins in obvious scorn at their daftness.

'Ask,' says Ranjal, who claims Guri has been charitable to her in years gone by.

'Did you send the dream?'

'No dream. Ask.'

The Olchibe enemy – yes, his enemies now – are yodelling at him to come on.

The mammoth who will always die stands like a sentient fog bank before him.

She has told him before she cannot remove him from this hell.

'Save my mammoth from his death,' Guri blurts.

Ranjal smiles her peg-tooth smile.

A hell-hour later the mammoth, snagged by a glancing spear, shakes it off.

Guri jumps down, and punches the Olchibe men witless as they attempt to kill their prisoners. The released men of the Marginal scamper away. Guri stands in limbo, sighing, patting the mammoth absently as sunlight curds the snow.

That night falls fast and in the hut he calls to no one. But the

271

two men who enter are only weary, and only ask him, or her, for shelter. One makes love to the woman Guri usually is by night. *Makes love.* Guri thinks he – she – must be a whore to like it so much. But then the man congratulates her on having been a virgin.

Next day Guri is male and light is there, but no one on the snow shouting. Only the solitary mammoth, blowing its closeted breath, the trunk searching out little dormant delicacies under the ice.

Guri mounts the mammoth. They wend westward, the direction the pale sun is not yet going in Guri's hell.

Now ten days went by on the plain under the mountains. Each day a year, of a sort.

Did the days seem especially prolonged? Not really.

The did what they always had, the campstead. The men hunted and played games, the women cooked and tidied. Taeb quarrelled with Swanswine. Curjai and Ushah looked at each other under their lids.

Wasfa fed her baby from the breast. It transpired she had been allowed to see this act. But by the end of the first day her milk dried, and the child did not appear to need it.

They knew. How could they not know, the evidence so garishly offered them, red, amber and blue.

Swanswine said he would take himself off. He might after all find others of his race roaming the plain of Hell now it was improved.

Taeb said nothing, but self-evidently she would put a bane on him if he did.

Behf and Kuul paid no one else much attention save Curjai, the accepted leader of the group.

Heppa and Wasfa were an innocent unit, sufficient to themselves and foolishly happy. But they also, by the third day, excluded the child.

Everyone did this. Even all the dogs.

The child did not seem to mind. He was swiftly independent. By the morning of the second day he had walked, and by afternoon run. He ate ordinary food from the second day as well, and grew measurably, escalating upward and filling out.

They watched his long-legged gallop over the rim of the plain, outracing the deer that had conveniently evolved, his fire hair streaming behind him. It was the fourth day, and manifestly he was more than eight years of age.

He never spoke to any of them. Not a single syllable, although he had a voice, for they heard him now and then singing. He was always gentle, not snatching or frenzied in the inarticulate frustrations of infancy. Perhaps anyway he knew none of these, for he grew so fast nothing was denied him. No sooner did he wish to do a thing than he was enabled to do it.

His eyes were very blue, more so than the sun, but in certain twists of firelight or sunset a glowing garnet crescent would curve between iris and pupil.

The child's skin was tawny amber, golden. He was in all ways perfect. And by the seventh day he was fourteen and by the eighth, sixteen, and a child no longer.

At this juncture they had come, mostly, not precisely to ignore – but to *overlook* him. He was like weather or morning or their own spuriously beating astral hearts: a fact, unconscionable, undeniable. *There.*

And he had almost done all this before, of course. He was an expert at faultlessly rapid maturation.

The evening of the ninth day, eighteen years and a little more, handsome and couth, coordinated and immensely strong, he strode away from the camp and did not come back.

On the tenth day, only then, they began to discuss him.

'Lionwolf. As he was. I remember him now,' said Kuul.

'He was a god,' said Swanswine. 'One of the mad useless gods of the Rukar.'

'He's a god again,' said Behf.

Heppa said, 'I never saw him then.'

Wasfa said, 'It's as it is.'

Taeb said something in the Gech tongue so smothered with magic and secrets they did not comprehend it.

The dialogue circled and veered everywhere and nowhere, meaningless, meaningful.

Curjai detached himself and went off too, loping over the nearer slopes of the mountains. Ushah who had been Ruxendra withdrew into her tent.

Curjai was in a whirlpool of thought. The girl had distracted him. He blamed himself not her, not seeing that it might have been neither of them that kept him from seizing on the child, attempting to adopt it when the rest let go. Not either of them, but some other thing.

But he, the red-haired being, god or man, both and neither, twice-dead, twice-born, he stood at some fundamental centre of the plain which had become, beside him, empty and bare, scattered only by stones and with the wind of Hell whistling mournfully as the blue sun sank.

> *Ask the snow what it is,*
> *Ask the ice, wind, sea and sky,*
> *Ask the land what it is,*
> *And the light and the dark that hurry by,*
> *Ask the beast and the bird,*
> *And the cunning, and those that lie,*
> *But of all that is*
> *What am I? What am I?*

Night came.

One by one the burnished tarnished stars of Hell lit up. The moon, which had been absent since the fourth night, rose on the brink of the plain, tiny as a seed.

He who had been Nameless, and Vashdran, and Lionwolf, stood sentinel of himself through the night and watched the occluded heavens of Hell wheel slowly over. The wind sang to him, and sometimes he sang also back to it in a bright bronze voice, old songs of the Urrowiy and the Olchibe, sophisticated songs of the central Ruk that Saphay, his first mother, had sung in his other boyhood. Or he sang mixtures, medleys, of all.

What am I? What am I?

It had always been his question, of the world and of himself. It is always the question, for men ask it too, but Lionwolf, bemused by his own terrifying power and glory, had never reasoned this out.

When morning stirred along the plain, the moon was still parked, a miniature white ball. It had got no nearer. And the wind still blew. Nothing had changed.

But then *he* turned, and *he* blew softly, and blew the wind away over the mountains and the last of the darkness with it. And reaching up his hand – the length only of his arm, the length only of infinity – he plucked the sun of Hell from the sky.

It was no larger in his grasp than it had looked above. A banner, the sun, blue as the flowers of the weed-of-light but dripping long discrepant flames of orange and yellow. The sky displayed clearly where he had dislodged the disc, a strange flickering and rounded hole that showed behind it a void, an *absence*.

The sun was neither hot nor cold to the touch, neither material nor of energy – what then was the sun?

When he released it, the orb shot upwards again and slammed itself back into the setting of the sky, which went black.

All around the plain was littered with trickles of electric azure and orange. Demented clouds gathered in the upper air.

A great way off Curjai, who had seen the sun dashed by some invisible force from its niche and then returned, believed he had had a vision.

But now a tempest of reborn winds and turbulence was pounding from all compass points. Thunder bawled, and the ground shook.

Over the plain something else was rushing.

Curjai, as he sprinted forward, saw the chariots tearing along. He had given up any sense of direction. The sky had only four matched quarters, all booming with storm and disturbance, and the sun, stuck back into its bloodshot socket, was blurred and static as if afraid to move ever again.

Yet surely the chariots were from the city, one of the twin

cities of Hell – Shabatu, Uashtab – they were black and brilliant, with spikes of hoarse light glancing from their runners. Not the weasel animals but the more ominous spider-horses drew them, their eight leg-divisions making slight work of the terrain.

The foremost chariot contained two figures, both dark, one clad in a pastel gown that might have been vividly blanched if the shade of the storm had not diffused it.

The rest of the chariots, five or seven of them – in the roused tumult it was hard to be certain – roiled after. The guards of Hell clustered in those.

Lightning irradiated the surface of the cumulus, east to west and south to north, fissuring the cloud like a plate.

Pieces fell on the plain. Curjai, running, stared at them and when they struck him shied. They felt like smacks and had a smell of salt and galvanism – they were shards of the *sky*.

Lionwolf turned and regarded the chariots.

He waited motionless as the mountains seemed to be, and the six or eight vehicles foamed in about him in a spray of disintegrated stones, under the seizure of sky-falling tempest.

The stone King of Hell stood above Lionwolf in the black and golden prow of his car.

'You have touched the sun.'

'Yes.'

Hell's King was the first creature Lionwolf, in his most recent incarnation, had talked to, yet he did it simply, graciously, those qualities conveyed in even so small a reply.

'I am Hell,' said the stone King. 'Do you understand this now?'

'I understand.'

'To touch the sun is to displace the atoms which I am.'

'This world,' said Lionwolf, 'must be displaced.'

'By you?'

'Who else?'

Beside the stone King was his black queen, Winsome. She was like a statue of flesh, warm but not yet alive.

'Do you see the city?' said the King. 'That is Thasuba.'

Lionwolf gazed through the wallow of the storm. A city lay there, the same city, with high, high walls.

The guards had descended from the chariots; they too occupied the plain, inscrutable and adamantine.

And this was the tableau Curjai looked at as he bolted towards it and the sky fell.

The mammoth, a great vehicle smothered in coarse white hair, suddenly stalled.

Guri tapped it lightly, behind the ear.

'On we go.'

But the mammoth would not budge.

All through the grey stillness of that day they had moved across the terrain of the private hell. Truly now private it was. No others were there, neither men nor animals. Nowhere on the open waste, or among the distant boles and arches of ice-forest, did Guri perceive a sign of life, not even the semblance of it.

But the peace which came from this vacant land had instilled itself into him. He did not mind aloneness, perhaps never had. And to be free of false comrades, and actively real enemies, was a kind of bliss after what went before.

He had not been thinking much of the way ahead, letting the mammoth mostly tread as it wanted. It was actually a female, old today, tusks yellowing and encrusted so he would need to scour them carefully in the evening, providing this remission from horror continued. She might have been, the mammoth, a herd leader. They were generally females. Curious that. He had known of course yet never considered it. They must be sagacious then, like a Crax. Therefore, did she understand more than Guri did?

Ahead – what was it? Just whiteness, what he had taken all this while for a tall featureless escarpment of hard snow against cold sky. Yet in fact—

Guri tipped back his head.

The snow bank rose up and up. And up. It rose into the

amorphousness of the low heavens, and even there he could see it now he tried to, flat and stationary behind the drifting cloud.

He turned, left, right. He craned once more upward.

The snow bank not only ran into the sky but also off to both sides. At ground level it curved a little as it went, he could make out now too, curling to accommodate stands of forest or high rocks.

Could Guri fly here? He could not guess, but nor did he wish to try. For he sensed what lay there in front of him and away on either side would ascend to some impressive height and there join another thing, a thing in that case like – a roof.

Without reason, with utter certainty, it came to Guri that he had reached the end of his hell, and then the unassailable idea that he – and it – were contained, not only within high walls, but inside a *box*.

SIX

Like a new coastline, most of the harbour swallowed, the lesser bergs driven away by fire and towing: a shore now of ships, four hundred and seventy-eight of them, long vessels and Mother Ships, approximately nine thousand men, some with their women and their sons. The holds of the Mothers were stuffed not only with horsazin, but with lowing cattle and disgruntled fowl, with stores and barrels of water and alcohol far in excess of anything previously got up for a voyage. The Vorms had rallied, then they had called to the Kelps, and perhaps more softly to the Fazions of the outer isles. For sure not many Faz came in comparison; only six jalees of theirs were out along the liquid sea of the harbour. The Kelps had sent eleven jalees of long ships and narrow boats. Best take as many of your fellow reivers as you could with you on such an expedition, lest they be tempted to swoop on the homeland in your absence.

But then, would any of them be returning to the homeland anyway?

Centuries of experienced raiding, adventuring, piracy, buoyed up the collected fleet. That and the fierce, wolf-god-smiting goddess, who came and went yellow-haired among them, lighting torches with her eyes, smelling always of perfumes from the far south.

And there were the hero-children, too. Five of them were present by then. Rumour said at least twelve more were scattered on various of the northern isles. Of those here now, two were Kelpish, and one Faz, and one a Vorm from further along the Vormland coast. The fifth boy came from the continent, southwards. He seemed the eldest though all were adultly old beyond their reported years. Either oddly or inevitably, these boys did not cleave to each other. Every one looked on the rest with a remote and collected suspicion. They had, at least all five currently here, been *visibly* unique until this gathering.

Their disunity may though have seemed bizarre. Beings of such unusual excellence had been expected to flock together. Also, the Vorms were disappointed in the reaction of their goddess Saftri. She treated all the boys, including the eldest, Dayadin, who had been stolen from the Jafn as her special treat, in the same almost unliking way.

'But to bring her joy, that was why Krandif took him,' Mozdif had complained to Jord.

'Joy he doesn't bring her. She sits apart, biting her nails at the delay in setting off.'

'Are gods ungrateful? Yes,' said Mozdif. 'And my brother dreamed it, too. What reward does he get? Not even a blessing.'

Saftri, in her god-house, had stopped biting her nails. They always grew back in minutes, oval and charming, irritating her doubly. Just as children unhealthy or otherwise unsuitable to the voyage had been weepingly farmed out at remaining villages, so she had given Dayadin to the willing guardianship of the local women, who reverenced him and lavished on him every care.

'He is not my son.'

That was what Saftri said, both to Krandif's crestfallen crew and to herself.

But this was not really it. Dayadin was, if physically quite unlike Lionwolf, so *very* like him. For both were or had been flawless, and virtually extraterrestrial in their glamour and otherness.

She had been smitten by this once, with Lionwolf. But even then, if she had been honest, Saftri must have acknowledged she fooled herself constantly into believing that he was in some weird way only human – or *super*human – rather than totally foreign. With Dayadin, who was not the child of her body, she refused a second encounter with the sharp-edged blade of maternal love.

Besides, she had sworn to him that once he had acted for her as the Vorm fleet's lucky talisman she would return him to his own people, the Jafn Holas.

With the influx of other black children, Saftri had thought Dayadin might seek her and demand she take him back at once, *four* more such talismans now being to hand. But he did not. His part-adult mind was only too conscious how his fame had grown for the Vormlanders, whose jalees were nineteen in number. He had saved men from sharks and breathed down a gale. It seemed even towards those who stole him he had a sense of duty.

If Dayadin was unhappy or disorientated none of them but Saftri had been shown it. He was princely, courteous, and reserved. He had trained the hovor sprite Hilth to help the women in daily tasks. Oh, the jolly laughter, seeing the pails of chipped ice or milk skimmed along by a little creamy wind – that was, once they got over their fright.

How long readying the expedition had taken, however. The men coming round to the venture, the getting up of ships, the repair of any damaged, or building for those lost, the embassies to other islands, the in-gathering.

For a human community they had been in fact remarkably speedy. But for the gods obviously, to whom this was nothing, how it dragged.

Each evening Saftri scanned the west and south. Sometimes she flew up to make sure. Was anyone – anything – coming? No, not yet.

Why did he idle, the atrocious Zzth? Had she really impaired him so thoroughly? Was he *afraid* of her?

'I am alone,' she said to herself or to her temple. How strange. The notion of Zzth's impotence made her . . . lonely?

She had noticed Best Bear's mother no longer wanted to visit the grave. Best Bear's mother spent time with Dayadin, who in turn seemed not repelled by her. The woman's hair was growing back.

'Best Bear,' said Saftri, again aloud.

With an astonished inner turmoil of temper and distress, she thought, *Why couldn't I have borne a mortal son? Why couldn't I have stayed a mortal? What has been done to me? Why? Why?*

A mile below the Vormland, with its ice and mountains, villages and graves, driven-off bergs, liquid sea and garnered shipping, black murder was slowly swimming round and round.

The stem of the large Vormish island grew down into the bedrock under the sea. Brightshade, second half-god son of Zeth, was perambulating in his legless manner, circling the stem, thinking his own whale *shape*-thoughts of discontent and mishap.

Zeth had cowed him. Never before had anything been able to do that. Brightshade had always been bombastically villainous. It was the norm for him – he was a giant whale. Now the affront of a bully greater than he had torn his limited and sparkling world in shreds.

He was here to kill the woman-creature he had seen off before. It would not be so easy this time.

But also he was here to mourn the subjugation of self, the unfairness of everything.

Finally he sank down.

He lay, as he had after his father's beating, on the floor of the ocean, sometimes sipping fish, but with no enjoyment. He brooded.

Without a qualm he would destroy Saftri and her insectile horde of men and ships. That was nothing.

And then he would smash the islands. He would smash it all. And go to his father with the wreckage on his back. *Look what I have done for you.*

The god would respect him then.

Surely?

Yet Zeth had betrayed him anyway. Lionwolf had been the betrayal. And then that fiery other something – the *other* birth, Lionwolf's daughter – and Zeth had no concern for any of that.

The hugeness of the whale, if he had risen, would have matched the Vormland. Even to mountains, even to ships and graves, for Brightshade's back had all of those features and more.

He liked lying coiled about them, unknown; some consolation.

Nor was this the moment. He knew when the moment was. He would sense and hear it too, drumming down through the stem of the island.

Departure. The voyage. The open sea.

The morning of departure came.

The goddess walked along the shore. She blessed the men and the jalees, the horsazin, the cows, the water. She had got her way. A thorough blessing was the least she could do.

The Vormland crews were still mentally teetering between distrustful apprehension and their inbred craving for adventure. To live a saga – that was no bad thing. This would be sung of, one day.

Saftri was rowed out to the second Mother Ship of Krandif's two jalees. The boy, Dayadin, went with her.

The shamans who at all other times would ride the ship alone apart from animals in the underdecks, or prisoners taken, lurked beneath one of the nine masts, where the canvas was about to be unfurled. They were always ambivalent about Saftri. Gods too should know their place, and this one did not.

'Gentlemen,' said the goddess, giving them a look of mingled distaste and scorn.

Only one leapt forward, gyrating before her on the deck, waving rattles of bone, were-lights spraying from his garments and saliva from his lips.

On the planks a symbol was spontaneously drawn in anaemic fire.

Everyone stared at it.

Saftri read it by her power in three seconds.

'Danger,' she said. She herself had decided to be valiant. Her mouth quirked. 'Oh dear.' She spoke in Rukarian, then added in Vormish, 'Thank you for your warning, sir. But don't be afraid. I'm with you.'

The shaman's mouth too did something, pulling back over long, darkened teeth, wolf-like.

Saftri felt a twang of annoyance. *Do I despise every male, god or human?*

But Dayadin said, putting fists to forehead in the respectful way, 'Father, you are here to help them, also. They *should* be brave with so much help.'

Mollified, perhaps, the shaman changed the shape of his mouth, but even so danced on about the deck creating other fiery symbols, yellow and pinkish, the tint of sick. These seemed meaningless.

'Why do you make up to him?' said Saftri. 'He and his stole you.'

'You want me for your luck. The sooner we reach the new land, the sooner I can go.'

'Perhaps they'll refuse to let you go.'

She thought, *Why am I cruel? Yes he is beautiful but he is not Lionwolf, nor mine.*

She thought how Dayadin had cried only that once.

She said, 'Forgive me. I'll keep you safe.'

Saftri had vowed to him she would carry him back across all lands, all waters, no matter what.

Dayadin said, hushed and like a child, 'If you don't keep your word, I'll *swim* back there.'

Yes, so you would. Maybe even you could.

'I will keep my word.' She heard with relief the protectiveness in her tone.

The land moved, so it looked. Like huge slabs of multi-coloured ice the vast flotilla separated from the shore and breasted the sea.

Beyond the harbour lay green open ocean, ruffled with white rollers.

Looking back – many, many did so – the flattened crag of the island, the mountains, one today with a sunlit cloud on its shoulders. The sky was pallid but otherwise clear. The village and the bluff, the temple with its shells, a pair of last unheeded smokes rising, and kadi circling in the still air: these were the finishing scenes of home.

Women who had been strident for going away cried. Younger children sobbed noisily, confused. Down in the holds the horsazin trundled and the cows mooed, while sails bellied to the off-shore wind. Krandif's men began to sing. Presently others joined them. It was one of the already-established sagas, of Gunri the hero and wise-man, who had founded not only the Vormland but the nations of Faz and Kelp also. A hymn suitable for everyone.

In this way, singing, under a clear sky and the watching of one golden cloud, the fleet sailed out on to uncharted waters.

Feeling the drum purr down to him through the island's stalk, Brightshade woke from a partial dream. But he was always in readiness, his armour constantly on him and in his mouth. Silent and leisurely, *shark*-like, his impossible mass uncoiled with the oiled ease of a serpent.

Above, far off, he saw the shadow-shimmer of disturbance as the sea was runnelled by the prows, keels and oars of nearly five hundred ships.

Brightshade's thick tongue licked out, and spooned up a breakfast starter of shoaling fish.

He knew pleasure now, was hungry now, had an appetite despite everything for the job in hand.

The fleet, all gleaming ignorance, forged on, and the great whale maintained a steady amused pace with them, below. He turned over as he did this, like antique collected treasures, past events of wrecking: jalees of a hundred vessels sunk, men swallowed whole – not to eat, merely to *keep* within his cavernous guts which were haunted always by the residue of humanity, as by the least soluble parts of ships.

To Brightshade the depth of the sea was warm with guarantees.

Morning intensified and peaked to noon.

Up there by now the sky was a jewelry blue and the sea had blue in it, as if the sky had spilled over. A single chain of icebergs marched miles off to the west, glittering and of unusual shapes like Rukar diadems and Mother Ships all masts and rigging of semi-transparent ice that glowed like beryls.

Fish in thousands inadvertently plunged up from beneath. The reivers did not deduce that something deep down and more than inauspicious had dislodged them, and only spread their lines and nets and hauled in the bounty. Fish did rise. It was just good fortune.

In the second of Krandif's Mothers Saftri sat on her carven chair, forward of the deck. This vessel moved by thaumaturgics as well as sail, needing little guidance on calm seas.

Something nibbled at her composure, unacknowledged. She would not look in at her mind to see what it was.

She had crushed the whale tooth with a flick of acid light from one hand. Sympathetic magic, worthy of minor Rukarian royalty.

There was no reason to think of the whale.

It was only a beast.

Besides, even if – well, she had decimated its father, Zeth. The mammal, despite its bulk, must be child's play for her now.

And yet the small stain thinly spread along her consciousness whether she glanced there or not.

In the afternoon the icebergs were behind them, as were the occasional minute and uninhabited isles they had seen.

Saftri knew the overview of this seascape from her flights, but from the water itself everything was different.

The bounty of rising fish had stopped.

Some of the women who rode with their men were already gathering the caught fish, dropping them in pots of vinegar. On the decks of the Mothers, other women had braziers smoking under fish strung up like necklets of soapy gems. The sea smelled of fish also. Out here the odour was particularly strong, curiously increasing.

He was lifting himself now, the giant shadow beneath.

He was driving his land-long body more swiftly – outstripping in a matter of minutes the ships above.

Brightshade nurtured his own *shape*-thoughts of the spectacular. He wanted to present himself to the fleet before he destroyed it. He wanted them to see and be quite sure of what he was, his illimitable size, his black brilliance, his horn like a tower of white onyx. He looked *forward* to confounding them first with *himself*, as the prologue to their death.

Was Brightshade aware that this was his recompense for Zeth's harshness? That the arch-bully had made him a bully too, where formerly he had been only ruthless, indifferent and mighty?

'Look,' said one man after another, one woman after another, 'what is that?'

'Where?'

'Ahead of us – to the star-side – *there*.'

'More fish rising.'

'A herd of the whale folk it is.'

A fresh wind blustered suddenly towards them over the crests of the sea. The wind was huge and it stank of fish-life and of the decaying loams and botanical submarine detritus that massed the ocean's lowest floors.

The ships rocked wildly. On their poles the sheets of sail wagged and cracked against their stays.

Saftri got up, as the shamans sprang yelping into the ship's bow.

Dayadin said quietly, 'It's land coming up from the bottom of the sea.'

Saftri as before felt herself gripped by terror. Memory was her enemy. All it would give her was the recollection of her journey over a diluvian back, her incarceration in mud, her freezing execution and her second death which, by now, she had almost managed to blot out.

Brightshade, night-in-day, rose from the sea.

So *softly, carefully* he came up, not wanting to dislodge too much. Not breaching, not splashing, neither striking with nor standing up on his tail to put out the sun. No, he must be subtle now if they were to see his glory properly. *Subtly* he arrayed the surface of the water with all his landmass magnificence, raising his head the last very high, and also the serrated fan of his tail, *demonstrating* them, while the horn on his kingly head spiked men's future and killed it.

He too had grown since last Saftri beheld him, since Lionwolf and Guri had traversed his back in a quest of two days. He had grown since Zeth last thrashed him, even, by a touch.

He heard them shrieking, felt the *shapes* of their mindless agony of fear and disbelief, the chaos as human hope gave way.

See me.

See.

Then from his blowhole he fountained out, with the utmost delicacy, a diamanté streamer of water, allowing it to fall down on them like the mildest tickle of icy hail.

The jumbled sea, displaced by his arrival – in spite of all his cleverness – had begun to seethe.

Men ditched in the waves clung to oars and the sides of vessels. Women held their children as if to press them back inside the womb – uselessly. There was no safety to be had.

Not only by the gargantuan size of the leviathan, instinctively they were educated by other elements about the whale. He was sentient, he *thought*. He was malign. He was death.

The shamans gabbled. Their fires created webs that were then disrupted by electric explosions. The explosions *stuck* to each other and plopped into the sea.

Gradually a silence closed over the ships. They froze in it. All outcry died. A preface.

Krandif, his own son in his arm, a lad of ten, terrified yet turning a hard man's face to nemesis so Krandif – even at the gate of ending – was proud of him, Krandif said to the silence in a whisper, 'Dayadin, son of Arok – find a song – find a way to breathe – *now* – or we die. You with us.'

Saftri was struggling with herself. She tried to energize her powers. But they were lamps without kindling. This, most horrible of all, was like some appointment she had had to keep – now three times.

Dayadin spoke, perhaps not with his voice. 'Hilth! Carry me—'

Attention only for the whale, still they glimpsed something else whizz through the sky. It was only part of the nightmare.

Brightshade though, with one sidelong sun-splinter eye, noted a child running over the air towards him, winged with a sort of fleecy breeze.

It would be nothing to snap up this bug.

Then Brightshade hears Dayadin talking to him, talking in *shapes*.

'How fine you are,' says Dayadin, in *shapes*, 'you are blacker even than I. You are black as the other side of a star.'

Brightshade's brain answers, nearly inadvertently, a *shape* – irresistible – of accepting gratification.

A second *shape* follows, which observes that Dayadin, though nowhere as black or vast as Brightshade, is for a human thing very black, better than most. *Courtesy?*

The hovor holds Dayadin before Brightshade's eye, which is small compared to the rest of the whale, but round and large as a wheel to the boy, a wheel or a window of stained glass.

Brightshade tautologically assures Dayadin, now in *shapes*, what he has already demonstrated: that he is able to extinguish him and all the other life over there in a matter of instants.

Dayadin neither replies nor seems interested, if anything disappointed. A vague *shape* filters to Brightshade that Dayadin thinks this would be a distinct waste of Brightshade's genius.

Brightshade looses the thread slightly of his murder mission. He is an adolescent in some ways. He wants to show off now, because Dayadin has something also about himself, something that burns and is wonderful. This something was all over the former foe, Lionwolf. It evoked envy and rivalry. But Dayadin is no rival. He is not anything to do with Zeth Zezeth. And yet he is – *godlike*. He is – like Brightshade. Dark as night and shining as day. A smaller package. An exquisite gnat.

Brightshade is aware of the hovor too, some non-corporeal slave. The child is a magician.

The whale twitches daintily and the sea gulps and crashes. The hovor topples about but never lets go of Dayadin. Who – *laughs*.

Brightshade thinks to him: *You must visit me, admire me. I can wait to batter and bone-break and drown those on the ships. Until you're done.*

Dayadin thinks back, *Why drown them? What do they count for?*

I have sworn I will.

Who could make you *swear anything?*

One there is.

Dayadin is about to go on with his persuasive murmur of *shapes.* But this is the moment Saftri the goddess regains herself.

Maybe it is Dayadin's risk-taking valour, or the fix she has got all of them into, some deep human idea of behaving honourably.

Whatever it is, and perhaps it is only solipsism, the power lamps flare on again.

Saftri stretches out her hands and opens wide her attractive mouth and over the ships of her people, over the heads of no longer gibbering shamans, she breathes her lioness fire. It goes itself like a tidal wave, and smashes into the mountain of Brightshade about the area of his ribcage.

She has aimed well away from Dayadin. She does a new thing next, casting a ring of air more solid than steel running half a mile upward and rather more down, about the reiver fleet, to protect it as the whale – as now he does – rolls and thrashes. Saftri has truly hurt him; worse let it be said than any preparatory punishment of Zzth's.

A kind of screaming fills the sky, high as a whistle, scalding the ears so again the people on the ships cry out in turn.

But Saftri sees her cordon of protection holds them against the jar of the outer waters. The water *inside* is only very choppy.

She means psychically to lasso Dayadin and bring him back, up over the cordon, but now she cannot find him.

Then she does. Although not with her eyes.

Dayadin, son of Arok, Nirri and Chillel, was spun round and round by Brightshade's paroxysm. The hovor wound Dayadin like a rope, clinging to him as much as supporting him. And in that timeless second Brightshade did what it had been in his thoughts to do, did it less from malevolence than from a desire to possess, which had now become automatic as all his colossal body rang with blinding pain. Choking and seared, Brightshade undid the doors of his mouth, the palisades of his teeth that were like domed buildings of zinc. Brightshade inhaled and swallowed. And Dayadin, son of Arok, goes down into the belly of the whale.

Ninth Volume

BLIND SEEING

The nostalgia the essential soul feels, when in the physical world, for the so-called hells and heavens of the after-and fore-life, compares directly with the nostalgia it also feels, when in the spiritual world, for the so-called real world of the flesh. The purposes however are different. The astral soul seeks review and integration of its physical lives in order to expand its wisdom. While, world-locked, it dreams of luminous places where it may enjoy – and suffer – those adventures physical life has denied it.

Kraag dictum: Southlands and South-East Continent.

ONE

His voice – shouting, tolling like a hoarse bell, descending to a ragged maniacal drone – was constant there as some fearful wind. At first the land, the walls of the house, seemed to quake. Then they became used to it. Now, if it should ever cease, what then? But perhaps it never would.

The travellers who had struggled in across the snow waste, blizzard driven, paused below the great house to gaze up at its towery and the sightless darkened windows, listening in awe.

The storm of weather was nearly over. A few flails of snow flared across the dusk.

What is this place?

It is a magician's mansion.

But that sound—

The torment of one he punishes.

Presently they moved away, plodding on towards the village called Stones, which they had been told of by other travellers met on the ice plains. They were all Rukarian, of the outlying steadings and villages, whose cores over the past two years had somehow fallen in socially and architecturally, like rotted vegetables. Stones it seemed for some reason still stood, though in poor repair.

They had heard of the sorcerous Stones themselves too, and took care not to go close to them.

From one of the high windows of Thryfe's southern house, Jemhara had watched the people come and go. She saw where they must be heading. She herself had been to the village yesterday, as sometimes she did when he was a little more sluggish. Then the magical house servants were sufficient to guard him.

He and she had existed here some months.

To begin with she had only been relieved to arrive, astonished and grateful when the house, at her request, opened itself to let them in. Thryfe had been in a stupor, the same stupor that felled him in the Telumultuan Chamber. Only three of the house gargolems remained active; the rest had disappeared. Also only two of the feminine jinnan spirits and one male jinan were there to tend the building. Above in the towery the wonderful scrying oculum had smashed itself to grains like sugar. Below in the subtor, though these doors too opened for Jemhara, there was nothing she thought she could understand or with which, therefore, she could help him.

Thryfe regained consciousness on the second day. During the first he was like a man near death. Then vitality came back, and the wordless shouting and roaring started.

It was impossible to quieten.

The gargolems saw to it that Thryfe stayed bound, for his own protection and hers. The jinnans soothed the hurts and abrasions he gained when striking out, resisting the padded bonds, howling until he choked.

Jemhara and the jinnans mixed curative potions or nourishing broths. When he grew intermittently enfeebled and almost docile, only moaning in that fearful low rasp, they were able to spoon some of these into him. He seemed unaware of it and of them all, or else saw them as shadows.

No conversation was feasible with either gargolems or jinnan. You could only issue instructions or receive general news. The masculine jinan did not talk at all. It was the handyman of the mansion, hunting and setting traps for food, feeding the lashdeer team, mortaring up loose tiles, and so on.

Jemhara did not talk to herself.

Deep in her mind she thought, *Thryfe now sees only Thryfe and the crime he considers he is responsible for.*

But it was more desperate than that, and perhaps she knew as much. Thryfe saw only *futility*. Nothing was of any use. No

act, however valiant, was worth the attempt. Facing the nega-
tive abyss, he refused to look away. It was no longer his rage
at himself or other men, or whatever unknown gods. It was
nullity he strove to embrace and, at the same moment, nullity
he raved at in utter revulsion.

He was very strong and of unusual endurance and his mage-
powers were of the highest order. For those reasons he had
survived, and because of that alone Jemhara had been able to
resuscitate him in the city. Yet she had brought him back to this
state. It was a living hell. It was cold and had no end.

Despair crept over Jemhara.

Her initial high hopefulness evaporated. Her own endurance
held but became wan. She felt old, she was bereft. Sometimes
she thought fiercely that she should have killed him outright in
the Insularia to spare him this. Occasionally she became
enraged herself, wishing to strike him, wishing to run away.

But she loved him, loved what he was or had been, and
could not leave.

The awful clamour of his voice, when it had sunk so low she
could not, waking from slumber, hear it, frightened her with
absence. She would rush to the room he lay in above the subtor
in case he had died.

She only touched him now and then. She believed he would
hate her touch. But now and then when he stretched there,
droning and muttering in half-sleep, she brushed one finger
over his forehead, or set it on the back of his hand.

Once or twice she dreamed again he approached to murder
her. Once too she dreamed she kissed his hand instead of
merely setting one fingertip on it. This dream but not the other
made her weep.

The evening after the vagrants had stared at the house and then
gone up to the village, Thryfe dropped into one of his more
docile ebbs. Jemhara went out of the mansion, and herself
walked away up the slope towards the Stones.

It took her as always about an hour and a half to cover the distance.

As she got nearer the moons were coming up, all three of them, and full, remaking night as day. The familiar curl of ice-forest spread across the vista. The village was over there, but in the bright moonlight she could not tell if fires or lamps were burning now.

She had not visited the Stones, unlike the village, since her return here.

There had been some slight alteration in the terrain; a ridge of impacted snow had drifted into prominence. When she had climbed it she saw the Stones about seventy paces away.

Jemhara stopped in her tracks.

Phenomenal always, now the enigmatic ring had become fantastic. For it had *grown*.

Before she had sometimes considered this might be happening, but never been sure. Now, like infants she had not seen for a while, the Stones had shot upward.

Not all were the same. Some had reached a height of fifteen, sixteen or seventeen feet; others towered thirty feet or more. And all were entirely and flamingly lit. They had assumed an unusual colour also. They were green.

The light slowly pulsed, but did not otherwise change. Each stone flamed like a jewel.

A sort of radiation seemed to come from them. She felt the skin of her face tighten, and the roots of her hair. There was a low audible vibrancy, almost like . . . music.

Jemhara formerly might well have retreated over the ridge.

But now the perhaps unsafe sorcery of the Stones lured her. After everything else, her ability to be afraid had lessened or rather grown unimportant.

She went on.

The jade light covered her, tinting her complexion and cloth-ing as it had the surrounding snow.

As she came among them she found the Stones had in addi-tion a scent. She did not know what it was. It reminded her of ripe fruit or salad from a king's hothouse.

The musical undertone played through her ears.

She stood at the centre of the ring and remembered how she had darted here as a hare, and Thryfe had pursued and caught her and the world been refashioned.

Looking at the coloured snow she thought, *Like myths of grass . . .*

Then she discovered that she leaned forward, bending to the ground. She did not know why. She took up a handful of the green-tinted snow, which here was loose and simple to get hold of.

The snow too carried the refreshing edible smell. It chilled her hand, and straightening up again she slipped it into the deeper pocket of her cloak. Probably outdoors it would not melt. Snow and ice now had this property: human warmth was not enough to quench them.

Suddenly, everything else ceased. The scent and sound and feeling of radiation. The brilliant green light went out.

That was like a blow. How dark the night of three full moons.

'What – have I done?' she stammered to the Stones, now huge dark monoliths. 'Have I offended you?'

Another strange thing happened then. A woman crossed over the new snow hill above. Jemhara took her for one of the travellers. But she had a curious appearance – rough and layered, with wild tufting hair, and in her hands, or so Jemhara thought, branches and twigs, also hand-like, which she must mightily have torn from the adjacent forest. The woman, passing over the ridge, grinned at Jemhara. Then she was gone – perhaps down the far side of the hill, perhaps into some spot the triple moonshine, oddly, had not reached.

In Jemhara's other lesser pocket something buzzed softly. She put her hand there, and located the twig from the rural temple, the twig that had seemed to direct her in the Telumultuan Chamber. She had forgotten it.

She eased out between the Stones. 'Pardon me . . .'

Looking back some minutes later, she saw them stationed, lightless still, glistening only faintly from the moons.

When, two hours later, she re-entered Thryfe's house, he

was already bawling again. She had heard the distressing outcry almost a mile off.

Jemhara went to the room where they had bound him.

All three gargolems had hold of Thryfe, who writhed and roared. He was like a deranged beast, no longer a man. She did not know him.

Because she approached him, the gargolems voiced a warning. Normally she kept back at the room's edges when he was this bad. Not now.

Thryfe did not, she thought, exactly see her, yet he reared towards her nevertheless, sensing something that must be to him an enemy or threat of some type. She would have to be swift.

Bringing out the snow, which had been coloured over green and now was only a mottled white, she ran forward and crushed it into his open bellowing mouth.

There were never any words to his tirade.

Now there was a word. It was the word of sheer extraordinary silence.

He froze there, as if contact with the snow had changed him to a pillar of ice.

Through his face, his body, behind the skin, muscle and bone, she saw something plunge that was like a boiling cloud. His eyes retained it the longest. They seemed to fragment in swirlings of smoke and fire. Then the cloud was gone, and still he stood there, static, and his eyes looked at her. They *saw* her.

Jemhara did not know what she had done. But she beheld he had come back into himself. Not in pleasure or relief, not to be thankful or generous or benign. But to be Thryfe the Magician – oh yes, to be that. So when he spoke to her she did not flinch either in amazement or pain.

'Here you are again. I told you once to stay far off from me. What a meddler you are, Jema. You can leave nothing alone.'

He straightened up and shook himself, and the gargolems and the great padded bonds were sloughed from him like slips of paper.

'Fetch water and wine,' he said to the jinnan which had wafted to the door. 'And something to eat. It's been a long fast.'

Jemhara raised her head.

He saw that.

Cold as the hell he had inhabited, he said to her, 'And I'm to thank you for my release? No. Why do you think I brought myself to this? It was my *atonement*, you stupid bitch. Once you undid my life. Now you undo my death. Get away from me. As I've told you before, you will prefer to take yourself off to any travel arrangements I contrive for you.'

She did not lower either her head or her eyes.

'I've done as it was given me to do.'

'Given you. *Who* gave it?'

'You,' she answered, her voice quite flat.

'You're mad, you little whore. Get out.'

'Yes, I shall go.'

She turned and moved to the door. Pausing there, she glanced back at him. He had left off looking at her.

Aloud she said, 'You're not such a weakling, my lord, as you like to think.'

Outside the room she whispered, 'If any god hears, help him, help him.' She did not ask for herself, knowing she was now beyond their help.

She went through the mansion and out into the night and began again to walk up the slope, this time towards the village.

Vagrancy had made them uneasy. Their nearness to the fluctuating, vivid Stones had increased this. They were glad eccentricities of the landscape hid the supernatural sight from them when in the village.

The next morning, as a powdery sun rose, some of the women went out to chip water.

A woman was already there.

She was beautiful, her black hair streaming down.

They could not read her face, even though her soul was now written on it. They could not read, after all.

'What is it, lady?' The leader of the travellers had nervously emerged. He identified this woman as somehow relevant, maybe dangerous.

'What do you need?' she replied.

They gazed at her, flummoxed by a vague potential cornucopia.

Jemhara was exhausted from her journey and her recent experience. She said plainly to them, 'A well of liquid water? And do you need fire?'

They *had* fire. It was kept alight with difficulty in a semi-sealed vessel, because they had no witch left to bring it out of the air. Water they only got by chipping.

Jemhara advanced to the container of fire and twisted its element to stay always alive when in the pot. She told them what she had done in brief sensible words. But as she talked the fire erupted in red florations – *muscular*.

Then she made a well for them in an old ice cistern. Jemhara unlocked the snow, the earth – she who could defrost ice. The water came, astounding everyone who saw, even conceivably Jemhara herself, for the fluid burst from the cistern and poured over the ground, and would not desist. Only far off did it freeze and become a slide. The children soon went there and skidded madly about. But in and by the well the water constantly flowed.

Jemhara next set about the shoring up and fastening of the village. She enabled, by her magic, roofs to coalesce and walls to congregate. With spells she laid thresholds and re-established broken rooms, bricks and logs scurrying at her command, while the travellers gaped.

Her heart was flung wide as any window. She wished these people to be secure and hale, so that they might be usefully available to Thryfe – to be, in fact, assistants to him on whatever course his Magikoy aptitude decided.

She had been so hurt – that was, grievously harmed – that she did not truly know what she did. Yet some stricture persisted. *Him* she would serve, even if indirectly, even if he had disallowed it.

When all was done, the travellers were uplifted to a fever.

She noted their tiny ecstasy with a dim gladness, seeing how they, like the water and the fire, flowered in the slipstream of what she had worked for them, such *little* practicalities.

But she saw too how she had warped and waned.

Jemhara, silent in their adulation, took herself off and left them the minuscule world of the village of Stones.

She had an itinerary she herself did not grasp. She wished to cast all segments of her awareness *elsewhere*.

She went away over the waste of snow, leaving her sorcerous abilities to become legends in altruism and power in the village. They did not know her name so called her *Ravenhair*. But Thryfe they knew of because she had, during her short sojourn, educated them. Thryfe therefore they valued, and would be prepared to assist.

Thryfe meanwhile dreamed of his mother.

As he watched, the black wolf rent her in bits.

He woke abruptly, and for some minutes did not know where he was, or *what* he was.

Then he recollected.

One of the jinnans was there offering him a snack.

Thryfe began to speak uncouthly to her. He curtailed himself and spoke with politeness.

'No. My thanks. It isn't necessary.'

He pulled himself up on the couch, longing to remain where he was. He was drained of energy and could sleep he thought for ever.

But as he strove between unawareness and consciousness, some other urge forged through his veins.

Thryfe thrust himself to his feet and balanced by the wall. When the jinnans came, both of them, to aid him, he showed them they must move away. They did so.

What have I become?

He did not know.

Memory was all a book of granite which had been scored

and *axed* with words he could not decipher. He saw what had occurred, and his part in it – or removal from it – but all that was as if some other had done these deeds, and some other had been written of.

Nevertheless, in the citadel of his intellect he *knew*. It had been him, right enough.

The pain flowed through and from him, endlessly renewed, like water from an unlocked well.

Like fire that cannot die.

He staggered again to the couch and lay down, and again dreamed. This time he dreamed of a woman with long black hair, lovely – and *prohibited*.

In the dream he embraced her. And she embraced him. Day broke like the well he had partly envisaged, light flowing forth as the water had done. Thryfe tried to hold his loved one back from the morning, her sweet face, her sweetest self – but she put him aside smiling. Out into the world she went.

And under the tree, where the ice hung like swords, the wolf came.

The wolf came and cut her into pieces.

Jemhara, leaving the village of Stones, did not visit the Stones themselves, although she had informed the villagers that certain marvels went on there which should perhaps be monitored.

She did not care. She found however she cared for human things. Love had taught her all about itself by now, and she gained solace from solacing *them*. But she was like a sort of ghost.

She walked across the land. She did this without analysis, in some way sure she was capable of survival, and in another unmoved as to whether she might be.

She did not affect her shape-change to the physical persona of a hare. She could not be bothered.

Jemhara came on empty farms wrecked under the innovative advances of snow. She came on deserted bothies where dead animals lay, their carcasses picked clean of flesh – and cleared of soul. Other villages she entered, where beasts and men were wavering, hung between body and spirit. She stole among them all, putting right what she could, adjusting, for by now Jemhara had a true perception of what was appropriate, either living or dead.

She saved many lives, giving gifts of constantly flowing water, enduring fire, salvaged homes and provender. Many took her for a great mageia, and often – since this was in the Ruk – for one of the Magikoy returned to them, a forgiveness of the gods.

Unlike Jemhara's scryer which had burst at the destruction of Ru Karismi, the great oculum in the towery of the South House had only displayed the message of the White Death, then mutely closed its eye. Perhaps even so its structure was made friable by the experience.

Though not a living thing, each of these enormous Rukarian magical mirrors possessed, like so many so-called inanimate objects, a fundamental life which developed in accordance with individual power, not to mention constant use. Thus, in some form, the oculum did live. And it was the transcribed image of another live entity, the rising of the whale called Brightshade on one of his calmer over-sea appearances, which had destroyed the oculum's fabric. None of them had ever been able to relay a picture of Lionwolf, save in – self-protective? – symbols. The firefex was shown, a flame-cloud, similar things. But this other being was a god-whale, and only his whaleness had been captured in the mirror. At that inevitably his *godness* damaged it. Maybe the oculums, or this one, had been prey to the defect of racism: thinking the race of animals less than that of humanity. If so, a high price to pay.

Thryfe, locked those years before in timeless lovemaking with Jemhara, had not received the oculum's signals, just as, for the same reason, he had not been present at the White Death. The oculum cracked and flew apart.

Ten days after Jemhara woke Thryfe from the last of his madness with snow from the Stones, he reappeared in the upper chamber. He was dressed in a workman's clothes, and followed by all three of the gargolems.

He ordered the room and the workforce, himself pitching in with the readiness of any trained labourer. His own lingering debility he ignored, along with those impairments which now stayed with him – a slight limp in the left leg, a stiffness in the fingers of his left hand, a tiredness of his eyes and lungs.

To such as Thryfe any bodily infirmity was to be treated with scorn. Either it would disperse with exercise or he would become accustomed to it. He could utilize other strengths to compensate.

The physical task was additionally good. He had been too long – *years* long – inactive, and he had thought too much.

Needless to say, the repair of the oculum was not a project for any ordinary workman. These also were Magikoy skills.

Passing between the lower subtor and the upper towery, he limped up and down hundreds of stairs, the gargolems with him bearing implements or finished sections of glass. Magery was stirred into every item, even the carefully ground lenses of the mirror-eye itself. Day and night the mansion was liable to echo now not to infernal shouts and cries but to the notes of hammer and burnisher, winch and counterpoise.

The commission took more than a month.

By then, though Thryfe still halted a little on the left side and must often flex his fingers to unknot them, he was generally healed and seemingly as vigorous as he ever had been.

As for the oculum, it began to operate again, slowly to begin with, itself relearning ability and force.

Beyond the house white weather scourged the landscape. Blue days went by. Storms returned.

In the magic mirror the first scene Thryfe searched for and was given was of the plains around the dead city of Ru Karismi.

Thryfe saw, as he had predicted more than two years ago, an uncanny change was now taking place there. The sheaths of snow and ice were granulating, becoming a kind of bitter little sand, composed of motes like marble salt. Here and there already a crouching mesa of ice had extruded from the expanse, where the sweeping up of the sands for some reason left it whole. Generally the level of the land had dropped.

This was like the great Uaarb, the ice desert of the farthest north. There, antique Magikoy teaching had it, weapons the like of those that had been deployed in the Ruk were once before unleashed, experimentally.

During the storms and snowfalls, if she was far from any settlement as frequently she was, Jemhara sheltered in snow caves, in ice-jungles, or sat on the open ground.

It was no longer complex to ward off the elements. She could erect a sort of cage of air about herself, or draw thick curtains of it over the doormouths of cave-holes and leaning byres.

Twice she came on caravans of wandering unhappy people. The first she gave her usual help, but could not advise as to where they should tend. She did not know herself where *she* should go. All she wanted was, after all, to go back to him. And that she could and would not do.

The first caravan decided for itself on the ruin of Or Tash. Something might be made of it, they said, for they had heard others were settled in there.

The second caravan reacted to Jemhara in another way.

Some of its members had already fled from Kandexa during the war. Others were from various more eastern settlements round about, which had either been wholly abandoned or simply ceased to function. The dying of all these outer environs of the Ruk was like nerves dying in a human body at some killing central injury a vast distance from the eventual paralysis. There were however with this caravan a group of people from the heart city itself, Ru Karismi.

These knew Jemhara, even in her spoiled clothing, which anyway had come to her from the city by the Gargolem's will.

'Lady – you are a queen.'

'No,' said Jemhara.

'Yes,' they insisted. 'The second queen of Sallusdon, King Paramount. His widow.'

'No longer.'

'*Yes*. How can you untie such a knot? You were crowned there.'

'I saw her crowned,' stated one of the older men, 'on the high terrace above the stair, sparkling. I saw it.'

Accused unfalsely of her royalty, Jemhara recalled how she assassinated Sallusdon at Vuldir's order. None of these people knew *that*.

'It's done now,' she said, meaning everything.

They had a minor mageia with them who saw to the fire and any healing. The woman was from some small Rukarian town and had dyed her hair pale blue – but now it was mostly grown out, a faded greying brown with pale blue streaks and ends. The mageia showed serene respect for Jemhara, not because she had been a queen but because she was a more puissant sorceress. She gladly let Jemhara work her prodigies in the repair department, assisting modestly if required. Jemhara next taught the witch, who learned quickly, the knack of melting ice. Other women included in the class were not able to learn. Obviously the lesser mageia was herself latently gifted.

'I wish you'd stay with us,' said the mageia. 'What you might be able to lesson me in – I'd be grateful.'

Jemhara shook her head.

All the others called her by royal titles, some elaborate in the Rukarian manner.

'Stop this,' she said. 'I am Jemhara.'

During that time the caravan had made a choice and moved on – or back – towards Kandexa, which lay many miles off on the north-western hilt of the continent's shore.

Jemhara was presented with a slee that had a tattered half-shell awning of silk. She refused a driver, handling the team of two lashdeer herself. Soon, seeing the witch bumping along uncomfortably on her sheep-drawn slederie raft, Jemhara invited the woman into the carriage.

Her purpose was as they journeyed to teach the mageia

whatever might be possible before she, Jemhara, went away. But strangely, after a while Jemhara found the older woman's company suited her. Sometimes they even laughed together. Hearing her own voice, laughing, Jemhara was always startled. But the ache of loss soon came back. It was, though the subjects were different, the same for all of them.

They had travelled nearly a month through the often falling, heavy snow when Jemhara understood that they no longer asked her if she would stay, and that when she spoke of her departure they smiled patiently, confidently accepting what she had not. Which was that they had adopted her and she would now accompany them to a ruined city by the sea.

After a particularly violent snowstorm, Thryfe was alerted one morning to the advent of a band of people under the mansion walls.

One of the gargolems went out, to which they haltingly explained that they wished to have a few words with the magus, should he be able to spare the minutes.

Thryfe, absorbed in rebuilding of oculum and self, had thought very little of humanity. Having betrayed it, what right had he to think of it at all?

But the crassness of that had begun to reveal itself to him. Guilt maybe was one of the most selfish and self-focused vices. It let you off any further attempt to aid or amend, saying you were beneath any virtue, so need not try.

He went down, in the elegant garments of what he was, a mage. He went down remembering that his vocation above all else was service, and that being allocated to a court of kings had never been his preference: he had envied those Magikoy who strove in the lesser towns and villages.

'Good morning,' he said.

The villagers nodded low bows and spoke his name with firm esteem.

He had assumed the storms must have caused them trouble in a dilapidated village.

They assured him that this was not the case.

'The lady came by, the Magikoy.'

Thryfe stared at them and for a second, despite Jemhara's praise of him to them, they feared his eagle's eyes. Then he had corrected himself, seemed only bleak.

'A Magikoy,' he repeated.

'Yes, sir. Like yourself. We called her Ravenhair.'

Thryfe knew no Magikoy woman by that name. He *had* known one who might go by it.

'All that she did for us, sir, prevented any damage from the worst storm. The fire still burns too, and the liquid water's constant. She taught us easy protective charms, she said they were only small things, but that wind blew slantwise and missed us.'

Another man said, 'I believe it was her own power she gave us, a tiny slice of it, or how else could we do such things, never being Magikoy-trained.'

'She is not—' Thryfe paused. 'She isn't Magikoy.'

He noted they did not credit this. They seemed to be thinking he lied to protect her in some way, when of course in reality—

Torrents of rage threatened again to smash through his brain and heart. He curbed them, wrestled them away.

That whore Jemhara, what did she play at? What had she done? How dare she do these things—

He said he would go with them to the village, make sure all was well.

They were delighted, like youngsters wanting to show off.

When they reached the village of Stones, Thryfe saw all they had said was a fact. Not an ice-brick was off let alone a wall down. Contented lamasceps foraged from lines of dormant grass that seemed less dormant than potentially *growing* under some trees. Water bubbled from a cistern with women chattering round it. The worst of the gale-blown snow lay in neat heaps over on the north side – where they declared it had drifted of itself.

'See how well the children are, sir. She blessed us, so I think.'

'Ravenhair,' he said. That was all. And then, 'But what then do you need from me?'

'Nothing, High Magus. It was she who said we should be ready to serve *you*, if you should require it. And we are. It seemed time we should come and tell you so.'

TWO

Curjai had reached the tableau of figures and chariots.

He seemed to himself to have been running for months.

The stone King stood in the prow of his car, with the gorgeous queen beside him.

All around grouped the guards of Hell, their snake-hair sizzling and the vizors hiding their eyes. There were no jatchas. In the traces of the chariots, the spider-horses resembled machines temporarily disconnected.

Vashdran stood unmoving also.

Vashdran was new as a new-minted coin of gold. He was twenty years of age, or twenty-two perhaps, and had been born without pain, and grown to his present stature and status in ten days.

It seemed to Curjai the tempest of winds and dislodged falling slates of sky was easing.

Cloud had closed over the sun that had been pulled down and then replaced, cloud like a bandage.

Vashdran turned to Curjai. 'We're going to the city over there. It's called Thasuba now, they say.'

'It's the same name, isn't it?' Curjai said.

'Yes, always the same name.'

But the name *Vashdran* – Curjai pondered it – that name too had altered itself into another form. Lionwolf.

'Lionwolf,' said Curjai softly.

'Yes?'

'Are we prisoners here again?' And asking, Curjai felt himself a child.

Lionwolf said, 'No, Escurjai.'

'Why do they stand there then?' Curjai said stupidly.

'They are waiting for me,' said Lionwolf.

'For – you?'

'Go on,' said Lionwolf quietly to the King and queen and the guards.

The guards went smartly back into their vehicles, and the spider-horses woke up. Legs and runners moved. The stone King's chariot also turned for the city.

'We'll walk,' said Lionwolf to Curjai.

A funnel of wind roared above. Another tile of sky flashed down between them.

Lionwolf raised his head. 'Hush now,' said the Lionwolf to the sky of Hell.

And the sky of Hell was hushed.

Thasuba's walls were high and white but the gates that led into it were made, or so they appeared, of polished bronze. Above them a trumpet or horn, visible only as a round O, expressed a mellow series of tones.

People crowded about the gates and were out on the plain itself, despite the still-ominous overcast, and going in behind the chariots of the Hell King Curjai and Lionwolf entered a wide square, surrounded by houses and mansions, with walkways and stairs going up on all sides.

'This city is nothing like the others,' said Curjai.

Even the people were more *actual*. Men and women held up babies to watch the brief procession. There were calls and applause, but the vapid praise-songs stayed unsung. Welcome to Thasuba.

The palace still dominated the heights. When they reached it, there were groves of trees like cedars, glass-trunked and crusted, as normal, with prisms of ice. The doors of this palace were silver.

Flowers were thrown as always. Blue and mauve and white,

some of the last with narrow stripings of dark pink. Looking into one, Curjai saw only calyx and stamens.

Going into the palace he found it uneasily partly familiar in a manner of the world. It was rather like, in its layout, the royal house at Padgish. A great hall opened with a floor of veined marble. Pillars rose at strategic intervals. There were windows that gazed on ice gardens elaborately laid out.

Everything had changed.

Curjai's mind had never had to strive to accept the ability of flight, let alone a fully able body. But now it circled warily the concept of the make-over of Hell. *This place is unphysical – anything may happen, and does—* Like a morose dog nevertheless, round and about this reasoning his mind went prowling, looking for another solution. Looking for chinks in the armour of the unreal. He had never heard of the Kraag, who would have told him nothing seemed more solid than what was unreal, since the unreal passed itself off constantly as reality. Curjai was uncomfortable, and as Lionwolf walked up the hall with the stone King, the black queen moving separately beside them, Curjai dropped back. He stood by a pillar and observed, and when a girl came to offer him wine, for the first time in Hell he refused it.

Lionwolf and the King were seated by one of the windows. The queen had seated herself at the next window along.

Curjai heard clearly what was said.

Soon he moved from the pillar and sat down himself on a bench against the wall.

Rays of the wounded day and the reflection of the garden ice shone sombrely through the hall. There were now no creatures in it but for those four.

'What then,' said the King, 'do you think of this city?'

Lionwolf said, 'Much improved.'

They spoke like royal men, equals.

They had cups of wine, even the King, whose stone lips parted to drink, the wine going down with no motion of the throat.

Lionwolf looked deep into the palace hall. He could see

when he did this the eddying currents that composed it, dispersing, reinventing, holding all together.

'Ask your question,' said the King.

'Ask yours.'

'Very well,' said Hell's King. 'What am I?'

Lionwolf's own question, constant and native to him as his glamour. He said, 'You, sir King, are the stony aspect of myself, my obduracy, barely flexible. And from your hard stones, as once you almost told me, I built my Hell and made you its King over me. About the same time as I put the blue sun of my shame into the sky.'

'And you, aside from myself, are what, Lionwolf?'

Curjai, listening, flinched at the voice of the King. For suddenly it was not all those voices it had been, but only one – Lionwolf's own.

And Lionwolf said, 'I? Human and god, lion and wolf, stone, bone, blood, shadow and light. But the shadow burns and the light has darkness in it. In fact I am like all the rest. A polyglot, an amalgam. I listen to myself now as if I listened to you, or to some priest or sage or mage. And he tells me, too, what I am I may never know, beyond what is now obvious to me. And that it does not matter.'

Ornate lamps had appeared and lit themselves on the walls. The queen had done this, no doubt. Like most of those who had mortal blood, Lionwolf could invent a hell, but he had had the luck to tempt into it one such as Winsome to illumine it.

He sat, meditating on everything.

His brain was like a labyrinth, but through the never-ending interlocking halls and arches of it he moved now without impatience, anxiety or anger. He looked in at rooms full of what he had already done, been, lived, and destroyed. The emotion suitable to each of these libraries of his first residence in the world waited inside the relevant room, to be put on like a garment, felt and known all over again, and with an added intensity. Or they might be left on their pegs and in their chests. Lacking them, he could review the events and states judicially, implacably.

I am no longer afraid of myself.

That had been his only true fear, mirrored probably by his distress at his father.

Yet he had another emotion now, far greater, far more passionate.

Lionwolf acknowledged that he did not know what he was, but he knew at last why he had come to exist and what he must therefore do.

It fills me with terror and—

He could think of no description for the other element of the passion. It poised perhaps between excitement and disbelief, humility and overtowering vainglory. But it was *himself*, or all of Lionwolf that so far he had learned he was.

A cool peace lay all through him. It had been there from the instant he became fully aware inside the reborn body of the red-haired child, on the initial day that body was free of Wasfa's womb. Before that he had only played, going in to see the baby inside her, the baby he was again to be, then whirling around the astral plateaux of his Hell – and other hells – and other othernesses, which like the second component of his passion had no words in any tongue to describe them. He had seen Guri then, Olchibe Uncle Guri. Lionwolf had said to Guri, 'Only call out my name.' Soon Guri would call, very likely without using voice or will.

And the world – that was calling already, louder than any trumpet, yet so very far away . . .

He might stay here for ever, and still it would be calling and still he could go to it at the exact and proper moment.

Lionwolf turned a little in the chair he had designed from the recesses of his brain – the non-physical stone quarry that was personified as the King of Hell. That *was* Lionwolf's Hell. Other men had been lured in, other women, to this war hell, guilt hell. They had shared portions of their unlives with him. Now they might even make the place their own.

Curjai sat disconsolate on a bench.

What was *Curjai*?

Fire. The smoky worldly fire of the fire god of his own

people. Attajos – a torch, a hearth, the volcano brewing its laval fountains in the earth's depths. Fire was Curjai – or rather, what Curjai must be.

Lionwolf laughed softly.

Across from him he saw the stone King had become another pillar of blue-greyish marble. Near the top, two black living eyes looked down at Lionwolf, then closed and were gone.

And she, Winsome, what was *she*?

Oh, but he had always known. She was Chillel who was the night. No wonder she had powers of light in darkness and could call moons.

Lionwolf got up. He went to her and stood before her.

'Do you know who and what you are, Winsome?'

'I don't care who or what I am.'

Outside, beyond the windows and gardens, amusement and music were sounding in Thasuba. The light was slowly changing too, lifting, healing. Was it possible to cure Hell? Why not, if he had been its architect?

Curjai, sitting kicking his heels like a boy of thirteen with two legs and feet, watched Lionwolf go out of the hall hand in hand with the queen. The King had vanished, the way he always did. Curjai did not think he had seen that happen. When the wine-girl came back she said to him, 'The sun is bright again.' Curjai walked to a window. The sun was bright, like a blue pearl with a heart of palest gold.

The lovers lay together on a bed of carved stonewood, heaped with furs and fine linen.

They coupled slowly to begin with, like an elaborately choreographed dance, then joined like serpents, thrashing and leaping in each other's arms. Flame and smoke, night and day, Lionwolf and Chillel.

Across the weird city of Thasuba a clean milky snow sprinkled down, then fluttered off. The sky became gradually more blue than the sun. Shadows flowed over the sharded barren plains beyond, making the ground flicker as if something grew there.

Quite a long way from the city, Behf and Kuul crouched on a slope below the mountains. They had been hunting, but taken shelter at a bizarre hallucination. The sun had seemed to be snatched from the heavens, and when it reappeared an insane tempest began.

'Is it him caused that?'

'The boy?'

'Vashdran – is that still his name?'

'Lionwolf,' said Kuul, frowning. 'It *means* that. A lion who mates with a wolf and produces one like him. They have a myth for it in Gech.'

'Him then?'

'*Him* then.'

When the storm dissipated, the plains cheered up remarkably. Hordes of deer went galloping by, nearly flirting with the hunters to follow, which they did.

Returning at sunset with four carcasses dragged on an invented sled – summoned out of the air, as they were getting used to doing – Kuul and Behf saw the camp had also taken on a new lease of life.

The makeshift dwellings looked much better. There were trees, some of which showed green – flowers were speared through the ground in what had become virtually forgotten colours, rich scarlets and cherries and honey yellows. Had Taeb done that?

But Taeb was in her bothy with Swanswine doing what came naturally, and doing it *very* naturally, judging by the row they produced over it.

Wasfa and Heppa were also busy, although much more quietly, in their own apartment.

Behf and Kuul gave each other a look, dumped the deer carcasses and went into their own shack with a pot of wine.

Ruxendra alone sat on a boulder with the dogs lying round her, staring with their large, gleaming, ale-brown eyes. The hound which had been Vashdran's, Star-Dog, started gently to whine. As the gold-blue sun went down in a garland of candy clouds, Ruxendra who was Ushah, and the jatcha who was now a dog, wept together yet apart in their own ways. As if finally realizing, both of them, that love, worse than dead, was gone for ever into another country.

THREE

That night Sallusdon, son of Bhorth, woke in his bed at Kol Cataar. Feeling him wake, the chaze snake woke too and draped its inquiring length about Sallus's wrist. *What is it?* unspeakingly asked the raised flat head, and, *Is it rats?* hopefully.

Sallus generally knew what the snake was thinking. 'It's nothing here. Out there . . .' Sallus pointed away and away, through the wall of the chamber, the other walls of the palace of ice-brick, the various walls of the tent-shack city.

After a short while Sallusdon lay down again, troubled. It was no use getting up and roaming about. Since the night when the chaze had first arrived, all those months back, any nocturnal excursion of his – even to the latrine – occasioned a worried check from guards, not to mention the new nurse; even sometimes Bhorth himself.

Sallusdon lay pensive, while the snake re-coiled itself against his spine and slept.

Had it been a dream? Sallus believed not. No, he had seen something, even through the medium of dreaming, that had actually occurred. And this something was horrifying, for though mostly amorphous visually, a glimmered shifting gloom, a *sense* of horror massed all through it.

The seen place was, he thought, the inside of some colossal building. That must be it, for objects – indecipherable yet omnipresent – loomed everywhere, and from these came a glow, greenish or pallid, giving a sort of illumination. But there was also mist or vapour swirling about, and even as you began to decide what *that* peculiar structure might be, or *that* one, the fog eddied between and all clues were lost. Liquid water lay over the floor, if it *was* water. Again it was not possible to be sure. Drips and gurnings, savage yet inexplicable noises filled the space. It stank, too. But even the effluvia was unusual and unnameable, aside from a distinct odour of fish.

In the dream or seeing Sallus had moved, staring around him, *experiencing* the horror. That was all. It was enough.

He lay wakeful an hour, then sleep reclaimed him. During the second sleep he had only his ordinary dreams – of running or flying in the air, of playing friendly with large beasts, and riding a sleekar chariot as his father did. Average things that were interesting but never too taxing.

The nurse woke him next, an hour after sunrise, as she always did.

Unlike the former nurse who had not prevented the chaze entering the room and fainted when it came back from death to be Sallus's companion, the new one was lively and alert, and not afraid of the snake. Sallus preferred and liked her, though he felt sorry for the other woman, now relegated to the outer ramshackle environs. Here, he had heard from guard-talk, she lived with a drunk who beat her. Sallus had attempted to improve her lot via his father, but Bhorth said she must learn her lesson. Life seemed full of such cruel lessons. Maybe even because they passed Sallusdon by, he pitied the ones who must suffer them.

Like, he assumed, the boy he had been inside the dream confine, wading in stinking water.

Over to the north-east in the Marginal Land, Guriyuve son of Ipeyek was musing on a similar dream.

Less than a year old, Guriyuve had escalated in his growing up as if he must correct delay. He was already like a boy of ten, strong and handsome, with long black crispy hair that Hevonhib his mother braided for him in the Olchibe fashion, fixing in small painted beads and tiny mouse or bird skulls.

Because of the production of Guriyuve and his own hunting skills, Ipeyek had been elected to a high position in the sluhtin.

He was the nearest they had to a leader now, for the Crarrowin, particularly Piamtak the Crax, kept the underpinning of any command. As Piamtak had remarked, exalting Ipeyek had eased the whinging of the old men. They could pretend they had a man in charge.

But the Crarrowin stayed powerful. They had let go nothing. And stripped of youthful men, for the most part the hunts and other masculine duties were still organized and performed by the women, while other women wove and cooked and worked the stills for alcohol.

Olchibe had always respected a Crarrow. It was not so hard for them really to give the Crarrowin the reins.

Meanwhile, two of the ancient mammoth females who had not gone to war and so been slain had birthed, one a pair of females, one a pair of males. Everyone was surprised, for double births were rare, the animals were old, and they must as well have retained the seed a greatly extended time – longer than their normal two-year pregnancy. It augured splendidly. A replacement herd was in the making.

Guriyuve was often with the mammoths. They grew fast, as he did. The sluhtin looked on approvingly as he showed such an able happiness with them.

He would be a hero. He would bring glory back, perhaps even the historic glory from the time before the Ruk smashed the Olchibe nation and took its land.

Living even in such a web of approval, Guriyuve did not become wanton or foolish. He reverenced the Crarrowin, his mother included, and was nice to the men. He saw himself, of course, as unique. He would be the one man equal to the women.

The dream, however, upset him.

Where had he been? In an ice swamp, he thought, like those he had been told of up near Sham. Mud and liquid on the ground; smoke, and vague fiendish lamps blurring in it.

He was trapped, he knew that much. And he had also been deserted by somebody he had, perforce and unwilling, trusted.

Having woken, Guriyuve wrestled all night with the demon

of the dream, and eventually slipped out of Ipeyek's shelter, along the cave halls full of bleary potted firelight and snores, towards the mammoth enclosure. Here he sat down with the four young ones, the old females drowsily browsing and paying little attention.

The young mammoths had, rather as had Guriyuve, grown abnormally quickly. A few months of age, they had more a look of two or three years, and already their tusks were showing.

They clustered round the boy and in whispers, not to annoy the older animals, he recounted his dream.

All the twins seemed concerned for him. They moved in and stood right against him, then kneeled down as their elders had for mounting.

Guriyuve fell asleep again leaning on their steamy wool. Then he only dreamed the average dreams of flying, or swimming in the depths of a liquid sea.

Across the length and girth of the continent, and now further off, northward beyond Vormish lands, the black sons with whom Chillel had impregnated men shared, unknowing, the same dream or trance. All saw it somewhat differently, but all saw it, *experienced* its murky detail and ambience of misery. Only those of the ships of the Vorm-Kelp-Fazion fleet knew why. *They* knew who it was and in whose wretchedness they had participated: Dayadin, son of Arok, there in the guts of Brightshade under the ocean.

For a while after he had been gulped down Dayadin was stunned, hardly aware. The ingestion had been like plummeting through a burning *fleshly* whirlwind, only to arrive in a sewer.

He had landed by luck or more likely design, for even in his own distress the staggering whale had wanted to safeguard this prize, on some type of raft, probably the side of a wrecked boat long since otherwise absorbed.

When Dayadin properly came to, he sat up. Above him the whale's stomach roof arched along great flexing bulging ribs of muscle. On every side matter, decay and fluid were gently lapping. In them bobbed every kind of junk once under the sun.

Some distance off bulked actual *banks* of debris. Here plants and white trees grew from the mire, and house-like structures leaned, perhaps made by other unfortunates who, sucked in, had died here.

Brightshade's innards, as with his disgusting botanic back, were not exactly like those of other sea mammals, even those of his own species.

He held a sort of breathable air, though it was more flavoured by unwholesome gases than not. In addition, his digestive tract was adaptable and also selective, in that his digestive acids might be diluted, or segregated from items he wished to preserve – at least for as long as the wish continued. These abilities were now automatic. As well they were. Dayadin was their beneficiary, even as Brightshade toppled over and over down into the depths.

By the hour Dayadin was once more fully conscious, the whale lay prone again on the sea floor. He breathed in slow waves, a respiration not general with his kind, sifting the outer waters spontaneously. Brightshade was not insensible, but he had sustained injury and was in acute pain. He was also afraid, with some cause. And through all that he had now forgotten snatching the levitating child. All Brightshade could think about was the blast Saftri had fired at him – and the imminent wrath of his father, Zeth.

Dayadin's subsequent movements did not disturb the whale's reflections. They amounted to no more than the passage of intermittent so-far-spared live fish through the murk of the abdominal pressure-cabin.

With vast reluctance Dayadin took a bit of floating plank from the fluid, and began to row his raft towards the nearer 'bank'. As he did this he felt a fluttering – and then a helpful push on the raft.

Looking behind him the boy saw that the hovor, Hilth, had also been gulped, very likely against his will. But finding a friend in need brought Dayadin to tears. He sat sobbing as he had done only once since his abduction, and let Hilth do all the work to bring them ashore.

The bank was as ghastly as he had expected. He sank in the mud, and in pretend streams that coursed over beds of jumble. Things gleamed fitfully through the perambulating vapours. Though by now he was getting used to the smell, the dangles of human bones and half-digested sea life made him nauseous.

It was the hovor who pulled Dayadin into one of the odd house-structures. Here in the almost total dark, with less vileness to gaze on, Dayadin became calmer. He sat on an upturned bucket left lying there, and the hovor folded itself round him.

'What shall I do? My father would want me to do something now. *He'd* know the answer. Like in the legends of heroes.'

Mournfully Dayadin peered into his own mind.

He had always blithely guessed he had powers, but they were now like limbs which had been robbed of circulation and gone to sleep.

Outside and around, Brightshade was also thinking of his talents and his daddy.

As the amalgamated day-night of the sea floor continued, moons and a sun rose and fell on the world above. The fleet and the woman were long gone.

The agony in the whale's side grew less. He had managed to attract a deep ocean shoal of blind fish to clean the wound and slather it with a kind of oily salve their bodies excreted. As a reward he ate the shoal. But he did so by discharging his juices selectively, even without recalling why. There was always something or other in his belly he wanted to hoard for a while. Dayadin, during this manoeuvre, had only an impression of flapping and exploding in the surrounding 'water', and a stench beyond all others so that he buried nose and mouth in his own whale-scented shirt.

Now that he was feeling rather better, Brightshade's *shape*-thoughts started to rotate like a wheel, searching for a solution.

Should he pursue the witch-goddess-human female, and again try to obliterate her? Should he give up on that and seek Zzth, begging forgiveness, entreating some extra aid? Zzth *had* assisted when Brightshade tackled the woman last with her hated son.

Glumly Brightshade knew, whatever *shapes* he entertained of victory, Saftri was now too much for him. While Zzth would *not* be forgiving.

As soon as he felt he could, Brightshade lifted up through the water to where the ton weights of it were less. He turned himself full north-east, a direction the fleet had not been going, the direction that was farthest, he hoped, from any land and any gods.

Off he sailed, under thick sheets of surface ice and wide open stretches of waves. Now and then when he risked going up for fresh air, he shattered the tough ice in preference with his pinnacled horn. It gave him a feeling of self-worth.

Once only he had an idea of something sitting inside him. But it was merely like one more thought-*shape*, a *stomach* thought, refined and deserving to be kept, if he could remember to.

A morning dawned and the whale was an incalculable distance from his starting point.

He rose to breach for a change through unimpeded water, attracted to the sunlight.

Maybe he had begun to be optimistic.

He should not have been.

Between the mighty head of the whale, ejecting tumults of water through the blowhole, and that attractive inviting sun, something was waiting on the sea.

Zeth Zezeth Zzth was himself quite recovered. He blazed with silvery goldenness, but his entire face had shaded to indigo. The malign side. What else?

Brightshade gave a hiccup of fear. It thundered all through him, knocking Dayadin and Hilth out of their mud-house, into the acidic lake beyond. As the hovor plucked Dayadin up, the boy shouting with sheer horror, their enclosed world again went sprawling, and any chance of rescue or protection ended.

Topside, Zzth was lamming into his son with whips of lightning and rods of malevolence.

Brightshade screamed.

The whole sea heard, and its cold blood ran colder.

No use to beg for mercy now.

The deity has given up his appealing man-god form. He has become a hurricane. He spins the whale, bashes him down and up, pummels him, throws him for miles, retrieves and stamps on him.

The atmosphere blackens. A storm is churning through. Tidal combers hit the sky as Zzth hits with his psychic fists.

Zzth offers no words. Yet his fury fills Brightshade's brain with *shapes* of viciousness and never-ending contemptuous hate.

Only when, resistless, blank and broken into pieces, the gargantuan mass sinks again into the deepest depth, can Zeth in his ecstasy of rage draw back.

Then the god shoots away up the sky like an arrow of silver, and with a strange howling. Could it be his volcanic violence has been too much even for *himself* to endure?

The whale has vanished and does not resurface.

If any flicker of being was detectable from Dayadin, now it is not.

Five shepherds stood just down from the important hut. Higher was the fifth of these.

'After the stars altered. Not after that,' said Higher, repeating what they had said earlier below in the village.

The others nodded. He was accurate. The heavenly iris of bright stars had diminished. And after that night not one of them had seen Chillel.

'You see her before then – you said she appear from air—' added another of the men.

'True,' said Higher. 'I did. *She* did.'

Several days, ten perhaps, had elapsed since the event. He remembered, however. Chillel had told him to go. Something was coming he 'must not see'. It might 'frighten' him. And he had been scared stiff anyway.

Now it was dusk, and the twilight empty of the iris stars, and

327

the village wanted to be told a story by their story-teller, even if the tale was – as always – obscure.

But they stood here, and had politely called to her five or six times, and got no answer.

'Big with baby,' said one of the men.

'Should women come up see?'

At this moment two things happened. They heard the black lamb they had gifted to Chillel bleat loudly, and the door was moved aside.

It was not Chillel who stepped out, nor for that matter a black lamb.

The lamb had become a full-grown sheep, with a king's ransom of curly fleece. Next to it was a young woman.

At a glance they saw this was *not* Chillel.

Indeed not. For though Chillel was young and exquisite, the girl was younger. She was, even so, fantastically lovely, and she had a look of Chillel. For example, her skin and eyes were jet black. However, the rich hair that streamed from her head was of a colour none of them had ever seen on man or woman. It was like the cup they had once been shown when some of the vagrant wanderers from an abandoned Ruk town stopped by. The cup had been gold mixed with copper, and they saw it by the red of the communal fire.

'Who are you?' said Higher.

'My name,' said the girl quietly, 'is Brinnajni.'

They had none of them ever heard a name like that. Yet they knew what it meant instantly. Rather than try to pronounce it, one by one they murmured, 'Burning Flame.' Except for Higher who, condensing pragmatically, said, '*Flame.*'

'Where is Woman Chillel?'

'My mother has gone away,' said the girl. She seemed resigned.

They beheld that in ten days the baby had been born, had grown, and was in village time by now at least sixty years of age – that was a damsel of about eighteen.

A *living* story – and not at all obscure!

They swallowed it complete.

'Are you to take her place?'

'For a while.'

'Then come to the fire. The magio must see you. Eat, and tell us a tale.'

The living tale smiled at them in a way that was, unlike her astonishing mother's, attractively knavish. And the sheep bleated again vociferously. Together, Flame and her black sheep went down the slope to the village.

'Once there was a hero,' began Flame, standing rather than sitting among the villagers. 'He was sailing across the seas of the world, when a great and angry whale rose from the deeps.'

'Ah,' muttered some of the audience, 'the *whale* story again.'

But it was not the story Chillel had told before.

'The hero, who was named Hawk-of-Stars, flew out to the whale to pacify it, and almost he had done this when the goddess of the area, mistaking what went on, struck the whale in its side with a bolt of energy.'

Flame's story-teller voice was thrilling, and she acted in gestures all she said. Chillel had never done that.

Coming to the energy bolt, Flame mimed it so vigorously, whirling on her heel, flinging out her arms, her fire-hair waving, that many gasped, and most of the children shrieked.

'Alas,' cried Brinnajni, standing now solid on the spot, her voice dropping an octave, 'Hawk was swallowed by the whale in this frantic moment.'

A groan from the crowd.

Brinnajni bowed her head.

The village waited on her, breathless.

Then she told them how it was within the belly of the whale. Obviously, although she did not say so, she, like all her brothers, had seen this in her sleep.

She described everything minutely, and how Hawk had rowed his raft to the foul shore. She did not say he wept. She knew that too was a secret.

'Many days and nights the whale lay wounded on the ocean

floor, until finally he dragged himself away northwards and eastwards, and Hawk, his prisoner, without a choice was taken also.'

Brinnajni described the journey now – fish which leapt, other marine life, the frozen cellars of the sea where all things had become like steel or diamond. These facts were to the village fantastic as any legend.

She did not speak of a god erupting from the sunlight to take vengeance – the third secret.

After an hour of the most vital story-telling they had ever heard, Brinnajni ended her tale just as her mother had, with it hanging in the air.

The village was used to that. Nevertheless, her performance had so enlivened them that several called out to her to ask what would happen to Hawk. Would he be saved?

Brinnajni looked about at them all, serene and yet cunning.

'Do you wish him saved?'

'Yes—'

'Yes, yes – a hero—'

'At what cost?'

'Any cost – it must be done.'

'Then,' said Brinnajni, 'you must let me go and do it.'

An astounded dumbness blanketed the spot.

After a while the woolly magio got up. He pointed at the black sheep, which had sat all this time to the side of the fire. He meant, We gave you a sheep, there it is, and now you desert the village, both you and your mother.

Brinnajni nodded in the terse village way. Her face was no longer playful, but adult and closed: no argument.

Higher went to the magio and said softly, 'Like the flowers in the glacier – and in the sky – come, and go.'

When Brinnajni walked back up to her hut, the sheep processing with dignity at her side, the shepherd people talked sullenly. Higher said, 'Chillel never say she'll go. This Flame told us she must. To save the hero.'

'She'll disappear anyhow, do as we want,' said another.

The magio had gone into his own hut and put the cord across

the top of the door which indicated he should not be interrupted.

That night every one of them, even he, dreamed of being in the belly of the whale, in the dark and muck and stink and solitudinous horror. Children woke screaming to be comforted by trembling parents.

They knew exactly what the dream was, but how Brinnajni had made them dream it they could not fathom. By the evidence she was a mageia herself. Her mother had been too apparently.

When she went away the next morning, setting off along the snow on a sled pulled by the full-grown, elegant sheep, her red hair flaring like her banner, no one attempted to detain her.

That year, which was a year only by the shepherd's calendar, all the sheep produced three or four lambs, a dead fruit tree put out bulbs of fruit inside its ice, and one night a piercing red star lit in the east and only faded three nights after when, presumably, Didri the star-lighter quenched it.

She had magic, the girl, and she put it to work.

When they were entirely clear of the village she spoke to the sheep, which – also exceptional from nearness to mother and daughter – sprang into the air.

Upwards they soared, sheep and sled and girl.

They flew fast towards the north, devouring the miles, literally as the crow flies.

Flame took no notice of what dazzled by below, and little of what went on in the sky. They were the everyday things anyway, snow and ice, ice-forests and wastes, sunrise and moonset, weather of various types – not all amenable, but no real problem for these travellers.

At some juncture certainly the girl on the sled flew over the eastern hilt of the continent, over the very snowbound garth where whale-gulped Dayadin had been brought into the world. This was not deliberate, nor that she be seen. Yet seen Brinnajni was. Nirri saw her, Nirri, wife of Arok the Chaiord of the Jafn Holas, the mother of Hawk-of-Stars Dayadin.

Nirri, who had been shedding tears as so often now she did in private, saw the red flag and the black fleece speed through the sky. Something plucked at her psyche. She got to her feet, dried her eyes, put on another necklace and went down into the joyless joyhall.

'I have seen a sign,' said Nirri, in the bell-like tone of a true queen.

But the flying Flame, even if she sensed any of that, did not pause.

She was already out at sea, over the ice plates and the dark, shining, shallow-moving waves with their frills of pallor, heading towards the far north-east.

Brinnajni could *hear* the whale. He was trumpeting like an elephant in distress, down there in the maw of the ocean. And she could hear the small, perhaps impervious heart of her brother Dayadin, ticking in the maw of the whale.

Unlike her brothers, Brinnajni had been born of *two* superlatives, each a god. And if one god had actually been dead when he got her on her mother, the result seemed unimpaired.

Winds came, clouds came, to pay court to her as she flew, and below the green outer waves tilted up to look at her with their subliminal eyes.

Guided by the mental bellows of Brightshade, who no longer made any physical noise at all, Brinnajni plunged towards the ocean at an area off all the maps.

As they entered the sea the black sheep turned and gave her a single glance. Brinnajni grinned. Where her mother's smile had undone a thousand hearts and sexual continences, Brinnajni's grin – clown-like and elastic on that lovely face – would also leave few unmoved.

The sheep ducked her curly head. She swam down into the core of the icy sea, drawing the sled and her adopted sister after. Flames are extinguished by water and sheep drowned in it. Never mind that. Not these two.

The ocean changed from greenish to ashy, ash to obscure blue, to blue-black.

Here were the drifting rifts of ice, the icy cliffs, the ledges stabbed to blue-whiteness by ancient shells and fossils. The pressure grew as all light was sucked away. Brinnajni felt this, but it did not impede her. Fish swarmed by, armoured like warriors to withstand the cold. Others watched unseeing, frozen till eternity should shed its skin. Down, down they went.

Suddenly, through the dimmest region of the dark, where the water pressed heavy as a quarter of the volume of the world, willing to crush anything that was not sparked with divinity or a similar talent, a black bulk became – not visible, but psychically tactile. Brinnajni felt it over. She knew she had found the sick-bed of the leviathan.

Brightshade was barely alive. Being what he was, however, he was not remotely dead either. An uncomfortable state. As much as physical hurt, his essential self had been ripped in tatters. He had forgotten all things except himself, a predicament suffering may induce in almost any creature. He had never needed love or kindness. Awe and fear he had always been able to inspire. He had never needed *help*. He had never needed to *think* aside from as a hobby; now this was all he could do. Brightshade *thought*, unloved and maimed, having no one to turn to and nowhere else, not even death, to which he could escape.

Settling like bubbles through the sea, the sheep landed the sled weightless on the astonishing country of Brightshade's head, just behind the forest-like mansions of the horn spurs, with the vast horn itself about a quarter of a mile away inside them. Everything was hung about with skeletons and ribbons of even gods did not know what. A dull moaning sounded, not in the ears but in the mind: Brightshade's anguish translated.

Brinnajni stepped off the sled. She walked up the headland. Standing on the skull of Brightshade, she listened intently, both to his distress and to the ticking of Dayadin's heart acres away below and behind, where the guts were.

After a while Brinnajni sat down.

333

She thought *inward* at the whale.

Poor child, said the thought, *shape* or not.

Something in the whale raised its little sad head, not at all like the gargantuan mound she sat on. A little beaten thing gazed up, all tears. Was it laughable? Was it absurd? Well deserved maybe, redolent with justice – but was it tragic? When the proud and mighty really fall, why not tread on them? Why not pick them up?

Gently, baby, thought Flame to Brightshade.

Did he, even for a second, reckon this elemental young woman was the very child or baby *he* had wished to eradicate? It seemed not. He was beyond jealousy, for now.

But, sobbed Brightshade, *but* . . .

Brinnajni began to sing a lullaby of the Jafn. It was the very one Dayadin himself had given to the sharks that sent them slooping off in slumber.

Brightshade's small interior child-head sank. He lay, metaphorically only, in the arms of Flame, and metaphorically only she rocked him to sleep.

Poor silly great walloping lummox. She was quite fond of him, already forgiving him for what he had done to Dayadin – who was almost Brightshade's own nephew. For now it would not matter.

Once the whale was deep in a trance Brinnajni returned to her sled. She flew over the whale's body, going back towards his belly. As before the prospect dazzled by below, only sheathed now in the pitch black of the ocean's foundation. Brinnajni caught sheeny glimpses of putrescence, jungles, swamps, and here and there a wormy perhaps-animal gawping at their progress, without eyes.

The sheep navigated their landing this time on the spinal cord, above the stomach.

Flame knelt down. They were in a kind of ravine between hills of detritus. Some of this was constantly dislodging and unravelling away through the sea.

Which was irrelevant.

She called in through the gallons of blubber and flesh, calcium and fluids, to the wet inferno where Dayadin lay.

The hovor, whom Brinnajni mentally made out at once, had hauled him back into one of the vile structures on the stomach's muck-banks. A white treeish something craned over Dayadin, with the hovor perched in it. The sprite had managed, using the art of its wind-power, to empty Dayadin's lungs of acid and guts of poisonous dirt. He lived. He was Chillel's. Of course he did. But that was all you could say. Every so often the hovor would leave the tree and breathe his fragrant snowy breeze through the child's nostrils. Brinnajni noted that. She spoke to the hovor with courtesy, giving it instructions.

She had many gifts, attributes and knacks. One was fire.

Saftri's blasting bolt, to this, had been rather pale. Like a laser the black girl's flame pierced the hundred barriers of Brightshade's body. She created a narrow fissure, narrow that was in comparison to Brightshade's size. Through it blood and tissue would have flowed off had the gap not been cauterized instantly by the very heat which caused it. The excavation took some while. And it made the sea grow white and boil so the fish fled before they were fried, and the sheep sunned herself, pleased to be warm.

When the appalling hole was all the way through to the stomach, out tipped assorted juices, dead digesting prey, and many of the trophies of Brightshade's innards. Bits of ships were there, *whole* ships sailing upside down, treasure-remains of several types, flotsam and jetsam; rubbish.

Last of all, propelled by the hovor Hilth, Dayadin, limp and eyes closed, was swum through into the open sea. Hilth let this clean water wash Dayadin, then he flitted along the whale island, carrying the boy before him. Hilth waited until Brinnajni had resealed the tunnel in the whale, padding and adhering and stitching with all her pharmacy of paranormal transplants, glues and threads. Satisfied she stood, and Hilth placed Dayadin in her arms. Hilth had apparently decided to have faith in *this* one.

Brinnajni sat back on the sled, her brother carefully

positioned on her lap, the hovor billowing in her hair. Hilth was a marvel. He had filled Dayadin with enough good air to last the journey.

The black sheep shook herself.

Very slowly now, to offset the oceanic pressures, up they all went.

In the aftermath of the fight, the garth had bowed in fateful gloom. Arok and all the able or passing for able men of the Holas had ridden out to meet the Vormland reivers. Only sixteen living men came back, including Arok himself. The larger part of their number, an army of forty, they brought home on the chariot floors, unhuman as logs – twenty-three corpses. Two more of the wounded died only paces from the garth gate. Once within the walls, the fires mage-tinted black to mark enormous lament, the white mourning garments donned, and yet another casualty dying – leaving them fifteen men, and many of these disabled – grief burst like steam. Wizened women screamed and fatherless babies shrilled. Two Endhlefons went by. And on the twenty-fourth day Arok went into the upper room a Chaiord shared only with his spouse, took down a sword from the wall and broke it in half with an axe.

Nirri, precipitated to her feet in the corner, was shocked. She knew what the ritualistic gesture conveyed: *So I have been broken and all that is mine.*

But she put back her shoulders and remarked, 'At least you did it up here. None of your people saw.'

'My people,' said Arok. 'My *people*. Who's left of my *people*?'

Nirri thought of the Jafn phrase for malign luck sometimes found in songs and legends. *We have a raven in the eaves.*

'Sir,' she said to him, 'brace up for the sake of the garth—'

And at that he turned on her and she reckoned she would get from him what she had so often had from her former husband the fisherman, a blow in the face. But Arok did not strike her with his hands, only with his next sentence.

'Don't give me lessons, you stupid shumb. Do you forget already we lost my son?'

To which Nirri replied in such a low voice he read her lips to hear it, 'Oh, was he solely yours?'

Arok strode from the room and down the ladder-stair and went out with the last men to hunt.

Nirri wept, huddled to a wall.

Initially, when he had returned with the dead and the news of Dayadin's abduction by the barbaric offal of Vorm – so delighted to collect such spoils they had made off at once, leaving the dregs of the Jafn alive – Nirri and Arok comforted each other. Even, once or twice in following days, they made love, hoping perhaps in unthinking instinct to conjure another child. But no other child came, and anyway how could he have been another Dayadin? Though Nirri did not herself know Arok's well-founded theory of the boy's conception, Nirri could not imagine a second hero would be birthed from her. They had mislaid the gift of Great God. No wonder now they could never be fortunate again.

Months evaporated in the Holasan-garth. No one knew where time went, now they did not use it properly.

An evening dropped, louring with the promise of deluging snow. Ten men and a pack of women came to the House door. Those that lived within the House went out and joined with the visitors.

'What?' said Arok, pushing out into the dusk to meet them.

He had lost weight since the reiver fight, looked gaunt and haggard. Despite always trying to put a brave face on like a mask to hide his wretched privacy and evil dreams, he saw they knew. They had judged him, his people, the ones Nirri had told him once to brace up before. Maybe they supposed he was even the source of their rotten destiny. Maybe they were right.

They told him, with obsequious mannerisms that made him want to put his fists into the jaws of the men and storm at the women young and elderly alike, that they wished to go elsewhere.

'We haven't enough men here.'

'What will we do now if others of the sea-scum attack us?'

Arok could no longer declare their Jafn allies would rally to them. He had toiled so fiercely to attach the potential aid of the Kree, the Banjaf – any who seemed willing to make a pact. And look how they had rushed here! God's eyes, even following the battle, none of them had come. A few commiserating messages only were sent. The 'allies' blamed everything for their non-presence, uncertain top-snow, illness in their garths, accidents, omens. None had come. None ever would.

'Where will you take yourselves then,' said Arok icily to his folk, 'if you leave your own place?'

'Chaiord,' said one of the young men who had survived the fight, a warrior about fifteen, 'we can go to the Kree. They'd welcome more men – women too, even the old ones. And our newborns.' He himself had sired six sons since his thirteenth year. He had fought like a lion. An asset. 'Chaiord,' said the warrior, 'why not throw in your lot with us? They'd honour you, and your wife.'

'So you'd have me bound as lesser kinsman with the Kree? The Kree that first banded with the Lionwolf and began all this?' The fifteen-year-old looked down. Arok thought, *Why shame him? We're shamed enough.* He recalled how he had always been lesser kin to the Holas, and only brought to lead the garth in default of others who had not survived the Rukar war.

'No,' said Arok. He stared away from them. 'If you will leave, then do it. I'll neither prevent nor bless you. Any who wants, let him be off. Make your way with the Kree if you like, prosper if you can. Never,' he switched his gaze back to them, dark as the threatening dusk, 'never return to this garth. When once you're outside, these gates will close against you for ever.'

Some of them grimaced, some looked sick. The antique widow who had been the ninety- or seventy-year-old's wife gave Arok the coldest glance. But he shook his head at her. 'You also, Mother. Though your man was a great warrior, if you choose to go away, you're none of ours. Erase your Holas clan name. Now you are *Kree.*'

Arok did not watch the departure of the column of men,

women, chariots, carts, and sleds; the lions and dogs and hnowas; the hawks that were their property and which he had allowed them to keep.

Even the House Mage and his fellows left. Without one word.

Nirri did watch. She stood up on the wall of the garth in driving sleet. It was the queen's duty to oversee the important arrivals or their going away.

When the exodus was complete, the garth was virtually empty. Five men remained, twenty women and six children, four of these girls.

Arok did not climb down to the statue of God in the below-stairs of the House.

If God did not already notice what went on, He was no God at all.

Against such a background, Nirri entered the joyhall and announced, 'I have seen a sign.' The eleven or so women and two men in the hall looked round. A baby started to whimper and the mother shushed it. 'I saw,' said Nirri firmly, 'a black sheep of unusual size pulling a sled over the sky. A figure sat on the sled, black like the sheep. And its hair was made of *fire*.'

When Arok came in from a desultory hunt, he and his three companions toting a seal carcass which fleers had already been at, the garth was in ferment.

It enraged him. All this spurious adrenalin.

'Is this your doing?' he demanded of his wife, having heard what she had reportedly said.

'No, sir,' said Nirri. 'I was shown it.'

'And you have hatched this smoke-brained scheme because you had a dream by a window?'

'It wasn't any dream.'

'What proof?'

'That I say it, and you have always known me for a proper Jafn who does not sleep save at the proper time, and also as a sensible woman who does not lie.'

Arok was taken aback. She did not frequently stand her ground with him. As a rule she simply stepped aside from his moods, letting him come round in his own way. This too was happening in the joyhall, with all the excited women and the now obviously influenced men looking on.

'Upstairs,' said Arok.

They went.

Arok paced about. The fragments of the dismembered sword lay in a corner still with just a shawl thrown on them. He indicated them.

Nirri said, 'All the more reason.'

'You say we too are to go off.'

'To the north,' said Nirri, 'where I saw the firehair go.'

'It was some gler, trying to trick you.'

'I've seen glers enough. This was no gler.'

'You're too uppity, woman. Did I wed you for this?

Nirri replied without a pause.

'You wed me because I carried your son, who was black as that figure on the sled, your boy that you loved, and I loved, I who bore him in that very bed there. Arok' – she seldom called him by his name save during sex; she had always been highly courteous – 'Arok, let's go northward. Make or take a ship. Follow the reivers. Find Dayadin.'

'Six men and a boatful of yattering women. And *where's* the boat to come from? We haven't a Mage either. What do we do for fire or to ward off tempests? Jafn aren't seafarers. We resign that to the Kelp and Vorm and Faz filth.'

'There is,' said Nirri, 'a Thing meeting spot along the coast, and a tall ship there, many-masted, like the Mother Ships of the reivers.'

'It's wedged in *ice*!'

'*Unwedge* it!'

'I should kill you—'

Some dam within her burst, as episodes of *Summer*, once in a thousand moons, undid the ice floes and flooded the land.

'Kill me then!' she shouted at him. 'Kill all the world! It was never *your* fault you were robbed of your son – nor any fault of *mine!* But *this* – *this* is your fault. What are you, you man? My lord – or some wretch from a midden? Take up your kingship, Arok, before all of it flakes from you. Why do you think your people left you? *Arok* – be *Arok*. Be the one who outraced the giant whale and saved me with him and gave me a life and a love and a child and all those things I never had. Be *Arok*, you man. Or I'll hang myself from that beam there. Where else but the Other Place can *I* go, if *you* are no longer *Arok.'*

He bounded towards her.

She thought now he truly would kill her. She stood straight. She had never felt more alive, or sure.

Arok fell at her feet and buried his head in her lower belly, against the mound of her sex. He, not she, wept. She stroked his white hair, knowing the battle won.

FOUR

Evening had descended early – the time spans of this contained world seemed to vary wildly. Guri by then had moved the mammoth away from the wall of the box which shut in his hell. They camped in a stand of cryogenized forest, under fir, eucalyptus and palm trees so crusted with ice they had become walls themselves, semi-transparent, a little daylight still kept inside. Guri made fire with a flint. He did it carefully, abstemiously, in the fire-pot he had somehow kept. The mammoth browsed on ferns, chipping off their frost carapaces with her curved tusks. He had delicately descaled these for her during the late afternoon.

Night filled the box that was the hell.

It seemed only peaceful and ordinary with the fire, the cold, the large beast steadily chewing.

And tonight no one at all came near, either to hurt or to cajole. Perhaps they had all been, those tormentors, those Olchibe bad companions, figments of Guri's own blame.

He had never known he blamed himself. Yet he must have done or how otherwise could it all have happened?

A means of escape from the box was less believable. Probably now he must linger here alone, if not forever then for aeons.

At least they – or he himself – had allowed him the company of the mammoth.

He dug into the snow beside the pot of fire. Rolled in his furs he slept.

A low wind was whispering over the forest ice when he

woke again. It was still night. *Two* mammoths were there now, grazing side by side, the second one a younger male whose coat had been beautifully groomed, *combed* even it looked. He was behaving civilly to the female, uprooting fern and small iced saplings for her, spreading them before her trunk and stepping back a little to allow her room to eat.

Someone sat across the fire.

Guri stared. He lifted himself up slowly.

'Well, Uncle. What an age you took to wake. I've been sitting here for hours, counting the leaves and needles in the ice. A million million and two I make it. What do you think?'

'Lion—'

'Uncle.'

'You're a dream.'

'No. Reach over and take my hand.' Guri did nothing. 'Then I must take yours.'

Right across the fire, through the craning flames which flared to lick unattended at his strong brown wrist, Lionwolf reached and caught the hand of Guri. The flames licked both of them then. They were only pleasantly warm, while the clasp of Lionwolf was like fire as it should be, burning, utter.

Guri snatched his hand away.

He looked at Lionwolf who was precisely as he had last seen him in the living world, a flawlessly made man of about twenty-three years, and in the dark blue mirrors of the eyes two slender crescents like polished rubies.

'Why are you here?' said Guri.

He shook. He did not know at last what he must feel. Floods of love and loathing crashed through him. Every memory shared and every joke and every bitter dismay.

'It's time,' said Lionwolf gravely, 'that we think about going home.'

'*Home?* Where's *home?*'

'The world, Uncle. Where else?'

'I'm dead.'

'Never stopped you before.' Lionwolf grinned.

343

Ruefully Guri said, 'I'm *twice* dead now. I came here for punishment and got it.'

'So did I. Now we move on to other events.'

'How?' Guri challenged him, shivering, his teeth chattering, maybe only with shock.

'First, we'll leave here.'

'I can't. There's a wall round it, a roof on it—'

'Oh, yes. But as you see, I and the mammoth had no trouble with those. Do you recognize the mammoth, Guri, by the way? He's the toy you gave me, the little psychic toy, when you were a ghost and I was just born.'

'You brought him into hell.'

'He came with me. Look at him now.'

They looked at the toy which had become, at least to all intents and purposes, real. He and the female were feeding close together now.

'I can never escape this country,' said Guri.

'I'll show you the way.'

Guri pulled a wry face. The shakes were going off. He felt only *shaken*. 'How'll you do that?'

'There was a hero called Lalt,' said Lionwolf.

'Some Jafn freak. Bright green of skin, was he, ah?'

'Not Jafn. Lalt is a hero of Simisey. No, you've never heard of Simisey. Listen. Lalt went down into the hells under or between the worlds. There he asked how he could see to travel in the dark, and they told him: You'll find your path more easily if you are blind. If you are blind, you'll have to.'

'Each of us,' murmured Guri, 'tries to find his way blind. Look where it takes us.'

'Get up, Uncle,' said Lionwolf, standing, hauling Guri effortlessly and unexpectedly upright also. 'Mount your mammoth and when you're sitting comfortably, bind your eyes with this cloth. Make sure you can't see a thing.'

'Then what?' Guri demanded.

'Trust me to lead you.'

'*You?*'

Before he could decide if he wished to say that or master it if he did not, the word had flamed from Guri's lips thick with contempt and allergy and accusation.

Lionwolf's face did not change. It was, Guri thought confusedly, always now partly melancholy, but too always clear and collected.

'I led you into an earthly hell before, Uncle, you and thousands of others. Now let me make amends. Let me lead you out of this one.'

Guri stood by his mammoth, leaning his head on her side. He stayed like that for more than an hour. Then, silent, he had her kneel, and got up on the wide familiarity of her back. Not looking at Lionwolf, who burned on motionless on the ground below in place of the fire which had vanished, Guri tied the black cloth tight about his eyes and, bending forward, hid his face in the mammoth's greasy hair.

Presently he felt her move.

He heard ice crackle underfoot. He heard the other mammoth treading in step with his own. He heard the slight night wind ruffling the immovable cryotites of the forest. He *heard* the presence of Lionwolf, son to god and mortal, twice dead and twice born.

Don't look.

Advance blindly.

The darkness and the light guide you.

Let them do what they must.

Curjai was listening to a boy singing in a high pipe of a voice, every note like a coin of silver.

As he walked into the great hall of the palace at Thasuba, Curjai saw a group of the priests who seemed to haunt each city. They were going slowly through the hall, swinging the censors of incense. Something was immediately startling about them. They had each a uniquely defined and human face. At the procession's head was the old child who had sung so peculiarly elsewhere. Now he sang like a well-tuned instrument. If anything, *his* face was older, but there was a look of absorbed content on it.

Curjai watched them pass, and when they were gone he strode towards the terrace at the hall's far end.

He had slept in a side room the night before. There had been a bed in it that reminded him almost painfully of royal beds he had seen at Padgish. They had never been for himself, then the invalid, but for men of standing. In the room he was waited on by two delicious women. But though he found himself aroused by their appearance and actions – slightly, unnervingly aroused, for sexual arousal was quite new to him – he did not invite either into the princely bed. After all, they were doubtless figments of the walls. To screw the brickwork did not appeal to him, when he considered it. It made him think, even so. Why he had never felt even a twinge of desire when formerly *alive* he was not certain. For sure he had been equipped for it, if not for everything else. It seemed to him he had learned to suppress desire at source before it could gain any hold. And why? Maybe on advice he could not recall from one of his king-father's judgemental mages – or even the shaman. With Ruxendra-Ushah he *had* begun to feel desire of course. But they had not consummated their mutual lust. Puzzling on this but only with half a mind, Curjai went on to the terrace.

It was open to the sky above, the city below.

He looked down and saw festive activities in the streets and squares. Nothing seemed to need doing here that was onerous or a chore. Crowds went along with flowers, and beating drums and choruses of laughter and music. From window-places banners and ribbons waved in a light breeze. The sky was deep blue, the sun blue only at its outer circle, the rest gold. You could still gaze straight at it. Sometimes birds flew over. They had the appearance of pigeons, or the long-necked gosands of Simisey.

Curjai looked further, and beyond the high walls of Thasuba he saw the plains dressed in fresh colours: tawny ochre, green, here and there rivered across by other shades of crimson and violet. Things grew there. Grasses, grains even, not that he had ever seen them in life to recognize them now. Flowers provided the extra colour. He could smell those, he thought.

Down on the plains men from the armies, presumably disbanded, rode in chariots or on the backs of horse-like creatures – these Curjai could make out. Deer ran in a blond ripple.

It was . . . warm?

Last night Lionwolf had gone away with the Queen of Hell.

Curjai wondered if he had been at last left behind in this afterworld he had claimed, truthfully, was like Heaven to him. He did not know if he was chastened or angered by dismissal. And if he was either, then as a man or a child?

Lionwolf and he – something bound them. *What* bound them? The boy's worship of the older boy? Something so minor? Or did it have weight and worth?

'Lalt,' Curjai said under his breath. 'Tilan.' Tilan, in the legend, had let Lalt bring him out again from death. But later they quarrelled. There came a battle between them. Lalt killed Tilan with his own hands. Then Lalt mourned Tilan for all the remaining years of his life. And all the fair women that he loved, the saga said, could not console him for the loss of his brother.

The sun – felt *hot*.

Curjai glanced at it.

For one dislocating moment he thought he saw part of a face and an eye glaring right through the sun, at him and at Thasuba.

It must be the face and eye of a god. One who was seething and – virulent.

Curjai steeled himself for whirlwind or hurled thunderstone, but nothing else happened. The impression of a watcher withdrew. Only the friendly sun beamed on. Whatever had looked in at this etheric world, that being could not enter, nor even send a token, or surely retribution would have sprung wolf-like on them all. Everything would have been smashed to pieces.

*

'Undo the blindfold, Guri.'

Guri undid the black cloth and dropped it. He did not undo his eyes.

Through the closed lids streamed light.

He heard a susurration all around. It reminded him of the noise of a woman's sleeve or skirt brushing as she walked, but much amplified.

There was a scent too. What was it? Like spices, was it? Or like bonbons for a celebration . . .

Another noise alerted him. The sound of things running, their feet beating on the ground, the sound of deer going pell-mell, but chariot runners too, whisking along as he had heard on the snows when he visited Lionwolf's earthly Gullahammer.

A stab of horror went through Guri. Great Gods – had the boy drawn him back into those wicked and ill-omened months?

Where temptations had not made him open his eyes, affront did.

Guri sat his mammoth, paralysed.

'Where—' he said. 'Where?'

'*My* Hell. It's healing. Don't you like it? It wasn't like this before, I can tell you. All stones and dross.'

Guri, paralysed on the mammoth, amid the standing corn.

'But—'

'Cereals and grains that grow. Grass that grows, the way it would around a hot oasis or spring.'

'*Green.*'

'Yes.'

'Yellow – butter yellow, like a pretty Olchibe girl.'

'Not *quite* as good as that, Great Gods witness.'

'Amen,' said Guri without thinking.

A herd of chariots was pounding through the stalks, broadly smiling men in them waving their arms. Lions drew some of the vehicles, deer drew others, and there were riding animals like horsazin, but neither horned nor scaly, nor smelling of fish.

'Lionwolf! Lionwolf! The war's over!'

'I know,' he told them.

Several jumped down, embracing him, slapping his

mammoth and Guri's on the side so the big beasts shuffled and squinted at them.

'We went along the plains,' said one man in a deer chariot, 'saw others there. Not all wanted to come to the city. They like the life among the fields. Harvest soon.'

These phrases, ideas – *fields, harvests* – seemed known to them not from hothouses or slots of dormant flora. They came from the far past, five centuries before in the days when winter was seasonal not ubiquitous.

But Guri stared on. He held out his hand and something small and flying settled on his thumb. It paused there, fanning its wings to receive the sunlight. The sun glowed through the wings, which were red as garnet, thin as finest Rukarian paper.

He did not know it was a butterfly. It flew away presently.

And Lionwolf and he rode on towards the city.

With the prolonged fiery sunset, a torrent of water dashed from the sky, tepid and fragrant, shining, making every wall and tower, gate and pillar, glitter in the hot sidelong shafts of the sun. As the downpour lessened, narrow waterfalls went on tinkling from the high cornices and edges of things, twinkling, turning the whole city into a vast, strung, sounding harp.

Rain.

Only genetically could they have remembered it. The ice-cold earth had not known rain as such time out of mind.

Curjai who, along with hundreds of others, had been standing out to be soaked in the milk-warm showers, saw Lionwolf coming up a stairway and next to him an Olchibe – not Swanswine but another, younger and thinner, but also scowling as Swanswine generally did.

Lionwolf took Curjai's right hand and Guri's right hand and put the two hands together.

'Curjai, son of the kings of Simisey. Guri, first captain of Olchibe's vandal bands.'

The two men looked at each other. Lionwolf added easily,

and without flourish, 'Guri, Curjai is my brother. Curjai, Guri is my uncle.'

Below trumpets were honking men in to another feast – perhaps for victory, or only for greed.

These three stayed on the terrace, with the rain spangling down. Nine moons rose in the east, three crescents, three halves, three full.

Curjai recollected how he thought he had glimpsed the face of the black queen in a moon, and the face of a furious god today, in the sun.

Guri said, 'If this is your hell, Lion, why are all these others in it? Aren't they real?'

'Their hells are enough like mine to make them seem to be here, or me seem to be in theirs. We come and go across each other's paths. Like life, do you think?'

It was so strange, the healed Hell, so strange and alluring. Everything had altered but did any of them know into what? They did not want to speak of it much.

The sun had still not sunk, and the rain still littered down, and the nine moons hung in the east as if shy.

A word quivered through the city. It came from the timpanic rhythm of the rain now so lightly hitting the stones. *Tomorrow* was the word.

'Tomorrow,' said Curjai. 'Do you hear it?'

'Tomorrow,' Guri said. 'I hear it plain in the Olchibe tongue. And you—'

'In Simese.'

'Do you hear it, Lion?'

Lionwolf looked into their eyes. He was no longer even Lionwolf. What then – *what* then?

'I *spoke* it,' he said.

Curjai said, 'What must we do?'

'Wait. The night will be a long one. Use the night.'

Men who died here in their afterlife, men like Choy and Lifli, where had they gone to? A better or a worse place? It was possible to stay here. To spend eternity, perhaps.

But for Curjai – he felt an alternative abruptly tug on him, drawing him – where? A plunge of fear – oh. He knew.

'We go back to the world, then,' he said. 'Well,' he added, straightening, 'this holiday has been informative.' He thought how he had been when alive, left on his rug by the door, without limbs, without a face, the looking-glass broken. And the loved warrior saying over the wall how glad the king would be that Curjai must soon be dead.

Lionwolf detected Curjai's thoughts.

He said, 'That was the previous life, Curjai. Not the next.'

Guri said, 'You mean we're to be born again in the flesh.'

'Yes, Uncle. Some poor mother will have to put up with us all over again.'

'The *flesh*,' repeated Guri, stunned. Then, 'How do we get there?'

'How we came here.'

The sun went suddenly. The whole of the east flushed to carmine. Overhead stars winged from their shells moltenly brilliant and laid in complex patterns.

'Death,' said Curjai. 'We have to die fully ourselves. As the others did.'

'How do you know this, Lion?' questioned Guri seriously.

'Because now I can read it on all of those men here – they have all done it many times. Dying in the world, entering an afterlife, returning through death to another mortal life.'

'Not you?' asked Curjai. 'Why not you?'

'My last life in the world was my first life in the world. Given such powers – yet so ignorant. No wonder I was adrift. But also it's true for you, Curjai, and for you, Guri. One human life. Then this.'

'Only one life – we are so young, then.'

'*No. We* are so *old*.'

'A riddle.'

Lionwolf said, 'I've found – not what I am, but what I am to *be*. When I reach it I must be thrice dead and thrice born. And you two lazy ones – Guri will be thrice dead and twice born. And you, Curjai, little brother, just twice dead and twice born.

351

Don't pine. That will be enough. There are other kinds of death we have all known. Even the false real deaths Guri has known here. But once we leave this curious region, death will be done with us, bored with letting us in and out.'

The rain was over. It had fixed itself up on the sky as more stars, better than the stars of Hell had ever been.

'We're gods,' said Curjai. 'It's that. I told you so.'

Lionwolf said nothing. Guri was offended. 'My mother was a *woman*. And my father mortal too. *Be* gods if you like, but leave me to make my own road. Great Gods hear it and amen.'

Tomorrow tintinnabulated in the last rain dripping from the high places of Thasuba.

One by one the nine moons separated and reached the apex of the sky.

By then Guri and Curjai in uneasy alliance had gone down to drink in the feasthall, where a wide pool spouted cooked fish and gorgeous girls wove about, dressed in veils like spun glass. The guards, vizorless, off duty, drank with the rest, snake-hair lying quiescent. They had eyes. All the dogs had them too, running here and there for titbits. Later Guri and Curjai would go out to look at the two mammoths on the plain, which were shedding their heavier wool in the low heat. Great sheaths of it lay among the trampled stalks. Evidently they had been mating.

And Lionwolf lay entirely mated in the arms of Winsome, in a room from one side of which a fountain poured over a pyramid of rock and away into the dark.

'Will I find you again?' he said at last to her. 'Or will you become Chillel made of obsidian ice, and hide from me?'

'Your light,' she said, 'will find me out, wherever I am.'

'Are we gods? What are *gods*?'

'It can never matter, beloved. It has only to be lived.'

'Then to us it does matter.'

'Least of all to us.'

She raised herself to lie above him, and gazing into his face she said, 'From nothing I was made – from night and snow. I am the vessel of what made me, who are three gods, or one god that has three persons. For this, and to be this, I was created and am. I am this cup. If you will drink, you will drink.'

'Those were the words you spoke in the burnt city of Or Tash, to all of them but me, and nearly drove me mad.'

'I am the cup,' she said again, 'and now I'm only and ever for you.'

He put his mouth to her, to her breasts, drew her like silk over his body, brought the centre of her darkness that was not dark, the midnight cup holding its pomegranate wine, to his lips. 'And I was so thirsty. How can you have guessed?'

After this long night it would be a while without intoxication. After this last night of Hell that had healed to Paradise. And *Tomorrow* breathed the rain beads on the stones. *Yesterday.*

FIVE

Asleep, he heard the oculum signal to him.

Still sleeping, he dragged himself off the couch.

He woke up only as he stood. Body first, mind second.

Then he ran.

The halt in his left leg was improved, Thryfe thought, even as he propelled himself up the stairway into the towery of the South House. But his left hand was if anything worse – like wood. He flexed it as he went. Entering the chamber of the oculum, he stopped dead.

The great eye was full of a laval amber. Through the amber shot cross-currents of blue and gilded white, and dim streamers of a variable red.

'Oculum, I'm here. Let me see.'

He had given up on his left hand and abandoned it to lie partially inoperable by his side. With his right hand Thryfe made a gentle pass over the thaumaturgic globe, as if to draw a curtain aside.

It drew.

It *drew*—

'Incendimus ar konturbatexis.'

Thryfe spoke spontaneously a phrase from the elder writings of his Order. This was not an incantation, more a kind of prayer: *Deliver me from such ruin-fire as this.*

He knew what he saw now. His brain held only that – was *subsumed* by that.

The oculum had grown red and gold, with a core of live whiteness. All the while, golden and orichalc, flares bloomed

354

like feathers and exploded like volcanoes. The urge to cover the eyes was very great. Yet also, impossibly, he was not blinded. Nor did the rebuilt oculum give way. If anything the uncontainable power now imaged there seemed to feed its own.

Formerly the firefex had been visible in the glass, the legendary bird that burned itself in the sun and rose from its own ashes more beautiful and more valid. Later, other half-seen ciphers, symbols—

But this was the sun itself.

This was the sun as once it had been before the age of ice.

'In the name of any god – is *that* what you are?'

Like a flower, the magmatic tumult resolved by closing up its petals, then drawing away and away, up into a distance and a sky more blue than blueness. There it blazed, and only there.

Below, a young man was seated on the side of a building, perhaps a terrace or balcony. There seemed to be a city beneath, but it was unclear. The young man turned his head and looked at Thryfe looking into the oculum.

The stranger had coppery hair and was blue-eyed, and his skin was tanned as if from a sunlight long since departed out of the physical world.

'Yes, that is what you are.'

'*Is* it?' said the young man. 'Is *that* truly what I am?'

There was an appealing innocence, a disquieting sophisticated humour, together terrifying to any observer.

'Vashdran,' said Thryfe. 'Lionwolf.'

'And . . .?' said the Lionwolf, sitting there and smiling at Thryfe, respectful and nearly humorously naive; prompting.

'And the sun. You are the sun.'

'Thank God,' said Lionwolf. He grinned at Thryfe the wonderful human grin he had gifted to his daughter. 'It could, couldn't it, have been *so* much worse.'

Thryfe woke.

He was lying half off his bed, his left hand dead under him, his eyes he thought already wide open.

A *dream*?

This time he pulled his body together like a rowdy and

undisciplined battalion, before driving them and it to limp up all the stairs.

In the upper room, the oculum was blank and cool. Day was beginning in the windows, slaty-skied, no hint of any solar disc, and the snow miles deep to every point of the compass.

Kandexa had surrendered instantly those years before to reiver squadrons of the Gullahammer. They for their part killed every Rukarian man, woman and child they located there, stole anything portable or herdable, and went away.

Due to the submission, however, less damage than usual had been done to the city's architecture. What had – due to the sprees of the invader – ice and snow had capitalized on inevitably.

A dreary hollow, Kandexa, echoing with silences and noises that were too loud.

It was in size below one-eighth of the circumference and volume of Ru Karismi.

Others were already in possession of certain areas. These had marked off their established zones with piles of rubble, packed ice, and derelict carts or slees. They had written up titles for the territories, for example: *The region of the West Villagers, The New South, Hopeful Still, Clever Town.*

All were guarded, some even by men who wore the mail of Rukarian soldiery. Either they were those who had made themselves soldiers after the war, or deserters from it.

When the caravan arrived, wending through the barricaded areas inside the crushed-in gate, it was challenged more than once.

'How many are you? We have many communities already here.'

'But we're all,' said the leader of the entering caravan, Gabram, 'Rukarians.'

'That's debatable.' This from a batch of 'soldiers' over whose improvised wall flew the red and silver colours of Ru Karismi itself. 'You're easterners, aren't you?'

'No,' said Gabram. 'Some of us are from *here*. And some from the City of the Kings.'

The interrogator spat on the ground. He said only, 'Try the New South. They may welcome you. They're running out of sheep.'

But they did not try the New South, which anyway they saw along a wide avenue now blocked by ice-bricks with metal shards sticking out of them.

A lower section of the city was vacant. Someone from the caravan had owned a house here. The lots were marked by fire. They had heard, twice small bands of reivers had come back to loot the remains of Kandexa. Gabram and his brothers decided it was best to dig in on this ground. They did. Within a few days then they too had their own district, spaces between existing walls filled by whatever lay to hand and even a title on the stonewood door that served as a gate: *Paradise*.

Perhaps the irony of the name, or just the general breakdown of law and livelihood, produced three raids on Paradise during the first month. Gabram's men repelled the raiders, all of them from other settlements in the city. And when one belligerent gang brought along their witch, Gabram called out the caravan's middle-aged mageia.

Up on the barricade she stood throwing psychic rays at the other witch down the street, who threw rays back.

Jemhara, who had been unblocking a well among the courts of burnt houses, heard the commotion as the older mageia was felled by a small flung ball of marble.

When Jemhara reached the fray, she bent first over the mageia, her friend by now, and felt her forehead to make sure the skull was in one piece. It was, so Jemhara climbed on the barricade in turn.

Her advent at the top checked some of the attackers. Some even called out obscenely to her, seeing she was young and attractive.

For all she had changed her nature Jemhara had, when feasible in her past, given short shrift to dangerous morons – and that method she had kept.

She concentrated her gaze on the cemented snow of the avenue. Within three or four seconds it was churning, fissuring, giving. Shouting and yelling, the enemy force sprawled every which way, until a gushing wave of melted ice rose and swept them, their mageia included, right along the boulevard in a screaming, kicking mass, smacking them into other walls and obstacles along the route, for a bonus.

The defenders of Paradise began to laugh. Gabram cautioned vigilance – but it was unneeded. Even hours, days later, the raiders had not returned. Nor did any of the zones mount an attack on Paradise thereafter. Word had got round, it seemed. Paradise had a Magikoy.

'Drink this,' said Jemhara, spooning a cordial into her witch-friend's mouth.

'There. Worth a bump on the head to taste that. Wine in it? Thought so, a good one. Don't cry, Jema,' added the older witch, moved at this concern. 'You and I both well know I'll live.'

Jemhara shook herself cat-like to cast off the tears.

She did not reveal she had not shed them for that. The cordial was one of those she had mixed for Thryfe in his mansion, and she had spooned it into him too when his delirium would let her.

That night Jemhara lay in her room, the attic of a small house by Paradise's eastern barricade.

She could not sleep. She could only think of him.

Near dawn, however, she dreamed. Waking from this dream she did not believe she had slept. The dream had only netted her in, a sort of trance that had nothing to do with unconsciousness. Two years ago and more she had sometimes sent her physical spirit through doors and walls of the world – but never *out* of the world. Not until now.

After the dream, Jemhara sat a long while by the slit of window, aware she had journeyed very far.

Below teemed the people from the caravan, intent on renovating their district. She had helped with this and would soon go down to do some more.

But the dream for now came between her and her duties. Even between her and her longing memory of Thryfe.

She knew who he was, the man – the deity – in the dream. Yet she had never before seen him. She too, like Thryfe, had missed his advent at Ru Karismi.

Once, nevertheless, she had met one who resembled him.

That had been in her primal adolescence, there in her hovel near Sofora. She had been working up a spell to punish some unwary person in the stead who had offended her. Suddenly, from a corner of the shack, a being stepped out.

She had in fact not been entirely certain of who or what he was, but canny from her awkward life she understood she had better kneel and kiss the floor at his feet.

Years after, having identified the visitor from the god-statues in Ru Karismi's temple-town, Jemhara boasted to a session of scholars at one of the libraries of magic she frequented. They had mocked her, naturally. Why should the god Zeth Zezeth have attended her silly little spell? And in his benign aspect too . . .

Jemhara did not forget his smile. She had been aware, though Zeth Zezeth the Sun Wolf did not touch her or speak, that he found her quite appealing. He seemed to approve of her. Few had. Few had *cause*.

It had stayed a small shimmering mystery of her existence, which she had never solved and finally seldom considered. Only when the city icons of Zezeth began to crumble in the onset of the barbarian war had Jemhara re-analysed what, if anything, this god might mean to her. Certainly he was not one of her natal gods; three others had been given her. Then Vuldir re-entered the picture of her days, and soon shifted her mind from Zezeth by sending her to entrap Thryfe. How could he have been so stupid? Yet . . . in a way, she had done it . . . And what followed that congress thrust everything other from her brain.

In the attic room at Kandexa, Jemhara compared the gold and silver god with the gold, fire and sapphire of the deity in her trance.

They were alike, vastly so. As brothers might be, or more perhaps a young father with a son curiously the same age.

Her trance had shown her Vashdran. She grasped this. Vashdran, the alien Lionwolf, and he was made in the image of Rukarian Zeth Zezeth, but for his colours and his beauty, which was greater – *greater* than that of Zeth.

In the trance too there had been an unknown city raised very tall, more elevated than Ru Karismi even, and set amid long meadows and fields of extraordinary growing stuffs. A procession wound slowly through the city lanes, chariots drawn by lions such as the Jafn favoured, or by lashdeer in the western way. Men were in these chariots, maybe two hundred of them, all exchanging banter both with each other and with an adoring crowd which danced, tapped drums and flaunted bells. A sunny day. The light had struck Jemhara even though in the trance she had been a bystander floating in the air, removed, involved only as audience and herself unseen.

At the procession's head, in a lion chariot of gold-trimmed bronze, rode the man who was also undeniably a god.

His face was mostly pensive. Sometimes he, also like Zeth, flashed out a smile like lightning to the crowd, or at two men who rode beside him. One of these was an Olchibe with leopard-coloured skin. The other was young and handsome, dark-haired, brown of complexion and eyes.

Though Jemhara had heard music and song in the trance, even portions of ribaldry and repartee, she heard nothing from these three despite seeing they sometimes spoke to one another.

Then the red-haired god looked over. He looked directly into her eyes. This Zeth had not done, to spare her most definitely, for now the direct look from this other was like an assault. Yet, too, an assault that enchanted, that *possessed*. None surely could ever resist, or want to.

'Greetings, Jemhara,' said the marvellous voice in Jemhara's trance-dreaming mind. The smiling mouth of the god did not move.

Jemhara did not vocalize. She was snared, could only listen.

'Life,' said the Lionwolf, 'how we struggle with it. But I've let go of all that. This is like dropping a burden. Simple. It *is* simple, Jemhara. Do you believe me?'

Now she could answer.

'Is it, lord?'

'Don't call me *lord*, Jemhara. That would be a craziness between us, you and me. When you see me next, I'll be a fool again for a while, a type of fool. Will you mind?'

The lunacy of what he said, which seemed entirely sane and lucid while he spoke, each time rinsed over her thoughts, scattering them. But he could read her thoughts. They made him laugh, she saw.

He was gentle enough, playful even. Not the maniacal warrior, the Jafn Borjiy who had provoked the destruction of so many and so much.

'Oh,' he said, 'pretty Jemhara. I'll have to learn again, out there, what already here I know. Don't expect wisdom from me to begin with. Not that you will. Here is the best news, then. A man is on the road to you. A man like a tower of ice with eagle's eyes. Who can *that* be?'

Jemhara's trance heart stopped, then surged forward. Lionwolf shook his head. His face was shadowed she saw when the smile left it, but not with any grief that could lessen or corrode. Even so, it seemed he had not forgotten who he had been, what he had done.

As she must one day learn, the evil past is to be given room, a little space to sit, for it must be available like any necessary reference book. No need, though, to fill the house with it.

'Until we meet, Jemhara,' said Lionwolf.

The chariots moved on, and Jemhara hung in the sunny air. Then she saw the dark Kandexan attic and the slit of cold dull morning, the city outside, and far to one side the distant frozen sea.

Only by rehearsing the trance all through again in her conscious mind did Jemhara reach its last moments, and hear again those words, *A man is on the road to you. A man like a tower of ice with eagle's eyes.*

361

Reaching this, Jemhara cried out.

As if by a broom everything else was brushed in a hundred bits into the storage bins of her memory.

Thryfe.

A god – even a god of madness and cruelty, perhaps a *dead* god – had foretold her future.

Ridiculously, Jemhara recollected the wicked steader witch of her youth, who had sexually abused Jemhara and beaten her into her first spiteful shape. The witch, as Jemhara's mother also had, once promised Jemhara a future magnificent love. Lying sops to summon obedience. *Realities?*

As the days moved over the South House and melted to nothing on the horizon, Thryfe divided his time between his studies and the needs of the village of Stones. He walked to the village every third afternoon, or sometimes took the sleekar to give the deer exercise. These had been his vehicle and team. He had abandoned them on entering Ru Karismi in the aftermath. Someone – or thing – had saved the chariot and kept it in repair. The lashdeer too had obviously been well cared for. He did not think gargolems had seen to this, for they were by then in the city all defunct, or had disappeared. But whoever it had been, Thryfe would not spoil their thrift by leaving the deer to atrophy in a yard.

The village did not require his assistance, but seemed always delighted when he appeared.

In lieu of other service, he started to teach some of the children who showed aptitude rudiments of magecraft. Most if not all the Magikoy were dead. Who knew, maybe emerging generations would supply replacements. Though where they could be tutored to the higher levels he had no idea. Not the Insularia. That potent complex was now like clinker from a burnt-out hearth.

The children were promising. Some of the adults too when they dared lurk on the periphery of Thryfe's classes. One young woman, who had never dealt a stroke of sorcery in her life, learned literally overnight how to bring fire – which she did not extract from the air, but out of her abdomen – rather in the Crarrowin manner. Thryfe then had the task of reconciling the woman's husband to her promotion to village mageia.

One superstition thay had all stubbornly grappled to them with bonds of steel was about the Stones themselves, up above the ice-forest. No one would go there. They told Thryfe that originally no one had *looked* that way after nightfall, for fear of noting any glow.

'The Stones are an enigma, but not anything to be afraid of.'

Nobody seemed convinced, even by this Magikoy lord they had sworn to serve.

In the end, Thryfe persuaded a party of them to go with him to the spot.

He had found, to his relief and satisfaction, that he had almost bottomless patience with the villagers. In Ru Karismi patience had worn thin as gauze against the arrogance and numbskullery of kings and courts.

He chose four of his brightest pupils, plus the new mageia. The village leader would have to come as a matter of course.

The seven of them went up around the forest in the dusk. A faint snow was drifting by and pearly ice-spiders spun their intricate webs. They met an enormous badger too, white as alabaster, just the tarnished stripe of cream along its forehead, trotting on shovel claws.

When they reached them the Stones were not as Thryfe recalled. They had *grown*, in some instances colossal, and they were black.

Only a single half-moon was up. It limned the Stones but nothing more.

Thryfe was taken aback. He had never expected they would enlarge, nor had he ever seen them wholly unlit aside from by day. With sunset they began, and ended with the dawn. The sheens and colours were malleable, generally running to and fro, but always *there*.

Something seemed to him inherently wrong, if not in gained size then in the absence of light.

Inevitably he thought then of the dream he had had of Lionwolf and the sun that Lionwolf was. Thryfe had tried to paint over the picture many times, putting it down to disorders in his own self-harmed brain. But always the original vision scorched through. What did it really mean? And now this – what did *this* mean?

He stood with the villagers for ten minutes.

Then he said, casual, 'No, it isn't a night for them after all.'

'But don't they always light up?' asked the leader, who knew too much for his own good.

'Not always.'

Thryfe sent them down to the village with this comfy lie. They were glad to be let off, he could see, even the fire-bringer.

Thryfe himself walked round the Stones. He did and said nothing, for they had been at all times objects beyond his scope. He had met no other Magikoy, let alone lesser magus, who knew of them and thought anything different.

Eventually, despite that, he put his right, still-functional palm on one of the lower Stones, which was only about twice his height. He had never touched them before. Had anyone? Maybe. Even as he made the move a sort of warning – no, not that, some faint, unidentifiable alarum not to do with fear, only readiness – sounded in his mind.

Under his hand a vivid emerald spasmed all through the standing Stone. As his hand of its own volition flew off, the ignition sped from block to block, until the entire ring of them blazed green.

Something emerald and flaming burst too in Thryfe's brain.

He tasted snow – and leaves.

The second, which had lasted a long while, became another second. Thryfe found himself again, upright and solid in the middle of fifty giant pitch black stones.

From his body the half-moon cast a sombre reflection on the pale ground. It seemed to be the copy of some other life-form.

Thryfe smelled Jemhara's perfume in the night and felt her finger tracing back the hair from his forehead. He knew what she had done, bringing him the snow, cramming it into his mouth. He *remembered* what until now he had never seemed to have been present during, let alone a part of – the howling limbo, the torture cell of smoke and chains, the double resurrection.

Stupidly he said aloud, 'But to bring me out of hell she too must have gone down into the Weapons Chamber. She must have suffered the ordeal of swords—'

The Stones were black.

Where had the moon got to? Ah, it was sinking along there, in the west. How bizarre, to sink in the west. Why did it do that? This earth – so strange to him. As if he had never lived in it till now.

He went over the slope and towards his house. Its windows shone a smooth non-frantic blue.

He thought of the night they had glittered whitely for a threat of danger. Why had he never before wondered how the shape-change to a hare of a limited and mercenary minor witch could have stirred up the sentinels?

His studies altered. Thryfe sat hour by hour in front of the oculum.

It was history he wanted now, the history of his life, and of one other's.

The oculum displayed the measured, conservative panoply of his own years, the vibrant, multi-hued scramble of hers.

He had been born in near squalor, among lamasceps and unknowingness. She too. His mother was slain in front of him. Hers cast her merrily out to the care of a fiend of a witch. He flew with eagles, she unlocked ice. He went towards the legendary Magikoy, she murdered her abuser and turned crook herself. As Thryfe walked from the Insularia a master magician, Jemhara skittishly studied in the libraries of the city and at Vuldir's orders seduced, wed and poisoned Sallusdon, King Paramount. Then Thryfe and Jemhara, those two disparate mortals, met.

Locked in an infinity of rapturous lust, she had loved him.

Let it now be said, *he* had loved *her*. How not? Each set free the other from approximately two decades, or with him rather more, of self-induced blindness. But only she had known she had received the gift of sight. Thryfe had bound his eyes and thrown himself into the pit.

Guilt – useless, perhaps unmerited. What anyway could guilt achieve? Throw *that* in the pit instead then, and leave it there.

He saw himself hung in smoulder and nullity in some crevice of the Telumultuan Chamber. He saw Jemhara run through the snow, a little black hare. He saw her enter ruinous Ru Karismi naked, and the Gargolem itself appear and succour her.

Oh yes. Only the greatest of the sorcerer kind could attract the attention of the Magikoy Gargolem. At the finish, not even the Magikoy had lured it from its obscure alternate universe.

But Jemhara *had*.

Thryfe saw her fall into the room of ordeal, saw her rent, slashed, cut to scarlet rags, as he had seen his mother. Watching this Thryfe held himself in fetters of iron. But soon he threw the iron off into the guilt pit. It was not appropriate any more. Then he wept, leaning his head on his dead left hand.

Defenceless, he beheld her healed, and then her rescue of him, her courage, her becoming the bait for him as eagle and predator, and how she did not know her own wisdom, only knew *him*, and waited there as he came at her to kill her, which he *would* have done had he been able.

At last Thryfe watched as Jemhara tended him, ordering his supernatural servants with ease. He saw her fetch and put the transmuted snow into his mouth. How he reprimanded her. How she went away.

Over the land she went.

Going ever into icy distance.

To his bewilderment, after that view the oculum would display no more of Jemhara. It turned opaque and refused to answer his request that it show him where now she was.

She then had become capable of shielding herself from *him*?

He deserved nothing better of her.

No, throw that too over in the pit. Who deserved *anything*? Alter and grow more worthy, and earn the rewards.

It was her pain clouded and blanked the magic glass, her pain, his.

What am I, that I can't find her?

He felt his power, both as a mage and as a man. He laughed.

He knew what he was. *Now* he knew, although it could take all his life maybe to learn and get it right. Finding Jemhara, to this, was nothing.

In the village of Stones they started up in dread. One of Thryfe's gargolems, two or three of which some of the villagers had glimpsed around the mansion, ambled into the street and halted by Ravenhair's well. Its voice was mild, mechanical, and gradually reassuring.

'He has gone on a journey, and sent me to school you. But best,' said the gargolem, 'you are coming up to the house.'

Several days and nights went by. No one went.

The gargolem, or one of them, was there every morning in the village and each twilight the same, always with a similar announcement.

The students who had been lessoned by Thryfe got over their fright at it first. One sunrise it made a slide all down a slope, for the younger children to enjoy when the slide attached to the well was too wet.

The students decided they would chance the mansion.

Also the mageia thought she might go up with them.

'It does no harm,' she said to her husband.

'Oh yes, *off* you go,' he said. 'Leave me to fend for myself, you thankless lump.'

The mageia called him a name not often coined by a decorous woman for her partner. Then she filled their hearth with a conjured fire, set a chicken sprung from the cold-larder ready cooked before him, with fresh-baked bread which had been rising dough a split minute earlier.

'Get on with you,' said the mageia. '*You* won't starve. And if you miss my company, there's always the carter's widow in the third house, the one you have a frolic with when you think I won't find out.'

Seventh Intervolumen

Whether I have been broken dead under a chariot or turned into a flaming star, if ever I see again the ones I love, I shall remember that once I lived and was one among them.

Bardic Lay of the Hero Star Black: Jafn

It had not been possible to return, not for two days and a night. All that while Saftri, goddess of the Vorms, had wrapped her fleet of Vormlanders, Kelps and Faz in a swimming inpenetrable fortress of air, and drawn a wind to blow them swifter than any could row, north-west.

She could have sped them faster. But seeing their hair blown forward and the very *skin* blown forward from their cheeks like bladders, not to mention how the sails banged about on the Mother Ships, she did not risk higher velocity.

All this speed was precautionary. Brightshade, though subdued, would recover. Zeth might even assist him in person. Then one or other or both of them once more pursue.

Saftri when Saphay and a princess had been trained in a sort of miserly aloof housekeeping. Waste nothing, and take care of what you have. Probably in her girlhood she had not practised these arts. Endowed with supernature she began to. So the ships belted over the sea until she felt sufficient miles of water had been opened between them and the giant whale. Only when they anchored in the lee of a field of small icebergs did Saftri go back alone to search for Dayadin.

She recognized the stretch of water where the whale had sunk after a while. A mark was on it, visible only to one such as she.

Saftri darted along the surface of the waves. But she could not bring herself to go down into them. Her last mortal memories of dying there put her off. She was, it must be said, *phobic* about most things submarine.

371

Needless to say, even so her psychic antennae soon picked up an absence in the sea rather than a presence. Brightshade had recovered himself enough to slink away.

Saftri searched then over a wider radius of ocean. She did it diligently, but with an increasing impatience and a flagging heart. Loss tended to make her irritable now. As much as Dayadin's awful plight engulfed in the monster's belly, she resented her own inability to reach him and smarted that she had not properly protected him.

He was a little boy.

In the end, she alighted on a floe of ice and shed tears of frustration and sorrow.

He would be dead by now. Yes, yes, he had been of exceptional calibre and obviously infused by some sorcerous force, but ultimately he could not withstand what had happened. The very thought of it – Brightshade and his *guts* – made her retch.

There had been a kind of ticking of Dayadin's life, too, somehow in the air. It had now faded from her inner ear.

What had possessed him to approach the whale? He had tried to save them all by flattering it – and she had not seen, not properly, so caught up in her own dilemma and the temporary sticking of her powers. Heroes, she thought. *Men*, she thought.

She visualized rushing across all the sea for ever, looking in vain for Brightshade. She imagined going down under the ice after him and knew she never could. Besides, who but she could predict what else might be sent against her people? She was responsible for *them*. She had brought them away to make them safe. One life, even a peerless life, against so many must not be allowed to count.

He too was dead.

The field of small bergs sheltered the fleet for some days and nights, including one sleep nocturnal-diurnal.

The ships lay between slender needles and curving cliffs, parabolas and concaves of ice, that had in them, often even in the dark, mystic, lit lamps of ultramarine, lapis lazuli or green turquoise.

Saftri, as she wafted in over this scene after her fruitless quest, thoughtfully took in the likenesses and difference of the fleet itself – lighted only by individual cups of oil or torches at the prows. The Vormish ships she knew well, with their decor of shark, whale and cow horns. The Faz ships were very similar. The Kelps however had adorned their one hundred and forty-seven vessels with shells, along with the rest of the paraphernalia. They had gods made of shells, too. Nasty-minded raven gods, or preposterous shell-scaled fish with double tails and elephant trunks. Out of deference to Saftri, the currently ruling deity, these abominations were stowed at the rowers' feet.

Saftri had more than once previously flown to and over the far continent, but going at a human pace now and on water, she began to note other features. Though she feared the deeps, the surface intrigued her. Tonight the gemmy lucific of the icebergs was enthralling, if only for a short while.

Altogether there were five Mother Ships in this adapted fleet. When she descended to the one that housed her, the Vormish shamans were performing one of their irksome and apparently irrelevant dances on the deck.

Shrieks and squawks and festoons of hysterical sparks enveloped Saftri. She swept through them into her between-decks hut. Here she glared about her. It was a ramshackle and unlovely space, and had the aroma of horsaz from below. Why had she always had to make do? The inhospitable east side of the exquisite palaces in Ru Karismi, the outcast and loveless bedroom where pregnancy, or awkward spirits, had seen her dumped when in her husband's Jafn garth, Nabnish's vile abode, Yyrot's over-hot or dissolving ice-pyramids; mud, misery and mess. Even her sea-tomb had been frigid and smelled fishy. Insult to injury. Finally a goddess – *this*.

Now I am a god, to which god do I pray?

Oh, send me something – her heart wrinkled in embarrassed yearning – *something I would – enjoy.*

Oh, send me someone I can never fail, said her inner heart, too shameless and low for her to hear. *I am so tired of loss.*

Their initial days at sea had been fraught.

None of the remaining Holasan-garth knew anything about shipcraft. Nevertheless a scatter of men from Holas villages, men either redundant through frailty from the war or, less usual, too unenthused to have joined it, came to assist instead the Chaiord with the weird Thing ship. Some of them were fishermen and whalers. They knew at least the vagaries of their clinker-built boats, how to row, how to raise or furl sail, to steer, to sniff out weather. Nor were they seasick, unlike twenty of the thirty-three Jafn Holas from the garth, Arok not excluded.

Nirri was immune to the spooning of the sea, as were eight of the other women, two of the men, and two of the children – one boy and one girl. No one could explain why this should be so. The fishers said it was a gift from Great God. Better not question, just get on.

They, these fishers, quickly taught the younger stronger women who were well enough, and the rest of the people as they adjusted, what must be done about the huge, idiosyncratic ship.

Seventeen masts? What odds. If you could manage one, that only meant managing it seventeen times over.

There were also five wise-women from the villages both inland and off the shore, and one werloka from another clan, who had, he said, been ousted by a younger – and less able he *also* said – fellow.

All these had come to Arok with the villagers, and been useful in first unearthing the ship from the ice.

The Thing had stood there since the dawn of the ice. Long ago Arok, then a boy, had been brought with his father and other kin of the Holas Chaiord to a meeting here with the Kree and Irhon, under green truce torches.

Each of the five wise-women was adamant. The ship might be used, but they must first ask her permission.

'A she?' queried Arok.

None of them deigned to reply.

The ship was buried to its or her waterline in ice. The Thing Place was surrounded also by a ring of black spar. He thought, even if they could raise the Thing it would fall to pieces.

From sunset to rise the wise-women went round and round with burning brands, calling to the ship, singing to it, sometimes stroking the surrounding ice sheet with fire, which made little impression. The werloka sat outside the spar ring, looking on. He had offered no comment on the efficacy of any of this.

After the sun rose the women came to Arok. 'Dig now.' So they dug, hacking away chunks of ice, permafrost and colourless dead snow. Then the women performed another ceremony, anointing the ship with an elixir, chanting to it of the sea.

'Bring the ropes now.'

Arok shrugged, annoyed by it all yet fearful too – but of the ship's shattering or coming out whole? He was unsure.

They tied on the ropes and only then did the werloka ramble about, attaching amulets, speaking in some garble. The other ends of the ropes were fastened to the last five chariots, with the last ten lions in the traces. The men would pull too, and some of the young women. Nirri stepped up, and Arok frowned at her. But she shook her head. 'You made me queen. Am I to sit on my rump when your people toil?'

Arok slapped the whip against the air and everyone began the task in a nimbus of thaumaturgic lights.

To start with it seemed impossible. He thought the lions, not to mention some of the older men, would drop dead. Then he heard a big awesome bark behind him. He knew the sound. It was ice breaking deep down. Then they put their last strength into the ropes and with a noise now of smashed glass, sawing blades, earthquake boom and wailing wood out the Thing came, showering them in a hailstorm of ice and frost.

It was intact. Or *she* was.

The long centuries of cold had turned her hull and masts to something like petrified light granite and her keel to hollow vitreous. Where there seemed any fault or flaw it was tended to by the whalers, who built their fires on the ice and smelted pots of liquid iron, or charred hard wood harder. The canvas came from a hundred or more abandoned little boats, sewn together with metal thread. By the time she was rigged, she had gone down along the sheet ice on runners and been towed out to anchor in the moving sea.

Arok stared at the ship. It was real then, all this. Now they would have to go.

'Name her,' ordered the werloka. 'You're the Chaiord.'

Arok glanced at Nirri. He was getting used by now to female things.

'Her name is *Hawk*.'

The day before they set out, as the last provisions were coming in and the last carpentry was effected on huts and shelters on deck and in the wide hold, which had also, like the rest, mostly been maintained by the ice, one of the fishermen brought in his son. Others had already brought their sparse families, a handful of women and two or three babies. The story ran that most of the original wives had left those men who did not join the Rukar war, connecting themselves to those who had and going south-west with them. These women here had been left by their husbands, and now found partners among men called formerly cowards. Well, the cowards were still alive thanks to their cowardice. However, this fisherman was different. He had been to the war, and come back. Arok had not known that, not till now. For the fisherman's son walked hand in hand with his mother, who held her head high as any royalty. The child was about seven from the look of him, probably not in fact.

'Do you allow it, sir?' asked the fisherman. 'She said,' he indicated his woman, 'you might refuse us, seeing why you want the voyage and all.'

'Of course I allow it,' said Arok, stiff as any mast on the ship.

The boy was black. He was another get of Chillel's, therefore Dayadin's one-third brother, if this man did but know it – and maybe he did.

But the fisherman looked at Nirri now, worriedly.

Nirri spoke in a dry little voice.

'What's his name?'

'Fenzi.' Arok saw Nirri's hand flutter out on its own, as if to call the child to her and hold him. She mastered herself. Admirable. 'Perhaps a good omen,' she said.

The sky was clear the morning they embarked. Gazing back at the shore Arok asked himself if he was the only one to see, abruptly, as though a blindfold disintegrated from before his eyes, how unknown the land was, his birthplace, sheathed in its infernal cold obduracy of white.

I won't miss it, he thought. *It's people you miss.*

Bad weather entered the equation on the second night. By then several were queasy, and with the extra momentum they gave way.

The worst side of it, Arok surmised between bouts of lunatic vomiting, was that the illness never truly eased, even in the intervals.

Meanwhile the ship was run quite spryly.

Cheese-faced, Arok watched the unnauseated ones striding about, swinging aloft over spars – *eating* Great God forgive them . . .

The weather settled, but his sickness did not abate. To his chagrin Arok found himself the last of the severe cases. By then most of them were bright-cheeked and cheerful, glad to feel better. But with every shift of the wind Arok leaned over the side, trying to expel his soul into the waves. The medicines of the wise-women did nothing to alleviate his plight.

He determined throughout this, and through an inevitable growing weakness, to uphold his position as Chaiord and protector. He stood on deck, and attended at the helm as the whalers steered the ship among currents and floating packs of ice. They knew such steering devices, having needed them for their own heavier vessels in the past.

Every so often Arok went unspeaking to the side, and returned shivering, pretending indifference. He took his temper out on Nirri, snapping at her, calling her names. Now she made no remonstrance. Well, she had got her way, had she not?

Nearly two Endhlefons had passed.

It was about midnight.

Arok stood in the bow, looking at the chill icicles of stars the whalers had begun to teach him. Until his belly, for the thousandth time, came looking up his throat for an exit.

'*Be damned to this – be cutch damned to it . . .*' Spitting and breathless, he felt a firm strong hand cup supportively over his forehead, as a kind father would do it with a sick child.

'Lift your head, Arok,' said a youngish man's voice.

Arok thought this must be one of his men. Impertinent – and odd. Usually they kept well clear of him at such moments, not to humiliate him further.

'The trick of it, you see,' said the unknown man, 'is to breathe with the sea. Some do the opposite in storm too, to quiet the gale. That's not so easy.'

Too far gone to resist, Arok said dubiously, '*Breathe* with it—'

'Look there. The wave rises. Breathe in. Yes, that's it. Well done. Now, watch as it folds over, and breathe out in company. It's that you help the sea then. Do you understand? You breathe as *it* breathes, and make it an ally. In turn—'

'I don't feel sick,' said Arok. 'By the hand of God, where's it gone?'

'Breathe now,' continued the kind and only slightly amused voice. 'Soon you'll keep pace without thinking.'

Arok felt his world hurrying back. His blood began to run normally. Presently he was ravenous.

He turned to discover who had been so intelligent – and the deck behind him was empty under the great billows of sails and sky.

Arok began to hear the tales then. He heard how the lions, restless in the hold and unruly when let on deck, had grown calmer. He heard how a baby crawling towards some unsuitable station of the ship was picked up and carried to his mother. She had thanked the man. *She* was the only one sure she had seen him.

'He was a noble, so I thought. And I thought, but that can't be right, all the noble Holas are standing with Arok there.'

Others said he was, though quite young – about thirty years – white-haired as the Jafn often were. Well built and worth looking at too, the woman who saw him said.

Arok, now hale and in charge, went to see the wise-women in their belowdecks bothy.

'Some say it's a ghost, ladies.'

They conferred.

'Not quite that,' said the oldest one.

'Nor quite alive. Alive *once*,' said the other elderly one.

'Surely then a ghost. As I said.'

'Can you feel the hand of a ghost on your head? Does a ghost pick up a baby and carry it, or groom lions?'

'We'll ask. In *our* fashion,' said the youngest, who was fifty years if she was a day. 'Get along with you, Arok.'

He sent them a present of beer and dried figs from the stores. But they did not produce an answer.

Islands showed themselves far off. They had met no reivers, no shipping of any sort. Sometimes fish filled the water thick as vegetables in a stew, at others they could make out no living thing other than themselves.

Before they reached the Vormland, Arok knew they would need to plan what must be done. There were too few of them to plunge in and seize Dayadin, even once they knew his whereabouts. But there would be unpopulated areas where they might enter, moving then by stealth against whatever dirty village of the Vormland had him.

One evening, as the stars were splashing their snow over the sky and the ship was at anchor, only a watch alert for it was a sleep nocturnal of four hours, the fisherman with the black son Fenzi walked up to Arok, the boy at his side.

'He has something he wants to tell you, Chaiord.'

'Do you?' Arok looked down at Fenzi, uneasy with hurt bafflement, almost envy, and curbing himself from such degrading emotions.

'The ghost-man on the ship is a Chaiord too, but dead,' said the boy without preface.

'Yes?' asked Arok, agog. 'How do you know?'

'He spoke to me. He said so.'

'You could see him?'

'Clear as you, sir.'

'What does he want on my ship?'

'He said he'd tell you, if you were willing to listen, one king to another.'

'What—' Arok paused. 'What was – is his name?'

Fenzi beamed, pleased to aid.

'Athluan of the Jafn Klow. He wed the yellow-flower-haired Rukar woman, Saphay, the lady who gave birth to the Lion-wolf.'

'Yes. I know whose mother she was.'

'Athluan said he would be down with the lions now, giving their manes a brush. He said they were old lions, and should be made a fuss of. But if you were to go down, he and you could talk a little.'

Arok pulled himself together. He thanked the sunny child and the perturbed father, and went over to where Nirri slept in their exclusive hut below the prowmost spar.

'I regret waking you.'

She sat up. 'Is something amiss?'

'Perhaps. Or not. Do you recall Athluan of the Klow?' She nodded. 'His undead spirit is aboard the vessel.'

Nirri made a small ritual sign, but this action seemed practical rather than fearful.

'What does he want?'

'To talk to me. To discuss the grooming of the chariot-lions it sounds like.' Nirri burst out laughing. Arok too, taking himself by surprise. 'He was guardian,' said Arok, 'to *him* – or would have been, but Rothger killed Athluan, and that began the feud that began the war—'

'Go down and see,' said Nirri.

Arok went.

The belowdecks were dim-dark and smelled of foodstuffs, fish, stale water, fowls and lions.

The lion shelter was in a large fenced enclosure and here they generally prowled, mourning their imprisonment. Only feeding times or excursions above interested them. Arok's own favourites were gone – wiped out like the rest at Ru Karismi. But these tough old beasts were worthy of honour and he could not, he thought, have killed them only to save them the voyage.

Coming into the enclosure he sensed a difference, and then even in the limited light he saw it. They had been smoothed, their claws well trimmed and the rings adjusted. Their manes were recently braided and full of beads and tiny nuggets of gold. Someone had been feeding them dainties too. *Someone still was.*

It was curious how Arok arrived at witnessing the ghost. There had, he thought, been nothing visible, but then the more he noticed about the lions the more he became aware of a figure just there – or *there*. The final view was precise. A white-haired man stood between three of the cats, placing slivers of what appeared to be deer-meat into their jaws. On his shoulder perched a striped hawk. The bird flared its wings and let out a thin screech and Arok jumped half a foot.

'Greetings in peace. A fine night.'

Arok was transfixed. The Klow too had been wiped off the face of the earth by Lionwolf in person, which was of course the proper resolution of his feud with them.

'Do you know,' said Arok, 'your people are all dead?'

'We all come to it,' said Athluan levelly.

'Some of us less completely than others.'

'Long ago, a ghost leapt through me when I was still a living man. Possibly that has something to do with it. Or the uncanny manner in which Rothger murdered me. Maybe that.'

Athluan moved steadily forward, and put out his hand.

Arok could smell a healthy human smell, washed hair and clothing. Reaching out, he clasped Athluan's hand. It was solid and warm. He knew it immediately.

'Oh, yes,' said Athluan. 'Well, it's hard luck to get so sick. Anything I could do.'

'My thanks. What now in return?'

'You must alter course.'

'Why?'

Athluan said simply, 'You're on the wrong track.'

'Vormland.'

'Your son isn't in the Vormland, not any longer.'

'Do you say – do you say—'

'No, I never meant he's dead. He lives. Another land, beyond the reivers' isles. He's there, where I suspect he has to be to fit with one more pattern of this strange design.'

'There are no lands beyond the north.'

'Another continent.'

'Why would you lie?'

'Yes, why? I've not lied.'

Arok prowled about as the lions so often did, setting them off. Everyone then prowled in circuits, only the ghost of Athluan and the hawk staying still.

'Then I'll ask another question,' said Arok at last. 'Why are you on the ship?'

'I've somewhere to go myself. And sometimes, Arok of the Holas, I like to do things as I'd have had to when made of flesh and blood. So I ride the ship and look at the stars. Sometimes I lie down to sleep a couple of hours. When you're dead you can do most things at will. Even choose not to. But I'm bound for the continent I spoke of. It's my pleasure to travel with you.'

'Are you always here?'

'Not always. Sometimes I go somewhere else to – shall I say *think*.'

'Where, in God's name?'

'There you have it,' said Athluan quietly. 'In God's name, and only God knows.'

'God,' said Arok; he muttered, '*gods*.'

'All of those. All part of the same material. As are we. How else do we get by at all?'

Arok turned his back, then childishly spun round again to see if Athluan would vanish.

Perhaps like a sensitive father playing hide-and-seek with his boy, Athluan had obliged him. Only the hawk circled high up a moment before dropping straight down to Arok's shoulder, with a definite weighty thud. It was still sitting there when he emerged again on the upper deck. Then it flapped off to a lower mast. Arok thought he would go back to Nirri and leave the watch to their own wakefulness. Sleep nocturnals were supposedly for slumber not canoodling. But his body seemed to have remembered Nirri's abruptly. It was itching to get at her. Sleep, like ghosts, could wait.

Under their own volition now, the fleet drove west of north.

The days were calm and cinder-coloured, the sun a smudge of lemon light. Enough wind blew to abet their progress. If the wind failed they surmised the goddess would be able to summon one. They were very confident in the goddess now, only careful of her temperament. Dayadin's devouring had been their main source of discontent, but this faded. The Faz, heartless perhaps or pragmatic, declared it a necessary sacrifice to the gods of the sea, one of which had either piloted or inhabited the enormous whale. Saftri after all had smitten the whale. The death of the child was therefore tit for tat. The Kelps made no comment. They had two such hero boys among their own jalees. The Faz for that matter had one. Even the Vorm-landers were left with one black child of their own. Used to deprivation and to going on in spite of it, they swiftly put Dayadin behind them in thought as literally they had in miles.

Krandif alone stayed unappeased.

He fumed and pushed off the would-be consoling hand of his brother Mozdif.

An evening came when the ships had stopped rowing, sitting a while so the crews could eat and drink, on a veldt of sea that still glowed blue from the leftovers of a sunk sun. Krandif lowered himself into the water and swam vigorously over to Saftri's Mother Ship. Men applauded his action, cheering, thinking the ship-lord used the freezing ocean for exercise, like the let-out horsazin who were frisking and playing all around in the waves.

Krandif drew himself up the ladder, fisted his forehead politely to the shamans, and took hold of Jord's arm.

'Where is she?'

'Our Lady – she's below in her hut there.'

'I'm going down.'

Jord looked unencouraging. As one of Saftri's priests he had responsibilities. 'Perhaps . . . you wait a while. She's—'

'In one of her moods she is?'

'As you have said it.'

'By my father's skull,' said Krandif, 'in one of *my* moods *I* am.'

Saftri heard the loud banging on her flimsy door, and caused it to fly open. There stood Krandif, his brows knotted, his mouth clenched.

The rage of men still caught Saftri off guard from time to time. In her former life she had had to be wary, and old habits were ingrained. But she said frigidly, 'What?'

'Do you never consider him?'

She knew exactly what he meant.

'Of whom,' she said, 'do you muse?' Somehow she had transcibed the syntax of Vormish to extreme Rukarian city-speak.

'The lad I brought you. The fallen star who was our luck. From his father and his people I tore him and gave him you, for your—'

'I never required him of you. You should have let him be.'

'—interest, to care for him, as would any of our kind.'

'I am,' said she with great hauteur, 'no longer a *woman*. And when I was, *never* of your kind.'

'Our luck's gone,' said Krandif.

'*I* am your luck.'

'You,' he said.

Foolish, Krandif. She had berated herself enough over the

fate of Dayadin, did not need another to do it for her. She flicked her slim hand through the air and a flame whacked Krandif flat on the cabin floor. He lay there and said nothing.

'Go,' said Saftri, 'before I am really angry.'

He got up, suppressing a series of groans. Above, Jord and another of the priests helped him along the deck.

'Gods are unfair,' observed Majord. 'It's their nature.'

Krandif shook them off at the rail. He called to one of the horsazin he rode on land and when it swam over he mounted it and was borne back to his jalee.

He stood on his own deck wrapped in a fur cloak, even now leaning a little from her blow.

Only to Mozdif did he say, 'When we are to come ashore, if ever there *is* a shore, I and mine go our own ways. Do you agree?'

Mozdif looked dismayed but he nodded.

As with gods, when Krandif really decided something you had better go along with it or the discord might never end.

The wind woke in the night.

It charged up from the bottom of the sea as the whale had done, throwing a waterspout hundreds of feet into the sky. They saw this in the distance and then the waves ran down on them, high as the houses of the Rukarians.

Sail clapped, jolted and split on the masts. It was black as all-night, no stars or moons, and the air was made of water.

'I said. Our luck he was. *Gone.*'

But there was no true space for maledictions or reproach.

Saftri poised in the prow of the Mother Ship, as always ignoring the antics of the shamans whose flung rainbow sprays seemed to do nothing but add to the confusion.

About the ships she built rings of protection. They held, then gave way, like walls that bricks fell from.

She breathed upward into the wind to disperse it, and it veered from her and struck this way and that among the fleet.

Three ships of the Vorms, two of the Faz, were already

capsized and going down. Men clung to broken spars and planking, whirled over and over by the blustering water.

Saftri threw herself upward into the wind.

She seized it with her hands. It felt to her like ropes. 'Is this *you*?'

Even in her strength, she sensed once more her powers were not now sufficiently vital. It must be Zeth Zezeth's doing, this tempest. The undersea was his country too.

All night she fought with it, *grappled* it, sometimes taking on inadvertently almost her lioness aspect. She kept some of the storm off for sure, but all of it she could not. Below her, ships were wrenched apart, spilling their souls of men and women into the sprinting sea.

At dawn the storm was abruptly dead, killed by her ceaseless assaults or, more likely, having lived to its full potential.

Bleached sunlight showed the water now spattered with the remains of things.

In all they had been robbed of twenty-one ships, including one of the Mothers with its staff of shamans. But the fleet had been blown on west of north; the wind had pushed them where they had been going, as if to jest with them – *See? This is what it takes.*

Saftri thought, *It was never him.* The tempest had been only weather. Despite that, she was proved unequal.

Other voices were muttering now on the vessels. The consensus was that with Dayadin's subtraction, the fortune of the fleet went too.

Before noon, across a long stretch of water, the shoulders of a mighty landmass gradually and mistily appeared.

Another great silence settled.

On every vessel, faces turned only that one way, eyes looked only in that one direction.

So. It was true.

Saftri, who had *known* it was, having seen the vast dish of land from the air on more than one occasion, felt herself vindicated. By mortals.

But the sight of the land rather than encourage them oddly

seemed to depress them. It was mostly that the solution of landfall had come too late to save their comrades, that the very
agent of their quick arrival – the wind – had deprived so many
of their number of ever benefiting from it. Also, the land scared
them almost witless. This was not the known and often
attacked South Continent. It was new, untried, and might be
infested with anything. Their legends were full of such regions,
shores discovered in unexplored seas where inimical creatures
lurked and dragons laired.

Stoically then, they set course for the coast.

The vista opened slowly and inevitably.

It was like other places, at least at first impression. Long
sweeps of ice aproned the littoral. Behind, the terrain went up.
Cliffs, maybe mountains, flat-topped, blurred by distance and
the foggy overcast, took on extravagant altering shapes – the
heads of colossal men or beasts, axes, anchors – as the mists
wrapped and unwrapped them.

'Something moves out there. Along the sea.'

Saftri too squinted her eyes.

The sun was at the zenith now, a halo with only an inner pin-
point of light. Quasi-lit by this, huge white triangular sails were
setting off from around the shores, sailing out to meet the
incomers.

'They want a fight? Are they *giants*?'

In murmuring clusters they realized the truth.

'Icebergs,' confirmed Saftri.

Though tapering upward, the bergs were tall and wide, as
was often the case. Sometimes too their kind might drift about
with unnerving speed. Generally, however, the advance was
ponderous and reasonably to be prophesied. They were
independent of each other also.

These moved in another way. They moved altogether and at
once, and very fast. Already it was possible to see the wind-
sculpted quills of burnish snagging what little light the sun
gave, and the caves and ornate pillarings, the cores of electric
blue, or the bizarre shadows of things trapped in them long,
long ago.

Straight at the fleet they came.

Five hundred or more great bergs, bearing down on ships and men.

There was shouting now and cries. The horsazin kicked and the cows mooed in the holds as at every upsetting event they had.

Majord stood at Saftri's side. She had not seen him arrive. He gaped at the iceberg fleet with open mouth. No well-rhymed hymn for *this* circumstance then.

Saftri rounded on him. 'We can't get wide of them. There are too many.'

Majord nodded his horrified head.

'*Look there!*' The shout went up from a hundred throats. A much smaller berg, only adrift and not part of the vast oncoming hunting pack, stood aimless and becalmed in their path. Two of the advancing icebergs slewed towards it in total and undeniable unison, and mashed it between them like two white doors slamming. All across the lessening margin of water there came a roar and a crunching. Slabs of ice flailed upward and crashed down, and waves peeled off, slopping cumbersomely into the fleet which juddered at their collision. Only as the displacement re-balanced did most of the reivers see that the little iceberg had been pulverized.

Saftri soared into the air.

She felt a type of frantic courage, a berserker genius she had only been told of, and based only loosely on her by now lowered confidence in godhood.

As the bergs sailed towards her adopted fleet, she sprang to meet them.

At the last instant, only then, utter terror swamped her. She saw their true form. Inside their pillars and delicate wind-carvings, they were all the same. They were all *pyramids* of ice, blue-green at their bases, dirty like uncleaned quartz, holed with mysterious glows that had nothing it seemed to do with daylight. *Pyramids.* Like that living tomb in which she had been cast up from the sea of her first death. Like the storehouses of Yyrot, Lover of Winter, where he had incarcerated her she thought until she was fit for the onslaught of Zeth's whale and her first death's re-enactment. But these rose far higher – twenty or thirty times the height of any man.

Saftri screamed. But the scream was like that of a preying hawk. She dashed in among the looming driving ice, screaming and pushing the shapes away from her – not with her hands but with blasts and missiles of her hypernormal armament. It was not enough. Clearly it was not. All about the bergs splintered and gave way, sloughing ledges and towerets and whole storeys of themselves into the exploding ocean, but even so they continued to swerve towards her and her fleet, their ragged ruins still vast enough to squeeze her, and all things only mortal, to a broken bloodless pulp.

Something in Saftri too gave way.

She changed, before she had known she could or would, into a detonating spiral of raw energy and fire.

In an abstract ecstasy of furious power she cut the icebergs to bits, revolving among them like a golden scythe. And while she did this she shrieked invective at Zeth and at Yyrot, two of the thirds of that unnatural god-thing, both her nemesis and her salvation. The atmosphere sizzled not only with psychic pyrotechnics but with off-colour language. Could even Yyrot fail to hear?

At last the thunders, cracks, crashes and sonic boomings ceased. Light died on a tapestry of choppy water and chopped up ice.

Saftri returned to her physical female form afloat in the lower sky, and gazing down saw the havoc she had created. She had brought defeat to the icebergs. Not one lingered there save in fragments.

Elated, Saftri glanced over towards the fleet she had rescued from destruction.

She had not rescued it. Oh, she had spared it the action of the militant bergs. But in doing so she had wrecked every last ship.

The ice had toppled in the sea, and the resulting tidal waves had over-washed and spine-snapped every surviving vessel in the jalees. All were gone, except for a flotsam of spars and oars,

planks and casks and shreds of sails; most of the cattle had
drowned and were lurching pitifully in the swell alongside
horsazin, men, women and children who were also not always
alive.

She had not thought – had she had the time – to protect them
too. Perhaps anyway it would not have worked.

Whatever else, that which the tempest had overlooked,
Saftri's rescue mission had annihilated.

Ashamed, she hung in the air, frightened as gods must be so
often at her act – well meant, and too much to survive.

She had sunk some of their boats before. That had been in a fit
of pique; she could not even remember why she had done it,
only that she reclaimed the men at once from the sea, alive.

It was harder this time to save any of them. Some saved
themselves, swimming, or riding the swimming horsazin. For
the rest, two living cows positioned on a raft of planks, children
locked in dumb fear in a series of waterlogged, refloated long
ships, gibbering shamans perched useless as wet birds on a
single horizontal mast – Saftri swept them all gently shorewards on a conjuring of breezes strong enough to assist, not so
strong they would make matters worse. But how impoverished
now the landfall.

The land was white, like all lands. Nothing special to it and
nothing welcoming.

As night gathered the haphazard camp was formed inland
from the shore ice. Fire fluttered in the dark, and women wept
and children gave in to terror. Only the four black children controlled this urge, although two of them had lost both parents.

The men came to Saftri in a body, Faz, Kelp and Vorm
together, with Krandif at their head.

She had set herself apart as she nearly always did, but no
shelter had been offered her and no fire. She did not need
shelter or a fire, of course. She was a goddess. Nevertheless.

As the men approached, the flame-light behind them, Saftri
stood up.

Krandif spoke.

'There has been Assembly. We're agreed. Hear this I say. Go away from us, go wherever you will, be it far, far off.'

Nonplussed, Saftri said, 'How do you dare—'

'*How?*' Krandif pointed around at the cold alien *familiar* landscape, the sea which had drunk the ships, the laments. 'Since you came to us, goddess, we have had too many troubles.'

'I protected you from them.'

'Fine to protect us from what you yourself brought down on us. That fire-wolf thing – *your* enemy he was, so it seemed. We only on his path to you. And the boy, the beautiful night child, the whale had him. And now this, the very country you made us come to in order only to please *you* – itself that country sends its ice to crush us all, and when you fight with it, everything's done for.'

Saftri turned her head. Her eyes glittered strangely. She was crying, but if they saw it made no difference.

They only ranged there in front of her, a tall fence of male hatred.

'What do your women say to this?' she asked after a moment.

'You shall hear, goddess, what the women say.'

He would not call her Our Lady now; she was no longer anything of theirs. He moved aside and out of the rank of men a single woman came. Her hair was still quite short. She was Best Bear's mother.

'Go away,' said the woman to the goddess. The woman's face was flat and expressionless, unafraid and unhuman. 'Go far. Never come back.'

Saftri flared like a torch. Fieriness streamed from her. Not one of them flinched. They looked at her burning there as if at an aggravating infant that shows off.

'I could blast your little lives to clinker,' said Saftri. 'Be afraid of me.'

'*Terrified* we are of you,' said Krandif leadenly. 'Look where you've brought us. My brother dead in the salt sea. That's where *I'm* brought by you. Go, you Unluck, go away. What can you do to us now worse than what already has been done because of you?'

Saftri trembled. She put out her light.

She rose into the air, stood in it looking down at them. But they paid her no attention now. The body of men and the single woman had already moved off, back towards the encampment.

'I saved you,' Saftri whispered.

How small the camp, how few the survivors. She turned all of herself away from them.

At a loss, Saftri-Saphay looked in the only other direction.

Above loomed the pitiless grim phantoms of the cliffs and mountains. She found herself beginning to walk along the sky towards them. There was nowhere to go, and for that very reason she went towards one facet of the nowhere. And this reminded her of something. At first she could not think what. Then the memory returned sharp as a razor. That time the tears had frozen on her face, but – outcast from the Jafn-garth – she had clutched to her one element that gave her warmth. It had been her own child, Nameless, Lionwolf. Her dead son.

But now all things were really gone. She walked the sky towards the uninviting mountains.

Such calmness of sea and sky seemed remarkable to Arok as the voyage continued. Blue days of sun entered nights fiercely embered with stars, and nearly always one moon at full.

The big ship ploughed her burnished path, going over more westerly now as the whalers steered her course.

No one had objected to taking the ghost's advice on that.

'Athluan is our good spirit,' they said. 'He was a brave warrior and a just king, who died in battle at his brother's hand.'

Steadfastly they refused any connection between the Jafn ghost and the Lionwolf. Athluan after all had been dead before the Lionwolf was born.

Often the ghost was absent. Then the voyagers would look

for him. Even Arok found he did so. Sometimes the hawk was up in the rigging when Athluan was nowhere to be found.

They had been at sea a great while. It was hard to imagine ground beneath you that did not tilt; views of hills or ice-jungle.

Arok, standing his watch on a sleep nocturnal, turned and saw Athluan also standing at the rail.

'In ten days you'll come to it,' said Athluan.

'The land?'

'The land.'

'And my son is there?'

'Yes, though you'll have to search him out.'

'Do you know where he is?'

'No. The dead can see farther than you, but not all the distance.'

'You know my son is black like the other child aboard – like a hero.'

'Like Star Black Made-of-God. Yes. I've glimpsed his first mother, too. Oh, not in the way we do it here. Between the spaces of the stars – like that.'

Arok breathed in and out, a kind of sighing. 'Chillel. She was the most enticing woman on earth, so we thought, all of us. Him too, the – *him*.'

'Yes. She was also god-created. A minor god of the Ruk.'

'It's puzzled me always, why she chose me. The other men all went after her, but me she picked of them all. I never forget it. *Here as wife*, she said to him – to Lionwolf. And he said, thinking as each of us did she was to be his, *Whose?* And she said *Now I choose* and he said to her *Who will you have?* And she turned and pointed to me. *That man*, she said, *I choose that man as husband.*'

'You loved her.'

'You couldn't miss loving her. Or hating her when she began to ride with any other man who wanted it – even the Vormish scum, and Faz. I threw her out of my tent. I'd had enough. But every man she cutched lived through the Death at Ru Karismi. I saw them after – thirty – fifty – I can't recall that, how many of us had dighted Chillel and so lived. One of them was one of the Rukar kings.'

'And he, too,' said Athluan, 'was chosen by Chillel.'

Arok's head jerked up. He glared, staring. '*Why*? A *Rukar*?'

'She was made by a Rukar god. I told you.'

'But he – and I? We two. Did she *want* us? Was that it? I suppose,' he said, dropping his voice, 'if I have to share that with someone, if he's a king it's not so bad.'

'You too were recently a king, of the Holasan-garth.'

'Not for so long. Nor when she picked me. Besides, she didn't seek out any of the other kings or clan leaders. That yellow vandal king, Peb Yuve, he wouldn't go near her. But there were others, and they only got her if they went to *her*. Why did she choose the two of us, Athluan?'

'I don't know. Perhaps time will reveal it.'

'There's Nirri now,' said Arok, looking at the moonlit sea. 'I don't love her, but she means a lot to me. She's a good woman. Hot in the bed as well. And she gave me my son, even if he was Chillel's too. Chillel never had to push him out.'

'One thing I do see,' said Athluan, 'Nirri has another boy in her now.'

'What? Why haven't the damned wise-women told me?'

'They haven't seen it yet.'

'A boy? A boy. Is he—'

'No, Arok. Pale-skinned like you or me. But healthy and as he should be.'

'He'll be born in another country.'

The ship rocked gently. It amazed Arok now that this accustomed motion could ever have upset him.

Glancing aside, he saw Athluan their benign spirit had gone away, the hawk too. Arok sensed they might be gone for good. Ten days, and then the new world. And – what? – eight months and then the new child . . . Did Nirri herself not know? He would take a bet she did, was only waiting to be sure before she told him. He would say nothing, let her have the glory of announcing that to him. Perhaps he did love her anyway.

Another sort of love, not rampant and searing, milder and calmer – like the sea now, and the sea's deep tender motion.

As the sun set dull red among the mountains there was a horned whale in the sky, made of maroon cloud. Every detail of it was exact – Brightshade to a T. From the blowhole curved up and over a spout of extremely bright stars. Ddir had been busy, apparently; stars *and* clouds for this latest artistic effort.

Below too something flashed and gleamed, but with an ebb and flow unlike that of anything in the sky.

Yyrot, Winter's Lover, sat on a mountainside, gazing down at the earthly light-source. Beside him sat a curious being. She was a woman – of a kind; and beautiful – in a distinct sort of fashion. She was covered in short sleek fur that took a reddish polish from the sunset. Inside this fur envelope her body was, plainly, that of a human female. Yet where her hands, aside from covering, were also human, her feet were enlarged versions of two clawed paws. Her head was a cat's head without camouflage, the ears placed high and pointed, the eyes, now shut, normally rounded. Behind her, her tail flickered to and fro. She was dozing, leaning on her partner. Once she had been Saphay's cat.

She still had a cat's lack of concern with most things not involving herself. At home, wherever their bizarre domestic arrangements might lie at the time, the cat and Yyrot-as-hound's thirteen children lived their own lives, hunting and fighting, eating and singing in unique voices. Sometimes they too mated. This rarely happened between two of at all the same type, rather between two of the most *opposing* types. Thereby they had already produced a bevy of even more eccentric creatures than themselves, if that were possible. Drajjerchaches and chachadrajes – dog-cats and cat-dogs. Credited and named in the mythic antiquity of Gech they, like the fabled ice-beast the lionwolf, were hybrids. And *their* offspring, which even Gech had not supposed could ever exist, went by the parents' name still, the drajjes being those most canine, the chaches those most cat-like. None of the grandchildren in fact resembled the founders of their line with their characteristics of pure cat and pure dog. But then neither did Saphay's cat much look like her former self. She *had* a name, however. Yyrot had given it to her: Shimmawyn.

Now Shimmawyn stirred and opened her round eyes.

Yyrot's interest in the rising and sinking light below had been put aside. He was standing up, as over the ridge of the ice-locked mountain another god came stalking.

Shimmawyn lashed her tail and sprang behind a convenient rock.

'Well, brother,' said Yyrot. 'You have brought splendid weather with you.'

Doubtless it was being around the mortal world as they had been now for twelve years or so which made them carry on like mortals to the extent of holding conversations. Half a century before, if anyone had told them they would be doing such a thing, particularly amongst themselves, could they ever have believed it?

Unlike Yyrot the second god did not evince his amenable side. His face was masked in indigo, and so was every inch of his golden skin. His hair was grey and spiked with small knives.

'Why am I here?' he demanded, stopping some feet away from Yyrot.

'Why *are* you? I have no idea why either of us is here.'

'This is not my domain. This is the shit-heap the woman I hate was aiming for. I am surrounded by those who enrage me yet slip from my grasp.'

'There, there,' said Yyrot, banal and remote.

Zeth Zezeth smote the ground with his look. Large clumps of hard snow went flying upward then down, thundering into murky valleys miles below.

Shimmawyn, unseen by either god, slunk off round the rocks and hid in a cave, and so beheld Ddir, the third of the triad, descend the staircase of the air outside. He peered in at her briefly but showed neither fascination or disapproval, moving on to join the other two.

Yyrot saw Ddir and nodded. Zeth cast him a blazing and poisonous glance. Ddir only sat down on a rock. Blandly he peered into space, his unmind on other priorities.

'What is that light down there?' Yyrot presently asked Zeth.

'That? Some rubbish of humans.'

'Do you think so? I am inclined to go and see.'

'Go then.'

'And you?'

'I will remain here with my hatred.'

Yyrot paused. 'Saftri, you mean.'

'*Saftri – Saphay—*'

'She is too strong for you now. Even for your whale. Did you kill him, by the by? Surely he also is too vigorous to actually die.'

'I neither know nor care. That cretin Ddir has slapped him up on the sky, you see? What message does that convey? If I come across the animal again I will blast him into three million crumbs. But she – I want her. I will have her. She will pay me. She will pay for ever. Meanwhile . . .' Zezeth hesitated noticeably, 'the boy is beyond me for now in his pathetic hell, but when he returns, this time *I* shall deal with him.'

Yyrot mused. The nature of his musings took shape in the snow in a series of well-executed carvings. They pictured Zeth Zezeth very much compromised in ways that were, in human terms, frankly indescribable.

Zzth saw them too.

The blue shade of his malignity began to infect even his hair.

He roared, 'Why have you aided them? Why did you make *her* an immortal?'

'Did I?' said Yyrot.

'You go against me. You are no confrère but an enemy, just as that star-fiddler is only a fool.'

'We are one,' said Yyrot. 'We have grown together. I am you and you are I, and both of us are him as he is us.'

'I am *myself*. Zzth, Sun Wolf.'

'Did you steal some of my ice pyramids and send them out along the ocean here?' Yyrot asked suddenly, an afterthought.

'I would neither tamper with nor utilize your icebergs. They are beneath me.'

'Then who, I wonder, moved them all? They vanished, but I detect their debris under the water, along with one or two ships.'

Each god then was for a moment alerted. Even Ddir seemed to be concentrating on Yyrot's words.

'Winter is here,' said Yyrot, 'adorable and perfect winter. Nothing can disturb the equilibrium.'

Ddir got up and went off. They watched him climb back up the invisible stairway. He had thought of something extra he wished to add to his whale-sculpture, and in a minute more they saw the result. One bright ray, perhaps from the all but vanquished sun, pierced through the cloudy belly of the whale, and out along it there glided an incredible thing, a *black* star that sparkled like all the rest.

Zzth struck the whole top of the mountain. Ice and snow erupted high into the sky, and Shimmawyn came running for her lover's protection.

Yyrot enfolded her in his dark hair. They winked out of the world.

Zzth stood alone, scowling down on the shifting lights below in the valley, which grew richer now the sunset faded.

Zzth hated Saphay and hated the frozen world. He hated Lionwolf more even than these – Lionwolf whom Saphay had enabled to rob Zeth Zezeth of some of his essence. The essence, though long since returned to him, he felt no longer quite fitted into the grooves of his deistic material. Lionwolf had contaminated it.

But Lionwolf would come back. The signals for that had been clear, revealing themselves inside Zzth's awareness at once. The Rukarian girl he had sent through the Afterlife to punish Lionwolf had only succeeded in galvanizing him. Yes, return was now inevitable, the parents had been selected. But there Zzth had some leverage. He had visited the prospective mother. This had not been during her current bewildering adulthood, but by travelling back into her past. Whatever mankind became, however many changes humans made to themselves, the past, the *beginning*, would always slip through under the correct stimuli. They had no real stamina, none of them. Their persistence in adversity's face was not noble endurance or fortitude – it was bloody-mindedness and idiocy.

And she, this woman with black hair, she would be worse than most. She had magical powers, but had been in her youth an evil-inclined harlot, abused and abusing, interested only in herself and her desires. It had pleased him enormously visiting her adolescence years ago, weaving with facility through time. He found her there concocting some dirty little spell to harm others. A pretty girl, yes, very attractive. He might sample her himself – in the coming future that was. Even to a god, action in finished time was impracticable. He had only been able to look at her and charm her with his smile. How properly flattered she had been. She had also, he guessed – *knew* – wondered why he had appeared before her, during the rest of her young life.

She would become an acolyte of his. What man could compare to Zeth Zezeth?

'Jemhara,' murmured Zzth aloud in the world he did not like, and for an instant the gold and silver of him showed through the raging blue. But only for an instant. He turned, as if listening. He had picked up the scent of Saphay's life on the wind. He too disappeared from the mountain, leaving only stillness and the light fluctuating far below.

Does suffering increase when you can no longer suffer? That is, when the wound that never closes has become unfeeling, nerves put out like candles – yet the nerveless wound stays agape and bleeding before your eyes.

Saphay, the goddess Saftri, had flown in over the high cliffs, but somehow gravity like a magnet had pulled her down to earth.

It was not that she pretended to be only a woman, outcast and trudging across the snow. She did not know what it was.

No thoughts came to her except all the memories of her son. Against the white world, these colours of fire and love. Night was sifting through the pallor after a lethargic crimson sunfall. Some cloud forms massed, not dispersing. She took no notice, not properly observing anything external. A god, she walked more swiftly than any mortal and no physical obstacle impeded her. She covered miles.

In the night darkness, stars above, she went down into a valley and halted, dazed by a race of light. It was a startling bluish green, luminescent, surging up along a hill near the valley's centre. Into the sky the glimmerings rose. The snow burned like emeralds.

I have heard of something like this—

After a second, Saftri who had been Saphay recollected. In Ruk Kar Is, a mystic area, Stones that lit, passing lambency from one to another, often coruscating all at once, immutable and never understood. Even the Magikoy had had no answer as to what they were or might be.

She had never seen them.

But here it transpired were others just like them.

The patterns, flitting, flaring, lowering like lamps, hypnotized her.

When she reached the spot the conductors had attained a climax of brilliancy and held it static. The whole night and all the valley seemed glowing. They *were* Stones, and very high, some over fifty feet she thought. They described the outline of the short hill, marching up and over it and down the far side.

She walked up with them, over and down.

At the foot of the hill stood a blue thing with knives in his hair.

'So you are here then, you nothing,' he said.

Saphay had no resistance any more. She looked at Zeth Zezeth and she let go. She fell. She was finished. She no longer cared.

Zeth leaned over her. How ugly he always was at such moments, a horrible sight.

Even gods can be mistaken. Behind Zzth a man had appeared, tall and far more blue even than he. The blue man was blued by rottenness, flesh dying on his dead frame. Then that was done with. Out of the chrysalis came a Jafn king, intact and presentable, rather more indeed, his white hair shining.

Is this the one who was before me with her?

Zzth heard the thought and turned.

Zzth was tickled, slightly. 'A ghost? How did you die?'

The ghost looked eye to eye with the god.

'I'm not dead, in that sense.'

'Yes, you are dead. Where is your shadow?'

'Where's *yours*?'

Zzth recoiled. Remarkable. But shadows were a sore point with him since Lionwolf.

'I need none of that.'

Athluan took a new tack. 'What is your name?'

'No, you could never have heard. A barbarian are you not? My name is Zeth Zezeth. And this cow is mine.'

'Not so. This is my world and she is my woman.'

'She is a goddess now.'

'Still mine,' said Athluan, Chaiord of the Jafn Klow. 'Still *mine*.'

'I shall kill her. Whatever she is now, I shall find a means. She was *mine*. I had her in the sea. What to follow, barbarian?'

This conversation, substantially, had come from before. Guri back then had been the ghost who crouched malevolently above the sleeping Saphay. And Guri, made irritable by Athluan's intervention, had sprung at Athluan, the kind of leap a cat would make, over and *through* the flesh.

And Zzth – he was a god by now far too meshed in human customs.

Athluan sprang.

Straight through the orichalc and indigo-ashen body of the god he flung himself, through a web of superphysical fibres and filaments, through a heart that was not a heart, a soul that was not a soul.

It appeared Zeth *felt* that. Like scalding water? Who could say? A hoarse cry broke from him and a thrash of galvanics to rival the iridescence of the stones.

As the Jafn landed beyond him, Zzth ripped energies from his own core and slung them. For a count of five heartbeats the ghost was riveted, outlined in incendiaries. He appeared to be alight. His body, which had seemed so real, frayed at its edges—

The Stones of the new-found country darkened – then cascaded.

Any other light was extinguished.

The nightscape stared like a green bone.

Zeth was flailing. He was being knocked from pillar to post of the monolithic segments, thrown at them, spun off and buffeted into others. In vain he hurled his power about him. The Stones *took* his power and used it for themselves, feeding from him, draining him, so in the end he slumped at every hammering.

Athluan, recovering himself, lay on the green ground watching.

He saw Zeth Zezeth battered one last blow, then ejected very fast and upward into the sky. Far overhead the god was slammed against some apparent roof – it was a thick cloud, sculpted like a whale . . . Bright stars above it seemed to shake at the impact but none came loose.

For a brief while Zeth was plastered there on heaven. He looked most like some strange four-legged insect someone had trodden on. Then the cloud went black, the world went black. Zeth had once more vanished from it, and so had the light of the Stones.

Soon after, Athluan was himself again. He crossed through the darkness, and now he leaned over Saphay.

Her eyes were open. She had looked on death. Athluan stared, expecting death's signature to be painted on the irises. But death, as now he knew, meant nothing so much.

He raised her in his arms and held her close against a heart which, presumably, no longer beat.

Before he planned, his mouth was on hers.

Athluan shuddered. She had a taste of eternity.

The kiss had lasted less than—

Less than for ever.

Warm.

'Where—' she said. 'Where?'

'Here,' he said. 'You're here.' And then, as before, he said, 'Tell me your name.'

'Saphay . . .'

'Hear me,' he said, 'Saphay.' He lingered on the name. 'Let me tell *you*. Long ago. The hero—'

'Star Black,' she whispered.

'Star Black, yes. He had a second wife after the first perished. She was white as ice and he as black as night.'

'Hold me.'

'I am holding you.'

'Where were you?' she said.

'Oh – I was in another place.'

'But not with me. Why not with me?'

'It happens that way. You and I are not alone in that.'

She moved. He held her closer.

She said, 'What has become of us?'

'Everything,' he said.

'Everything.'

'Listen,' said Athluan. 'Star Black and his wife lived together for a great while. At last he must leave the world.'

'Don't leave me,' she said.

'Ssh. This is a story. Star Black said to her, I am always with you. Nothing can divide us, death least of all.'

Saphay turned her head on his arm.

'We're divided.'

'Not by so much.'

'I must be dreaming you,' she said. 'Even now I sometimes sleep and dream. Even of you. That's what it is. I never loved you,' she added bleakly. 'It was *that* one I loved.'

'You loved me. And I loved you. From the moment I saw you in the ice. But the love never grew. It hadn't any chance. Not then.'

Where he had been, when outside the world, there was no time. It was now therefore as if only yesterday he had held her, only the day before that he found her in the pyramid of ice surrounded by jewels of blood.

She moved from him presently. They both got to their feet. The hill was dark though all about now it was possible to see tiny pinpricks of vague light on the crags around, herdsmen's fires most likely. The land was not unpopulated. It was just that neither of them had yet looked for anyone else.

'Well,' she said.

They began to walk across the valley. It was like all such areas. The snow was crisp and glacial forest rose either side, now and then seeming to breathe as white bats fluttered in and out of the ice-caves which had formed between the trees.

'Where are we going?' she asked.

'To a house over there.'

'Is there a house?'

'A sort of house, ruinous.'

'Cold comfort. Cold unkindness. Like all this world.'

She so often sounded, this goddess, like a child. She was consumed by shame and distress and, worst of all, by an unrelenting hope. Athluan was as she remembered him. He had not grown older since the day of his death, while she had added ten or eleven years to her span before immortality checked it. They were now therefore almost of an age, she and he.

The 'house' appeared. It was a long, log-built brick, most of its roofing down, outbuildings reduced to single frames of wall or heaps of rubble.

'We can make this better,' he said.

The scene changed. The house was whole and upright. It was no longer any building of the new continent, but the Klow House, with the Jafn sword lying horizontal for peace above the door.

404

No lamps burned in the high windows, however.

She thought, as they went on towards it, *He summons the illusion of shelter – but his honour won't allow him too many lies. The House will stay dark, and empty.*

It did so.

No Jafn warriors guarded the doorway or yard gates. No man or woman was there but for Athluan and Saphay, who anyway were neither, only a strayed ghost and a despised goddess.

The joyhall rang as they moved through it, not with the sound of them, but with nothingness. But up the ladder-stair they went.

Oh – the room . . .

As she followed him into it, it woke and became a flower of colours and illumination. There was the lamp that might be turned to provide a more sombre glow, the axes, bows and other weapons gleaming in the firelight on the walls, the bed with its furs and chequered quilts.

'You're a mage now you're dead,' she remarked tactlessly. 'There was another I knew like that. His name was Guri. An Olchibe spirit, who became the guardian of my – of—'

'Our son,' said Athluan. 'Lionwolf.'

She stared. Almost in fear she said, 'But he was not your son – do you still think *that*—'

Athluan said gently, 'He was my son because you were wed to me, you bore him under my roof and, if I'd lived, I would have given him his name. To all eyes he would have been mine. Neither of you would have come to any such pit of grief as you did when I was taken.'

'Athluan . . .' she said, in her low child's voice, 'what would you have named him, our – son?'

'Conas. For my elder brother who died.'

'Conas—'

'I've met him, Saphay, our son, some while ago on a shore by a sea. He knew me. We spoke of you.'

She put her face in her hands and began to cry.

'Everything's been done wrongly.'

'No, Saphay. By the most twisting and tortured route, the arrows are flying to the targets.'

'What do you mean?'

'I hardly know. It's not yet the time to know.'

'Conas,' she wept. Then she looked up at him. 'How curious – in your language it means *as a lion.*'

'So it does.'

When he advanced towards her her stance became rigid.

Athluan halted. 'Are you afraid of me?'

'Yes,' she said.

'And I of you, goddess. But it's too late for that.'

He put his hands on her then and his mouth on hers.

Like before . . . so like before—

She remembered *him*.

Love him? Whom else could she love? *That* had not been love at all, that other passion.

But the touch of lips that woke her in the heart of the ice – Athluan, who brought her back to life with his kiss.

On the bed they fell together, hungry as wolves and lions.

The first time, far off in that other country, he had paused at the brink of having her, finding she was not virgin – startled, dismayed. She saw him remember. He laughed aloud. And then his body came home to hers and the pleasure of so many years' delay burst inside the pair of them, wave on wave, like a sunrise, which ebbed only finally to great tranquillity.

'Don't leave me,' she said again.

'My love, I must. How else can I come back to you?'

'Riddles – silly Jafn word-games—'

'I'm dead. Let me be born again here. I'll find you, or you will find me.'

'You'll be human.'

'Learn a way to make me immortal then, my wife.'

She lay watching him, frowning.

'Will you stay – at least – till morning?'

'At least till morning.'

The lamplight faded slowly through the night. The firelight dimmed. Over the window the vine that only bloomed inside the bedroom rendered a faint musky scent. And once, when they had again made love, in the after-stillness she thought she heard men singing below in the joyhall. Everything passes, everything returns. She was not a goddess nor he a ghost. At least, till morning.

'Yes,' said Arok.

He spoke brusquely, then turned and saw the fisherman standing there looking as usual uneasy, with the boy Fenzi by his side.

'He wants to speak to you, Chaiord. He's had a dream.'

Arok gazed into the face of the boy. He was not like Dayadin, though of the same hue and comeliness.

'Yes, Fenzi, what was this?'

'Sir, I saw Dayadin your son. I saw him before in a dream, only then I thought it was me – a frightening shut-in vault, a kind of indoor swamp—' Arok caught his breath. Quick with reassurance, Fenzi added, 'But now he's free. Our sister set him free.'

'Sister?'

The fisherman lowered his eyes. 'He speaks of having an older sister, but my woman and I have no daughter.'

'Dark as me,' said Fenzi, 'like Dayadin and the others.'

'The "others" being other children like yourself, born among the Jafn?'

'And in different lands. There are very many of us. But only one sister. She's like us, but has bright hair, like a fire.'

Something shot through Arok's mind, angering and alarming him, but peculiarly intriguing him also – so Lionwolf had fucked her too, Chillel. And unlike all ordinary men who had her, Lionwolf had been able to leave on the subsequent off-spring one marker of his own – his bloody hair.

'So Dayadin is with your sister.'

'She's called Flame.'

'Where?'

407

'I couldn't see,' said the child. 'But it was a nice place. Not like the other.'

To his appalled helpless shock Arok felt tears run from his eyes.

Useless to hide them.

And the boy – the boy reached out and patted Arok's arm in the friendly way of an elderly father.

'You'll see him soon, sir, I'm sure you will, Great God grant it,' said the fisherman.

It was almost midnight. In the dawn, they would behold the new land kneeling up on the water.

Riadis detested the mages. They had had no interest ever in her son, not even when he had been dying.

Yet every day for almost three years she had invoked their permission to enter the god-hall, and there she went round to almost every one of the gods.

'Send me a sign. Let me know of my son.'

This she repeated to all the images, the grey winter god of ice and snow, the gods of wind and night or sea and mountains, the horde of them standing there in painted whale ivory or stone. Even to the god of the dromazi, the chariot and sled beasts, she went. He was a compendium of man and dromaz, his back with two humps and his long-nosed face the dromaz face, with great petal ears. At the ends of his man's legs were the big pads of his kind, and his hands were like that too, if smaller. He was coloured fawn and his eyes were black polished agates.

'Send me a sign. Have your people seen him after death? Have they carried him on their backs behind the neck, or drawn his chariot? I know,' Riadis said in a quick rough voice, '*there* he has all his limbs. If *there* exists at all.'

To each of the gods she went, hurrying to and fro under the high narrow window with its strips of stained glass. She poured motes of incense, offered blossoms from indoor lianas, wine

and confectionery. To the god of the dromazi, Obac Tramaz, she
brought bunches of live grass cut in the hothouse.

'Send me a sign.'

Only to the god Attajos, Maker of Fire, did Riadis not go or
speak. She turned her shoulder to him so her chestnut hair
fanned in a satin smoke.

Attajos had been her son's father. The king, her husband,
who could fill ten other wives and countless concubines with
babies over and over, had never been able to seed Riadis. But
the god spat his fire on her foot, ankle and leg, and when she
recovered from the pain she had found herself carrying.

Curjai the king had named him. Escurjai among his friends
and kin: spirit, heart, mind.

He had had all of those. Only a faultless body he did not
have.

Today Riadis completed her usual circuit of the god-hall. She
had little else to do. None came near her now except her
women, or the clan shaman who could sometimes give her a
little comfort. For a queen she had a secluded and unfruitful
existence.

Obac Tramaz was the last god before she reached the end.

From her basket, Riadis drew out the fresh grass. She prepared to lay it down.

'Mighty Obac, send me—'

Something.

What?

A glitter over the black eyes of the god. Some trick of the
window light.

Uncontacted, and on its own, an object flew from the offering tray that held yesterday's bunch of grass.

Riadis saw the object roll across the altar and, with a click,
down on to the floor.

As she stooped to retrieve it the remembrance woke in her
how, five days after Curjai's death, one of her attendants had
stumbled on a loose tile in Riadis's apartments, and when she
stepped away the tile lifted, and there lay the small bow one of
the warriors had fashioned for Curjai.

She had thought *that* might be a sign from her son himself. *See*, perhaps he said, *now I can shoot with a bow, having both arms and legs in the afterlands.*

The thing which had fallen to the floor was about the size of a large ring, some adornment say of the king's. It was a firm seed-head, perhaps from the grass or from some other grain that had become mixed with it. As her fingers met the oval seed it split. Out came a sprig, uncurling to living green.

Riadis turned the morsel in her fingers.

Had Obac Tramaz given her the years-demanded sign?

His sculpted sheep-camel's face was friendly, but then it always was.

Riadis crossed back through the hall and, emerging, found two of the mages, who had paused in weighty discussion of some esoteric trivia to do either with sorcery or with their priestly function concerning the gods.

They did not acknowledge her, nor she them.

It was the shaman, Korch, she meant to seek. He belonged to her own clan, and had travelled with her to Padgish those many years before when she was given to the king. Riadis came of a royal herder family living among the eastern uplands.

Korch was in his tibbuk or smoking room. He had been inhaling fumes from some burnt substance and the air was thick with the sharp reek of raw caramel.

By now the curtain was pulled back. She might go in.

As Riadis did this Korch got up and wove towards her, eyes inflamed.

'Something you must see.'

'Something I must tell you.'

They both spoke at once, but each heard the other.

'Does it have to do with—'

'With your dead son Curjai? What else?'

'I had a sign from Obac – a live shoot in a head of grain that was cut and dead.'

'I've seen the afterlands,' said the shaman.

Riadis made a gesture of fear and protection.

'Is Curjai—'

'Go to your room, queen, and take out that bit of mirror I made you keep, the costly glass that you broke when Curjai looked in it and was made despairing. Send away your women. I'll join you in an hour.'

Riadis stared at him.

Then she fled from the tibbuk, through the dense trunk-pillared corridors of the palace to her room and her carved chest. The mirror bit was wrapped in a piece of tiger-skin, a wonderful and rare pelt allowed only to the royal houses.

She held it there for some time, tracing the pale dark stripes, stroking the paler amber of the fur which, when you turned the surface, went to purest white.

She thought how quiet the palace had grown, as if it held its breath, this place that had never bothered much either with herself or with Curjai. Outside too a restless wind which had risen with the sun lay down on the ice-tasselled trees.

She had not yet removed the mirror when Korch arrived at her door.

In the mirror, a fragment no larger than a man's hand, the woman looks at the instruction of the shaman.

She sees appear a sweeping landscape clothed in growing fronds, a vast city to which Padgish is a pebble.

Within the city a crowd sings and lauds a procession of men and chariots that is riding out into a wide square space. The foremost chariot is drawn by animals that Riadis does not recognize, although they seem to her somewhat like tigers – but they are maned, and in colour grizzled.

The driver of the chariot is a god.

By no possible means could even a fool miss this fact, and Riadis is no fool at all.

Who is he? Is he the fire god?

No, she does not think he is, for Attajos is very dark of skin and hair, with golden eyes. And this god is red-haired with golden *skin*. These eyes are blue like the sky above the city.

She only sees the god a moment anyway.

Curjai rides there at his side.

Curjai. Him she knows instantly. She has always known him to be exactly this. A handsome man, about twenty years now, of a light yet muscular physique, his eyes like the hazel gems men dig from mountain caves. His hair is a mane to rival those of the chariot-cats, to rival even that of the red-headed god.

Curjai.

'*My son,*' she mutters, too proud to be silent yet careful not to unseat the spell.

When she speaks, Curjai however seems to hear. He half looks at her. For a fleeting second he smiles, showing all his fine white teeth. He has every limb. He is a man – she had always known he was this, inside the body he had been born with. How marvellous he was always, then too, undeniably then. His nature and his dreams. His leaps of humour and pooling gentleness, his *kindness* to *others.*

My son.

Riadis sees there is another man in the front chariot too, but she pays him no heed except to note he has a skin she has never seen, a yellow one.

Ahead of the chariots, across the city square, there is a wall of pulsing light. It seems to beat like a heart. It is somehow terrifying and steadying all at once.

The chariot is going away from her towards the light. All the chariots, all the men, are doing the same.

The glass clouds.

Before she can prevent herself Riadis cries out—

The vision blanks.

'Bring it back!'

'No, queen. I can't show you more. Some secrets the gods have to keep, or they'd send us insane.'

Along the up and down tumbles of the land of Simisey, lying alone in a ruin, another woman is sobbing for her child. The goddess Saftri remains a woman, remains Saphay. In sleep, she saw him. When she awoke, he, and her lover's arms, were gone.

But more curiously, elsewhere, a human woman of the

Olchibe stands dry-eyed, gaping at the sudden removal of a mirage on the snow. From the other two, the queen and the goddess, this woman, a young Crarrow, is separated by much more than miles, lands or seas. However she too has beheld a chariot drawn by lions which, actually, she does not quite identify. In the chariot she saw two shadows, one shining and one darker, and also a little Olchibe boy who turned on her a look of such utter insolent astonishment, the Crarrow girl had wanted to reprimand him. Too late anyway. The mirage faded. And she must go back to her sluht. In the distance a snowstorm is starting, up in Gech by the Copper Gate and the mighty city of Sham.

My son, say the whispers. Saphay and Riadis know why. Only the clever Crarrow, trotting back through the ice-woods, is again surprised. Has she seen a vision of the man who will be born to her? Indeed she has.

Beyond the pulsing light lies an open plain covered in stones and shards.

It is the first plain, cold hell, under a watery veined sky that presents no sun of any type or tint.

The chariots fan out. Men dismount from the vehicles, which disappear with their various animals like smoulder.

'I fear this, Vash,' said Curjai, apparently forgetting Lionwolf's reinstated name, and also not knowing he or some facet of himself had recently smiled at another, elsewhere.

'And you were the one who told me of Lalt and Tilan,' said Lionwolf.

'They quarrelled. One killed the other, and died too, inside his own heart.'

Guri said morosely, 'It's uneasy for us. This is the first we ever had to go *back* into life.'

'Vash!' Curjai gripped Lionwolf's shoulder.

One by one, without any fuss, the other fighters on the plain were winking out like blotted stars.

'It's so simple?' asked Guri.

'Not for us.'

'Ah? Do you *know*, Lion?'

'Something in me knows. In all of us something knows.'

Every other man was gone. The plain was vacant.

Then it was not.

Over the stones came bowling a high plume of blackness, a kind of tornado, twisting.

Lionwolf gazed up into it.

He had never feared anything save his father, and himself. Those fears were gone, presumably for ever.

'Run, Guri,' he said, 'run, Curjai. Run with me towards it.'

They darted forward, three lions now, lion of Olchibe, lion of Simisey, and Lionwolf, son of god and mortal.

They met the funnel of blackness. It curled them up. It tore them into shreds. There was no agony, no horror. It felt *right*, as a sword feels right that is made for you and put into your hand, as a kiss does from one you want, as day does breaking, as hope does always, even when it can never be realized.

Tomorrow, sang the plain on one long monumental chord. *Yesterday.*

Riadis jumped to her feet.

A spark from the brazier had flown off and lodged in her skirt. She beat it out in three slaps.

The hole scored through the cloth into her flesh. A miniature triangle on her thigh was already scarlet and blistering. There would be a scar. No doubt of it.

Greater than the discomfort, the sureness.

'*Attajos*,' she said.

... Unended ...
Next

No Flame But Mine
Book Three of the Lionwolf Trilogy

GLOSSARY

Bedfreh – Literally a blanket; sexually over-willing and amenable: Jafn

Bit – Human chattel: Ranjalla and southern north-east

Borjiy – Berserker, fearless fighter: Jafn

Chaiord – Clan chieftan/king: Jafn

Chachadraj – A cat-dog, product of the mating of a cat and a dog (see also **Drajjerchach**): Gech originally

Concubina – Unmarried royal wife: Ruk Kar Is

Corrit – Demon-sprite: Jafn

Crait – Type of lammergeyer: Rukarian uplands

Crarrow (pl. **Crarrowin**) – Coven witches of Olchibe and parts of Gech

Crax – Chief witch of **Crarrowin** coven

Cutch – Fuck: Jafn and elsewhere

Dilf – One of several forms of dormant grain and cereal: general, but found mostly in more fertile areas

Drajjerchach – Dog-cat, product of the mating of a dog and a cat (see also **Chachadraj**): Gech originally

Dromaz (pl. **Dromazi**) – Type of camelid: Simese

Endhlefon – Time period of eleven days: Jafn

Firefex – Phoenix: Rukarian

Fleer-wolf – A kind of wolf-like jackal, known for its lamenting cries: general to the snow wastes

Flylarch – Pine-like berried plant: general to the continent

Forcutcher – Insulting variation, of obscure exact meaning, deriving from the word **cutch**

Gadcher – Eyesore (compare phonetically with the ascribed name of the Hell hounds – which would seem to indicate a kind of pun): Jafn

Gargolem – Magically activated metallic non-human servant; the greatest of these creatures guarded the kings at Ru Karismi prior to the White Death: Rukarian

Gler – Demon-sprite: Jafn

Gosand – Type of wild goose: Simese

Hirdiy – Nomadic band: northern north Gech

Hnowa – Riding animal: Jafn

Horsaz (pl. **Horsazin**) – a breed of horse apparently part-bred with fish; scaled and acclimated to land and ocean: Fazion, Kelp and Vorm

Hovor – Wind-spirit: Jafn

Icenvel – Type of weaselish thick-furred rodent: general to the continent

Insularia – Sub-river complex belonging solely to, and solely accessible to, the **Magikoy**: Ru Karismi

Jalee – Fleet of war vessels, including Mother Ship, usually thirteen in number, though sometimes less or more: Fazion, Kelp and Vorm

Jatcha – Hound of Hell, compare with 'gadcher' (Jafn): Eyesore. A pun?

Jinan/Jinnan – Magically activated house-spirit: Rukarian – normally **Magikoy**

Kadi – Type of gull: general to the continent

Kiddle/Kiddling – Baby or child up to twelve years: Olchibe

Kiss-grass – Rare soft grass-like plant, favoured by mammoths as a delicacy, either in thawed or dormant state: Olchibe and Gech

Lamascep – Sheep of long, thick wool: general to the Ruk

Lashdeer – Fine-bred, highly trained chariot animals used for high-speed travel over snow and ice: Rukarian

Mageia/Magio – Female and male witch or lesser mage: rural Ruk Kar Is, and elsewhere in the north

Magikoy – Order of magician-scholars, established centuries in the past; possessed of extraordinary and closely guarded powers: Ruk Kar Is and elsewhere in the Ruk

Maxamitan Level – Highest level of achievement available to **Magikoy** apprentice; the next step is to become a **Magikoy** Master: Ruk Kar Is

Mera – Mermaid: general to the north

Morsonesta – Burial ground located in the **Insularia** of the **Magikoy**: Ru Karismi

Oculum – **Magikoy** scrying glass, or magic mirror of incredible scope: Ruk Kar Is

Ourth – Elephant or mammoth: Olchibe

Scrat – Type of rat; see also **scratchered**: general to Southern Continent

Scratchered – Basically, over-used: Jafn

Seef – Demon, type of vampire: Jafn

Shumb – Something valuable now spoiled; may carry a reference to the sacked city of Gech, Sham: Jafn

Sihpp – Similar to **seef**: Jafn

Slederie – Primitive land-raft drawn by sheep or sometimes dogs: Ruk and south-east

Slee – Riding ice-carriage: Rukarian

Sleekar – Deer-drawn ice-chariot: Rukarian

Sluhts – Communal tent/cave/hut dwellings: Olchibe

Sluhtins – Large city groupings of **sluhts**: Olchibe

Soint – Obscure insult, seeming to have to do with either genital or lavatorial practices (?): Jafn, but also elsewhere in the north and east, including Ruk Kar Is

Subtor – Lowest underground chambers of magician's house: **Magikoy**

Tattarope – Snake of corded, rope-like skin: Uaarb and far north

Thaumary – Thaumaturgic or sorcerous chamber attached to main hall, for use mostly by mages of a garth or House – even the chieftain does not enter here uninvited: Jafn

Tibbuk – Room kept for the inhaling of various smokes to do with scrying and prophecy: shamanic Simese

Towery – Complex of towers connected to each other by walkways and/or inner passages: **Magikoy**, Ruk Kar Is

Vrix – Demon-sprite: Jafn

Weed-of-light – Forest-growing ice-plant, having blue flowers: north and east

Werloka – Male witch: Jafn villages

Woman bow – A bow which can fire only one arrow at a time (male bows can fire, normally, up to four arrows at a time, depending on the skill of the archer): Olchibe